As the fury of his [passion]
more became aware
receptacle for his lust. She lay beneath him,
slender girl, with smooth white skin and firm young
breasts. A virgin no more, yet still innocent of the
pleasure of union. She was sobbing helplessly, her
chest shaking, and her eyes, when they met his,
were clouded with pain.

Now that he was no longer tormented by the
immediacy of his need, he felt a surge of sympathy
—and regret. If only he had not been so strongly
aroused! Gently, he ran his fingers over her body,
touching her cheeks and wiping the tears away.
"Forgive me! I could not control myself. I've been
denied a woman too long—and you were far too
tempting." He met her eyes and flushed, shamed
by the reproach he saw in their depths. "It can be
good. I can show you. . . ."

His hands caressed her shoulders tenderly, and
when she pulled away, he let his fingers pass the
softness of her breasts and circle lightly over her
exposed hips. Gently he lowered his face to hers
and kissed her on the lips. She felt his touch with
astonishment. The demand, the force that had
frightened her and hurt her had vanished.

Alexei was in control now, and determined to
right the wrong he had done her. "Yes, my little
one, again. I cannot leave a woman as lovely as
you so fearful of mankind. But you must give yourself to me willingly."

Her body responded without her willing it. Her
flesh, where he touched her, throbbed and tingled.
Slowly, Kirsten moved up to meet his thrusts, a
new desire growing in her. . . .

Rapture's Rebel

Iris Bancroft

PINNACLE BOOKS   LOS ANGELES

RAPTURE'S REBEL

Copyright © 1980 by K & I Enterprises, Inc.

An original Pinnacle Books edition, published for the first time anywhere.

First printing, July 1980

ISBN: 0-523-40521-9

Cover illustration by Bill Maughan

Printed in the United States of America

PINNACLE BOOKS, INC.
2029 Century Park East
Los Angeles, California 90067

Chapter 1

Kirsten Gustafson rested her slender fingers on the wooden embroidery hoop that lay on her lap, her head tilted in attention. Something had changed in the sounds of battle that came from the city below. She held her breath, sorting out the rattling of gunfire. The cannons had ceased to fire. A faint frown creased her smooth young forehead, and she glanced down at the sampler that lay half-finished in her hands. She hoped to hang it over her marriage bed when the war between Russia and Sweden ended and Knut Ivarson came from Uppsala to claim his bride.

Her fine features worked nervously. Life had not been easy in the months since the main spear of the Swedish army had left Turku to cross Finland in an attempt to rid the land of the Muscovite invaders once and for all. She had never felt so frightened, yet she had stood her ground with courage. The cold of winter had come and gone since first her mother had urged her to flee to Sweden, but Ranghild Gustafson was too weak to travel herself, and Kirsten had refused to leave her invalid parent, despite her longing to be free of the fighting. Yet the knowledge that escape was possible, that were her mother stronger they could flee across the Gulf of Bothnia to Ahvenanmaa and from there be transported to Stockholm, saved the sensitive girl from total despair.

1

Now it was too late. All roads to safety were certainly closed. The Muscovites had reached Turku.

It had been a strange battle, far longer than Kirsten and her mother had expected, since the defenses were terribly inadequate. All the strong men from the town and the surrounding countryside were in the army—or gone north into the wilderness to escape the fighting. The protection of the city was in the hands of the very old and the extremely young.

In the sudden silence, Kirsten looked down toward the city. It lay before her in the sunlight, a beautiful sight. There was the great castle of Turku, stark and grey, filled with tradition and memories of past glory. Clustered around it for protection were the city offices, stone structures too, but lacking the majesty of the castle. Beyond them were the homes of the townsmen, poor wooden structures with flat facades and tiny gardens.

Near the harbor, at the mouth of the Aurajoki River, were the square buildings where cargo was stored and traded. But the docks were empty now. What ships had not been commandeered by the Swedish army had been taken north by fleeing merchants.

The homes of the wealthy merchants and the Swedish government officials were, like Kirsten's, perched on the low hills that surrounded the town. As the daughter of one of the few prosperous Swedish traders, Kirsten had visited many of those homes during holiday seasons in the past. But the socializing had ended when the fighting drew close. Now all the Swedish merchants and their families had returned to Sweden. The city of Turku was occupied almost exclusively by Finish women and men who had not yet reached, or were far beyond, fighting age.

The occasional rattle of guns ceased. Startled, Kirsten searched for the cause of the silence. The pall that lay over the city was more frightening than the fighting had ever been. For the first time in days, Kirsten realized that even the sounds of the birds were stilled. She gazed at the sampler in her lap with a feeling of helplessness. She had received some comfort from pretending there was some purpose in her labors. But she could deny the truth no

2

longer. It was all over. Before her life had even begun, it was going to come to an end.

One by one, the noises of nature resumed. Inhaling deeply the sweet fragrance of the lilac buds, Kirsten waited for the roar of battle to resume. But the silence continued. All she heard was an occasional rattling of a gun against a stone wall or the slamming of a distant door, and a sort of hum that seemed to rise from the throats of the dispersing army.

Dropping her sampler on the bench, she hurried up the path to the steps of the stone mansion that had been her home for as long as she could remember. She was a lovely girl, tall and slender, with rose-pink cheeks and clear, white skin. Her blonde hair hung in long curls around her shoulders, and her deep blue eyes were filled with sadness. Her lips, bud-like in a shapely chin, seemed perfectly matched to her long straight nose and slightly flared nostrils.

Her slender legs moved smoothly. What a joy to be alive on so beautiful a day! Unconsciously, she began to skip. And then she remembered. This lovely morning would be the last she would ever see.

Halfway to the house she stopped. "Mother! Come quickly. Something's happened. The firing's stopped."

The front door of the house opened and Ranghild Gustafson emerged, resting heavily on a sturdy wooden cane. She was dressed in a simple gown, without any of the hoops that were all in vogue, yet there was no question of her aristocracy. A white linen collar edged her low neckline, exposing the swell of her full breasts. Her face was pale under her wide-brimmed hat, and her blonde hair, lightly flecked with strands of white, was combed into a neat bun on the back of her neck.

There was no doubt as to her relationship to Kirsten. Their features were as identical as if they had been twins, and only by a careful study of the shadows on Ranghild's face could one realize that she was more than twice the age of her young, vibrant daughter.

Kirsten caught her mother's hand and they stood side by side looking down at the capital city. "What does it mean, Mother?" Kirsten's voice still held echoes of hope. "Do you think the Russians have gone?"

3

Ranghild shook her head and pointed her cane toward the edge of town where a large army of men were beginning to fan out through the empty streets. "No, my darling. I fear the worst." Her voice broke, and she wiped a tear from her cheek. "See, over there where old Carl and his grandson manned the cannon?" Her cane moved toward a small rise where two bodies lay sprawled beside an ancient artillery piece. "I fear it is all over. The Muscovites have won."

Her arm crept around Kirsten's shoulders. "My darling, we must hurry. What lies ahead if we wait for the invaders to reach us is more terrible than death. Come. Your father will greet us in heaven."

Kirsten looked longingly up at the deep blue of the sky. Overhead a bird flitted past, singing wildly. It was the first time she had heard the lilting song since the fighting had begun. Then, watching the flight of the bird as it soared over the roof, she followed her mother around the house toward the forest.

She had no illusions as to what lay ahead. Her mother had spoken of it often in the three years since her father had died in the influenza plague of 1710. The Swedish armies, which had occupied Finland for longer than she could remember, had been pushed back by the invading Russians. And now, after a last-ditch battle waged on the outskirts of the city, Turku had fallen.

All the defenders were dead. And the women, traditionally considered the spoils of war, were at the mercy of the conquerors. If she and her mother did not go through with the pact they had made with her father and take their own lives, they would be raped by the invaders—raped not once but many times and then they would die violently, their torture providing the last amusement for the hardened troops.

A great ache filled Kirsten's breast. It wasn't fair! She was only sixteen. She had never even had a chance to live.

Her step slowed, and her mother turned. Below them a new sound had started. Even from the distance of almost a half a kilometer, the screams of the women cut through the air with terrible urgency. But there was no one to help them—no one to stop the heartless assaults.

4

Ranghild drew her daughter into her arms. "Oh, my dearest little Kirsten. I know how you feel, and I want nothing as much as I want you to have a chance to live! But you refused to leave when you had the opportunity, and what lies below and will reach us soon is not life. It is terror and horror beyond belief! Do you think your father did not love you when he made us promise to do this thing?" Her tears swelled uncontrollably, and she brushed them from her cheek. "Come, it will be over soon and we will be at peace."

Still Kirsten did not move. As she glanced about the garden, her kitten ran out from under a bush, leaping wildly at a passing butterfly. A sob racked her body. "Oh, Mama! I can't leave Fluffy for them to hurt!" She broke away and ran toward the white furry ball that tumbled over the smooth patch of grass. Picking the kitten up, she cuddled it in her arms and walked reluctantly back to where her mother waited. There was no way out. No way except the one offered by her father.

Her deep blue eyes met her mother's, and she felt a new surge of courage. Why was she being so foolish? She knew how it hurt her mother to do this. Determined not to aggravate her mother's sorrow any further, she led the way down the path to the door of the sauna.

They had prepared everything earlier in the spring, when it became clear that things were not going well for the Swedish army. The door to the small building shut tightly. Fresh air came in through small holes near the floor. Kirsten herself had stuffed rags into each one of the openings while her mother had filled the firepan with fresh wood. Death would be easy and swift. They would close the door, light the fire, and wait while the air turned bad. Unconsciousness would come first to soften the moment when life would end.

They removed their clothes out of habit and folded them neatly, piling them on the stone bench just outside the sauna door. As she removed her slippers, Kirsten remembered again the wonderful times she had had in the sauna with her parents. It had always been their favorite winter retreat. As a child she had sat between the naked bodies of her mother and father, watching the perspiration form until, with a shout of joy, her father would swing open the door and lead the way into the snow. Naked and overheated, the three of them would dive into the icy whiteness, shouting and screaming in delight. Then, when they began to feel the cold at last, they would return once more to the heat of the sauna.

But there would be no joyful exodus this time. The sauna that had been the source of so much pleasure in the past was destined to become her tomb. When the soldiers reached the Gustafson estate, they would find the dead bodies of two women. And a kitten. Fluffy would be with her. Kirsten nuzzled her face against the small furry body as her mother closed the sauna door. She would not leave the cat to starve.

Alexei Mikhailovich Leonidovich rested his hand on the hilt of his long battle sword and paused in his climb. Staring at the tear in the bright blue sash from which his scabbard hung, he cursed his shortness of breath. His horse was still in town where he had stabled it himself. But he had been too restless to remain in the quarters that had been appropriated by the officers—and unwilling to join in the general debauch.

He turned and looked back at the city. In spite of his long experience in the army, he still found the mayhem that followed conquest disgusting. As soon as they had entered the city, his men had gone wild, tearing young girls from their mothers and taking their pleasure in the streets like animals, as they had taken the farm women they had discovered as they advanced. He cursed aloud. Why did men turn into beasts at the sight of women?

Alexei growled. He needed a woman, too. But not that way! He tugged at his long beard, uncomfortably aware of the hard swelling bulge in his loose trousers. The sight of the men coupling with their victims had affected him despite his irritation with their bestiality. He needed release soon, if not with some female he found desirable, then by his own hand.

Pensively, he continued his climb, aware that he was no longer young enough to make such an ascent without a shortness of breath and a pounding in his chest. Still, it was good to be away from the city. The screams of the women were too much to endure. He cursed under his breath. What did they hope to gain by such irrational noise? And what did they expect? They knew the soldiers had been without females for many months.

But it was always like this. Whenever the men started to search a city for women and housing, they ran into screaming, hysterical creatures. It almost made taking them not worth the effort.

Up on the rise, in the peaceful garden that crowned the hill, there was no screaming. Alexei wondered if the house was empty. Most of the Swedish aristocrats in Turku—and in all of Finland—had fled long ago. Then he saw the sampler on the bench.

"Holla!" He tried to keep his voice from sounding too demanding. "Holla! Anyone home?" Picking up the sampler, he began to circle the house. The odor of freshly burned wood lay heavy in the air, yet he could see no smoke. More curious than worried, for he felt confident that his men could put out any fire that might have been started by a fleeing Finn, he stepped into the birch woods.

He passed a group of small buildings that served as storage as well as stables. They were empty. Cursing, he pushed open each door. The story was an old one. The owners of the house had released their servants and sent them up north to the wild country. And all the supplies had been taken by the Swedish troops as they retreated. Alexei shook his head and tugged again at his beard. It was a wonder they hadn't burned the house. So many of them did.

Burned . . . He remembered his original reason for searching the grounds and hurried back to the path, the pressure in his trousers somewhat lessened by the diversion. Suddenly he found himself in a small clearing, in the middle of which stood a tiny wooden hut. On the stone bench at the door was a neat pile of women's clothes.

He recognized the building immediately. The Finns were notorious for their saunas. The odor of burning wood was strong now, and he headed for the door. It wouldn't be locked, of that he was certain, though he was confused as to why any woman would seek shelter in such an odd place.

The door did not respond to his pull, and he stepped back in surprise. Grasping the handle once more, he pulled again, and this time the door opened easily. Propping it open with a rock, he stepped inside, his forehead stinging from the sudden blast of heat that slapped him in the face. He coughed when the stale air filled his lungs. Stepping away from the door, he gasped in the fresh air and then, holding his breath, he went inside the small building. What he saw brought a curse to his lips. Two naked women lay sprawled before him.

They were clearly mother and daughter. The older lay on her back on the highest bench. The younger one had evidently been kneeling beside her mother, for she had fallen from her perch and lay on the ground, her head close to the wall. She was by far the most beautiful young thing he had ever seen.

Beside her, its extended paw clutching a ball of cloth, was a small white kitten. And all three of them appeared to be dead.

Chapter 2

Kirsten opened her eyes and stared about her. Was this heaven—a spiritual copy of her own drawing room? In her semiconsciousness, she was aware of a bird chirruping on the windowsill. Tremulously, she reached up and touched her cheek. It felt just as it had when she was alive.

Everything was as it had been! The chaise on which she lay was under the open windows. The furniture had not changed in the spirit world. The satin-finished wood glowed with polish and the deep pile of the carpet stood up on brilliantly shining floors.

In langorous curiosity, she searched the room for the souls of her mother and father, but they were nowhere to be seen. Instead, she met the gaze of a dark man dressed in a blue uniform. It wasn't her father. Was it an inquisitor sent to examine her before she was permitted into paradise? Her heart fluttered in sudden fright. Was this Lucifer himself?

When he caught her eyes, the man rose, clearing his throat as he approached the chaise. "Good! I began to wonder if I had been too late to save you!"

The fog cleared, and Kirsten found herself staring at a thick-set man with greying temples and a pointed beard. His eyes were kindly, but behind the surface friendliness was a hunger that sent a shiver of fear through her breast. Suddenly aware of her nakedness, she sat up and protected her feminine parts with her hands. "What happened? Where am I?" Her eyes widened. "Who are you?"

He bowed from the waist, a crooked smile on his full lips. "Colonel Alexei Mikhailovich Leonidovich of the Imperial Cavalry." His eyes prodded hungrily into the curves and crevices of her body.

She felt her skin grow warm as a pink flush touched her cheeks. "How did I get here? I'm . . ." Her fright spilled over. "Mother! Where's my mother?"

The colonel settled himself beside her, his hands nervously clasped in his lap. Kirsten watched them uneasily. They seemed to have a life of their own, and they threatened to pull themselves from his control and overpower her. She moved away, pressing against the carved arm of the chaise.

"Your mother is dead." He hurried on, as if fearful that she might break down, or accuse him of murder. "I pulled both of you from the sauna as soon as I found you. I think it was your kitten that saved you. She dislodged a ball of cloth from one of the vents, letting in just enough air to keep you alive. Though just barely. If I hadn't come along, you'd have been dead, too." His eyes caught hers once more and held. "Why did you try something as foolish as that?"

She stared at him in silence, unable to stop her trembling. When he reached around and pulled her close to his warm body, she was too terrified to protest. Tears trickled down her cheeks, and her voice shook. "You're Russian, aren't you?"

She knew the answer before he nodded. The uniform was unmistakable. She tried to still the trembling of her lips and failed. "Are you going to rape me?"

He smiled and took her chin in his hand. "Where did you get that idea?" He paused and drew back his arm. "What is your name, child?"

"K-Kirsten. Kirsten Gustafson." She spoke so softly he could hardly hear, and her eyes were wide circles, staring up into his. "My mother told me that's what would happen."

He rose abruptly and strode across the room. She was only a child! The pressure inside his trousers increased. A child, yes, but a most beautiful one. He turned and looked at her, huddled fearfully on the chaise. Her well-formed breasts were hardly concealed by her slender arm, and the blonde growth of fine hair that she covered with her hand teased his senses. More than anything, he wanted to take her, to throw her onto the floor and smother her with his own demanding body.

The throbbing in his groin increased, and he cursed under his breath. Damn! If only she were less of an aristocrat. If only she were just one of the common females of the town, then he could take her without guilt.

"Confound it, my dear, you make it most difficult. I have been too long without a woman to cater to your youthful sensibilities. You sit there all exposed as if you dare me to touch you!" He stormed across the room and pulled her up into his arms. "Yes, dammit! I am going to take you! But whether it is rape or not is up to you!" His compelling gaze held hers. "Has your mother taught you nothing? Do you dare to stand here and tell me you are not aware of the needs of a man?"

Slowly, she shook her head. She had failed to follow her father's orders. Despite her efforts, she was alive, and in mortal danger, just as she had been told she would be. But the man who stood before her was not quite the beast she had been led to expect. He had not taken her as she lay unconscious, nor had he killed her, finishing the job she had bungled so badly. "Mama said—" She stopped. She couldn't help him in his atrocity. She would tell him to leave her alone—that she would kill him if he touched her.

But when she spoke, the words were altered by her fear. "You won't hurt me, will you?" Her lips trembled, and tears spilled from her solemn eyes.

He cursed once more and released his hold. "Not if you answer me. Do you know what I must have?"

Her eyes widened in renewed fear, the threat inherent in his words forcing her to respond. "When I got engaged to Knut, Mama told me what I would have to do to please him. I know—" she dropped her gaze to the bulge in his trousers and then looked away, frightened by what she saw—"what you will do."

Alexei exhaled loudly, a hint of a smile touching his

11

lips. "Thank God! Lie down, then. I will be ready in a moment."

She did not lie down, however. Instead, she perched on the chaise, her hands clasped so tightly her knuckles turned white. Her mind was racing. She had learned as a child to make the best of whatever situation she found herself in; Arne Gustafson had had no use for helpless women. Obviously, she would have to survive in this new life, for she had no courage to attempt again what she had failed to achieve as she crouched beside her mother.

She watched transfixed as Alexei slipped his trousers down until they hung over his boots. His manhood sprang out, hard and thick, a dark red knob at the end shining with moisture. She stared at it in horror and the trembling began once more. "No!" Her voice was barely a whisper. "No! You'll hurt me! Please, don't!"

He looked at her sharply. His need was becoming too great for him to cater much longer to her fears. Lifting his trousers so he could walk, he reached her side. "Lie down. It will be easier if you are on the floor."

Her eyes on his demanding member, she sidled onto the carpet. If he dropped his trousers again, he would hobble himself. She moved inch by inch until she was just out of his reach. He turned, supporting himself with his hands as he knelt before her. Once more the top of his breeches fell over his boots.

In that moment she was on her feet and running. She reached the door before he was up, and she turned the handle frantically. It was locked—and the key was gone.

Shaking, she turned and looked back. He was on his feet, his member swinging toward her like a spear. With a scream she tried to avoid his strong hands, but he caught her around one wrist and threw her violently onto the rug.

Shrieking and kicking, she pushed at him with her arms until he caught her flailing hands and pressed them against the floor. His full lips covered her mouth, smothering her cries, and his heavy body settled between her legs. There was nothing she could do to protect herself. She was pinned down, helpless against his assault.

She felt her flesh tear as he entered her, and her mind reeled at the sudden pain. There was a movement within

12

her, but she was only vaguely aware of it. Her body was tense with her rejection of his act, his smell, his weight. She acknowledged only the searing agony.

The force of his need was too great for him to exercise further control. In the back of his mind was a small regret that she had turned his desire into rape. But he was far too aroused to care much. He felt a surge of relief as he penetrated her tender body, and then the drive for satisfaction took over, wiping all awareness of her fright from his mind. Panting from exertion, he pinned her to the floor, hammering her down in a final burst of passion. Then, with a groan, he lay still, resting his entire weight on her slender hips.

As the fury of his passion subsided, he once more became aware of her as more than a receptacle for his lust. She lay beneath him, a slender girl with smooth white skin and firm young breasts. A virgin no more, yet still innocent of the pleasure of union. She was sobbing helplessly, her chest shaking, and her eyes, when they met his, were clouded with pain.

His voice was angry and hurt. "Why did you fight?" He rose to his knees, wiping himself on his soiled kerchief. "Dammit, girl, you only hurt yourself more! It would have been better for you if you had accepted it."

She made no answer. As he released her arms, her hands sought the tenderness between her legs, as if to protect it from further assault.

Now that he no longer was tormented by the immediacy of his need, he felt a surge of sympathy and regret. If only he had not been so strongly aroused! He had hardly been able to enjoy her virginity. And her fighting could have added to his pleasure instead of interfering, if he had been less driven. But she had tempted him too much with her nakedness and her firm breasts and that fine blonde hair. When she had fled, it was as if some floodgate had broken in his brain. If only she hadn't tried to run away!

Gently, he ran his fingers over her body, touching her cheeks and wiping the tears away. "Forgive me! I could not control myself. I've been denied a woman too long—and you were far too tempting." He met her eyes and flushed, shamed by the reproach he saw in their depths.

"It can be good. I can show you. It doesn't hurt all the time."

He stroked her smooth cheek with his fingertips, caught one of her curls in his hand and twisted it gently. She was so very young! She couldn't be much older than his daughter, Anastasia. The vision of his own child floated before him and he shuddered. God forbid that she should ever find herself in a similar predicament! "It was just too much when you tried to run away from me. Why did you do that, after you said you would let me take you?"

Kirsten chewed helplessly on her lower lip as he spoke. Then, her eyes still holding his, she caught her breath. "You hurt me! Why did you hurt me?"

His hands caressed her shoulders tenderly, and when she pulled away, he let his fingers pass the softness of her breasts and circle lightly over her exposed hips. She was so beautiful! If only she would release her genitals so he could show her that a man could give pleasure as well as pain. As one hand continued down her leg, the other ran up her arm. "Please forgive me, my dear. I could not . . ." He paused. He was repeating himself unnecessarily. Gently he lowered his face to hers and kissed her on the lips.

She felt his touch with astonishment. The demand, the force that had frightened and hurt her had vanished. His fingers caressed her shoulders and her hips. When he ran his hand up her arm, she felt a tremor that started in her shoulders and moved quickly to her groin. Her tight grasp on her genitals relaxed. She felt suddenly confident that he would not hurt her again. The weapon with which he had taken her hung soft and harmless between his legs.

Still, she was not completely reassured. "Why did you hurt me?"

"Didn't your mother tell you? It always hurts the first time. But it won't hurt again, not if you do as I tell you."

The shaking that had almost stopped began once more. "Again?"

He was in control now, and determined to right the wrong he had done her. "Yes, my little one, again. I cannot leave a woman as lovely as you so fearful of mankind. It can be good—" He saw her wince, and he caught her

14

hands in his. "But you must do as I tell you. You added to your own discomfort. Now you must give yourself to me willingly."

She met his eyes again. Now that the shock and terror were past, she was remembering some of what her mother had said to her when they spoke of her coming marriage to Knut Ivarson. She had forgotten it all in her fright. "What must I do?" She covered herself once more. "If it hurts again, will you stop?"

He smiled, his eyes caressing her gently. "It will hurt a little at first, maybe, but not as much as before." He was aware of his passion rising as he touched her soft curves, and he lifted himself to his knees above her, ready once more to take her. "Spread your legs and wrap them around my hips. I will enter carefully."

He was true to his word. Kirsten felt a jab of pain as he pushed past the tender lips, but she deliberately held her body loose. The discomfort lasted for a moment and then, gradually, he stirred the passion that lay unawakened within her. When he felt her respond, he bent and kissed her eyelids, letting his mouth trail down to her lips. His voice was filled with a new tenderness and passion. "You're so beautiful! So very beautiful!"

Her body responded without her willing it. Her flesh where he touched her throbbed and tingled. Slowly, she moved up to meet his thrusts, a new desire growing in her. This was what her mother had said it would be. It would build and grow.

He shuddered suddenly above her and pressed her to the carpet. Confused by the abruptness of his action, she tried to push him up again, tried futilely to resume the sensation she had only moments before learned to enjoy. But his weight was too much for her.

Pinned down, she felt a flood of disappointment. Was this all there was to the pleasure—that there be no pain? She trembled convulsively, and he smiled into her clouded eyes.

"See? It can be good, can't it?" With a smile of self-satisfaction, he rolled beside her on the floor. Once more his organ was flaccid.

She closed her eyes and felt the longing that shook her

body. There had to be more than this! If there was nothing else, she could endure it. But in their private talks her mother had not spoken of endurance. Ranghild Gustafson had been a passionate woman and she had taught Kirsten to want—to expect—much more.

Alexei was on his feet now, buttoning his trousers. "I told you it could be good!" There was a smugness in his expression she could not help but resent, yet she dared not show him her disillusionment.

"Yes." Sensing his wish for her acceptance, she closed her eyes in assumed ecstasy. "Oh, yes."

He pulled her up. "Come, my dear. You can't stay here all alone. It isn't safe. I will take care of you, at least as long as we are stationed in Turku. You're far too lovely to be shared with the others."

She gazed at him with wide, innocent eyes. Despite her disappointment in what had just taken place, she thought that her father had not been quite correct in his evaluation of the results of conquest. Instead of peril and death, she had met a man who promised to care for her, a man who could take her father's place and protect her from hardship. And all he demanded was that she feign enjoyment when he took her. He was not the enemy, despite his uniform. He was her friend.

Suddenly she remembered. "My kitten?"

"Your cat is dead." He saw her face wrinkle in grief. "I'm sure we can find another for you. As long as I'm around to care for you, I will do what I can to make you happy." He touched her shoulders, letting his fingers run through the strands of her long blonde hair. "You are such a lovely child!"

He waited while she dressed, and then he helped her bury her mother. She kissed her mother's cold lips and then watched in silence as he laboriously shoveled dirt into the shallow grave he had prepared.

He smiled indulgently when she insisted on a second grave for her kitten. Watching her cradle the tiny body, he wondered that this could be the same female who had served him so well as a woman. Yet he was charmed by the union of childishness and maturity that met in her expression. It would not be difficult to love such a one.

16

Mixed with his appreciation for her beauty was an awareness that her life would be far from easy. He could shelter her from the debacle that filled the streets of Turku for as long as he was stationed in this godforsaken country. Maybe, when he left, he might even take her with him. But sooner or later the time would come when he could no longer keep her under his protection, and then he would be comforted by the knowledge that she was no longer a frightened child who feared a man's touch. Even now, if she had to, she could survive in the streets of Turku, for she had learned not to resist the inevitable.

Chapter 3

Viotto Hannunen cursed under his breath and crouched farther into the shadows that served as temporary shelter not only for him but for three other Finnish soldiers who had miraculously escaped the final push of the Muscovite army. In the distance, the shouts of the triumphant invaders posed no immediate danger, but until he was certain no advance contingent was approaching quietly, he preferred to exercise caution.

Viotto was dressed in the uniform of a lieutenant in the army, a position not often awarded to Finnish recruits. But Viotto was not typical of his fellows. Born in Turku, he had been raised in Uppsala, and had even attended the university for a year. He had returned to Finland when the fighting broke out between Sweden and Russia, right after Charles the Twelfth's magnificent victory over the Russians at Narva, in Estonia.

He had married that same year—a gentle girl whose father owned the farm next to his own, for he had no illusions as to the position he might expect to hold when the fighting was over. As a Finn, educated or no, he would have little opportunity in the business world. Besides, he loved farming, loved the closeness with animals and the feeling that he was near the source of all life.

He had barely consummated his marriage when the fighting began in earnest and he had been forced to leave

19

his bride alone while he took his place at the head of his men. Now he had no one left to lead except the three who huddled fearfully beside him.

Once again he reviewed the battle. The Muscovites had attacked with a viciousness no one had anticipated, yet he and his men had been ready for them. But Viotto's anticipated victory did not materialize. Though many of their men fell, the Muscovites continued to attack, pouring over the field like a swarm of rats. And at last they had triumphed.

The sounds of the victorious army altered subtly. Viotto rose and signaled his men to do likewise. "We're safe for now. They're making camp."

The three men rose and stepped hesitantly onto the path that snaked its way through the underbrush of the birch forest. They were similar only in the uniform they wore and in the length of their beards and hair. There had been little time for niceties like shaving since the fighting began. All, like Viotto, were blond; all had dark, haunted blue eyes that reflected the horror of the recent battle.

In age, they were quite different. Two of the men were mature, rough soldiers, men who until recently had spent most of their time behind their plows. The third was a youth, not much more than fifteen years of age. His fine beard was almost transparent, and his slender frame showed his weariness.

Viotto rubbed the uneven growth of his own chin. He disliked beards with a passion, if for no other reason than the fact that every Muscovite wore one as a religious and filial duty.

He held up one hand as a signal for silence. The distant sounds were unmistakable. Tent stakes were being hammered into the ground. Exhausted by their victory, the conquering army was preparing for sleep.

"Filthy serfs!" Viotto's words were a curse. "Filthy Muscovite serfs! They win with numbers! Man to man they would have no chance against free men defending their homes!"

The three soldiers muttered their agreement. Only the youth frowned in confusion. "Would we have fought better with King Charles at our head? Why does he not return from Turkey? Doesn't he know his country needs him?"

The two older men turned on him with growls of anger. One spoke for them both. "How dare you speak ill of our king? Never has Sweden had a better monarch, or a braver one! It is we who have failed him!"

Viotto held his piece. He shared the youth's resentment of his king's absence, but he knew only too well the fierce loyalty of most of King Charles's subjects. It had served the army well to encourage such devotion. Now, certainly, was not the time to pull the only strength his men had left away from them.

"Tuomas! Halle! Enough. Errki will learn when he puts on a few more years. Do you think I led you from the field so we could stand here and argue? We have work to do. Between here and the coast are many small farms and tiny towns filled with women and children who will feel the brunt of our defeat. We must move fast so we can warn them."

He met his men's eyes. Tuomas and Halle, both strong men, looked back without flinching. But young Errki could not hide his fatigue. Viotto rested his arm on the boy's shoulder. "Take courage, lad. We cannot give in to our weaknesses now. You can rest when we reach Turku."

"Sir, can we at least take the time to hunt for food?"

Viotto reached into his inner pocket and drew out a strip of dried venison. "Here, eat this as we walk. It will renew your strength." He ignored the lad's embarrassed look. "Take it! That's an order!" He pushed the strip of meat into the boy's hand and hurried away. His own stomach growled with hunger, but he had no time for such frailties. His bride was one of the women who had to be saved.

As he led the way along the path, he thought again of the fine features of his Ruusu. She was eighteen, five years his junior, but she was already a mature woman, filled with the strength needed to live through difficult times. Her golden hair ringed her face like a halo, and it was as thus he always thought of her. An angel, watching him depart, her hand raised in a final salute. She had hinted that their love was bearing fruit. He inhaled deeply

21

and thrust out his chest. Maybe she was already carrying his son!

Viotto Hannunen glanced back at his three followers. Halle and Tuomas were striding stoically along, their eyes searching the woods around them. Young Errki walked between them. He was still munching on the venison, and his pace was strained to keep up with their wide steps. Viotto slowed down imperceptibly, repressing his own impatience.

Errki was not a stranger to his lieutenant. Viotto had known the boy's parents before the great plague of 1710 killed them both. It had been on Viotto's suggestion that the lad had been accepted in the army as one of the allotment from his village. Viotto had smoothed his first introduction into the rough life of a warrior, and had watched his proud assumption of military duties with satisfaction. Errki had learned to care for himself. He was sharp and well acquainted with the woods. And he had the ability to fend for himself when orders from above were slow in coming. Of the three, he was the most independent and capable.

The moon rose, its light filtering through the fine early leaves of the birch trees. Suddenly a doe broke from the brush ahead. Viotto signaled a halt. The doe stood for a moment, staring at the intruders. Then she was joined by her fawn and the two vanished into the forest. Viotto raised his arm and waved his men forward.

The woods ended abruptly. Before the travelers lay a typical farm community. Small buildings clustered in the center of the clearing, surrounded by well-tended farmland. Pigs and sheep filled the barnyards, and from the squealing that filled the air, Viotto could tell that spring foaling had already begun. A kid bleated piteously, startled by some night sound, and its nanny called in comforting response.

On the far side of the village was a corral filled with horses and cows. Viotto frowned. Ordinarily, most of the cattle would already be out at pasture in the open country. Pray God the delay here would not be too long!

"It looks as if they're already preparing to leave. Come

along. We might be able to help them." As he spoke, Viotto strode down the path into the town.

The townspeople were awake, silently moving from their houses, loading wagons with furniture and other valuables. When they saw the four men approach, they stopped their labors and huddled together in the street.

Viotto stopped before the pitiful group. One old man, almost too old to hold himself erect, stepped forward. "I am Viljo, the city elder. What is your purpose here?"

"We come to warn you of the advancing Muscovites. We are all that remains of an entire battalion of brave men."

The old man snorted. "Brave! Brave with women and helpless children! Look!" He turned and pulled one of the women forward. She was of stocky build, with hair flecked with grey and fine lines breaking the smoothness of her cheeks. But it was her eyes that held Viotto. They were deep blue and icy cold.

The old man turned again to Viotto. "This is Mija Agricola. Her husband was murdered by a party of soldiers who passed through here only a week ago."

Viotto felt a surge of apprehension. "They are ahead of us, then?"

Mija tensed her jaw. "The Muscovites? No! It was not the Muscovites who killed my man and violated my body! What reason have we to trust you any more than them? You wear the same uniform! Soldiers are no friends of the farmer, even when they come from the same country!"

Viotto grabbed her by the arms and shook her. "What are you saying? Our own men? Did they do this to you?"

Viljo pushed himself between Viotto and the woman. "Let her be! Can you not see that she has suffered enough?"

Abashed, Viotto released his grip. "I'm sorry. I did not mean to mistreat you, nor do we intend to harm you. We have families of our own. We want only to help you escape."

Mija stood where Viotto had released her. Suddenly she looked up into his face. "The bastards! They were in and out before we knew what had happened. They, like you,

23

offered to help. But we soon learned that they had little to offer. They wanted to take our chickens. When my Paavo tried to stop them . . ." She paused, her eyes filling with tears. "They ran him through with a sword. At least he didn't suffer—or live to see . . ." Again she lowered her eyes. When she met Viotto's gaze again, her cheeks were wet. "Who is the boy?"

Viotto turned to Errki. "He is a soldier, like the rest of us. But—" he stared at the lad in silence—"he has no family. He knows the land north of here. He traveled once to the wilderness, where those who flee can find refuge. Would it help were he to lead you?"

Viljo rested one hand on Mija's arm. "You must understand this poor woman. She has been treated most badly by her own countrymen. But what happened to Mija and Paavo was not repeated in the rest of the town. Paavo was a strange man. He was too ill to join the army when the recruiters came, and he showed no sympathy for those who went. He was an ill-tempered man. Even Mija will agree with what I say." He glanced at Mija, who was speaking quietly to Errki. "We will accept the guidance of the lad, if he is willing to travel with us." He pointed in the direction of the wagons. All was confusion. Women were dropping pots and pans and bulky hand-sewn quilts on the floor of their carts, leaving little room for the cattle. An old hag rushed past, a well-worn cradle in her arms.

Viljo threw up his hands in a gesture of helplessness. "What can I do? She needs that pile of wood as much as I need a silk gown, yet she is determined to carry it with her. None of them pay attention to my directions. It is hard to be old! I can no longer raise my voice to demand obedience."

Viotto felt a smile touch his lips, and he fought to repress it. "I will help, if you wish."

Under his guidance, the wagons were unloaded. Furniture was placed behind blankets and warm clothing, and both gave place to animals and chickens. Ewes with young were herded into the larger carts. Yearlings were tethered behind the wagons and strong oxen were harnessed to the heavy loads. Horses were saddled in preparation for the journey.

All but three horses were mounted by the strongest boys. Viljo led these to Viotto. "The lad will ride at the head of our caravan. You must take these beasts to speed your travels."

Viotto accepted the gift with a solemn nod of thanks. Many miles of rough travel lay ahead of the refugees. If they suffered too many delays, they would loose much of their stock on the way. Horses, the least productive of farm beasts, would be the first to be abandoned when the journey grew difficult.

Viotto signaled to Halle and Tuomas, who took their mounts and leaped onto their backs. Then he turned to Errki. "You must take no chances, nor must you delay. If you learn of Muscovites on the road ahead, take to the woods. If you have to abandon the animals, release them from their halters. Leather will be useful to the fighters up north. Abandon cows and laying hens last of all, for they will provide food, not only for the caravan, but for the men up north when at last you reach them." He met the boy's steady eyes. He was so young! "Try to bring everyone to safety." He clenched his jaw in thought.

When he resumed speaking, his voice was low. "If you see that the enemy is too close, let the caravan separate. You take the young boys and lead the way to safety." His eyes held steady. "Do you understand?"

Errki nodded. "Yes, sir. If I can bring the boys to safety, they can become soldiers, like me."

Viotto nodded. It was hard to leave such important decisions to a child. "Above all, Errki, avoid fights! Something has happened to change the Muscovite army. It is not the same as it was even a few years past. I doubt that even King Charles could overcome them now, were he as badly outnumbered as he was at Narva." He frowned. "When you reach the north, seek out Esko and tell him of our defeat. The king must be notified. All of Sweden will be lost if we cannot stand before the Muscovite hoard."

He stood silently, his hand on Errki's shoulder. He had not failed to notice the bond that had developed between the boy and Mija Agricola. "Above all, Errki, take care! Try nothing hazardous. Avoid confrontations! Remember, your duty is to deliver as many of the villagers as survive to the northern settlements, where they can assist in the fight for freedom."

"Sir, I will be careful!" Errki looked back toward Mija, who smiled at him from the seat of her wagon. "It has been a long time since I had a granny to care for. Mija Agricola is—" He hesitated, lowering his eyes, a flush growing on his cheeks. "So like my mother." When he looked up his eyes were clouded and tears streaked down his cheeks. He rubbed them away impatiently with his sleeve.

Viotto gave the signal to move. He was growing restless. Ruusu needed him, and he was wasting time with other people's grandparents. But he hid his eagerness until the pitiful caravan was lost in the woods. Then, handing the reins of his horse to Halle, he waited while his two companions led their mounts from the field. When they too were out of sight, he knelt and struck his flint near a pile of straw.

As the flames licked at the edge of the field, he hurried to join his friends. They did not look back at the glow that spread slowly over the fields of half-ripened winter wheat.

Three more times during their journey they stopped to assist lone women to start the trip to safety, and each time Viotto's impatience increased. Ruusu . . . Her face swam through his consciousness as he lay down to rest, her bright smile beckoned him to hurry when he felt his mount lag. He cursed each stone that caused his horse to slip. Most of all, he cursed the soggy road he was forced to traverse.

Ruusu. She needed him, and he was not beside her!

As he stirred his companions on the third morning of their travel, he vowed he would not stop again for rest or food until he held Ruusu in his arms. But his determination could not increase the pace of his horse. As they moved south the ground grew more soggy, wet from melting snow and spring rains. Footing on the slippery path was unsteady, and any attempt at speed risked the safety of them all.

"Damn!" He pulled on his reins to keep his horse from stumbling. "If only spring thaw had not come so early!"

Tuomas stirred from his own private reverie. "If the

battle had been fought in winter we might not now be fleeing! No Muscovite army can keep up with Finnish soldiers on skis!"

Halle chuckled. "Aye! Remember that battle near the crescent lake? They fired at everything that moved—and hit nothing! We swooped in, set their camp ablaze, and were gone before they knew what happened!" The militant humor that had been lacking throughout the long journey lifted his spirits. "It is far easier to fight in the winter—at least for a good Finn!"

"And to travel!" Viotto rolled in the saddle as his horse recovered his footing. "The stones under the muck! And time is so important to us now!"

Tuomas's face grew sober. "At least we have heard no more of the renegades who attacked Mija and Paavo. My farm is nearby, and I have been dreading what I might find."

Viotto studied the lightly rolling land. "You're leaving us then?"

"As soon as we reach the crossroads. I will go directly to the woods where we will rendezvous for the journey north. I have not forgotten your instructions."

"Good!" The uneasiness that had been eating at Viotto's thoughts throughout the day grew more insistent. "God be with you! May you find everything well with your family."

They reached the intersection of the two roads, and Tuomas raised his arm in salute. "Till we meet again, Lieutenant. May God be with you!" He turned to Halle. "And with you, too. I will be waiting." Leaning forward in his eagerness to be gone, he guided his mount toward his home.

Viotto and Halle continued on their way in silence, each lost in his own worries. Viotto saw in his mind's eye the narrow path that led from the main road to his small farm. His thoughts traveled down the trail to the door of his cottage. Ruusu stood at the open doorway, her eyes aglow, a cry of welcome on her lips.

His horse stumbled, and he pulled his thoughts back to his present dilemma. He wanted to run, to speed over the ground to be near her. But he was forced to move at the pace of a snail.

Halle said his farewell to Viotto just as the sun hung heavy on the horizon. "I must head due west now, Lieutenant. I will make what speed I can to the meeting place. God be with you."

"And with yours!" Viotto's face was solemn. "May all be well at your house—" he lowered his voice—"and at mine."

The weight on his shoulders lifted when he at last saw the clump of fir trees that marked the border of his land. Soon he would be home, and Ruusu would be in his arms! Too impatient now to ride, he dismounted and, reins in hand, led his horse up the hillock. His heart was pounding, and he tried to tell himself that it was with anticipation of holding Ruusu once more. But the fear that had been riding with him throughout the long journey surfaced, and he knew at last that he might face that which he dreaded the most.

He began to run, slipping on the wet grass beside the road, tugging at his horse's reins. "Ruusu!" His cry echoed hollowly back from the distant forest.

"Ruusu!" Still no sound. Flushed, he forced himself to slow to a walk. "Fool!" He spoke aloud, and the sound of his voice was reassuring. "Do you expect her to hear you from here? Wait! Don't get overwrought! Call her when you can see the house!"

Straining to control his eagerness, he turned down the trail. This was what he had envisioned when, alone at night, he had dreamed of returning to his bride.

"Ruusu!"

A cluster of birds rose screaming to the sky. Then silence once more fell over the woods.

"Ruusu!" Viotto could not conceal the panic in his voice.

A scrub jay squawked loudly from a tree and then blue wings beat against the sky.

Still no response.

"Ruusu!" He forced himself to speak lightly. "My love, your man is home at last!"

A crow swooped from a hanging branch, startling his horse.

"Ruusu!" He ran now, his heart pounding in terror. "Ruusu!"

In the red glow of the setting sun, the small cottage seemed peaceful. But Viotto did not see the peace that surrounded him. His eyes rested momentarily on the empty barnyard, on the grass where no chickens nested, on the open gate. He quickened his pace. When he reached the gate he paused. The brook that ran behind his farmyard gurgled softly. An owl hooted.

The barnyard was empty.

With a taste of bile in his mouth, Viotto pushed through the gate. As he pulled it behind him, his fingers closed over a scrap of cloth. Automatically, he stuffed it into his pocket and ran forward. But he did not call out again. He dared not face the silence he felt sure would follow.

She lay just outside the back door, her naked body twisted where it had been thrown. In the pink afterglow of sunset, her face seemed still to hold some life. Her legs were streaked with blood, and her eyes stared blankly at the darkening sky.

With a cry he was beside her. She did not move. He reached out and touched her face, and his hand recoiled at the cold of her skin. He looked about wildly. They must be nearby. The signs of violence were still too fresh.

Rising, he carried the fragile remains of his happiness into the cottage and laid her on the bed. He stood for a moment, gazing at her slender form. Then his hand touched the slight swell of her belly. She had spoken the truth. His child—their first child—had died before it had a chance to see the light of day.

Gently pulling a blanket over the ravaged body, Viotto dropped to his knees and folded his hands over the still form. Maybe they would come back, wherever they were, and kill him too. His bride was dead! His happiness was ended. He had been off helping others when he should have been with her. With a sob of anger and despair, he lowered his head on the silent corpse and wept.

He buried her by moonlight, wrapping her still form in a blanket before he lowered it into the earth. When the mound was patted smooth, he stood silent, staring into the darkness. His jaw was clenched, his eyes dry. The cold hard lump in his chest grew. He had seen enough as he moved through the cottage to be certain that his wife's assailants had been Muscovites. They had startled her, taken their pleasure, and left her to die, driving his cattle and goats before them.

A breeze stirred his hair, whispering its way through the fir trees. It was time to go. Halle and Tuomas would be waiting.

He reached into his pocket and drew out the fragment of cloth. He recognized it now. Colonels in the Muscovite army wore them tied about their waists. This piece had been torn off when it caught on the fence, probably as the officer watched his men ravage their frail victim.

Viotto returned to the main road without looking back. As he reached the rise in the hill, he gazed down at the sleeping city of Turku, visible in the distance. He would meet Tuomas and Halle and send them on their way. And then he would return. Somewhere in Turku was a Muscovite colonel with a torn sash. And that was the man he knew he had to kill.

Chapter 4

Kirsten rested her hands in her lap and gazed down at the activity below her. A large procession had arrived in Turku that morning, after Alexei left her, and she had been filled with curiosity regarding it all day. The officers, with Alexei in the lead, had ridden out to meet it. She had recognized her lover even from the distance.

Now at last he was on his way up the hill. With a smile she put the finished sampler down on the bench beside her and rose to get a better view of his ascent. As usual, he carried something in his arms. He had not forgotten to bring her a gift.

In the weeks since he discovered her half dead in the sauna, he had become an established fixture in her home. Not that he never took her into town; he seemed to take pleasure in showing off her beauty to his inferior officers. But he seemed happiest when he had her to himself, when he could touch her smooth white breasts with his fingers and kiss her lips.

Other than expecting her to be available whenever he felt a need for her closeness, he made no great demands upon her. Once the first terror of his lust was past, she learned to accept his importunities with quiet reserve. She was available, welcoming him without protest. But she also endured his lovemaking without enthusiasm, except when his query as to her satisfaction forced her to pretend a pleasure she did not feel.

In moments of private honesty, she admitted to herself that she found his behavior somewhat ludicrous. Ludicrous and even boring. It was ridiculous that a grown man should put such stock in an act that lasted for so short a time—and brought her so little reward.

Smoothing out her skirt, she brushed the thought from her mind. She was wrong; he rewarded her each time he climbed the hill. Didn't he bring her a new gift every evening?

He was puffing now, and his eager pace slowed down. She smiled indulgently. In spite of the frightful beginning, she took honest pleasure in making him happy. It cost her very little to accept his caresses, and it did so much for him.

"Kirsten!" He gasped for breath as he topped the rise and appeared beside her. "My dearest! Come and kiss your Alexei!"

His arms folded around her and his thick lips pressed against her throat. She felt a sudden warmth that spread throughout her body. It was always like this—in the beginning. The promise . . .

She pulled back, gently touching her face where his thick beard had scratched her cheek. Then she ran her fingers over the thick curls that concealed his chin and let them rest on his mouth. "I missed you, Alexei. Do you have to spend every day in town?"

"More so now than before, my sweet. The tsar's representative has arrived to take over the civilian affairs of the country. We are no longer in a state of war. The Swedes have been defeated. It is time we settled down and rebuilt the country."

"The tsar's representative? Does that mean you will be leaving?" She could not hide the fear in her voice.

"No, my dear, at least not immediately. And when I do go, you will come with me. I will not leave one as gentle as you to be abused by men who have no sensitivity to the wonder of your beauty."

Kirsten smiled and slipped her hand into his. "My father warned me, long ago before he died, that the Mus-

32

covite soldiers were cruel beasts. He told me I would be assaulted and murdered. Because we feared such a fate, my mother is dead." She drew him onto the path and began to walk toward the house. "I wish he had known you. He would not have then feared for our safety. And maybe, then, my mother would still be alive." Her voice broke. "Then I wouldn't be alone so much."

He laced his fingers with hers and pulled her into his arms. "Your father was not as wrong as you believe. Had you been less of a beauty . . ." He stroked her hair, letting the long blonde ringlets slip through his hands like a stream of water. "Who knows? If your mother had remained alive things might have been worse. If she had tried to stop me from—loving you—I might have had to kill her myself."

She glanced up at him quickly, a frown wrinkling her brow. "Please, Alexei! Don't say things like that! You would never hurt anyone. You're too kind."

"Ah, my little Kirsten, you are too trusting. Have you forgotten that I hurt you, when first I took you?"

"But you had to! You told me so yourself. And my mother said it would hurt. You are not like my father said you would be."

The sound of his laughter rang through the air, clear and free, like the joyful expression of a young man in love. "To think I had to travel across Finland to find you! It was God's will! I have never known a woman so trusting—so open and sweet! My wife—" He frowned. When he was away from her, he tried not to think of the sour-faced woman he had married to assure his position as an officer in the imperial army. "Even my daughter thinks sophistication is attractive in a woman. From the time she was a small child, she has been the smooth manipulator of men. But you are different. Do you think for a moment that I will let another man hold your charms? You have given me back my youth." He took her hand from where it rested on his shoulder and placed it over the swell in his trousers. "See what you do to me, my dear? I can hardly wait to taste the wonder of your charms."

Kirsten repressed a smile. How foolish this man was, after all! Her father had thought the Russians would be

33

beasts. He had warned her that she would be beaten and raped. Instead, she had fallen into the hands of a man who treated her like his favorite daughter, and who asked only that she accept his lust without protest and that she pretend, at least once in a while, that he pleased her with his attention.

She remembered the screams that had reached the hill that first day when the Muscovites reached Turku. Maybe she had been fortunate to encounter this particular man. He asked very little for all that he gave. She had her own home, he brought her the best food available, and he indulged her every whim.

Sliding her fingers from his grasp, she prodded at the bundle he had slung around his shoulder. "What did you bring me, Alexei? Is it a new dress?"

Alexei moved her hands back onto his abdomen. "Later, my sweet. I have dreamed of holding you all day. I must see you now and touch the smoothness of your skin. When we are resting I will give you your gift. Then I will be relaxed and able to appreciate your enjoyment. Now—" He put his hands over hers and closed them over the bulge that had grown hard under her touch. "Now I can think of nothing but love. "

Kirsten glanced up into his eyes. Sometimes, when he showed such eagerness, she knew he was willing to be teased. But his glance was serious, and his eyes burned into hers. She would have to wait. His need for her body was too great.

She fumbled nervously with his buttons and suddenly he burst free. With a cry of assumed delight, she slid her hands into the dark folds of his trousers and closed them over his swollen organ. Despite the deliberateness of her action, she felt a sudden surge of warmth between her legs. But she ignored the sensation. Her pleasure would have to wait until he was asleep.

Her mother had found her once playing with the soft wetness between her legs, and she had been strangely understanding. "It will do you no harm, my dear, for now, at least. But you will have no need for such play when you are married to Knut. A good man is all any woman needs."

She knew now that her mother had been wrong. This

34

man was certainly good to her. Yet when he lay exhausted and satisfied, she was still tense and filled with longing. Only her own fingers satisfied her need.

She felt the pulse of his desire and she tilted her head up, seeking his lips. Each time it was the same. The touch of his tongue against hers, the feel of his surging desire, set her pulse pounding. Her response was only partially assumed, for in the back of her mind was a hope: *maybe this time I, too, will feel the thrill that sets his heart racing and his temples pounding. Maybe this time . . .*

As they reached the steps, Alexei withdrew her hands from inside his trousers. "Go ahead, my dear. Tonight I want to hold you as I did that first time—as we lay on the floor in the study. I want to enjoy your naked innocence, waiting for my love to waken your passions. Like a fairy princess, unaware of the power that lies in the kiss of her lover."

Kirsten brought her hands to her face and inhaled the musky odor that remained on her fingertips. The fragrance stirred her passions more than his touch ever could. With a teasing glance into his dark eyes, she hurried up the steps. Leaving the door slightly ajar, she slipped into the hallway and vanished into the study.

As she slipped out of her dress, she thought again of her mother's words when, after her engagement to Knut was solemnized, she stood watching him return to Turku, from whence he would take ship for Uppsala. "The love a man shares with a woman is very beautiful. God made our bodies so that we could take pleasure in union. In a marriage where love is mutual, children are born healthy and strong. Cultivate your ability to take and give ecstasy. There is no sin in such love."

Would she have a child by Alexei? The possibility was disquieting. Brushing the thought from her mind, she folded her dress and placed it neatly on a chair. Alexei showed a marked enjoyment of games such as this. But her natural response to his presence was to push against him in an attempt to satisfy her own desire. Once he thrust himself into her moist vagina, a pressure within her body drove her to rotate her hips. But in this game such an act was not allowed until he was writhing in passion, and then it was too late. He would shudder, lie still for a moment over her, and then roll onto his side, leaving her empty and strangely frustrated.

The late afternoon sun streaked at an angle through the window, touching her naked body with warm fingers. With a sigh she lay down on the settee. He would enter suddenly, express surprise at her presence, and then . . . Her fingers dropped to the soft down that covered her most private parts. When they slipped between her legs, she felt a wave of relief, and then she began to tease the small button. A warmth spread to her breasts and her cheeks took on a rosy glow. Deep in her abdomen, a throbbing began, and she convulsed involuntarily.

A step sounded outside the door and Alexei stepped into the room. He had waited longer than usual. Maybe this time it would be different. Maybe this time she would feel in his arms the same pleasure she aroused with her fingers.

He strode across the room, pulling open the slash in the front of his trousers as he advanced. Through half-closed eyes she watched his pretended surprise and his sudden look of tenderness. Then she was lifted up and placed on the floor. There, on a rug her father had brought home from one of his journeys, he took her.

As usual in this game, she had to work to restrain her urge to meet his passion with her own. Biting her lip, she forced her body to remain still until at last he began to increase his thrusts, and she knew she was expected to respond to his presence. He moved swiftly over her, pushing himself deep into the warmth between her legs, and she circled her feet around his hips and rose to meet him. Her hands were stroking his back, pulling him deeper.

He shifted and pulled her arms to the floor. "Alexei! Please!" Her cry was involuntary, more a prayer than a call of passion.

His response was to increase his pace. In and out he pushed. She found herself counting the times, praying that he would last until the strange tension that filled her body was released.

Her desire increased. Four, five, six . . .

His weight slammed her to the floor, pinning her hips

down and holding her still. She felt the convulsions of his organ, felt his body jerk above her. "Kirs—" His attempt to speak her name ended in a groan.

When he relaxed above her she felt his weight on her hips and she braced her arms against his chest to keep him from crushing her breasts. He sagged on her hands, moaning quietly, his face pale and drained. "Kirsten! My sweet little Kirsten!"

She knew by heart the response he expected. "Alexei! Oh, Alexei, it's so wonderful!"

"It is good, is it?" His voice slowly returned to normal. "Does your Alexei make you happy, my little Swedish princess?"

"Oh, yes." Deliberately, she kept her voice high, as if she had trouble gaining her breath. "Oh, yes!"

He lay over her until the color returned to his face. Then, with a groan of pleasure, he rolled onto his side. The cool air rushed over her damp abdomen, licking at the moisture that oozed between her legs. She lay still. Maybe he would leave her now, and she could use her fingers to fill the longing his brief presence had aroused.

He propped himself on one elbow and kissed her cheek. "We will be leaving soon, my dear. You must be ready to move with me."

"Yes, Alexei." She tried to keep her voice bright. "I will do whatever you want. Where will we go?"

"Maybe to Moscow! Would you like to vist my homeland?"

She had no desire to leave Turku. "Of course. I only feel safe when I am with you."

His finger ran down her body, stopping to circle the dark rose of her nipples. Closing her eyes, she waited for the surge of passion to subside. She wanted more. But she knew he had nothing left to give her. Gradually, the pressure in her abdomen lessened. When she opened her eyes again, they glowed with a different light. "May I have it now, Alexei? Your present?"'

He chuckled and stood up, tucking his flaccid organ into his trousers. When he returned, he held the bundle in his hands.

She took it eagerly and tore the cords. It fell open suddenly, spilling brilliant blue over her legs. "Oh, Alexei!" Something heavy dropped to the floor, but she hardly heeded it. "How beautiful! Is this gown for me?"

"Who else could wear it, my dear? It is blue like your eyes, blue like the summer sky over Moscow! Tomorrow, you will wear it to the ball we are holding at the castle to welcome the governor. And you will wear what you dropped so carelessly to the floor, too. Pick it up, my dear, and tell me how you like it."

Kirsten did not immediately obey his command. First she held the gown before her, a flush of pleasure coloring her cheeks. It was an exquisite gown with a fine, tight bodice and long puffy sleeves that were laced down to the wrists with gold cord. The neckline was low, and she could tell it would expose the swell of her breasts in the latest fashion. The skirt was wide, shirred heavily around the waist. All that was missing was a hoop. But maybe, if she searched her mother's wardrobe, she would find one that would serve.

Then she glanced down at the floor and forgot such unimportant considerations. A chain of gold lay at her feet, set with sparkling gems that caught the rays of the setting sun, breaking them into a rainbow of colors. Bending, she lifted it to her throat. "Oh, Alexei! Diamonds!"

"And worth a fortune, my love. You will wear them tomorrow night—and many more times." Gently, he took the jewels from her hands and tucked them into his pocket. "But that is enough now, my sweet. Now you will pull on your new dress and let me see how well the blue touches off the whiteness of your skin."

It took no persuasion to get her compliance. She pulled the gown over her nakedness and then stood quietly while Alexei buttoned it up the back. He took the necklace from his pocket and fastened it around her throat. Then he stepped back and gazed at her with unconcealed admiration. "You are so slender—so delicate. I had trouble finding a gown among those left in the town that would do honor to your fine figure. We can be grateful I succeeded. The army tailor has no skill for such delicate work. He cannot even mend this tear in my sash so that it looks like new. Turn now, and let me look at you!"

Kirsten ran her hands up her bodice as she twirled about. The round white swell of her bosom was exposed temptingly, and she felt that for the first time since she had lost her virginity, she was truly a woman.

"Magnificent!" She basked in the wonder of his appreciation. "You look magnificent!" He gazed at her in solemn admiration. "Tomorrow night, you must be most circumspect. You are my woman and no one else must think for even a moment that he can take you from me. With my protection, you will have a life of luxury. I will provide you with a home of your own in Moscow, and I will visit you often. If you allow others to take you from me you will be ruined forever. You will be passed from one man to another, and all the dire things your father predicted will occur. Will you remember this, and stay close to me tomorrow night?"

"Of course!" She smiled beguilingly. "Why would I want to leave you? If I cannot stay in my own home, then I have no other place to go."

She was in his arms again, and his lips folded over hers. His touch lit the fire that lay dormant in her breast, and she felt the warmth between her legs increase. When he stepped back, she could see the outline of his desire beneath the loose hang of his trousers.

"Come, my dear. The sight of you in so lovely a gown has roused my manhood. You are a witch! I touch you, and I become young once more. Tomorrow others may enjoy your beauty. Tonight you are mine. I must possess you once more before I sleep."

She did not protest as he fumbled with her gown. When it lay abandoned on the settee, she led the way into her mother's bedroom, for there was the only bed large enough to hold both her and her stout lover.

She lay naked on the coverlet and watched him undress. His erect organ stood out before him as soon as he removed his trousers, bobbing heavily as he hurried to discard his shirt and leggings. Then he was beside her, inside her, and resting above her, his lust abated after a few quick thrusts.

She made no protest when he rolled over on his side

and began to snore. But as soon as she was certain he was sound asleep, she rose silently and drew on a robe. As always, she would not sleep until she had washed the evidence of his lust from her body.

Chapter 5

Knut Ivarson stopped his pacing and gazed sullenly at the panorama of university buildings that lay spread before him. "Damn all cowardly Finns! They'd leave their own mothers and sisters to the Russians! Why would they bother to protect Swedish women?"

Olaf Anderson rose from his chair and walked to his friend's side. "Come now, Knut, you exaggerate! You know the Finns have proven themselves to be able soldiers, and they fight viciously to defend their homes. They are loyal to King Charles, too."

"Loyal? Then why do they run for the north when the recruiters arrive?" He slammed his fist against the frame of the window without any awareness of the pain. "Blast it, Olaf! We aren't talking about the relative merits of Finns or Swedes as soldiers. We're trying to save Kirsten, my affianced! If the Muscovites have reached Turku, her life—her honor—may be in danger! We are too late!"

Olaf shifted uneasily. "Easy, Knut! Surely her mother will have the sense—"

"It is precisely because of her mother that she is now in risk of her life! Her mother is crippled, and Kirsten refused—*refused*, do you understand—to leave Turku without her, when escape was still possible. You heard Harald. He tried to persuade her to leave with the others and she would not go. And now . . ."

41

Olaf leaned against the wall, following his friend's pacing with his eyes. "I know, now she is in danger. You have told me that a thousand times already. Are you going to keep up this nonsense for the rest of the war? Knut, what has happened to you? You have always been the man of action. Knut Ivarson, the graduate student guaranteed to act first and think later! Are you now content to pace back and forth in your room like a caged beast? Has your commission in the army robbed you of your power to move? You can't help her if you remain in Uppsala."

Knut paused, his face red. "Is that what you think, Olaf? Do you think that all I have done is to rage and complain? Do you really think I'd allow Kirsten to be—" He stopped, his face working. For all of his anger, he could not speak the word. "I have been pounding on the commandant's door all week, attempting to get permission to take a force across Bottenhavet Selkaeril! And can you believe it? I have been ignored! My father could buy and sell the commandant twice! And he dares to keep me cooling my heels in his reception room!"

Olaf dropped into a chair and draped his leg over one arm. "He's doing it, isn't he? You bluster a great deal, my friend, but you have let him keep you here for almost a week since Harald brought the news of the latest defeat."

Knut hammered his hand on the heavy oak table that occupied the center of the large room. A candelabra in the middle of the smooth surface bounced as his fist landed, and the small flame flickered feebly. "Damn it all to hell! I will take no more of this!" He swung about, clamped his hat on his head, and stormed toward the door. With his hand on the doorknob, he paused. "Are you coming with me? Or are you only good in the role of a gnat, tormenting a man into fury?"

With a chuckle, Olaf rose, grabbed his hat, and joined his friend. Arm in arm the two youths descended the broad staircase and stepped into the cool of the morning rain.

Knut Ivarson, the taller of the two, was slender and fine featured. Only his tailor knew that he spent more money for his lieutenant's uniform than most captains earned in a

42

year. His blond hair was covered, as was the fashion, with a neatly groomed wig, and his face was clean shaven.

Olaf bore no resemblance to his friend except in the color of his coat. His face was pale, not tanned by the sun, and his light-brown hair showed beneath his unkempt wig. His eyes, too, were brown, not blue like his companion's. Unlike Knut, Olaf was short and stout, more like a baker than a soldier. But his soft pudgy features belied the sharpness of the mind concealed beneath his bright new hat.

The path that led from the dormitory to the rest of the university buildings was crowded with students rushing toward their classes, but Knut paid no attention to the young men who hurried past. He had been one of them only a few months before, but now he was a man of action.

When he reached the city streets, he turned and hurried toward the barracks. But in spite of his continued speed his pace changed. He walked now like an officer, ready to return the salutes of his men. When he reached the commandant's quarters, he drew himself erect. The guard saluted stiffly.

"Lieutenant Knut Ivarson, requesting to speak with Commander Hansen!"

The guard saluted again and stepped inside. When he returned, he saluted once more. "Lieutenant, sir! You are to enter."

Knut pushed his way into the dimly lit office with a firm step. Just inside the door he paused and saluted, and he remained at attention until the commander returned the greeting. Then he stepped forward, his hat cradled under one arm. "Sir!"

"Yes, Ivarson!" Commander Hansen's voice was sharp. "I know why you're here. And I know you think I have ignored your request, just because I did not comply with it immediately. But I have had my reasons. There are ten Finnish soldiers here, remnants of one of the top cavalry forces to go against the Muscovites. They just arrived in Uppsala this morning, and all have volunteered to return to Finland to accompany you on your raid." He paused and shuffled through the papers on his desk. "You are to leave tomorrow. Remember, you will be in enemy territory and you will be outnumbered. I expect no heroics! Do what you can to find your women and then return."

Knut frowned. "*Our* women?"

"Yes. The Finnish soldiers have wives in Turku. Their goal is yours. You will go in and out quickly. That is the key to success. Every moment of delay adds to the risk. Do you understand?"

"Yes, sir!" Knut was too delighted to be perturbed by the slight to his intelligence. Saluting smartly, he turned on his heel and stepped back into the bright sunshine. The morning rain was over—and so was his long wait.

Waves slapped monotonously on the side of the small skiff. Knut stirred and glanced for the hundredth time at the faces of his men. The expression on the face nearest him was typical of them all. The skin, still pale from the long winter, was flushed with a tint of red, the jaw was set and hard, and the eyes were focused on the approaching shore. Knut had looked into those eyes before and had seen in them the same dedication that drove him onward. The commandant had been wise in his choice. Every man in the boat was determined that this mission would be successful.

Other than their faces, there was nothing to identify these men as trained soldiers. All were dressed, as Knut was, in simple peasant garb. All had the soft high boots worn by Finnish farmers, the best footwear for swift travel over the water-soaked ground. All wore dark caps that they could pull down over their heads. They carried knives and muskets concealed in the folds of their baggy trousers, and swords muffled at their sides.

They had left Uppsala the morning after Knut's conversation with the commandant, and had arrived at Ahvennanmaa that afternoon. Carefully avoiding the small coastal town, they had beached their craft on an isolated strip of sand and, after a short rest, had continued on their way, The delay was deliberate. Knut did not want to arrive in Turku until well after sunset.

They stopped at a small island near the Finnish coast and muffled their oars with rags. There they waited until

Knut was satisfied that their arrival would be unobserved. Then, silently, they approached the mainland.

Knut had no difficulty guiding the small craft through the narrows to a stretch of shore some distance from the town. As the boat hit the sand, the men leaped out and together pulled it behind a large rock. Further concealment was impractical. If they did not succeed in launching their vessel before dawn, their project would be a failure.

Signaling silently, Knut led the way from the beach. Almost immediately he found himself in a birch forest. The shelter soothed his raw nerves, but he showed no change in his behavior. Like eleven ghosts, the men moved up the narrow path, each one alert to the slightest change in the night sounds that surrounded him. Their plan was simple. They would remain together until they approached the city. Then each one would seek out his own woman. They would rendezvous again when the moon was at its zenith. More time they dared not take. Any woman not found by that hour would have to be left behind.

A noise on the path ahead sent the men scurrying silently into the underbrush. From his place of concealment, Knut watched the empty woods that lay between him and Kirsten's home. He prayed once more that she would be there, that no misfortune had driven her away.

Ranghild Gustafson's determined face floated into his thoughts, and he wondered if he would have trouble convincing her daughter that it was time to leave. "Help me, God. It is sometimes difficult to handle a young woman, and I must make her understand."

The path ahead was still empty. Carefully, Knut crawled from his hiding place and resumed his journey. When he glanced back, his men were moving quietly behind him.

An owl hooted overhead, swooping down on an open meadow just as Gnut approached. He paused and watched the predator as it barely touched the ground. But when it soared again into the sky, it held a mouse in its claws. His rescue must be just as smooth. Squaring his shoulders, he moved ahead.

He knew the countryside as well as any of his men.

Mostly flat, with small rises that in mountainous Sweden would be ignored, the land of Finland stretched endlessly before him. In the past he had traveled inland to the tiny lakes, marveling at the emerald green of the rolling hills. But he had not been charmed by its verdant lushness. Winters, he knew, were far colder than those in Sweden, and in the summer insects threatened the sanity of any man foolish enough to travel without adequate protection.

But Kirsten loved everything about Finland. Not surprising, of course, since she had spent all of her life in Turku. She spoke with enthusiasm of the "icy fairyland" created by the winter snow, and of the wonder of spring after the long period of cold.

"It's my home, Knut, and I love it! When the sun sets over the water, it paints the sky gold, and the sea glows! I will go wherever you want me to, when we are married, for I will be your wife. But now I want to live only here. Look, the sun is setting! Have you ever seen anything as lovely in Sweden?"

Knut had refrained from responding. He knew that the mountains of Sweden held more rugged beauty. But Kirsten was only a child. She would learn to love her new home when she became his bride.

He gritted his teeth, and once more prayed that Ranghild Gustafson would do nothing to interfere. The woman had been sickly when last he saw her, and now she could not let her own disability harm her daughter.

The silent party reached the end of the forest. Now there would be no shelter. Farms, cool and empty in the moonlight, stretched between them and the sleeping city.

Knut waved his arm. The first man behind him crouched and ran through the unplowed field. Knut watched until he reached a small clump of trees. Then once more he signaled. A second man followed, moving silently like a wild creature.

One by one the men started their perilous journey. Knut watched until the last had reached the first clump of trees and the first to go had vanished in the distance. Dangerous as the crossing of the open farmland might be, there would be more hazards within the town. Sentries might challenge their approach, or a dog might bark and signal

46

their arrival. The Muscovites would be quartered in the homes, and if one of the Finns found his wife lying beside a Muscovite pig . . . Knut cursed silently. They had all agreed that the safety of the mission was more important than vengeance. But emotions were unpredictable.

His fingers closed over the knife that hung at his waist. If some Muscovite devil had harmed his Kirsten he would have trouble controlling his own anger.

By the time he reached the hillock where the Gustafson estate was located, he had regained his control. With a glance at the moon, he slipped into the birch woods and approached the clearing from the rear. The house was dark and silent.

When he came upon the graves beside the sauna, he paused in alarm. One large cross had been placed on the long mound, and beside it a tiny cross protected a small pile of dirt. His initial shock and fear vanished. No human inhabited that tiny grave. And no adult would have bothered to dig it. Kirsten was still alive and her mother lay buried. At least that hindrance was gone. Knut stepped over the grave without a further glance.

And if Kirsten were not alone when he found her? His pace quickened. He would face that possibility when he reached it. He would feel no regret if, as he led his child bride to safety, he left the body of her attacker behind. There was no longer any doubt that someone—some man—had arrived before him. Kirsten had not dug that grave by herself.

In spite of his apprehension, Knut smiled. How like his sweet bride to charm her captor into helping her bury her mother! He felt a perverse comfort in the knowledge that some Muscovite soldier had been touched enough by Kirsten's plight to do such a kindness.

And then he put such friendly thoughts aside. He faced many dangers in the next hour. He could not afford to weaken himself with sympathic understanding of the enemy. His knife felt hard against his leg. His hand tight around its hilt, he crept silently toward the darkened house.

47

Chapter 6

Little had changed since the day many years before when he had said his farewells to the child who had been promised to him. There, to his left, was the swing on which he had sat with Kirsten and told her that her father had consented to his plea for her hand. The memory brought a smile to his lips. She had been such a child! Twelve, and bursting with mischief. Yet her response had been all that he could have wished for.

"I'm a woman already!" Her clear young voice belied her words. "I began my flow when I was eleven. Why do we now have to wait?"

He had taken her hand and brought it to his lips. "Because, my dearest, there is more to being a woman than that. You have much to learn before you will be at home as the wife of an officer in King Charles's army. You must study the manners of society." She looked confused, and he hurried on. "Don't fear, your mother will teach you." He held up his hand to still her protest. "Your father is a wise man. He loves you and wants you to be happy. Do not fight his decision. See? I am willing to be patient and wait."

Her expression clouded. "Why don't you argue with him? I thought you loved me!"

His thoughts wandered back to the lusty female he had held in his arms the night before. He had the appetite of a

49

man accustomed to self-indulgence. He wanted a wife who would not be frightened by his desire.

"I do, my dear. But you must wait, and talk with your mother. She has much of importance to tell you, now that you are to be wed. When we marry, I want a woman in my bed—not a frightened child."

She had seemed disquieted by his response, and he had cheered her with a kiss and a pretense at adult conversation. He had returned to Sweden with mixed feelings. Her innocence was so charming! Silently, he prayed that she had matured without growing hard.

The house was silent. He moved slowly around it, studying the windows. Was he too late? Had she been torn from her home?

He stopped abruptly. Ahead, near the well, a candle flickered. Drawing into a shadow, he watched as a woman's figure appeared. She was dressed in a long dark robe, and she moved steadily toward him.

When he first saw her face, he felt a jolt. The delicate beauty of her features sent his pulse pounding. She had grown into a far more lovely woman than he had dared to expect.

He stepped from his place of concealment, his arms extended. With a gasp of surprise, she turned and began to run toward the back door. The candle fell to the ground, landing on the damp grass and sputtering before its flame flickered out.

"Kirsten!" He barely whispered her name, but she spun around at the sound of his voice and stood, her eyes wide with alarm and surprise, waiting for him to reach her side.

"Knut!" She was whispering. "How . . . Where . . . I thought you were in Sweden!"

He did not bother to answer her questions. His arms went around her, pulling her close, and he pressed his lips against the fullness of her mouth. Her lips parted, and her tongue reached out to touch his. Startled by the implied desire in such an act, he drew back and gazed into her face. "Kirsten, did they—?"

She did not answer, but neither did she flinch under his gaze.

"Are you alone?"

She lowered her eyes. "No. Alexei . . ." She gazed up into Knut's face, her eyes wide. "He—I—I couldn't stop him!"

The tension in his arms increased. So the worst had happened! He felt the swell of her breast against his chest. No, not the worst. At least she was alive!

He leaned quickly down to kiss her lips, his mind racing. She would have been so perfect! Such lovely features, and a father prepared to provide a dowry that would augment his own wealth quite satisfactorily.

Her eyes pleaded for a response, and he kissed her again, unprepared to answer her question. Marriage was impossible now. But that should not deprive him of her company. Many officers had mistresses as well as wives. He let his glance wander over her delicate features. He would be justified in leaving her, now that she was no longer worthy to be his bride. But he could not bear to leave such beauty in the hands of the enemy. "No, my dear, I am not angry. And we will speak of all this later. I am thankful that you are alive."

A faint smile lit her face. "Alexei is really very kind. He only hurt me when—"

Knut put his hand to her lips, his face filled with sudden hate. "Spare me such details! You will come with me now. Is that your mother's grave?" He gestured toward the mound.

A tear inched its way down Kirsten's cheek. "Yes." Her voice wavered. "We were to die together, but Alexei found me." Her expression brightened. "Now I'm glad he did! You've come to save me!" She told of the pact, and how her kitten had kept her alive. Knut scowled when she spoke of Alexei's attack, and she quickly ceased to speak. She gazed at him in awkward silence, but he seemed unwilling to be pacified.

"Please, Knut, don't be angry. Alexei has been very good to me. He has let me stay here, in my own home, and he has brought me food and wonderful presents. He promised that he will take me to Moscow with him when he leaves Finland."

Knut's jaw tightened. "He will take you nowhere! You are coming with me, back to Sweden."

She hesitated for only a moment. "Then I must say farewell to my mother's grave. Come." Pulling herself from his arms, she led the way to the sauna. The long mound stood out bleakly in the cold moonlight, and beside it the tiny grave seemed, for the first time since she had dug it, to be the work of a foolish child.

When Knut pointed toward the miniature cross, she blushed. "My kitten. It was he who brought air into the sauna and kept me alive until Alexei arrived." Her voice stilled. Why did everything she said sound like the ramblings of a child?

He drew her back into his arms. "Then the kitten deserves an honorable burial. Oh, Kirsten, when I think how nearly I lost you forever!" He kissed her again, her lips, her eyelids, the delicate upturn of her tiny nose.

Suddenly he released her and glanced toward the house. "The Russian. Are you sure he is asleep?"

"He was when I left him. And he usually sleeps very soundly after—" She averted her face.

He laughed nervously. "He deserves to die! The bastard! How could he?"

This time it was her hand that stilled his lips. "Please. What will you gain by killing him? He has been kind to me."

He had regained his control. "And we will only draw pursuit if I injure him. I made a vow that I would not attempt any heroics. Your safety, and the safety of the other women we are rescuing tonight, is more important than vengeance." He glanced toward the dark windows. "Besides, if he had not saved you, I would never have held you again. I owe him his life, if only for that." Resolutely, he took her hand. "Come, it is getting close to dawn. We must hurry."

She moved forward with him. Then her bare foot encountered a hard rock and she cried out in pain.

He turned to silence her, and for the first time realized that she was dressed only in a robe. "Can you get some sturdy clothes without waking the Muscovite?"

She nodded. Before he could speak again, she was out of his arms and running toward the house. When she returned, her appearance brought a smile to his lips. Her gown was typical of the peasant attire preferred by her mother. Her long wool skirt hung loosely about her ankles. Her white blouse was covered by a dark bodice that laced up the front, pushing her full breasts up even higher than nature had created them. On her feet were a pair of sturdy shoes such as he had seen on farmers' wives. He rose with a sigh of relief. She was, in spite of her fondness for her dead kitten, a woman grown. Her ability to see the reality of war and accept it proved her maturity.

She stopped at arm's length from him. "Is this all right? I wanted to wear one of my gowns, but—" She smiled suddenly. "Will I be able to have pretty clothes when we reach Uppsala?"

He pulled her into his arms, chuckling. "Don't worry your lovely head about such things." He spoke reassuringly. "I will have the best dressmaker in Uppsala at your service." Without kissing her again, he drew her toward the forest. "But unless we leave soon, I will be able to give you very little. We have only an hour until it is time to rendezvous."

She glanced back as they reached the edge of the clearing. The graceful walls of her home glowed in the soft moonlight. She caught her breath and stood gazing at the empty windows. She had been happy there. Then she turned resolutely toward the forest. Alexei would miss her. She glanced back once more. She would miss him, too. He had been good to her.

Knut tugged on her arm and she ran down the hill. All that was past. Now, with Knut at her side, she was ready to face the future as his wife. And that, she was certain, would bring her only happiness.

Chapter 7

The men were waiting when Knut arrived. Each led at least one woman, who crouched behind him, her head lowered in shame. Only Keikki had four females huddled around him, and he held his head high. "Halloo, Lieutenant! I have been most fortunate. My wife and daughters found shelter in a cave I had prepared for them before I went to war. They have been saved from the lust of the conquerors."

Knut felt a momentary resentment. Why hadn't Kirsten's father thought of that before he died? But his expression remained cheerful. "Good! And the rest of you? Are you satisfied that you have achieved what you set out to do?"

There were a few muttered words of assent, accompanied by sobs from the women. Then, suddenly, Jussi stepped forward. A tall man, he had held his head down, but now he drew it up and faced his fellows. "My wife was not fortunate enough to have so wise a husband as Keikki. I left her at the mercy of the conquerors. But she loves me in spite of my stupidity, and for that I am grateful." He pulled her into his arms and held her close, lifting her chin up so she looked him in the eyes. "I hope you will forgive me, my dear. You are a brave woman—and a good one."

His wife smiled, at first feebly, and then with sudden

pride. When he released his hold, she turned and faced the others with a new look of dignity.

One by one, the other men faced the shame their wives had suffered. Only one couple, after staring quietly into each other's eyes, turned and looked away. The woman's head was lowered, and her eyes were filled with tears.

Knut glanced back at Kirsten. But there was no shame in her face. He looked quickly away. It would not be easy to tell her that their relationship had been changed by her experience.

Abruptly, he shook his head. That could be settled later. Now they had to make their escape. Quickly, he turned and led the way through the underbrush to where the boat lay hidden.

He stopped at the shore, his heart beating wildly. The sea was tossing wildly, and the water was covered with whitecaps. Resolutely, he climbed into the skiff and assisted each woman to settle herself. Then he leaped onto the shore and joined the men as they pushed and tugged until the boat rode in the rough waves.

Immediately, the men climbed inside the skiff, rowing fiercely, their backs straining as they pulled against the force of the water. The boat shuddered as it pulled free of the sheltering cove. A high wave towered above the curved side and collapsed on top of the already dripping passengers. The women gasped in alarm and the men, straining at their oars, struggled to keep their seats on the slippery boards.

Knut sat at the helm, his arm resting on the steering post. As the water hit, the post was torn from his grasp, and the ship began to wobble helplessly in the water. Cursing, he caught the post and strapped it firmly. Another wave like that and they might never make it to safety.

Once more the men pulled on their oars, and the skiff shot forward. But another wave rose up overhead. With sudden resolution, Knut veered from under the towering water. He beached the boat north of their point of departure, at least a mile farther from the occupied city.

Once more the men set about protecting the skiff from view. When they were content that it was covered as best they could, they hurried into the shelter of the forest. Kirsten followed Knut, running much of the time to stay near him. Her hair trailed over her face, dripping water that ran down her nose. Her gown clung to her legs, and her blouse outlined the swell of her breasts. She shivered as a cool wind whipped at her skirt. But she kept pace with her protector.

Had she been foolish to leave the shelter of her home to travel with Knut? Impatiently, she brushed such a disloyal thought from her mind. Her father had approved of Knut's wooing. Of course she belonged beside him.

Shielding her eyes from the rain, she glanced about her. One by one the men had dropped away, each into a hiding place. She wished there was some protection to be had against the downpour.

Abruptly, Knut came to a halt, and Kirsten almost ran into his back. She watched as he knelt and crawled into a cluster of bushes that surrounded a large rock pile. She knelt and followed him.

A small opening appeared in the rocks and Knut pushed through it. When he did not reappear, Kirsten gathered her courage and crawled after him. The opening was small, and she wondered how he had managed to enter through it. But the cave in which she found herself was quite adequate, and dry. Kirsten had no difficulty sitting up in the dark space which, she felt sure, had been the winter lair of some wild beast.

Something brushed against her hand and she jumped.

"It's all right." Knut's voice was close to her ear. "The den is empty."

She shuddered. Never could she remember being so cold! As if in response to her thought, Knut's arms folded about her shoulders. He held her thus for a time and then, with a sudden decision, released her. "Take off your dress. We can warm each other better if we don't have wet garments between us."

Kirsten thought for a moment of the spiders and other insects that generally inhabit caves, and then, putting her fear aside, she obeyed Knut's command. He took her skirt and blouse from her and spread them out near the opening of the den, where a slight wind stirred their folds. Then he pulled her back into the darkness.

They lay together in a hollow and the closeness of Knut's body comforted Kirsten's fright. His breath was warm against her cheek, and he cradled her. She felt his desire grow between them, and her awareness of his need stirred her. Her mother had told her that uniting with Knut would be more than just endurable. Unconsciously, she tightened her buttocks against the hardness of his masculinity.

He shook with sudden passion. "Kirsten, my darling!" His breath was warm against her ear. "I worried so for you. Ever since your father consented to our engagement, I have dreamed of holding you in my arms."

She knew now what he meant, and it was as if a light had brightened the depths of her mind. He had said the same words four years ago, and she had stepped into his arms and kissed him. Then she had not understood his unspoken disappointment. Now she had lost her innocence. Deliberately, she turned in his arms and pressed her body against his. If it had been no sin for her to submit to Alexei's demands, surely she was doing no wrong to accommodate the man she was to marry.

The pressure of his lips against hers grew suddenly hard. With a groan, he rose to his knees above her, letting the hard spear of his manhood push between her thighs. Silently, she let them fall apart, arching her back to let him enter. Her lips parted, and her tongue pushed out to tease his.

She expected nothing. Yet she hoped that at least some of her mother's words would be fulfilled. As Knut began to move about her, she felt a tremor begin in her legs that spread through her body.

She was not aware of the moment when she forgot what she was doing and allowed herself to be lost in her own sensations. But the moment did come. Once Knut stiffened above her, and she suspended her passion, expecting that her growing ecstasy would come to an end. But he did not grow still, as she expected, nor did he roll away and begin to snore. Instead, he continued to thrust himself into her body, stirring the heat of her passion.

58

The explosion began deep inside her, and it traveled like a string of rattling gunfire up to her head. She had feared the insects that crawled around her—now she forgot they even existed. She had compared Knut's touch with Alexei's. Now she knew only that he filled her body and forced all thinking from her mind. She cried out and tightened her legs around his hips, pulling him to her with such force that he could not but comply. And then, pressed close against him, she lost all of her control.

She was still trembling when he rolled beside her, and she clung to him, reluctant to let such ecstasy subside. She tried to speak, to tell him of her excitement, but her tongue would not form the words. Gasping for breath, she lay beside him, aware only of the heat that rose from her steaming abdomen. Then the cold of the night air touched her belly, and she shuddered. "Oh, Knut! I—" She clutched at his chest. "I love you!"

Was there a delay before he answered? "You are a magnificent woman, little Kirsten! We will have many hours of pleasure together." His voice was more chill than the wind that whistled through their narrow shelter.

"Hours of pleasure? We have a whole life! My father consented to our wedding before he died."

Again the delay. "Yes. I know. But—" The silence was more obvious now. "My father would never approve of a marriage between an Ivarson and a—" He paused, and she could almost hear him thinking. "A woman who has known other men."

"Other men? Knut, what are you saying? I was raped by Alexei! I gave him nothing! He forced me. Am I to be condemned because of fate? Even when he took me, my thoughts were of you. I remained true!"

The warmth between them had cooled. Suddenly, she felt cold and very alone. "What do you expect of me? Why did you take me away from my home? At least Alexei showed me some respect!"

He was on his elbow now, and though she could not see his face in the darkness, she was certain he was smiling, and that his smile was not friendly. "Respect? When he took you at will? Is it the clothes he brought you that you believe showed his affection? Come, now, Kirsten. Don't act like a child! You were his property, no more. And when he left Finland, he would leave you behind. Then where would you be? I took you with me because in Uppsala you will at least have some security. I will provide you with a good home and servants. Even my father will not be opposed to such an arrangement."

She wished desperately that she could see his face. Could he possibly speak thus to her, after all that had just passed between them? "But you are my fiancé!"

"Many intended marriages have never taken place because of the war. Please, Kirsten. You will be happy."

"But our friends! I—my father knew many people in Uppsala. What will they think when we do not get married? I will live in shame! How can you do this? Don't you love me?"

He brought his lips to her ear and nibbled gently on the lobe. "Of course I love you. This has nothing to do with love. It just is not possible for an Ivarson to enter into any but a most honorable marriage." He continued quickly, before she had a chance to respond. "Please, let us not speak more about it now. You will feel better after you have had a chance to consider."

Her voice was tight and hard. "I want to go back."

He snorted, but he did not respond.

Suddenly cold, she rose to her knees and crawled to where her clothes lay spread out on the floor of the cave. They were wet and clammy, but she pulled them on nevertheless, shivering as the damp cloth touched her warm skin. Then, trembling with suppressed rage, she crawled back into the interior of the cave, keeping as far from Knut as she possibly could. He made no move to approach her.

She dozed, her head resting against the rocky wall. She woke when light began to creep into the crevices of the rocks, and then she realized that the rain was over.

The first gun shot shattered the morning stillness, sending echoes throughout the rocky cove. Startled, Kirsten backed into the shadows, just as Knut pushed past her. He had pulled on his trousers and shirt, and he grabbed his weapons as he exited from the cave. Then he was gone from her view.

Kirsten started to follow, but as she reached the mouth of the cave a scream tore into her consciousness. Even as the fighting was progressing, someone was attacking the women. Too terrified to move, Kirsten crouched down and stared through the thicket that concealed the cave from general view.

A ray of sunlight lit the area immediately before her, showing up each movement of the defending soldiers and their sudden attackers. There had been a flurry of shooting that followed Knut's exodus from the cave. Now the fighting was already over. Only the screams and cries of the women persisted.

One of the women ran past, her blond hair shining in the sunlight as it waved behind her. She was crying out fiercely and her gown trailed her in tatters. Close after her, his trousers open, a burly man advanced with long, easy strides. Then suddenly he was upon her. He lifted her like a doll and pushed her down upon his erect organ. Her legs flailed in the empty air, and her hands clawed at his arms, but he paid her no heed. Over and over again he pushed her down toward him, and each time she screamed.

He stiffened suddenly, crushing her to him with a roar. Then, like a child discarding a rag doll, he tossed her body to the ground. She fell with her buttocks up in the air, and then another man appeared behind her. With a shout of triumph he fell upon her, tearing into her tender flesh. She shrieked as he tore through the soft skin of her buttocks, and as he drew back for another thrust, Kirsten saw blood gush from between her legs.

The sight froze Kirsten to the spot. She could not take her eyes from the vicious scene, nor could she move to help the hapless victim. Her own screams stilled by her terror, she stared at the ravaging intruder. He finished abruptly, pressing over the still form of his prey until she was lost in the grass on which she lay. Then he rose, wiped himself on his victim's skirt, and gazed about him. Kirsten shrank back into her cave, but his eyes passed over her hiding place without a pause.

Suddenly he lifted his arm. "Hans! Ingemar! Let's be off! There's nothing else for us here!"

Kirsten gasped, aware that her heart was beating wildly. These men were not Muscovites! The bulky man and his vicious companions were speaking Swedish.

She watched in horror as fifteen men assembled in the morning sunlight. More than one rubbed at dark spots that marred the red and white of their uniforms. Two ambled up carrying women over their shoulders, and Kirsten could see that the females were still struggling to be freed. She shuddered again and closed her eyes. If she had followed Knut or if she had tried to run away from him, as she had considered doing, she would have been one more victim of the renegades.

A command sent the men straggling out of sight. Kirsten sat quietly long after the sounds of their retreat were gone. Little by little the morning voices of the woods resumed. A bird soared overhead, singing shrilly. A squirrel scolded noisily from a nearby tree.

Moving slowly, Kirsten crawled from the cave. When she had cleared the brush from her path, she stood for a moment staring about her. Bodies littered the forest floor, still bodies, with blood drying on open wounds. Knut lay almost at her feet, a bullet hole through his chest. He was still, but his chest moved ever so slightly, and when she touched his cheek, he moaned. Rising to her feet, she gazed up at the sky. Had they traveled too far for her to attempt to return? And if she did try to reach Alexei, would she be able to avoid the renegades who had killed her companions?

Once more she studied the forest. The attackers had headed south, of that she was sure. And Turku lay to the southeast. If she left immediately, she might make it back to her home before sunset.

A groan drew her eyes once more to the ground. Knut's eyes were open and he was gazing up into her face. "Kirsten, you must help me! Please!"

She looked down for a moment, her thoughts racing. Then she bent and tore a strip from her petticoat. If she was to help Knut, she would have to stop the flow of blood.

Chapter 8

There were moments, in the bright heat of the day, when Kirsten wondered at the wisdom of her decision. Knut floated between wide-eyed awareness of the danger they faced and an innocent childishness, his face clear of any but youthful memories. She had barely looked at the terrible wound that cut across his chest, even when she bandaged it, and the sight of the blood-soaked shirt filled her with an uncontrollable nausea. She felt certain that he was dying. Yet she could not leave his side to seek safety. In spite of his recent rejection of her, he was the only hope she had, now that she had been taken from Alexei's protection.

Alexei. He would be searching for her, she hoped. If he discovered her here, would he kill her in a fit of rage? Shuddering, she brushed the thought from her mind. She had been prepared to die once before. Surely, it could be no more terrifying a second time.

And when Knut died? She touched his cheek lightly with her fingers. It was warm, and his nostrils flared slightly with each breath. She would decide what to do when that happened, not now when he lay struggling to survive.

But the question gnawed at her consciousness. Could she return to Alexei? She gazed through the forest at the now smooth waters of the bay. Never! Alexei shared one emotion with Knut: he wanted to keep his women to himself. She shook her head, as if to wipe the thoughts from her mind. Had anything really changed because of this one night?

She knew the answer even before she felt the warmth spread through her body. Everything had changed. She knew now that her mother had been right. There was more to union than quiet acquiescence. Knut had stirred her responses as Alexei never could.

A faint moan escaped his lips, and she bent low to hear what he said. "Kirsten." He was himself again. "You must pull me into some shelter. We are in danger here."

"Yes, Knut," She swallowed hard before continuing. "But you are too heavy for me to move. I've already tried."

She waited for his anger, but none came. Instead, he lapsed again into unconsciousness, and she returned to her musing. What did it matter that they were in danger? Death was inevitable, wherever they might hide.

For the first time since the sudden attack, she examined her feelings toward the man who had rescued her from her Muscovite captor. Why did she not feel sadness, as she had felt for her parents?

She let her eyes rest on the quiet face. Knut was handsome enough. His deeply tanned face was strong and manly, and his blond hair crowned his features like a golden halo. Often his blue eyes had filled her dreams. But now he had destroyed her dreams with his harsh views. He would not marry her, if he lived. She would be an outsider in his world, a woman he used but did not love.

Why, she would be no better off with Knut than she had been with Alexei!

Yet Knut was dying. Surely she should feel some sorrow, some regret. But there was none in her breast.

"I'll cry later." Kirsten touched Knut's hand and gently squeezed his fingers. "When I have put my mother's soul to rest, I will be able to mourn for you."

Her words brought her a strange comfort. Of course! That was her problem. Too much grief dulls the sensibilities. And she had faced sorrow enough. Relieved, she lifted his hand to her lips. If only there were no further disturbances, and he could die in peace.

A fly buzzed around her head, and she brushed it aside impatiently, suddenly aware that the insects had taken over the forest. They covered the bodies of the other victims of the attack, and unless she kept them constantly at bay, they threatened to smother Knut.

Shuddering, she rose and covered the corpses with dry leaves. She dared not touch the bodies, nor did she look at them as she worked. A twig broke behind her and she jumped. Ghosts! Shaking with fright, she returned to Knut's side. He returned the pressure of her fingers, and she felt a surge of relief. He was still alive!

But now she could not remain seated beside him. Her back was too vulnerable. Silently, she crept to his side, pressing herself into his embrace. His nearness diminished her terror. Clutching his hand in hers, she fell into a troubled sleep.

She awakened suddenly, aware that more than spirits inhabited the woods. Someone was watching her. Her awareness kept her still, even in her fright. She had heard of the wolves that ate the carcasses of abandoned animals.

"Dear God," she prayed fervently, "save me from the horror that surrounds me. Let my death be swift."

The leaves behind her rustled. Someone was moving in her direction. Clamping her eyes closed, Kirsten continued her prayer. "Mama, Papa, protect me! Help me now!"

"What have we here?" The voice was melodious, filled with a firm strength that was oddly reassuring. "Halle? Tuomas? I believe this one's alive!"

Another voice responded from a distance. "Viotto, I've uncovered another body. They've been here, that's clear. But who has covered the corpses with leaves?"

The warm voice spoke again. "I think I have the culprit." She was aware of someone close beside her, and in spite of her fright she opened her eyes wide.

She found herself gazing into the face of a man, a young man with deep, sad eyes and a firm jaw. His features were fine and even, and even the ragged beard could not hide his nationality. A Finn! Then she saw his uniform, and she smothered a cry of alarm. The men who

65

had destroyed Knut's well-formed plan of escape had been dressed in similar clothes.

The firm lips spread out into a smile. "Halle! Help me! I have a live one here!" At that moment, Knut moaned again. "Two, by God! All of Finland is not dead, after all."

More rustling of leaves, and two more men approached. Like the first, they were dressed in the uniform of the Swedish army. They stopped beside her, their arms hanging awkwardly at their sides.

The first man met her eyes once more. "My name is Viotto Hannunen. I and my men have been traveling through the countryside warning everyone to flee before the oncoming Muscovites. How came you here? I recall no farm this close to the Selkaeri."

"I am Kirsten Gustafson." She noted a sparkle of recognition in his eyes, and then they closed down once more. "This is Lieutenant Knut Ivarson, my—" She paused. He was her affianced no longer, by his own words. "A friend who tried to rescue me from the Muscovites. We were waylaid by—"

"By a group of renegades." The eye flashed again. "We seem forever behind them. If God is just, he will lead them into an encampment of Muscovites, and they will suffer for their crimes. Do you know which way they were heading?"

Kirsten gazed about her. The memory was still too vivid for close examination. Yet she recalled that the big monster of a man had led the way south.

"Lilja!" Halle's voice rang in command. "Come and look at this man! He is injured!"

Immediately, from the shelter of some underbrush, a gray-haired woman approached. Beside her was a young girl whose face was familiar to Kirsten. It was Siiri, the young maid who had often come up from the town to assist her mother with the cleaning of the big house. Siiri curtsied awkwardly, a faint blush coloring her cheeks. She refused to meet Kirsten's eyes, and when she regained her balance, she turned to whisper into Halle's ear. Kirsten turned her attention to Knut.

Lilja was kneeling beside him, gingerly touching the bloody bandage. Then, with sure hands, she removed the wrappings and gazed at the wound. She rose abruptly and pulled some moss from a nearby rock. Placing it over the wound, she wrapped it firmly, this time with fresh rags torn from her own petticoat. Kirsten watched with growing relief. But when she looked up at the others, her fear returned. The faces that surrounded her were filled with anger.

Halle was the first to speak. "You are Kirsten Gustafson?"

Kirsten nodded.

He turned to Viotto. "My daughter tells me that this woman is the mistress of a Muscovite colonel."

Viotto's eyes widened, but he did not reply.

"She has gone willingly with him to many of their socials. And she has been seen wearing gems taken from the homes of the mayor and the governor, both of whom fled at the approach of the enemy."

Viotto's eyes burned into Kirsten's. "Is this true? Have you become a willing associate of the enemy?"

Kirsten felt her fear return. "No! He—" The memory of that first day returned with a rush. "He forced me! I was alone! My mother is dead!" Filled with sudden self-pity, she began to weep.

Viotto's eyes did not soften. "Did you accept his gifts?"

Kirsten nodded. It had seemed so right at the time. But now . . .

"What shall we do with her?" Viotto turned to his companions. "She is so young. Surely we cannot hold this against her.'"

The anger on the other faces did not fade.

A cold fear gripped Kirsten's heart. "I want to go home!" She met Viotto's eyes, her own wide and pleading. "Please! I want to go to my home!"

"You care nothing for this man?"

Kirsten looked down at Knut. Already, Lilja had found long poles and had formed a litter from his jacket. The peasants were preparing to take him with them. If he lived, it would be because of Lilja's handiwork.

"I . . . I can do nothing for him. I know nothing about medicine. Had you not arrived, he would have died."

"And you do not care?"

She felt a flash of anger. Of course she cared! But he loved her no longer. When she spoke, her voice was dull. "He doesn't want me. He was sorry that he tried to save me." She lowered her eyes. "I want to go back. Please, let me alone!" It was a cry of anguish. Too much had happened to her in too short a time. In her confusion she saw no choice. Alexei had been kind to her. Maybe, if she chose her words carefully, she could keep his sympathy.

Viotto stared at her in silence, the last faint spark of pity almost buried behind his anger. "You choose the Muscovite?"

Her voice was barely audible. "Yes."

He turned abruptly. "Tuomas, Halle, we part here. You risk too much each moment you delay. Can you take this soldier with you? If he lives, he can help to break the Muscovite chains."

"You insist upon returning to Turku?" Halle's voice was troubled.

"I must." Viotto looked past his friends toward the distant, invisible city. "He is there, somewhere, and I must find him. Maybe this woman can help me."

Farewells were swift but emotional. The men embraced and then, with solemn faces, lifted the litter from the ground. Suddenly overcome by a new panic, Kirsten ran to Knut's side. But he lay silently, his eyes closed. Only the faint movement of his nostrils told her he was still alive. Lilja walked by his side.

Overcome with despair, Kirsten fell back. She was not needed. Knut would be better off without her. Her head lowered, she returned to Viotto's side.

His voice was hard. "Do you know the countryside? Can you lead the way back to the city?"

She shook her head. Her father had not permitted her to leave the estate except in his company, and on established roads.

"Well, can you show me the path you took from your home? Surely you paid some attention to where you were going!"

"We were in a boat. The high seas forced us to land."

He shrugged his shoulders. "Well, it matters little. I know the path reasonably well. You will follow me." He began to turn and then, suddenly, he confronted her once more. "Do you know of a Muscovite colonel with a torn sash?"

She gazed at him with new alarm. "No!"

"You have seen no one like that?"

"No." The first response had been instinctive, born from her wish to be left alone. The second one was more considered.

"'Will you help me search for him? If you do, you will more than make up for your disloyalty."

Once more the rush of anger. Who was this stranger to judge her so harshly? What right had he to decide whether she deserved forgiveness or not? What did he know of the problems of being female?

She felt him grasp her shoulders. "Answer me! I must have that man!"

Still she did not respond.

He shook her fiercely. "Speak! Are you hiding him? Do you know who it is I seek?"

At last her voice returned. "What do you want of him? What has he done to you?"

"He raped my wife! He murdered her! And he destroyed my son, whom she carried!" His eyes were cruel and icy cold. "Speak! What do you know of such a man?"

Kirsten recoiled. This man was no more to be trusted than any other. "I know nothing. But I might be able to help you find him. What does he look like?"

Frustration clouded Viotto's eyes. "I don't know. But his sash is torn. I have a piece of it here." He pulled the blue rag from his pocket and waved it before her. "Have you seen a man with such a piece missing from his uniform?"

Kirsten felt a shock of horror. Could Alexei be the culprit this wild man was seeking?

No! He had taken her with force, that was true. But only the first time. In the days since his initial attack, he had spoken often of his daughter, of his home in Moscow, of his longing to be rid of the violence of war. He was a gentleman pushed by fate into the uniform of a soldier. Even as his mistress, she had had more affection and attention than she might have expected from Knut—whether as his woman or his wife.

Would Alexei rape a woman, murder her and her un-born child, and leave the body to rot in the sun? Never! She knew him. He was foolish, like an old man. But he was never cruel.

"No. I don't know any such man. But there are many officers in Turku." Her heart felt suddenly lighter. "How can you expect to find such a man? Wouldn't he simply get a new sash?"

A crafty glint appeared in Viotto's eyes. "Yes, of course. But he could not hide from me. The newness of his sash would tell me what I needed to know. I will have him! and when I do, I will kill him! You will not help me?"

Kirsten pressed her hand against her breast. Could this fearful man hear how loud her heart was beating? "I will try. I will do what I can."

With a grunt of satisfaction, Viotto turned and walked swiftly down the narrow path. Kirsten fell in behind him. She would have to stay with him until she recognized her surroundings. Her breath was labored, not from the strug-gle to stay close to the speeding guide, but because of the fear that obsessed her. If Alexei was the villain of whom Viotto spoke, he surely deserved to die. But she had to be sure. Before this wild man performed his act of ven-geance, she had to know.

Her world, the small bits of security to which she clung, was crashing down around her. And only if she found the man Viotto searched for before he met Alexei would there be any chance that she could salvage enough of her life to make the future endurable.

Chapter 9

Alexei stood at the edge of the garden, the sampler clutched tightly in one hand. He had awakened late in the morning, stretching out his hand to touch the nearness of Kirsten's body. But the bed beside him was empty.

Further search showed her to be nowhere in the house. The garden offered no more information until, quite by accident, he turned his foot on the stump of the candle.

He picked it up, cursing loudly. She had gone out, as he knew she often did during the night. Possibly to clean herself. He smiled wryly and tugged at his beard. He had little use for such devotion to washing. Like most men of his time, he was convinced that too much cleanliness weakened the body.

With the practiced eye of an experienced soldier, he searched the ground. She had been running when the candle fell, and she had spun around on one foot and hurried back, away from the house, to where a man waited. Much as he wished that he could see abduction in the clues that lay before him, he felt a growing conviction that she had gone voluntarily.

By God's grace, she would reach safety. Alexei scowled and tugged hard on his beard. He had seen too many times what could happen to a woman alone discovered by some of his serf-soldiers. One lone male companion would be helpless against a company of Muscovites.

He gazed silently at the growth of birch trees into which she had vanished and then, with a resigned shrug, turned and strode into the house. The new civilian governor, Sascha Andreovich, had issued orders for all the occupying officers to attend him for a morning conference. He barely had time left to dress and descend the hill.

But his thoughts followed Kirsten. She was such a sweet child, so gentle a mistress! And he had had such plans for her. "I will find another." He was barely aware that he spoke aloud. "There must be some child in the city who has not been destroyed, one who still has Kirsten's innocence." There was no conviction in his words. He had seen too many bitter, fearful females.

As he tied his torn sash, he thought once more of the farm woman whose struggle had resulted in her death. She had been a magnificent female. Even the quick glance he had given her had shown him that. Young, but one who had known love, one who could give love. If only he had reached her before his men.

Impatiently, he tried to brush the thought aside, but it refused to vanish. He had allowed his men to march ahead, aware of their eagerness to reach Turku, where the prizes of war awaited them. He had heard the screams when he was still too far away to respond, and when he at last ran into the clearing, he could see that he had arrived too late. Nevertheless, shouting in anger, he had raced across the narrow meadow, tugging impatiently when his sash caught on a post.

She was unconscious, and for that he was thankful. Gregor, the most violent and uncontrollable of his men, had her in his grasp, and he barely paused in his attack as his colonel approached.

Alexei had turned away in disgust, hurrying into the woods to conceal his weakness from his men. And as he retched painfully in the bushes, he heard Gregor bellow loudly. A body fell into the undergrowth. The animals were through with their pleasure and their victim was dead. He wiped his mouth on the frayed end of his sash and stepped back into the clearing. She lay twisted on the path, blood caking on her legs. The grasses that draped over her face were not stirred by her breathing.

72

The vision remained to haunt him. Often, when he woke with Kirsten beside him, he gazed at her innocent beauty and the memory of that victimized farm wife came to his mind. Her husband, if she had one, was probably dead too, killed in the fierce fighting that had preceded the final conquest.

Alexei was the last to arrive at the new Governor's Palace. He returned the salutes of the guards and marched purposefully into the conference room. The governor cleared his throat and tapped a small dagger against the hard wood of the table. "Colonel Alexei Mikhailovich Leonidovich, we have been awaiting your arrival!"

Alexei saluted briskly, his stern expression concealing his irritation. "Yes, sir! I regret if I have caused you any inconvenience. I had some trouble at my home."

The governor chose to ignore the apology. He rose and began to pace behind his desk. "I bring orders from the tsar. He sends his congratulations on the success of your action. Sweden is crushed. Never again will we suffer the humiliation of Narva."

Alexei suppressed a bitter smile. He had heard of the disgraceful defeat, when five thousand troops were captured by Charles the Twelfth and a small defending army of no more than three hundred. But the tsar's forces had been restructured after that disaster. The new army was invincible. He and his fellow officers had proven that.

Captain Ilyan stepped forward. "Your honor, are we to understand that Charles has been captured?"

A look of impatience crossed the governor's face. "No! He has escaped our allies, and is at this moment in the court of the Turkish monarch, organizing their combined forces for some form of devilment. He is, unfortunately, a formidable soldier, one the tsar respects. He cannot be ignored or brushed aside like some troublesome gnat."

The governor began to pace again. "Gentlemen, I will expect your reports tomorrow. Anton, Boris, you and your men will remain here in Turku. Nikolai, Vladimir, Jascha, you will take your men and return to Moscow. Ships will arrive in the harbor to transport you within the week."

He paused and suddenly Alexei realized that his was the only name not yet mentioned. "Alexei, your request to retire has been granted. You will go directly to St. Petersburg, where you will serve the tsar. You are aware, I presume, that the port city is close to completion, and that the seat of government has already been moved there from Moscow."

There was a murmur of voices around him, but Alexei gave them no heed. Often, in the final years of fighting, he had feared that he might not survive long enough tô reap the rewards of his labors. Now, at last, the day had come. He was going home! His thoughts leaped ahead. He would bring his wife from Moscow, see his children, now grown and with children of their own. And he would install Kirsten in a home of her own near the city's edge.

The governor had moved on to discussing the planned establishment of guard stations throughout Turku. Alexei let his thoughts continue to drift. Military matters concerned him no longer. Kirsten . . . His dream broke. Kirsten was gone. Staring up at the ornate carvings that edged the ceiling, he admitted to himself that he could not leave Finland until he knew her fate. Simple child that she was, she had endeared herself to him. And he had enough ghosts to haunt his sleepless hours at night.

When the governor indicated that the conference was concluded, Alexei filed with the others from the room. He was barely aware of the enthusiastic talk of his companions. For him, the fighting was over. He was through with violence, with bivouacs and forced marches, through with burning heat and freezing cold. Through with killing.

He had never dared to speak of his private dreams to his fellows, not even with Jascha, with whom he had grown close. Soldiers were not supposed to long for quiet hours of meditation, for delicate statues and fine works of art. They were not supposed to value music above a military march, not expected to dream of playing the harpsichord or of composing music. Soldiers were hard, tough men who loved fierce combat. Hardy men who did not wince when the enemy was disemboweled and women were raped.

It had surprised Alexei that his fellows had remained unaware of his fine sensibilities. They had not seemed to notice that he avoided the streets during that first rush of

74

conquest, and they had shown only envy when the woman he chose clung to him with some form of loyalty. And he had never bothered to tell them that he did not force his women. He courted them as if they were virgins, speaking gently to them and taking them only when they showed a willingness to permit him such familiarity.

Except for Kirsten. She was the first woman he had taken with violence. Always there had been some female who appreciated his gentleness. Some, as his fellows would attest, had loved him devotedly. Why, then, had he behaved so brutally to lovely, virginal Kirsten?

He knew the answer. He had worried it through his thoughts often in the weeks since he had taken up residence in her home. She had been such a surprise. So lovely—and so naked! His need had been roused by his long abstinence, and by the sight of that farm woman. She had been the kind of female he would choose, and the anger in his soul at his helplessness left his heart raw. But there had been an ache in his groin, as well. He had been too late to save her, and when he looked at Kirsten, lying helplessly on the floor beneath him, he had felt a kinship between the two. In his kindness to Kirsten, he was assuaging the guilt he felt about that unknown victim. Yes, he would have to find the girl, if only to assure himself that she had not been harmed by his men.

He trudged through the streets of Turku and up the narrow path to Kirsten's home. But he did not enter the house, pausing instead at the edge of the garden, where he had ascertained that she had vanished. Once more he glanced down at the ground. If the path she had made was as clear in the woods as it was in the garden, he would have no difficulty following her.

Impulsively, he took a step into the woods and then, with a sigh, he turned and strode into the house. He had some final work to do. The governor expected every paper to be in order before anyone could leave. He removed his dress sword and hung in on the bed post. Then, taking his portfolio in his arms, he headed for the study.

His thoughts refused to be corralled, no matter how hard he tried. The wind whispered at the window, and he looked up expectantly. But the glass was empty. A bird

75

whistled somewhere in the garden and he rose to look out. But the path was bare. The house creaked in the wind, and he looked up in anticipation. Immediately, silence surrounded him.

Yet, perversely, the study was suddenly filled with ghosts. There, sitting wide-eyed on the settee, was Kirsten, her hands pressed fearfully over the silken down that covered her feminine parts. Her transparent form was barely visible on the velvet cushions. Behind her . . . He had never seen her mother alive, but the figure that materialized in his imagination was Ranghild Gustafson. And in back of her, more ethereal than the others, was the form of a man. Alexei's tormented mind identified the final specter as that of Kirsten's long-dead father.

"I didn't harm her! I didn't want to hurt her! I want to take her to St. Petersburg with me, where she will be safe."

The two spirits were silent, and Kirsten's big, frightened eyes stared at him unblinkingly.

Suddenly aware that he was speaking aloud, Alexei rose and stamped across the room. "Damn it! You are the ones who deserted her! You left her to the mercy of an invading army! If I had not come—"

The ghosts faded as he approached. Once more he was alone in an empty house.

Impatiently, he gathered his papers and stormed down the hill. He was losing his senses. Ghosts, indeed! It was his conscience. And he could not allow his conscience to interfere with his duties.

When he stamped into the officers' quarters and slammed into his room, he barely attracted the notice of the few men who saw him. Nor did he join them for the evening meal.

It was past midnight when at last he folded his papers in a packet, tied them securely, and lay down on the narrow bunk. He, more than the other officers, understood the tsar's desire for the voluminous reports. After the fiasco at Narva, the army had been revamped. And it would be again, if there were any indications that it was growing weak or ineffectual.

Sleep did not come immediately. Once more the visions

of tearful women tormented his rest. And as he watched them pass, the conviction grew that he would only find peace if he held Kirsten once more in his arms. She represented all the misused females in Finland. Only by making her happy could he wipe the guilt from his soul.

Chapter 10

"Alexei!" Kirsten struggled to control the wavering in her voice. Behind her, hidden in the shadows of the underbrush that surrounded the garden, Viotto whispered, "Louder! I must see him before I leave!"

Kirsten shuddered. Her companion had spoken few words during the walk from the bay, but what he had said filled her with terror. More than once she had been forced to gaze at the ragged piece of blue sash, and each time she became more convinced that it did indeed belong to the stout Muscovite colonel who had become her lover.

"Call him again!"

She looked back, gauging the distance between her and Viotto. If she ran now, could she reach safety before he caught her? If Alexei saw her running, would he not shoot the man who pursued her? A shiver ran up her spine. She wanted no more killings!

"Alexei!"

The evening songs of the birds were stilled at her cry, but no sound came from the darkened house. Kirsten felt a faint stirring of hope. Maybe this evening Alexei had remained in town.

"Call again!" The voice behind her held a note of impatience.

"Alexei!"

Still no response.

Viotto materialized beside her. "Go into the house. Find him. I will wait here." His voice was harsh. "Remember, say nothing about me. And bring him out where I can see him. If you fail, I will know for certain that he is my man, and I will kill you both while you are asleep."

Kirsten inhaled slowly, struggling to regain her calm. She was filled with confusion. Despite the evidence, she could not believe that Alexei was the beast Viotto was stalking. He was too kind.

Alexei had spoken to her of his longing to leave the battle, of his hatred for the violence and the raping. And she believed him. In the quiet hours as they sat together in the study, she had come to know—and if not to love, at least to understand—the strangely tortured man who had taken her virginity. With a silent prayer for Alexei's safety, she crossed the garden and entered the house.

The hallway was dark except for faint patterns of light that stretched across the thick rug where the still-bright sky reflected through the narrow windows. Suddenly, memories of her childhood crowded in upon her. She had believed, then, that the long hall was inhabited by the ghosts of the men and women whose portraits hung on its walls, and she had refused to enter the haunted corridor without one of her parents at her side.

Filled with the old fear, she clutched at the handle of the door. "Alexei?"

The only response was the hollow reverberation of her echo. A shiver of fear convulsed her, and she ran across the hallway to the study door. The catch caught for a moment, and she felt perspiration, in rivulets of distilled fear, claw its way down her back. Terrified, she pushed against the reluctant catch, and burst suddenly into the safety of the familiar room.

It was empty, but the chair which Alexei occupied when he worked had been pushed away from the desk as if he had left it abruptly. One paper lay on the floor. She automatically picked it up and positioned it in the middle of the desk.

But her fear continued to grow. He was gone. She had been away for only one night, and he had abandoned her.

Maybe the renegades had come upon him and killed him, as they had killed Knut's followers.

When she returned to the hallway, her childhood memories were under control. It was not ghosts of past generations who gave her reason to fear. What threatened her were living men bent upon the destruction of the small security that had been given her by a kindly fate.

She walked the length of the hall, deliberately studying each dark shadow. But Alexei did not lie dead in the darkness. A growing feeling of relief added to her courage. As she returned to the stairway that led up to the bedrooms, she gazed directly into the dim faces of her ancestors.

Yet she did not call out again, even as she mounted the steps. Her room was as she had left it. Her robe hung neatly in the wardrobe, her bed was smooth and untouched. The bed in her mother's room was rumpled. Alexei had left it unmade, as was his custom. Automatically, she began to smooth the sheets and pull up the quilts.

She felt a shock when her hand encountered the stub of the candle, and she picked it up in alarm. A ring of dirt covered the wick. It was the same candle she had dropped when she heard Knut's voice. If Alexei had found it, maybe he was searching for her, after all.

With a new feeling of hope, she ran to the wardrobe and threw open the doors. It was empty. His sword, the few garments he had carried up from his quarters in the town, were gone.

She stood immobile, her mind racing. In one moment of weakness she had destroyed the small hold on security that God, in his strange ways, had provided her. Alexei, lover and father combined, had not been willing to wait for her to come back. She was alone.

No—not quite alone. Hiding in the woods was a madman. Would he kill her, now that Alexei was no longer available?

A door opened somewhere below, and footsteps moved through the entryway. Alexei? Had he managed, somehow, to escape Viotto's vengeance? With a cry of pleasure, Kirsten ran to the top of the stairs. "Alexei?" It was a whispered prayer.

The figure of a man stood outlined against the long pattern of light, a tall, slender man with a ragged beard. Viotto! He moved smoothly up the stairs, like a mountain lion intent on his prey. He stopped beside her and gazed into her face.

She met his eyes without wavering. "He isn't here."

His eyes were angry. "I don't believe you! You are hiding him. Why? How can you feel sympathy for a man who has raped your country? How can you protect a man who kills women and children?"

"You're wrong!" The fear had left her. Whatever he planned to do, she would not succumb to his hate. "He is a good man. But he is not here."

He grasped her shoulders and shook her. "Where are you hiding him? Tell me!"

She did not respond. With a muffled curse, he released her and began to search the rooms.

Kirsten followed behind him, her heart pounding. She cried out in protest when he emptied the wardrobes, throwing the clothes on the floor, and when he pulled up the bedclothes to gaze under the high beds.

When he had contented himself that no one was concealed in the bedrooms, he hurried downstairs and repeated his search. Kirsten ran behind him, struggling to replace each item he upset, praying that he would soon be finished, that he would leave her to repair the damage he was perpetrating.

When he had searched the cellar, he returned to the study. Kirsten was frantically replacing chairs, smoothing drapes, unrolling rugs he had pulled up in search of a secret trap door. She barely paid attention to his return. But when he did not speak, she glanced in his direction. He sat quietly on the settee, his head buried in his hands.

Her anger at his behavior melted, replaced by a flood of pity. How could she have failed to understand him? The Muscovites had raped and killed his wife. She should have offered comfort. Quietly, she crossed the room and perched beside him.

"Viotto, I'm sorry for your loss. But it could not have been Alexei. I know him. He is a good man—a kind man. The person you want must in Turku."

"Did he have a torn sash?"

82

Kirsten was silent.

"You won't answer! You have refused to answer because you know he did." His eyes widened. "You have been deceiving me all along. He *is* the man!"

"No!" Kirsten was startled at the terror in her own voice. "Not Alexei! He would never harm a woman! He has been kind to me!"

"Kind?" Viotto rose and pulled her to her feet. "Kind? What perverse picture of kindness do you have? He has taken you time and time again! You have told me so yourself! And he forced you! Do not deny it! Can you say that he would not attack a woman when you yourself have felt the power of his lust?"

Kirsten lowered her eyelids to shield herself from his penetrating gaze. But she could not let his challenge go unanswered. "He only forced me the first time. Why do you speak to me of such things? He has been good to me. Why don't you believe me? Do you think I would want to return to him if he had not?"

His lips were on hers so suddenly that she had no time to resist. His arms pulled her close, circled her, crushed her to him with such force she could not breathe.

When at last he released her, she gasped for air. His face was filled with anger. "Is this what it takes? He has held you in his arms, so you love him. You are loyal because he has filled your body. You don't know what loyalty is! A good woman would fight such an attack even if it meant she would die!" His features twisted in pain. "And each time he took you, you would hate him the more!'"

She struggled to free herself, but his hold was too fierce. "No! It isn't true! He was all I had! I was alone!" Her anger was rising. With a sudden shake, she broke free. "What do you know of a woman's troubles? I tried to kill myself when the Muscovites came, but he found me and brought me back to life. My mother was dead. My father had died during the year of the great plague. I was alone."

She gained strength with each word. The memory of her helplessness was so intense. "What was I to do? And then he came, and he was not the ogre I expected. He was kind, considerate, loving. Yes, *loving!* He did not hurt me after that first time, and he treated me with consideration. He did not beat me, as you do!"

It was too much. Tears streamed down her cheeks. She buried her face in her hands. Why, when it was so important that she be strong, did she show such weakness?

Viotto's hands grasped her shoulders, and she felt a change in his approach. "I have not beaten you! When have I hurt you?"

"You are hurting me now! You do not understand!" She challenged him with her eyes.

The momentary gentleness faded from his face. His voice was hard. "Now it appears you are alone again. And now I am here. What must I do to change your loyalty from the Muscovite to me?"

Their eyes met. The fire in his burned through her consciousness, stirring a warmth deep in her breast. Startled by her own responses, she lowered her head.

In a single motion he swept her from her feet and carried her from the room. He mounted the stairs two at a time, kicked open the door to her mother's room, and threw her on the bed.

She lay staring up at him, her heart pounding. "I hate you! Leave me alone! I'll kill you if you touch me!"

He laughed sardonically and then, with a deliberate calmness, removed his clothes. "You will kill me! Don't be ridiculous. Why should you do that? All I am going to do is turn you from a traitor back into a loyal servant of King Charles!" He paused in his disrobing and met her angry gaze. "Take off your dress!"

He was naked now, and he towered above her, his face red with a mixture of anger and passion. "Take it off! Or do you prefer that I tear it from your body?"

She obeyed, her eyes following his movements. Then, still filled with apprehension, she lay back, covering her breasts and the pale down that crowned her legs with her spread fingers. Her fear left her as she waited, to be replaced by a smoldering anger. How dare he treat her in this manner? She dared not try to escape. He was too strong and too swift a runner. But she would resist him. She would fight him all the way.

Still he did not move. He stood beside the bed, his face shadowed in the gathering gloom. Gradually his features seemed to melt. The angry frown vanished, the eyes grew gentle. Was it her imagination? Was it a tear that streaked down his cheek?

He knelt on the edge of the bed and leaned over her, his hands trailing lightly over her bare breasts. "Ruusu! Oh, my darling!"

The sudden change frightened Kirsten. Had he gone mad? Did he believe she was his dead wife?

But her fear vanished as he lay beside her. His arms were firm as they pulled her close, and his lips, when they touched hers, were gentle and loving. His body pressed close against hers, warm, demanding, sending shivers of anticipation down her thighs. Her need for love, for kindness, was too great. She could not resist this new approach.

He spoke the name again, and his lips met hers, drawing her to him, stirring her heart, wiping away the confusion and hurt. She felt as if she were entering a dream world where nothing was quite real. There was no anger between them. Only love, and an indescribable tenderness.

The tenderness grew slowly into a surge of passion. Her body was hot, burning, on fire with a desire she had not known she could feel. She tried once to collect her thoughts, to remember that this man was her enemy, to remember that he threatened her peace. But the thoughts would not come. All she knew was the closeness of his embrace, the pounding of her heart, the pulsating of her longing.

He did not take her quickly, as Alexei did, nor did he use her in the manner that had seemed natural for Knut. In Viotto's arms, Kirsten felt loved, wanted, needed. It mattered not at all to her that the name he whispered in her ear was not her own.

A tingling began in her legs and spread throughout her body. She was aware of nothing except the movement within her, the pressure of his lips against hers, the growing passion that obliterated her thoughts. At first timidly and then with increased fervor, she arched her hips below

85

him, rising to meet his desire. She felt herself sink into semi-consciousness. Her mind was floating, feeling only her need for his love and his closeness.

Above her, his face so close it blurred, he moved relentlessly, stirring his own passion, carrying her with him into heights she had never known existed. And then it began. The explosions in her groin moved up her body, convulsing her with such force she cried out in alarm. A faint smile lit his face, but he did not slow his rhythm. She was helpless, seized with a wild, mindless sensuality. She closed her eyes, unable to look into the depth of his soul, afraid that she would lose herself forever in his power.

A voice she did not recognize as her own drew her back to a recognition of what was happening. Stars flashed behind her closed eyelids. She pressed against him, matching the rhythm of his thrusts with an upswing of her hips.

When his body stiffened above her, she felt no regret, only a force that drew her close, that curved her back to meet him, that blended her soul with his. They were one, united in a passion she had never known she could feel.

His hips pressed her down, resting heavily against her, pushing her deep into the down of the mattress. He held her as if he were loath to let her go. His head fell beside hers on the pillow, and from his lips the name once more spilled. "Ruusu, my love!"

Kirsten lay quietly, feeling the dampness of his body against hers, aware that his cheeks were wet with tears. She tried to sort out her feelings, but she could not. All she knew was that she wanted to be near this man forever.

Then she felt a new desire, a longing to hear her own name on his lips, a need to know that he returned her passion, a desire to have his ecstasy rise for her nearness, not for his longing for a dead wife.

The chill night air wafted over her body. He had pulled himself away and thrown his legs over the edge of the bed. He sat facing her, a contrite look on his face. "Forgive me! I don't know what overcame me. I . . . I must have been mad."

He rose and began to pull on his clothes.

She lay still, too stunned by her emotions to move. The chill breeze lapped at the warm moisture that covered her body, and she longed to have him close once more. "Viotto . . ." She barely whispered his name.

He turned quickly, the anger rising, wiping the love and tenderness from his face. "I have asked you to forgive me. I have no excuse for the madness that came over me. It is not my habit to take women against their will. It will not happen again."

"It's all right. I . . . Was Ruusu your wife?"

His jaw tightened. "Don't speak her name. She was a pure woman, loyal to me, even to her death."

Kirsten was suddenly aware of her nakedness. Rising, she pulled her gown over her body. "I meant no harm. You called her name. I understand. You miss her as I miss my mother. I will not stand in the way of your—" She did not complete her sentence. She had seen his eyes, and she knew that the hate had returned.

The gentleness in his face was gone. His lips were clamped together, his jaw was stiff and hard. Had she almost abandoned Alexei for this creature? Was he right, that her loyalty could be purchased by an hour of delight? She shuddered. If he spoke the truth, she deserved his contempt.

Yet, he had been so loving, so gentle. In his arms she had felt at last all the ecstasy her mother had promised would be hers in the embrace of the man she loved.

He strode from the room. Drawn by a power she could not ignore, Kirsten followed. But even as her body moved, her mind recovered from the spell that had temporarily destroyed it.

She had been mad! How could she have responded with such enthusiasm to such a wild man? She hated him; a passion that left room for nothing else. And he hated her— he had said as much before he forced himself upon her. He had said it again while she was still too weak from the overwhelming passion to answer. He hated her for her compliance, her helplessness. Hated her because she had chosen to live with a Muscovite rather than die at his hand.

Well, she would not forget that hate again! She would stay with this man until she could find Alexei, so as to keep him from reaching his goal. And if she could find a way, she would return to her Muscovite lover. She would walk away from this madman with pleasure, back to where she had found respect and affection. She would leave him and she would never think of him again.

But even as she formed the words, her heart told her that she did not speak the truth.

Chapter 11

Kirsten and Viotto ate in silence, a meal she prepared from dried meat and vegetables stored in the cellar. In the darkness, the single candle Viotto permitted her to light barely illuminated the table, but when she rose to light more he restrained her.

"No. One candle, back here away from the window, is not apt to be seen. But I have no wish for visitors of any sort. Clearly, your lover has moved into Turku. Let him remain there until morning, when I can pursue him."

Kirsten opened her mouth to protest. What right had this man to speak so disdainfully of Alexei? Had he not taken her with equal force? But she abandoned the thought quickly. She could not yet contemplate all that had happened to her in the last hours.

Throughout the remainder of the meal, Kirsten waited for some sign from Viotto that he, too, had been affected by the closeness they had shared, but he remained stiff and formal. When they were finished eating, he rose politely and drew her chair from the table.

"I recommend that we retire early. There is little that can be done in such feeble light, and I wish to enter Turku before the change of guard. It is far easier to slip past a tired man than one who has just awakened."

"Why do you speak as if you are certain it is Alexei you seek?" Kirsten held tight to her courage, and as she spoke she searched her memory for any conversation between them that might have pointed him in that direction. She could remember none.

"Do I say that?" There was a cruelty in his eyes she had not noticed before.

"I have the impression that you do. You said just now that you wanted to pursue him."

He faced her directly, his eyes holding hers firmly. "Is he the one I seek?"

Her heart was thumping, and she wondered that he could not hear it. "How do I know? Was I there, watching what happened? All I can say is what kind of a man Alexei is. And I know he could not be so cruel."

"You know? Tell me again about your first meeting.'"

She closed her eyes against his penetrating glare.

"Tell me!" His voice was louder, and his hand grasped her wrist in an iron grip. "Say it all again! All of it!"

She started slowly, speaking in a voice so low he had to bend close to hear. "He rescued me from the sauna, where Mama and I had gone to—to join Papa. When I regained consciousness, I was lying on the settee in the study."

"He had not covered your body? Hardly the act of a gentleman. Can you be sure he had not taken you already, while you were still unconscious?"

She blushed and chewed on her upper lip. Why was he forcing her to repeat all of this? Had he no sensitivity? Could he not see that it pained her?

"Well, did he?"

"No." She did not look up.

"How do you know? You were not awake."

"I know. I . . ." She could not say the words. She had felt the pain as he tore through her maidenhead. "And then he was ashamed that he had hurt me." Her eyes opened wide, meeting his in unabashed pleading. "He was kind to me then. And he has been kind ever since. We have spoken of many things together. I know he could not countenance such behavior on the part of his men, and he would never treat a woman in that manner himself."

"You have talked of many things? Is it possible he has mentioned events you dare not relate to me?"

She cursed her inability to meet his gaze. "Never."

"Well, it matters little. I will speak to him before I kill him. I must hear it from his own lips. And I will know if he lies. I will see it in his eyes."

Kirsten shuddered. She had come to know Alexei very well in the time they were together. He had spoken of many things that troubled him. But he had spoken, too, of his dreams, and they were what had endeared him to her.

Yet there was his torn sash, and the ragged piece Viotto carried with him. She pulled away and moved toward the staircase. It was better that she not think of such things. They only filled her with confusion.

He stopped her before she left the room and took the candle from her hand. "We must leave this here. We can go upstairs without it. Come."

She followed him without protest. Her heart was beating wildly, and her throat was dry. Would he take her again? She tried to tell herself that she dreaded such a possibility, but deep in her breast she knew she wanted his nearness.

When they reached the door to her mother's room, he dropped her hand. "I believe I saw another room just to my left. Is there a bed in it?"

"Yes." Her throat hurt, it was so dry.

"Goodnight, then." She could see his broad shoulders outlined against the pale light that came through a window at the end of the hallway. He stopped when he reached the door to what had been her room when she was a child. Her lips parted in anticipation. But he only said, "Do not try to get away. I am a light sleeper."

Now at last the anger that should have protected her from her emotions surged forward. Without responding, she stepped into the room he had allotted her and slammed the door behind her. She was breathing heavily when she reached the bed, and she fell upon it with a sob.

The tears came then, searing, burning tears that rose from the bottom of her heart. She cried without trying to understand her sadness. Pressing her body into the softness of the bed, she pounded her fists against the pillow. "I hate him! Dear God, how I hate him!"

And then she remembered Alexei. Dear, sweet, gentle Alexei, who had shared this very bed with her before it was defiled by the violence of Viotto's attack. She sat up and stared at the wall that separated her from her tormentor. "I must save him. Even if he is the man Viotto seeks, I am certain he is not the villain that he would appear to be. He is a gentle man. And you will not kill him!" The last words were directed toward the wall with such vehemence that Kirsten stood up.

He was lying on her bed now. His body was resting on her sheets. His strong arms were thrown akimbo on her pillow.

She was drawn inexorably to the wall near the place where she knew her bed was positioned, and there she rested her cheek on the plaster. "Why?" The tears were flowing again. "Why did you not leave me alone?"

Suddenly fearful that he might hear her, she returned to the bed. She undressed quickly and lay between the sheets. But she could not rest. The fragrance of his body clung to the bedding, and the dampness they had created had not left the inner shelter of the covers.

Viotto went swiftly inside to the room he had chosen. It would not do to take her again, though his body yearned for her touch. He had shamed himself enough as it was. How could he speak of consideration, of gentlemanly behavior, when he longed to crush her in his arms again?

He closed the door, removed his clothing, and climbed onto the bed. His body felt tense, like a bow, taut and ready to spring. Why had he chosen her room? There was a perfume in the pillows that reminded him of the sweet scent of her hair. The mattress was soft and yielding, as her body had been when he took her. Soft and warm and responsive to his desire.

"Damn!" He was on his feet and at the door. He would take her again! Who was she but a slut who had abandoned herself to the enemy? Surely she deserved no special consideration. There would be no man who would deny him the right to use her as he wished.

His hand on the doorknob, he stopped. Use her? Despite all he knew about her past, she was still innocent. But she had given herself to another. With the same fervor? Was her rapture all a lie, a pretense she had learned in the arms of the Muscovite?

"I was a fool to take her with me. I should have sent her north with Halle and Tuomas—with her fiancé."

Knut, that was the weakling's name. Knut Ivarson. He had heard of the family when he was in Uppsala. They were proud folk. Had Knut really intended to marry the girl?

"Never! Not Knut Ivarson! But I'll warrant he took her. He had her too."

His bare feet padded lightly on the wooden floor as he moved across the room to the window. The faint light of a half moon lit the garden.

"Ruusu!" There was a tone of panic in his whisper. What had he been thinking? That he should have met Kirsten before he married his wife?

He snorted impatiently. What conceit! Kirsten came from a family almost as revered as Knut's. She would have ignored him had he met her before the fighting began.

Tossing the covers over the foot of the bed, he lay naked, staring at the ceiling. Fool! Idiot! Madman! To allow a need for Kirsten to soothe the longing for revenge that was due Ruusu!

Well, he would put an end to it. He was a man. He could put thoughts of her aside, as he had shunted her into another room to sleep. And he would not forget his goal of revenge. Even if he died with the villain, he would be satisfied.

At first the odor of burning wood blended with Kirsten's dreams. She was a child again, and her father had started the fire in the sauna, in preparation for an evening of relaxation. The first snow had fallen. Cold snow and the hot sauna. She felt a rush of excitement.

But the odor was too strong. Was she inside the sauna already? Perspiration covered her body. The crackling sound of fire was in her ears.

Startled, she pulled on her clothes. In the faint light of dawn, she could see smoke curling in under the door, from the hallway.

"Viotto!"

She screamed the name and ran to the door. It was still cool, and she pushed it open. Smoke was everywhere. She inhaled, and the heat seared her lungs. Then she was coughing wildly, holding onto the wall for support, a strange dizziness threatening to overcome her.

Strong arms encircled her waist, and suddenly she was lifted up. Still coughing, she felt herself being carried down the stairs, through the door and out, at last, into the glowing dawn.

He did not stop running until he stood in the middle of the garden, staring back at the inferno from which they had emerged.

Kirsten stirred. "Please, put me down."

He seemed to come to life at her words, and she realized that he had been standing motionless, staring at the burning building with great sadness. She felt the ground beneath her feet, but his arms remained holding her erect. "Are you all right? I thought you were going to faint."

She hardly heard his query. Her home—the house her father had been born in, and in which he had died—was burning before her eyes! With a cry of protest, she broke free of his hold. She reached the well before he could catch her, and pulled up a bucket of water. Then she was rushing up the steps, heaving the bucket before her.

A column of steam rose from the overheated door, but the flames remained as bright as ever. But she did not wait to see the results of her efforts. She was back at the well, dipping the bucket down for more water.

He caught her as she hurried toward the flames. "Kirsten! It won't help! You can't do anything!"

"But I must!" She felt the tears well in her eyes, and she pushed them back. "My mother's picture! And Daddy's! They're going to burn up!"

He took the bucket from her hand and placed it on the ground. "Where are they? Maybe I can rescue them for you."

She pointed to the study. It was glowing from the small fires that had already begun near the doorway, but the flames had not yet started to eat their way through its treasures. The paintings, two miniatures, hung on the far wall. "There! If I lose them, I have nothing left to remind me of them."

"You have your memories. Surely no fire can take them from you."

"Please!" She was pleading, and he could not face her eyes.

"Step back, then." He waited until she was a distance from the house, and then he pulled off his jacket and wrapped it over his hand. The glass in the window flew out as he hit it, and then he was up and in the room. He moved swiftly, rushing across the study to where the pictures hung. With one motion he tore them from the wall and stuffed them in his loose breeches. Then he was on his way back.

But the fire blocked his way to safety. Fanned by the air that had entered when he broke the window, it leaped across the room, eating at the deep pile of the rug and engulfing the settee.

Kirsten screamed, "Viotto!" and ran toward the place where he had vanished from her view. "Viotto!"

He landed on the ground at her feet, fire licking up the back of his jacket, which he had pulled on as he crossed the room. She moved toward him, but he shouted, "Stay back!" and began to roll in the grass. The flames died quickly. He lay before her, panting from the exertion.

"Viotto!" She was on her knees beside him, her hands on his shoulders. His face and hair were singed from the heat, but though she smelled the strong odor of burning flesh, she could see no injury.

It was then he held up his hands. They were raw and painfully red. "Don't touch me. Take the miniatures from my pocket. And then bring me the bucket of water. If you can get the salt from your storage cellar, pour some into the bucket. Hurry!"

As she ran for the bucket, Kirsten tucked the portraits into the small pocket that was hidden beneath her apron. Then she was back at his side, the bucket spashing as she lowered it to the ground.

Viotto sat up and submerged his hands in the liquid. She returned with the salt and poured it in as he directed. Then she sat down on the grass beside him. "I'm sorry. I should not have asked you to risk your life for my pictures."

"I need no thanks." His voice seemed unusually harsh, and she felt a momentary pique. Then she remembered the pain in his eyes as he held up his hands. "I did it of my own volition. Maybe some day you will come to realize what they stand for. And then you will return your loyalty to your own people, where it belongs."

She retreated at his words. Did he have to vent his anger on her? Could he never show her any kindness?

He seemed not to notice her dismay. "We will stay here as long as we dare. I suspect there will be no one from Turku who will come to fight the blaze. The Muscovites seem to relish the sight of enemy homesteads burning to the ground. But if they do start up the hill, we must be prepared to flee. You will have to stand watch near the steps, at least until my hands have recovered enough for me to move.'

The day dragged slowly forward. The sun seemed to crawl up into the heavens. Her greatest fear was that Alexei would appear, drawn by the sight of the fire, and that she would be unable to stop him from confronting Viotto. She took comfort, during the early hours, in the knowledge that Viotto would have difficulty holding a knife or a gun in his bruised hands. But that comfort vanished when she realized that he would ignore his pain in his eagerness to avenge himself on his enemy.

When at last Viotto appeared at her side, she felt as if a weight had lifted from her shoulders.

"Come along. Lilja warned me not to trust your medication. I have friends who can help me. We will go to them."

It was only as they slipped together into the woods that Kirsten realized she had missed an opportunity to escape.

Chapter 12

They reached their destination just as the sun touched the horizon, lighting the streaking clouds with gold. Kirsten could see that Viotto was noticeably weakened by the journey, yet he had refused to rest.

She was aware that she had missed many chances to leave her companion. He had plodded ahead of her, his head high, holding his hands up in the air to mitigate the discomfort. She could have left him at any time; yet she had not. And now, standing at the edge of a clearing, she felt certain she had waited too long.

"If, pray God, she has lived through the rampage, my sister dwells in that house. Come along. We might as well know the worst. If Sirkka is dead, I must face it eventually."

The cellar door flew open as he approached, and out from the darkness ran a small girl. "Uncle Viotto!" Her voice was high with excitement. "Mama! Uncle Viotto has come to save us!"

A tall woman appeared behind her. Sirkka was tall and blonde like her brother, with broad shoulders that told of her days of hard labor on the farm. Her hair was rolled behind her neck in a soft bun, and the scarf she had pulled quickly over her shoulders had a large tear over one shoulder. Even in the dim evening light, Kirsten could see the sadness in her eyes. But her strong lips turned up

97

in unconcealed delight, and she threw her arms around her brother's neck with no sign of embarrassment.

Kirsten drew back, suddenly aware that there was no one in the world to greet her with such happiness. Immediately, Sirkka released her brother and reached out for Kirsten's hand. "I am Sirkka, Viotto's sister. You must forgive me. I have not seen him in over a year. I feared he was dead." She looked nervously toward the darkening woods. "Come inside. We have remained out where all can see us long enough. It still is not safe. There are Muscovites everywhere."

Viotto seemed to have recovered his spirits, for he glanced from his sister to Kirsten with a sardonic look. "Ah, yes, little sister. We must be hospitable, even to those who side with the enemy."

Kirsten wondered why she had shown him any loyalty. She should have left him to find this place alone.

He nodded in her direction. "This, my dear, is Kirsten Gustafson. It is her wish to return to one Alexei Mikhailovich Leonidovich, a Muscovite colonel. Have you seen him? Or have you heard any rumors as to his whereabouts?"

Sirkka ignored his rudeness. "You are welcome in what is left of my home, Kirsten. I remember seeing you ride in a great carriage beside your father when I was younger. You always seemed more like a little princess than a real girl. I am pleased to meet you at last."

Viotto seemed determined to be cruel. "You have not heard of her perfidy? Others in the province seem to know her better. Halle's daughter showed righteous aversion to contact with a traitor."

Sirkka glared at her brother. "I know not what reason you have for bringing Kirsten to my home. But remember this: it is my home and I make her welcome! You may treat her as you wish when you leave, but here she is an honored guest."

Viotto lowered his eyes. "You're right, little sister. I'm sorry to have offended you. Forgive me! I did not mean to mar our reunion with rudeness."

Immediately, Sirkka was smiling. But her smile vanished again, and a frown furrowed her brow. "Have you

98

heard from Veikko? I have been so worried about him. I have heard nothing since the appearance of the Muscovites. Was he transferred to your battalion, as he requested?"

Viotto rested one hand on his sister's shoulder and then, with a wince, lifted it again into the air. "I bring sad news, little sister. Veikko fought near my side when we made our last stand against the oncoming hoard, on the plains of Hameenlinna. He died with your name on his lips."

Kirsten turned away, unable to look into the grief-stricken features of the young widow. But she could not stop her ears. The wail of agony seared her soul. This was what war was all about—not grand marching and cheering crowds, not proud young men standing tall in new uniforms. War was death and mourning and living out a life in loneliness. War was misery and rape and skulking in cellars to avoid assaults.

If ever I live to remember this war, let me remember this. May I never boast of cousins who marched to their deaths, as if there were greatness in dying. And if I have any sons, may I teach them to hate the smell of battle, Kirsten thought as she stared at the distant forest.

When she looked back, the mother and child were locked in each other's arms, crooning softly to each other, their cheeks wet with tears. Kirsten turned to Viotto. "Did you have to tell them right away? They were so happy to see you."

His lips turned up in a sardonic smile. "And let her worry, torn between hope and despair? She is a woman grown, Kirsten. She can face trouble." His expression softened. "I am here to comfort her now. Should I tell her just as I leave, and then send her north to safety? That would be far more heartless."

"You are leaving?"

"As soon as my hands are healed. Sirkka knows many herbs that will sooth such injuries. And when I can hold a knife again, I will pursue my hunt."

"Must you continue? Killing one man or a hundred will not bring your Ruusu back to life."

"No. You are right." His voice was deep, and filled with

hatred. "But it will be balm to my soul. For only then will her death be avenged!"

Kirsten slept that night on a blanket in one corner of the cellar. Once during the night little Eila awoke, and Kirsten heard Sirkka, her own sorrow still fresh in her voice, give comfort to the weeping child. When at last the two voices were quiet, Kirsten lay listening to the crickets and wondering whether she would ever again see true happiness.

Eila stirred again, murmuring her father's name in her sleep, but this time Sirkka did not interrupt her own heavy breathing. Kirsten shifted for the thousandth time. In all her life she had never slept on so hard a bed. At last, resigned to a night of wakefulness, she propped herself up against the wall.

It was then she realized that there were only two others in the cellar. She leaned forward in alarm, and gazed through the darkness at the place where Viotto had spread his pallet.

It was empty. She rose nervously and moved softly toward the thin beam of light that shone through a crack in the cellar door. He was not anywhere in the room.

The hinge squeaked as she pushed her way out into the night, but the steady breathing of the two females continued without interruption. A half moon hung low over the arch of the trees, and in its faint light the road snaked its way past the farmyard, on into the dim recesses of the forest. A chill crept over her. There was no doubt of Viotto's destination. Turku lay only a few miles beyond the first rise in the roadway. He had gone to search for Alexei.

She stood gazing toward the town, lost in contemplation. Then, her heart heavy, she returned to her bed. There was nothing she could do except to pray that he be disappointed in his search.

When she woke again, the sunlight shone through the crack in the cellar door and Viotto was sitting beside his sister, his hands held out before him. Sirkka was pouring a thin oil mixed with herbs over the tender, raw skin.

Kirsten rose and moved beside him. "You left us last night. Did you return to Turku?"

He smiled. "Yes." But the smile could not hide his disappointment.

She felt suddenly lighthearted. Alexei was still safe.

"You seem relieved. You have no cause. I learned where he has gone. He is not in Turku any more. It seems he was transferred to St. Petersburg. But there is a rumor among the peasants that he has not departed from Finland. He has delayed in order to learn what happened to the young girl he kept in the house on the hill." He met her glance with open amusement. "It seems I have you to thank once more. You are the cause of his delay. If he is persistent, and I suspect he will be, I will have time to recover. And then we will let him know where you are hiding."

Kirsten trembled. Alexei loved her! He had not abandoned her. He wanted her back.

But she would have to get away from Viotto. She was not willing to be used as bait for his plans to take revenge on a man who had not been proven guilty of any crime.

Viotto stared with a mixture of awe and despair at the delicate features of his unwilling companion. Happiness fought with concern, each struggling for dominance over her spirit. At last the smile that lit her face seemed to illumine the room with a brightness far greater than that of the sun.

He struggled to look away, but he could not tear his gaze from her beauty. *If only she felt such love for me!* As he framed the thought, he felt a rush of shame. She was a traitor. And he had yet to avenge the blood of his dead wife and the son he had never seen. Suddenly he wanted to destroy her happiness.

"I will find him, rest assured. And soon! My hands are already better. Alexei has headed east."

She turned then and ran from the cellar. Behind her, she heard Viotto speak sharply to his niece, and then little Eila was by her side. Together, they went into the sunshine.

Kirsten gazed at the child with dismay. Had Viotto instructed the girl to keep her company so as to limit her opportunities to escape? If so, he would learn that she was not that easily controlled.

She paused and looked around at the untilled fields. "Have you lived here all your life?"

"Oh, yes! Papa—" The child's face clouded, but she continued with only a small catch in her voice. "Papa was born here, too, and Grandpapa before him. Mama was born on the other side of the hill, where Uncle Viotto and Aunt Ruusu live." Eila's eyes were wide in innocent curiosity. "Is she dead, too?"

Kirsten took the small hand in hers. It was not right that children should see so much of death that it no longer frightened them. "Yes. She was killed—by the Muscovites."

"Uncle Viotto used to bring her to visit us after church every Sunday. Do you think she and my daddy can visit each other now?"

"Maybe they can." It dawned upon Kirsten that she had not thought about church since the day Alexei arrived and pulled her from the sauna.

"Why do you want to go back to the Muscovite? I thought they were cruel men who raped women."

The use of so raw a word on the lips of a young girl jarred Kirsten, but before she could protest, she remembered. How could it be avoided? The world was more brutal now. Gentle thoughts, like gentle people, belonged in the past.

"He isn't like some of them. He is very kind to me. Like a father."

"He didn't rape you?"

Kirsten wondered if the child knew the meaning of the word. "I think we have spoken enough about soldiers. How large is your farm?"

Eila's eyes widened. "Oh, let me show it to you!" She was bouncing up and down, like any happy eight-year-old from the untroubled past. "Come and let me show you where I used to play."

"Is it safe for us to roam about?" Kirsten intended to protest no more. The farther she could go from the house without alarming the child, the more easily she could make her escape.

"They won't know! Uncle Viotto and Mama can talk for hours without even thinking about me. Come on! I'll race you to the river!" She was gone before Kirsten could utter another word of warning. As she trudged behind the skipping child, she began to formulate her plan.

Eila ran to the largest tree and buried her head in her arm. "One, two." She looked up. "You're supposed to hide! Don't you know how to play?"

Kirsten nodded. Immediately the child continued. "Three, four, five, six, seven . . ."

Kirsten ran down the bank, her eyes searching the ground. When she found a protruding root, she stopped.

"Eight, nine . . ."

Kirsten dropped to the ground, sprawling out so her right leg was bent under her. "Oh!"

"Ten! Here I come, ready or not!"

Kirsten lowered her head and then slowly lifted herself up, as if she had just recovered from the fall. "Eila, help me. I think I've sprained my ankle."

The girl grabbed her arm and tugged. But Kirsten made no attempt to rise. "It hurts too much. Maybe I can get myself up if I crawl over to that tree."

But even when she stood balancing herself on one leg, she showed no ability to hop unless she had some support. Eila took her arm and tried to help her, but she was too short.

Eila knelt down. "Maybe I can wrap it in my petticoat. Does it hurt very much?"

"Maybe you had better get your mother. I don't think you're strong enough to help me." Kirsten hoped she would be forgiven for deceiving so young a child.

The tiny face twisted, and Eila began to cry. "Mama will be angry at me! She has warned me not to go this far. She'll beat me!"

"You can tell her I made you come here. Tell her it's all my fault. But please, get me some help."

The sobs grew quiet. "What if the soldiers come while you're alone?"

Kirsten was beginning to feel desperate. Would the child never leave? "It's all right. Go! My ankle is beginning to throb."

As soon as Eila was out of sight, Kirsten rose and began to run through the woods, parallel to the road. She stopped once to look back, and she realized that Viotto had joined his sister in a run toward the river. He knew what she had done!

Then she turned and hurried on. Until she found Alexei, she would have to be careful not to be caught by Viotto. He would not again be careless enough to let her escape. But to hide would be easy.

When she reached the black scar that had been her home, she paused. Maybe she had risked too much to return to Turku. But Viotto had said that Alexei left the city, taking the eastern road toward Helsingfors. She had to begin her search from the same starting point.

Nevertheless, she paused before she started her walk. If Alexei were searching for her between the town and the sea, then she would surely never find him. But now was no time for uncertainty. She would go east. And if God was good, he would lead her to where Alexei waited.

Chapter 13

The litter bounced roughly, and with each downward movement the searing pain in Knut's right shoulder grew more intense. There were noises, too, the voices of men and women, the rattle of—were they swords? and the crunching of feet on the untrampled forest floor.

Litter? He was a soldier! It was unseemly that he ride on his back. Grasping the rough branches that formed the sides of his moving bed, he struggled to raise himself. A sharp, knife-like pain shot through his arm, and he fell back with a moan. Immediately, a female face appeared above him. He blinked at it in confusion. This was not Kirsten! The creature who gazed down at him was old, with ragged grey hair and a crooked nose, more a witch than a woman. But her deep blue eyes were kindly.

Her lips parted in a crooked smile. "Good! You're awake. You have been wandering for a long time."

"I . . ." His throat felt raw, and a stab of sharp pain accompanied every breath. "Where am I? Where is Kirsten?"

"Kirsten?" The face twisted into a sneer. "The girl who was going to let you die? She went back to Turku."

This time he succeeded in raising himself on his uninjured arm. "She can't do that! I just saved her from . . ." The full import of the woman's words reached his mind.

"Let me die? She loves me! You cannot speak that way of her!"

"A fine way to show love! She was lying almost under your body when we found you, and other than covering your wound with a strip of her petticoat, she had done nothing to help you. You can thank her for your long illness! Had I been there to treat you when first you fell, you would have been on your feet long ago."

Knut felt a personal affront at her insult. "Why has she gone back? Just because she knows nothing of medicine?" He gazed at the woman with sudden alarm. "Did you force her to leave?"

"Me? Force her to go from your side? My poor boy!" The grating voice broke, and Knut saw a light of pity in the blue eyes. "No one forced her to do anything. As soon as she saw that I could care for you, she asked Viotto to take her to her home." The hand that stroked his forehead, wiping the hair from his eyes, was gentle. "You must not fret about her. She isn't worth your sorrow."

"How dare you?" The violence of his response was paid for in sudden agony. Pausing to collect his strength, Knut barely whispered his challenge. "How dare you speak thus of your betters?"

"My betters?" The old woman scowled. "A female who gives herself willingly to the enemy? A free woman who chooses to return to slavery? I cannot accept such as my betters!"

She walked in silence for a time, watching Knut's face. Then her anger seemed to vanish. "You must rest. There is much healing to be done before you will be able to march on your own legs again like a man."

Knut closed his eyes. Kirsten was gone, and after all he had gone through to save her. How could she be so ungrateful? Could it be that she objected to his decision not to marry her? He brushed the thought aside impatiently, but it returned to haunt him. Could that truly have been what caused her to desert him when he needed her the most?

He struggled to recall her face when he had told her. Had she shown disappointment? Surely she realized that a woman who had been taken by another could not become the wife of an Ivarson. If only she had had the sense to hide, to run into the forest and conceal herself. How stupid to attempt suicide in the sauna!

She had been so warm, cuddled in his arms as they lay inside the cave. No woman before her had ever been quite so—yielding! True, she had learned how to respond from another, but if she had been willing to claim that she had avoided capture . . .

That was it! He would have to find her and tell her his plan. She would return to Uppsala with him then. All she would have to do was pretend that she had never been taken by the Muscovite. It was a small lie, one they would keep between them. He could be gracious, after all. She was only a child! He opened his eyes. "Poor girl! She was so frightened! The only place she knows to go for safety is her home. When I found her, she was hiding in the cellar. The Muscovites had not discovered her, though God knows they searched."

A strained smile cracked the wrinkled face. "If that is what she told you, let it be. Now close your eyes. I'll not have my handiwork destroyed by a feckless invalid."

Knut obeyed gratefully. He had had enough of talking. Something in the old woman's answer made him uneasy. Yet there were many questions not answered. Where were his companions? Had any survived the attack that had destroyed their rest? And the other women. There had been screaming when he fell. Were any still alive?

He looked up again, but his companion was gone. And the beast to which his litter was strapped seemed to be moving through a thick, hot fog.

The jolting had stopped. Knut opened his eyes and stared about him. Everything was different. The thick, heavy smell of sweating horseflesh no longer surrounded him, and the bands that had held him safe throughout the journey were loosened. His litter lay inside an oval building with walls of dried animal skins supported by slender saplings. The curved ceiling was broken by an uneven hole in the center. The only heat came from a fire in the middle of the hut, directly below the hole.

He thought at first that he was alone, and then he saw

the old hag, sitting close to the fire, sewing on a piece of cloth. She was dressed in a heavy wool gown with a wide white neckpiece tied close at her throat. Her bodice was a dull red, almost brown, and her skirt, dull purple in color, was covered in front with a white apron. On her head was the triangular scarf popular with peasants both in Finland and in Sweden.

She rose when he stirred, and hurried to his side. "Aha! You are with us again. You have wandered in the spirit world for these last months, all the time we traveled up the coast." She paused, a sly smile on her face. "How do you feel? Sit up, and I'll give you some food."

"Where are we?" Knut made no attempt to conceal his impatience. "Who are you?"

"My name is Lilja." The old woman curtsied awkwardly. "As for where we are, why, we are here, of course! In the north country, where women are safe from attack, and men can tend to hunting."

Knut drew himself into a sitting position, aware with sudden pleasure that the pain was gone. He waited restlessly while the woman ladled out some stew from a large pot that hung over the fire. He took the bowl from her and insisted upon feeding himself when she carried it to him.

She settled quietly on a cushion beside him. There was no urgency in her face, no indication that she had other chores to attend. She gazed at his face in silence, waiting for him to finish his dinner.

As he ate, Knut gazed about the strange hut. He had little doubt that he was exactly where she claimed—in the north country. He had heard of it during his days of training in Uppsala. The Lapps lived above the point of land that connected Sweden with Finland, but they seemed not to resent the invasion of Finnish farmers who had fled north to avoid the war.

Rumors regarding the occupation of the renegades varied according to source. Some said the fleeing farmers hid in the thick forests because they had no wish to defend their country. But there were some who believed that the runaway farmers were fighting, in their own way, for freedom. It had always been Knut's preference to believe the latter.

He tilted his bowl and let the last drops of warm soup run down his throat. Then, resting the bowl on his lap, he turned to Lilja. "I am a lieutenant in King Charles's army. I can be of great help in organizing those men among you who choose to do battle with the enemy."

Lilja stared at him without answering, and he noticed that the skin at the corner of her right eye twitched continuously.

When she persisted in her silence, he felt a surge of irritation. "Are you suddenly dumb? Why do you not answer me?"

"I was thinking, young sir." She rose. At the door, a thick fold of skin that parted when she pushed it, she paused. "I will get Halle. He will know how to answer you."

Halle arrived before Knut could rise. He stood just inside the hut, across the fire, and saluted smartly.

Knut felt oddly relieved. Here at last was a soldier! Halle was a tall, strong man, with broad shoulders and a weathered face. Under his thick beard, his chin jutted firmly. His uniform was tattered but clean, and his breeches, loosely fitting as was the custom among the peasants, were patched liberally.

"Good day, sir, I am glad to see that you are better."

Knut returned the salute. The return of established patterns of behavior comforted him. "Help me up. And find my coat. I have wasted enough time in bed." As he spoke, he rose by himself to his feet. "How long have I been unconscious?" It felt good to move about, to stretch the muscles of his legs, though they were weak. He flexed his shoulder and felt no pain. "How long have I been ill?"

"Two months, sir." Halle's response was sharp and quick. "We saw your ship, but we are not sailors. We dared not put to sea. So we took you with us. Now that you are well, I can escort you across the marsh into Sweden."

Knut shook his head. He had no wish to return to Uppsala a failure. "Where are my men?"

"All dead, sir. We buried them before we started our journey."

"Dead? Every one?" Halle nodded, and Knut continued. "And the women?"

"Those we could find were dead, also. Except for one, the one who was with you."

Knut was growing impatient. "And where is she?"

"Gone back to Turku. Didn't Lilja tell you? She went with Viotto."

Knut frowned. He had hoped that the old woman was lying. "And who is Viotto?"

"Our lieutenant, sir."

"He has not returned?"

"No, sir."

"Well, then, I will take charge. There is much work to be done before we can launch an attack on the Muscovite strongholds."

Halle shifted from one foot to the other. His face was troubled, and he chewed nervously on his hanging mustache. "Sir . . ."

"Yes?" Knut knew when determination was needed. His jaw set, he waited for the soldier to continue.

Before his unyielding gaze, Halle hesitated, chewed again on his mustache, and then lowered his gaze. When he looked up again, his eyes were dull, as if he had deliberately vacated them. "I will call the men, sir."

Knut watched Halle depart with a smug confidence. It was simple to handle the peasants if one knew what to do. They could not stand up against orders properly given. He had no doubt as to what the man had wanted to say. Many of the people who hid in the woods were too cowardly to fight.

The flap of the door was pushed aside, and Halle entered with a mended jacket. "Sir, my wife has patched the cut, where you were wounded."

"Good! Give her my thanks. Did you bring my sword and my musket?"

"Yes, sir. They are outside. Shall I buckle them on for you?"

"No. I can handle them myself. Go and call the men."

As he strode around the fire, Knut inhaled deeply. Such

a pleasure it was to be alive again! As for the men who waited outside, he would handle them. He had no doubt regarding his ability to turn the worst cowards into a fit army.

As he stepped into the sunshine, he thought ahead to the day when, as a result of his efforts, Finland would again be a part of Sweden. He would be rewarded, certainly. Maybe King Charles would even place him in charge of the whole army, under himself, of course. Silently, he thanked God for providing him with such a magnificent opportunity. And then, a half smile on his lips, he turned and met the steady gaze of his ragged recruits.

Chapter 14

Kirsten stood for a moment in the center of the dusty road and gazed at the farmhouse. Then, her feet dragging, she crossed to the door. Her knock sounded loud and hollow in the stillness.

No answer. The farm was empty, like all the others she had passed in her days of walking. She longed for the sound of a human voice. Anyone, even a soldier, would be welcome!

But this time she did not resume her journey. If she had to, she was determined to enter the house uninvited. She could walk no farther. Not this day.

Fear had nipped at her heels during the first hours of her travels, fear that Viotto would appear suddenly and take her back. Fear that Muscovite soldiers would appear and put an unpleasant end to her search, fear that some wild beast would spring from the woods and end her life.

"Halloo!" The sound of her own voice startled her, and the natural cries of the wilderness stopped as if waiting with her for some answer to her call.

No response. A frog croaked in a nearby pond, and a hundred small sounds answered. She grasped the knob and twisted it. The door sprang open. But it stopped abruptly, and she realized it had hit a barricade inside. Someone was there—someone who dared not show herself.

"Please!" Kirsten put all of her fatigue in her plea. "Please let me in! I'm all alone, and I am so tired!"

A step sounded, and the barricade was pulled aside. The hinges squeeled as they moved, and Kirsten, who had been leaning against the panel, tumbled into the darkness.

A hand reached out and caught her, pulling her to her feet. A strong female hand, callused from hard labor.

"Hurry! Help me put the table back. They might get in."

Overcome by an irrational fear, Kirsten clawed at the heavy wooden plank. She felt it move, and then the door was once more sealed. She leaned back, panting from the sudden exertion. "I'm Kirsten Gustafson. I've been traveling from Turku, sleeping in the woods when I was too exhausted to continue. Thank you for letting me in. I need to rest."

Her hostess moved in the darkness, and suddenly her face was illuminated by a beam of light from the setting sun. "I'm Leena Jotuni. Are you sure you were not followed?"

Kirsten gazed at the women in surprise. "No. I don't think I've seen anyone on the road for the last three days. Is someone searching for you?"

"They all are! But I'm too smart for them. I never come out in daylight. And I've learned how to be invisible in the darkness." The voice rose in pitch as it reached the end, and Kirsten felt an eerie sensation as she tried to understand what was being said.

"Invisible?"

"Yes. I know the words. I learned them from—" The voice stopped suddenly. "Are you a spy? Have you come to find me so you can tell them where I am?"

The face that stood out in the red-hued rays was strangely misformed. The eyes were wild, with a shadowed depth that sent shivers down Kirsten's spine. They darted about, studying her from head to foot, then settling on her face. Kirsten tried to hold them steady, but they refused to be caught, flitting about like wild moths.

Her mouth, too, worked unsteadily, opening and closing as if she needed that orifice for breathing. But the most disturbing were her hands. They scraped on the wood of the table, pulled at her gown, pressed themselves against the white neck as if the woman were determined to choke herself, and then, without a pause, resumed the scraping on the wooden plank.

"Please. I'm just a woman trying to escape the Muscovites. And I'm so tired! I need to sleep."

"That's what you say! But I know them. They've sent you to rob me of my food."

Kirsten's stomach growled at the thought of something to eat. But she dared not increase this strange woman's suspicions. "I don't need to eat. All I want is a place to rest. Please, I won't do anything to harm you."

Leena leaned forward suddenly, her face only inches from Kirsten's. Her breath was foul, and Kirsten exerted all her self-control to keep from pulling back.

At last Leena straightened up. "You poor child! You must be exhausted! How long have you been walking?" The wildness had gone from the wrinkled face, and the voice was filled with concern.

Kirsten was slow to answer, too shocked by the abrupt change to know what she should do. "I've come from Turku. I've been walking for days without resting. I need a bed. May I rest here?"

"Why, of course, child! Come along. I'll see if I have some soup."

The soup was not much more than flavored water, but to Kirsten it tasted delicious. It was the first hot food she had eaten since the evening meal she had shared with Viotto in her candlelit kitchen.

She watched the old woman nervously throughout the evening, but the strange wildness did not return. However, she spoke almost continuously, chattering on without waiting for any response from her uneasy guest.

"My son, he's out in the field working. A wonderful lad he is, just like his father. He'll be back for supper soon, so we'll have to be finished or he'll suspect that I'm hiding you. But maybe you would like to meet him. You seem an upright girl, one not yet spoiled by the—" Her face twisted for a moment, and then grew smooth. "We must look out for the enemy, my sweet. I'd sooner you be dead than live to endure their assaults!"

115

Kirsten felt a terror grow within her. The trials this poor woman had endured had destroyed her mind.

But Leena spoke in a normal tone now. "Come along, my dear, I will show you to your room. It was my daughter's, and I keep it neat for her return. But I'm certain she will not object to sharing it with one as lovely as you."

Kirsten glanced out through the half-boarded window. The sky was dark except for the stars. The moon had not yet risen to cast a silvery glow over the ghostly scene that lay before her.

The farmyard, in the blackness, seemed untouched by disaster. A deer grazed near one fence, and in the gloom it looked like a placid, domestic beast. For one moment, she had the eerie feeling that Leena was speaking the truth, that her son would be returning from the field any moment.

Leena threw open the door with unconcealed pride. "You must be careful not to disturb her things. Smooth the bed carefully when you rise in the morning. Kerttu is most fastidious about her possessions." She stepped across the room and folded down the blanket. "Sleep well, my dear. And do not fear. I will watch. They will not harm you."

Kirsten repressed a shudder. But the eyes that met hers seemed calm and free of madness. "Goodnight, then. And thank you again for your kindness."

In answer, Leena bent down and kissed Kirsten on the cheek. Then, before the surprised girl could think of a response, she turned and was gone. The door closed softly behind her.

Despite her exhaustion, Kirsten did not sleep easily. She lay for a time staring about the room, wondering what kind of girl Kerttu might be, and where she had gone. Maybe she was married, and lived on a nearby farm. But why did Leena keep her room for her?

Then the answer came, and its logic put Kirsten's mind to rest. Kerttu must have gone north. And Leena, maybe because she wanted to be available to help her husband and son if they returned home, had not accompanied her. Relieved by this solution to the odd circumstances that surrounded her, Kirsten fell into a deep sleep.

Deep it was, but it was not untroubled. In her dreams, Leena returned, crooning a lullaby softly.

Kirsten stirred, and the singing continued, low, soft, gentle, and very close.

Suddenly she was awake, her body tense with an unformed dread. It was not a dream. Leena was in the room, standing at the head of the bed. The moon had risen, and in the pale light her sharp features seemed indistinct and ghostly. Her eyes were mad again, and her mouth was twisted.

A glint of metal caught the moonlight. Startled, Kirsten tensed her body. She felt sweat form on her forehead, and she stared at the shining object in terror. Leena stood poised above her, a sharp knife in her hand.

With a scream, Kirsten rolled from the bed. She did not wait to see how Leena responded, though she heard a thud that led her to believe that the knife had cut through the mattress. Scrambling to her feet, she ran from the room. At the foot of the stairs she paused to listen. Leena was sobbing helplessly, crooning nursery rhymes.

She appeared suddenly above Kirsten. She was walking slowly, her arms cradling an invisible figure. And then Kirsten knew the full horror of this house. Leena's husband and son had been killed defending the house, and before the Muscovites could enter, she had taken a knife and murdered her own daughter.

The terror of that long-past night still lingered to haunt the unhappy mother. She had saved her daughter from assault by brutal men, but at the cost of her own sanity. And now she stood on the stairs, reenacting the scene that would remain with her until the day she died.

Silently, Kirsten walked to the door. In her fright, the table that had seemed heavy earlier in the evening moved easily in her hands. The door opened just enough for her to squeeze through. Then she was gone, leaving the madness and terror behind.

She felt no need now for sleep; terror had given her new strength. Her thoughts raced back to the pact she had formed with her own mother, the one that had ended in her mother's death. For the first time since that terrible

117

day, she understood the torment that had filled her mother's soul.

She reached into her pocket and caressed the small oval frames of the two miniatures. The feel of the wood gave her new courage. It also reminded her of Viotto. He had risked his life to save them for her. As she trudged along the road, barely aware of the sharp stones that cut into her worn soles, she tried to understand the man. He had shown no sympathy for her on their journey from the coast to her home. And he had taken her with a force that had left her breathless. She remembered all he had said that fateful night. "A good woman would fight such an attack even if it meant she would die. And each time he took you, you would hate him the more."

He had said it, and then he had forced her onto the bed. And he was right. She hated him! He was cruel and spiteful and he was determined to kill Alexei, a kind man who loved her as if she were his daughter.

Yet the image of Viotto's strong body brought an ache to her groin. She could not push him aside, nor could she ignore the passion he had stirred within her. He haunted her footsteps throughout the long night, and for the first time since her escape from Sirkka's cellar, Kirsten knew that she wanted Viotto to follow her.

"If he finds me, it will prove that he loves me, after all."

The words were barely on her lips before shame and anger pushed them away. Never! He wanted only one thing from her: that she identify Alexei so he could kill him. His thoughts were too filled with the need for revenge for him to think of love.

He had told her, on their journey back to Turku, of how he had discovered his wife's body, mutilated and torn, lying at the door to their cottage. His voice was filled with pain. And for the first time she envied him because his response to terror and death was anger and determination to get revenge. Leena, who had faced similar terror, had turned into a mad creature, endlessly reenacting the horror.

"But he's mad, too, in his way. He will remain so until he rids his soul of the longing for revenge. Another death

118

cannot wipe out a first one. He could kill Alexei a hundred times, and Ruusu would still lie buried."

She felt a new understanding as she listened to her own words. Only life would wipe away the scars of war. Life and forgiveness. The past had to be put behind.

She prayed for Viotto, prayed that he would find the peace that gave her her strength. Deep in her heart she felt a new confidence. If he ever reached that blissful state, he could love again.

She sat down on a large rock to rest. He might find his peace, but she would not be near to share his love, not if her search was successful. She would be in St. Petersburg, with a man who loved her in his own gentle way, a man who carried his own burden of guilt.

And would she be happy there? She rose, brushing the question aside. It was too much to ask for happiness. In these days of trial and death, the best to be hoped for was peace.

The rough gravel dug through the thin soles of Kirsten's boots. They had been thicker when she started her journey, and warmer, and the birch trees that clustered alongside the road had been a brilliant green. Summer had come and gone and she had barely been aware of its passing.

Had she left Sirkka's house a week ago? A month? She did not know. Days had blended one into the next with such smoothness she had not been aware of the passage of time.

But she did remember Leena's house. That had been only a few nights past. Or was it a week? Kirsten shuddered as she remembered the terror that dwelt in that house of horror.

Days and nights had meant little to her since her flight from Leena's raised knife. She had walked until she was exhausted, slept until she was awakened by some unexplained forest noise, and had risen to continue her journey. She had traveled every small road, questioning the few women she met, facing the disgust on the faces when she explained that she was actually searching for a Muscovite colonel.

But nowhere did she receive any real assistance. The women she met were not as strange as Leena, but their suffering was fresh and their hate strong. She tried once to speak to a sad-faced woman about forgiveness, but her words fell on deaf ears. "I am to forgive the men who assaulted my old mother, who robbed her last hours of peace? I am to forgive them, after they snatched my infant from my arms and killed her with their lust? Don't speak to me of forgiveness! I am not God!"

And so Kirsten had hurried on, knowing only that wherever destruction lay, the Muscovites must be nearby.

She looked up. Ahead, a signpost pointed the way. Helsingfors lay straight ahead. She was not sure of the best road to St. Petersburg, for she had never paid much attention when her father spoke of foreign lands. But she did know it lay somewhere to the east. And Helsingfors was east of Turku. She was on the way to her goal.

As she resumed her journey, she gazed about her. Most of the birches had lost their leaves. Soon the land would be covered with snow. She shuddered when a chill breeze lifted her lightweight skirt and teased at her bare legs. She was not dressed for the cold. If she was not soon successful in her search, she would freeze to death.

The thought frightened her, and she brushed it aside. There would be some help soon. She would find some clothes, or some kindhearted woman would give her some. What was important was that she not abandon her hunt.

She did not allow herself to contemplate the immensity of Finland, nor did she acknowledge, even in her innermost thoughts, that she might never find Alexei. She did not think of him as her lover. He seemed more the father she had lost in the plague, the only man she could trust to treat her well, the only man who had shown any concern for her that was not marred by wild passion. For the closeness he had asked of her held no passion in her memory. She had allowed him to do what he would and he had been kind. He did not stir her emotions and leave her filled with confusion.

Knut Ivarson was seldom in her thoughts, and when he was it was as a judge. He had made it clear to her that he no longer considered her his equal. She was a fallen woman. He had not even recognized the possibility that she might have given in to Alexei because she was afraid and helpless, a child in a world of lustful men. He had tossed her aside. He would accept her only as a mistress; she was not worthy to be his bride.

A noise in the distance pulled her thoughts to immediate alert. Someone was coming! She listened for a moment and then, her heart beating in terror, she ran into the woods. The sounds were unmistakable. Soldiers!

But the bare trees offered little protection. Without bothering to return to the road, she ran parallel to it until, suddenly she was in a clearing.

This had once been a prosperous farm, with a large house and two enormous barns. Now it stood empty. Ashes marked the location of the house and one barn. The other had survived the inferno, at least in part.

On the far side of the clearing was a small lake, sparkling in the noonday sun. Kirsten paused to listen. The trampling footsteps were nearer. And this would be just the sort of place where they would pause for a midday rest.

Inside the one remaining barn, the charred remains of a carriage offered her adequate cover. Between it and one corner, boards had formed a sort of cave, and into that Kirsten crawled. She would have to pray that the soldiers did not disturb the ashes. The footsteps were close now. She had no more time left.

The advance scouts appeared first. One hurried back down the road to inform the column that they had found a resting place. The others set about drawing water from the lake.

They made no attempt to search the barn. It was clear to her that they had marched for many kilometers, for they seemed tired, and many lay back to rest as soon as they had finished eating. The officers sat on chairs taken from the backs of pack horses, and she strained to overhear their conversation.

She learned little from what she heard. Though she recognized one of the officers as a man she had met while in Alexei's company in Turku, she could not understand what he said. Alexei had always spoken Swedish to her. These men spoke only Russian.

They did mention Helsingfors, and she decided that they were headed toward that town. But having gained that knowledge, she let her mind wander. Leaning her head against the wall, she fell into a light sleep.

She awakened when the command to march was given. Bridles rattled and scabbards slammed sharply against stone as men rose and prepared to leave. Suddenly she was aware that her legs were cramped. By the time the soldiers had passed from her view, the muscles in her thighs were screaming for relief.

She rose and stumbled from her hiding place. Her first thought was for food. Her highest hopes were rewarded when she found a half-eaten loaf of bread between some rocks.

Her stomach more full than it had been in weeks, she headed for the road. If she was lucky, some woman farther on might take her in for the night. But in the meantime, she had many miles to cover.

After the first painful steps, her feet adjusted to the roughness of the gravel, and she began to move more steadily. Her hands strayed into the pocket of her dress, caressing the small portraits. The touch of the wooden frames comforted her, as if she were holding her mother's hands.

As she had done many times before, she brought the portraits up to her lips and kissed them. They smelled of smoke, and the odor invoked the image of Viotto. With him for her ghostly companion, she hurried on her way. And his presence gave her the feeling of security without which she would have been lost.

Chapter 15

When she reached the next road sign, Kirsten paused and studied the road. There was no doubt about it. The column of marching men had not continued toward the town. They had turned here, away from the Gulf of Finland and from the small fishing village.

She stared in the direction the Muscovites had gone. Was this, in fact, the shortest way to Russia? If so, she should take this road. But the air was growing colder. Before she journeyed farther, she must procure warmer clothing.

Her stomach growled, and her hunger won the day. If the Muscovites had not yet invaded this town, maybe she would find both food and clothing. Pulling her sleeves down to protect her bare arms, she hurried toward the red roofs that lay ahead.

She paused again when she reached the quiet houses. Maybe she had been wrong in her assumptions. It was possible that the soldiers had avoided the town because they knew it was already vacated. She had passed through many tiny villages that were empty and abandoned.

A cold wind from the Gulf ruffled her hair and sent a chill up her arms. With a growing feeling of desperation, she gazed at the silent houses. She had no alternative. If she wanted to live through the winter ahead, she had to find warm clothing. Much as it disturbed her to enter another's home uninvited, she would have to search until she found what she needed.

"Hello!"

She turned with a start, and met the clear blue eyes of a girl of seven.

"I'm Liisa. Who are you?" The long braids that hung over the slender shoulders were thick and shining. But what surprised Kirsten most were the eyes. They harbored no memories of past terror, nor fear of future harm.

"I'm Kirsten Gustafson." She looked at the silent houses. "Where's your mother?"

A brilliant smile lit the innocent face. "Mama's at home. Come, I'll bring you to her." As she spoke, Liisa took Kirsten's hand and tugged at it gently.

She skipped alongside Kirsten, heading toward the water. Then she turned into what appeared to be an empty courtyard. Kirsten shuddered. Would she find a repeat of the horror that had almost destroyed her at Leena Jotuni's farm? Was it possible that this child, like poor mad Leena, was simply unable to accept the terrors to which she had been subjected? Was her bright innocence really a sign of hopeless madness?

"Liisa! Where have you been?" The voice, even in its sharpness, was filled with warmth. "I've told you not to wander too far from the house! What if the signal was given for us to leave, and I could not find you in time!"

A plump woman stepped into view. Her hair was silver-blonde, her braids were neatly pinned behind her neck. Like Liisa, she seemed content, and not in the least affected by the terror that had possessed every part of the countryside through which Kirsten had traveled.

"I'm sorry, Mama." Liisa ran to the woman's side. "I didn't go far, really. And look what I found! A lady. Her name's Kirsten."

Abashed at her ragged appearance, Kirsten curtsied, "I hope you will forgive me. The child was so hospitable." The eyes that met hers were filled with kindly good humor. "I find it hard to believe that anyone can be so free of fear. Is it possible that the Muscovites have not visited your city?"

The woman smiled, and Kirsten saw in her face the same

124

love and gentleness that had always shone in her mother's eyes. "God has spared us—at least until now. But we understand there are soldiers about, and we realize that they will come soon. The old men are busy repairing the boats, and we will leave as soon as we receive the word. My goodness! Where have I left my manners? Come inside. The young ones will come running when the boats are ready. And in the meantime, I have a duty toward a guest. I have fresh fish, caught early this morning. Liisa! Hurry inside and set another place for our visitor. Quick, now!"

Liisa sprang to life, running across the courtyard and vanishing into the kitchen. Kirsten followed her at a more dignified pace. Her thoughts were confused. It was impossible that in the middle of devastation, such an island of peace should remain.

"Hurry along now, Kirsten! I was just calling Liisa in to eat. Everything's hot!" A chubby arm was wrapped around Kirsten's waist. Suddenly, the woman pulled away. "There I go, bossing you around as if you were my own little sister. And I haven't even told you my name." She stopped and faced Kirsten. "I am Dorotea Hamina. I gather my daughter has already introduced herself."

Kirsten nodded, repeated her own name and the explanation that she was searching for—she paused, unwilling to alienate this kindly woman. "I am looking for a close friend, whom I lost after the Muscovites took over the city of Turku."

Dorotea smiled knowingly. "A soldier, eh?"

Kirsten nodded.

"Well, I'm sure you can take a rest from your search. You must be footsore and weary. And I am willing to wager you have not had a good hot meal in many a day!" Dorotea took Kirsten's hand and led the way to the table.

The kitchen was spotless, like kitchens Kirsten had seen in the happy days before the fighting began. There were, as far as she could determine, no signs of the famine that plagued the countryside through which she had passed. As they entered, Liisa pulled a third chair up to the neat table and then climbed into her own place. Kirsten sat down and folded her hands for grace. It was not that this town was unaware of the devastation that surrounded it, only that for some unknown reason it had been passed by.

The food was, as Dorotea had claimed, both fresh and hot. Kirsten relished the sweet tartness of the fresh fish and the rich, dark bread with which it was served. Liisa chattered merrily throughout the meal, describing her morning wanderings. And Dorotea showed disapproval only when, hesitantly, the child admitted that she had wandered almost to the end of the street.

When they were through, Dorotea set her daughter to cleaning the dishes and then, once more clasping Kirsten's hand in hers, led the way to an upper room. It too was immaculate. A bed, with blankets smoothed over it, stood in one corner. A small dresser occupied another wall. Close to the door, facing the small window, was an enormous wardrobe.

Dorotea threw it open and pulled out an armful of dresses. "Take your pick, my dear. When we sail, we will have to leave all of our possessions behind. It will comfort me to know that at least some of my clothes have been put to good use."

An excitement possessed Kirsten. The gowns were most of them far too large for her, but she found among them some that Dorotea must have worn in her younger days, for they fit better. She chose a pair of heavy boots that might have been made for a young boy but that fit her quite comfortably, and a dress that spoke of styles long since abandoned. Yet the gown was warm, with long sleeves and a full, heavy shirt.

Dorotea insisted that she also accept a heavy wool cloak. "You are welcome to leave with us, if you wish. But if you are determined to continue your search, you will need this far more than will anyone who departs in the boats. We will be too crowded together to feel much chill."

Kirsten accepted the gift thankfully, reaching up impulsively to kiss the plump cheeks of her benefactress. But Dorotea seemed unwilling to accept such appreciation. "What have I given you? Nothing! All that has happened is that you have helped me save a few more of my belongings from the Muscovites. And you have provided me with the opportunity to share the bounty of God with one less fortunate. Come. I will show you the boats."

From what Dorotea and Liisa had said, Kirsten expected to see a flotilla of small boats in the harbor, but to her surprise and dismay, only one small boat floated at anchor. About ten others were resting upside down on the docks, their bare hulls partially covered with black tar.

A number of old men and very young boys were busy forcing the tar into the cracks, some of which were wide enough to let light shine through. Where the caulking had been completed, other men were busy spreading paint over the entire surface.

Kirsten was overcome with despair for these trusting people. She had seen many soldiers pass near the town. How much longer could they be expected to stay away from such a prize? Little Liisa tucked her hand into Kirsten's and hopped merrily in place.

"We're going to Sweden! Have you ever been there? I understand the streets are paved with real stones, big ones, as big as I am. And the buildings are roofed in gold!"

Amused in spite of her distress, Kirsten smiled down at the child. "Uppsala is a beautiful city, and an old one. But there is little gold on the rooftops." She saw the disappointment in the trusting eyes. "But it is still a wonderful place."

Liisa smiled happily, slipped her hand free, and ran to play with some other children who were starting a game of hide-and-seek.

"Dorotea . . ." Kirsten wondered how she could warn this friendly woman of the danger that was approaching. "Is it not foolish to put your trust in these old boats? Wouldn't it be far safer to journey, as I have, overland? There are soldiers throughout Finland, that is true. But it is not impossible for small groups of people to avoid capture as they seek shelter in the north country. Surely, your lives would be less threatened on land than they will be at sea, in such fragile crafts!"

Dorotea smiled knowingly. "It would seem so, would it not? But we have had the word. Come, I will introduce

127

you to our oracle, who speaks God's word to us. It is only a short way to the home of Katri Relander."

Kirsten followed reluctantly. "But, Dorotea! It makes no sense. Why should God save one town, when all the others have been destroyed?"

"Maybe the others have not served him as faithfully." Dorotea paused and met Kirsten's troubled eyes. "You cannot deny the evidence of your own eyes, can you? We are here, safe, unharmed by any violence. Can you deny that God's is the only power strong enough to work such a miracle?"

"But I have seen soldiers on the road. They are all around you. How can you be sure they are not planning some attack that will come when you least expect it?"

"Ah, that is where Katri serves us—and the Heavenly Father! She will warn us of such danger, and then we will leave. She is a holy woman, and we can trust her word."

"But what if the boats are not ready? You will sink and drown!"

"If that is the will of God, so be it! We follow his guidance."

Katri greeted her two guests at the door of her house. She let her hands rest briefly on Dorotea's head, as if giving a blessing, and then she turned to face Kirsten. "Welcome, little sister. Welcome to God's haven."

Kirsten gazed up into a pair of eyes that met hers without flinching, staring as if they saw through her body. The woman herself was tall and thin. Her face had the aesthetic look of one devoted to prayer and solitary contemplation. Her golden hair, braided as was the custom, was wrapped about her head like a halo.

A sick feeling of terror flooded over Kirsten. She had seen that look before, in the face of Leena Jotuni. Katri was mad, totally, completely mad. And the town had accepted her madness as a sign of God's grace.

She sat in silence as the two women conversed, too amazed and unnerved to respond in more than monosyllables to questions addressed to her. The town was doomed! Whatever opportunities might have existed for escape were gradually closing, of that she was certain. The Muscovites had plans for these unsuspecting people. And Katri, with her mad belief in her own knowledge of God's will, had won the town over. They had hung their hopes for the future on the word of a madwoman.

The following morning a noise wakened Kirsten. Terrified, she ran to the window and gazed into the street. Huddled together on the pavement was a group of five women and three old men. One of the women carried a child in her arms, and another held the hands of two toddlers, half pulling them along as she walked. All were gaunt, with terror-filled eyes and bony faces. The children's bellies bulged out abnormally. These travelers had seen the face of death. She wondered hopelessly if the small children would survive the starvation through which they had passed.

Then Dorotea appeared, her arms out in welcome. And that day there were many more at the table.

The hungry continued to arrive throughout the morning. By noon, there was little that could be done to help them. Homes that had been partially empty were filled with the sick and dying. And the wardrobes of unused clothing were stripped bare.

In the late afternoon, Kirsten pulled Dorotea aside. "How do you expect to take so many with you? Can you not see that the boats will barely hold you and your families? When you fill them with the old and the sick, they will sink the first time you encounter rough seas!" She paused to watch a new group of arrivals straggle toward the open door. "I should not speak, maybe, since you were so generous with me. But I do not plan to travel with you across the water. These people give themselves to you for protection. They do nothing for themselves. They are helpless! And they will only impede your voyage. Because of your kindness to them, you will surely be captured or drowned!"

Dorotea smiled. "I do not ask that you understand. If these people come at this time, it is because it is God's will. If we fail to take them in and help them, we do not deserve to survive."

Kirsten looked at the last to arrive. Liisa went to the corner of the courtyard where they sat, a plate of hardtack in her hands. As she watched, the old men grabbed at the dish, pushing aside the feeble hands of the children. They ate their food without looking at the pleading eyes of the young ones who had received nothing.

Dorotea seemed not to notice the selfish thoughtlessness of the men she sought to help. She smiled sweetly at Liisa and ordered her to bring more bread, and then she turned again to Kirsten. "Katri has told us how we must behave to remain in God's grace. But you are not bound by our vows. You are free to go at any time. We will not hinder you in your journey."

But some inner reluctance kept Kirsten from departing. Whenever she met Liisa's trusting eyes, she knew that she could not leave this little girl unprotected. When the house grew too crowded for Liisa to keep a room to herself, Kirsten took the child in with her, and she slept each night with her arms protectingly around the frail shoulders.

During the days, she kept Liisa constantly in view. She felt overwhelmed by an unreasonable lethargy, as if she were part of some terrible nightmare, waiting for disaster to strike, yet unable to do anything to get away.

She gained some comfort from watching the boats. One by one they were placed upright in the water and, despite their makeshift repairs, all seemed to remain afloat.

That small consolation was destroyed when, on the fifth day after her arrival, she reached the docks to find all but one of the ten boats filled with water, their decks awash. She had feared the effectiveness of the caulking, and now her worst fears had been realized.

Her apprehension grew as she watched the men pull the crafts onto the dock. It was then that Katri appeared. She gazed calmly at the worried faces of the workers. "Do not doubt, my friends. God will care for us. He will stop the leaks with his hands and carry us to safety."

Kirsten listened to her with a feeling of horror. How could men, even old men, believe such nonsense? Surely they remembered their days as sailors. How could they forget the force of the sea?

But the men nodded gravely and returned to their work. One boy began to whistle cheerfully as he helped apply more tar to the cracks, and no voice was raised to

130

object to his unreasoning happiness. Beside her, little Liisa laughed lightheartedly.

Her heart beating wildly, Kirsten ran from the docks, pulling Liisa behind her. When she reached Dorotea's house, she released the child and sought her mother.

"Dorotea, you must come with me! Katri is mad! She will kill you all!"

"Katri is blessed by God. He has given her the power to hear his voice."

"No! She is cursed! She has lost her sense! Her eyes see not what exists, but what she wishes to see. And she hears words that are not spoken. Dorotea, she is mad!"

"Oh, no." Dorotea showed no sign of uncertainty. "Katri is chosen. She has always been quiet, seeking God's truth above all else. In years gone by, she might have entered a nunnery, for she had no wish to marry. In our small Lutheran church, she is like a clear light."

Dorotea's voice warmed. "Katri, like all of us, worried greatly about the closeness of the Muscovites. We heard their gunfire to the north of the city, and we trembled. Only Katri did not waver in her faith. She went to the church daily, praying before the altar while we stumbled about in darkness.

"Then, after three days and nights of uninterrupted supplication, she heard God's judgment. She had reached his ear. And because of her devotion, we have been saved."

Dorotea paused dramatically, her eyes alight. "What she said that day has proven to be true. The Muscovites passed us by in their rush to reach Turku, and they have not returned. We all have faith now. We know that if danger approaches, Katri will warn us in time. We will be out at sea before they can reach us, and God will stop their bullets if they try to fire upon us as we depart."

Kirsten shuddered. There was no way to reach Dorotea. She and all her neighbors had chosen the path to follow, and they could see no other. They no longer could see the possibility that Katri spoke out of her own inner terror. She was mad, and the town had gone mad with her.

Still there was no evidence that Katri was not speaking the truth. Each day dawned bright and cold, and though the flow of farm folk into town continued, it began to

131

abate slightly. Yet Kirsten could not remain still. One morning, she approached one of the old men just as he finished painting the bottom of one of the boats.

"Old man!" He turned and gazed at her in silence. "Would it not be far safer were you to slip, a few at a time, along the shore until you reached a place closer to Ahvenanmaa? There is still some traffic between the island and the coast, and there are men there who would take you all to safety."

The grey head shook solemnly. "Oh, no, young lady. There would be greater hardships by land than by sea. We are, after all, people of the sea. We have been fishermen for generations. God knows what is best for us. He will take us where he wills."

Suddenly a scream tore through the air. Kirsten clutched at Liisa's small hand and squeezed it tightly, but her own fear could not be disguised. Liisa began to wail piteously, clutching Kirsten's skirt for protection.

Another scream shattered the morning. Kirsten wrapped her cloak around Liisa to shield her from whatever might appear. Yet she saw nothing unusual on the streets.

Then, with a rush, the townsfolk appeared. In twos and threes they ran from their houses and moved toward the wharf. Behind them, their gaunt faces looking like skulls, came the farm folk. Some stumbled as they walked, and though Kirsten watched with growing apprehension, she could not see them rise again.

Katri was the first to reach the docks, and her shout rang out loudly across the heads of her followers. "To the boats! Quickly! To the boats!"

A few of those in the forefront shoved their way onto the docks and stumbled into the floating hulks. A child, pushed from behind, fell into the water, and only the quick action of his mother saved him from drowning.

The first boat was filled, and yet the crowd on the dock grew. They pushed each other forward, heedless of the press that threw more victims into the water. And then the first boat began to sink. Packed from stem to stern, it took on water until with a strange sucking noise it vanished from view. The startled passengers struggled to stay afloat, but Kirsten saw with horror that many pushed at the weaker ones. She saw Katri then, her arm raised above her head, her mouth open wide as she screamed for assistance. And then she was gone, drowned in the horror that she had perpetrated upon the village.

Increased cries of alarm drew Kirsten's attention back to the mob. She could see the soldiers now, strong, burly men in blue, their guns pointed toward the crowd, their faces set. Some few eyed the plump village women with obvious lust. But most seemed unconcerned by what lay before them.

A command rang out, and from the center road, a horseman appeared. Kirsten gasped. Was this Alexei who directed the ravagement of the town?

But the man who appeared was a stranger. Tall, with a jutting jaw and bushy beard, he gazed at the throng as if contemplating its fate. At last his voice rang out. "Get them in lines! Three abreast! Get a move on! We have a long journey back to Mother Russia!"

The words cut through the crowd like a fire. Russia? God had promised them they would be safe in Sweden, through the lips of his spokeswoman, Katri!

But the culprit was nowhere to be found. Only Kirsten had seen her go down, in the last moments of life still praying to God for salvation.

She let the storm of anger wash over her. Now, when it was too late, the town had awakened. They were cursing Katri, but Kirsten knew their cries of anger were in reality directed at themselves. Katri had not forced them. Usually sober, thoughtful people, they had allowed themselves to be deceived.

Kirsten saw the light of understanding in the eyes around her. Katri could not be blamed for their agony. They had brought it upon themselves.

A shout rang out, and the loud cries of fright turned to sobs. Once more the voice sounded. "In threes! Quickly!"

One of the soldiers stepped before the horseman. "Sir! Shall we wait for any more people to come from the farms?"

"No! We have accomplished our purpose. The tsar wants men and women to work his fields. Men are hard to find except for those too old to labor. But the young boys will grow. Vladimir was right. Leave a pocket of land undisturbed, and the fools rush in to fill it. There must be five times the population of this one village here for our picking."

He turned then and rode away. But his words rang in Kirsten's ears. It had all been planned.

As she moved from the docks, Liisa pressed close under her robe, she glanced back at the water. One of the Muscovite soldiers had pulled Katri's lifeless body from the water and thrown it onto the wharf. It lay, eyes wide, one finger pointing upward, as if even in death Katri was urging the townsfolk to look to God.

Chapter 16

Liisa tugged at Kirsten's arm. "Where's my mama? I want my mama!" Her voice was frightened, and the hand that clutched at Kirsten's dress shook with terror.

"Don't worry, Liisa. I'm sure she's somewhere. We'll find her, if not now then later, when we stop to rest."

"But I want her now! Please! I'm frightened!"

Liisa was not the only child who responded to the sudden appearance of the soldiers with fright. Some of them, who had been playing on the wharf, had run toward their homes when the soldiers appeared, and they had met their mothers in the streets. But Liisa and a few of the younger ones had not been swift enough. They were crying now, and strangers were trying to comfort them.

"Faster!" The cry ran out over the sobs and the cries of despair. "Line up in threes!"

The women beside Kirsten formed into lines of three and began to move forward. Kirsten fell in behind them, her arm around Liisa. But she did not look ahead. She searched the wharf for some sign of Dorotea.

Just before she lost sight of the docks, she turned and lifted Liisa into her arms. "I see her! There, far behind us. But we'll go back to where she is the first time we rest."

Liisa stretched up to see where Kirsten's finger pointed, and when she saw her mother, she broke into a smile and struggled to be free. Kirsten put her back down.

With a cry of "Mama!" the child broke from the protection of Kirsten's arms and began to run toward the dock. Immediately, a soldier stepped into her path and caught her up in his arms. Kirsten repressed a cry of protest. This was one of the men who had shown the most obvious lust.

"Feodor! Get a move on!" The sharp call brought the man to attention. With a grimace, he dropped the child and pushed her toward Kirsten.

"Take care of your brat, woman! Next time you might not get her back!"

Liisa was sobbing when she crawled under the thick cape. "I want my mama. Why won't they let me go to my mama?"

"Don't cry, Liisa. You'll be with your mother soon. The soldiers just don't understand. They think you belong to me." She squeezed the slender body close to her, and felt the small arms reach around her for security. "You know I'll take care of you until we can get you back where you belong."

"Yes." Liisa's sobs subsided. "Is Mama all right?"

"She seemed fine, didn't she? Of course, she's worried about you, I'm sure. But maybe she saw you when I held you up. And we'll get back to her, don't you worry." Remembering the horrors her father had described, Kirsten wondered if the little one beside her would survive.

The pace chosen by the soldiers put an immediate strain on those people who had most recently arrived from the surrounding countryside. Still weak from lack of food, they stumbled often as they walked, and Kirsten feared that they might fall in their steps. The woman beside her stumbled on a small stone in the street, and Kirsten reached out and caught her in her arms. "Good woman, are you all right?"

"I am dying! We are all dying! But there will be some of us who will leave this torment sooner than others."

"You must not speak so! You must have hope. If you are resigned to death, it will come for certain."

"It will come, either way. I pray only that for me it will come soon. I have borne enough hardship."

Kirsten was silent. What answer could she give someone

136

who had abandoned hope? Especially since, in her own breast, a new optimism was forming.

They were going to Russia! Alexei was also moving in that direction. If she was fortunate, they might meet on the road, and then she could gain his protection, not only for herself but for Dorotea and Liisa. And if the worst happened and she did not pass him, she surely would find him when they arrived at their destination.

Although Kirsten was hardened by her long walk from Turku, the forced march still was difficult. No time was allowed for rest until the town was far out of sight. Even as they passed into the barren countryside, coated in a fine dust of snow, the first victims dropped to the ground. The woman beside Kirsten fell again, and this time Kirsten was not quick enough to catch her. Those behind stepped around her, but no one tried to lift her to her feet.

Kirsten felt a sharp rush of anger. If the officer could be believed, the soldiers had been ordered to deliver these people to Russia. But if they did not slow down the march, everyone would be dead before they reached the border.

Her anger was replaced by despair. "I don't even know her name. When I pray for her soul, I cannot say for whom I pray." She was barely aware that she spoke aloud. "I talked to her, but I don't know who she was." She looked back, but the fallen figure was out of sight. As far as she could see, the ragged line stretched behind her. "God rest her soul!"

The sadness remained with Kirsten for the remainder of the day, a strange sadness, mixed with both anger and confusion. She had been the only one to warn of the danger of complacency. She had spoken to Dorotea and to the old men of the danger that surrounded them. But it gave her no joy to know she had been right in her fears. She thought again of Katri, dying abandoned in the water, in sight of the destruction that had overtaken her mad dream. For these people there was no hope. The unknown woman had spoken the truth.

She glanced at Liisa. The child was walking easily now, her arms swinging beside her as if she were on a pleasant hike. Maybe some of the children would survive.

Survive for what? Kirsten recoiled from the thought of what might lie ahead. The children were the most vulnerable, for they still had faith in the goodness of their elders. They had not been prepared, as she had been, for the worst that might happen. If they lived to see Russia, how many of them would remain alive long enough to return to their homes?

The sun was early in setting, and in the glowing twilight the chill of the day grew more intense. Liisa, her face pinched with cold, huddled against Kirsten's warmth. When the child stumbled, Kirsten lifted her up, cradling the sleepy child in her arms. The blonde head fell against her shoulder, and soon Kirsten was aware that for Liisa, at least, the first day of the march was over.

They stopped when she had begun to fear that they would march all night. A command brought the column to a halt, and another shout sent the exhausted villagers into a field alongside the road, where they sought what shelter they could find in the stubble of last year's harvest.

Taking advantage of the confusion, Kirsten moved purposefully toward the back of the line until at last she saw Dorotea's worried face. The anxious mother had been able to dress in clothes as warm as those she had given Kirsten, and she held in her hands a thick cape for Liisa. The child stirred as the robe was pulled over her shoulders. "Mama?" Her voice was soft, warm with the sweetness of an innocent dream.

"Mama's here, Liisa. Go back to sleep. Mama's here."

As Kirsten settled herself beside the mother and child, she thought of the statue of the Madonna she had seen in an old abandoned church that had once belonged to the Papists. She prayed that this mother could protect her child from the danger that lay ahead. Then her body relaxed for the first time since the arrival of the soldiers. She lay back and gazed at the glowing sky. She wondered how the same God who could put such beauty in nature could permit such ugliness in the hearts of mankind. Sleep came at last, without bringing her any answers to her impossible question.

* * *

The days that followed were filled with terror. The soldiers rose at dawn, stepped from the tents they had pitched the night before and kicked the prisoners awake. Many did not respond to the jostling. The farm women died first, too weak from months of starvation to withstand the rigors of the march. Children, too, were among those left behind when the walk began. Mothers, holding cold corpses in their arms when daylight dawned, were beaten and forced to abandon the tiny bodies to the wolves.

Kirsten grew inured to the most blatant signs of suffering, but many she could not ignore, or forget. The gaunt faces haunted her when she closed her eyes at the end of a day, and each night she prayed that the end, for those who could not continue, would be swift and easy.

The lucky ones were those people who went to sleep at night and did not wake again in the morning. The most pathetic were those who fell on the road and were left to freeze, their cries of agony tearing at Kirsten's consciousness. For as the marchers who still could walk passed them by, they stripped the fallen of their clothing. Even in her horror, Kirsten could understand. The dead had no more use for protection against the elements.

On the sixth night, a new feeling seemed to suffuse the camp. The soldiers gazed restlessly at the prisoners, as if suddenly seeing them. One in particular, a woman from the town whose husband had been drowned in the crowded boat, seemed to respond to their lustful glances. Silently, she rose from where she crouched and crept toward the sentry. In the light of the fire that burned too far from most of the prisoners to give them any warmth, her cheeks seemed flushed with a strange fever.

The sentry caught her hand and pulled her toward him. "Feodor! Nikolai! Evgeni! Look what's come to entertain us!"

Kirsten shuddered. Could it be that Irja did not know what lay ahead? Had she never been warned of the viciousness of the Muscovites? But even Kirsten had not anticipated the full horror of what ensued.

The four men laughed coarsely as they led the girl to their tent. One, slapping her on the backside, asked her what she was called. And then the party vanished into the tent.

The laughter continued at first. Irja joined in, her laugh almost happy at the warmth and the food she was given. But a note of desperation soon appeared in the girl's voice. When the men began to grunt, Kirsten glanced down at Liisa. The child slept peacefully, seemingly untouched by the fear that surrounded her.

Kirsten attempted to ignore the noises, to join Dorotea and Liisa in sleep, but she could not. She huddled, wide-eyed and tense, listening as one man after another took his pleasure.

But she was not prepared when the screaming began. Dorotea woke with a start and clutched at her daughter. Her frightened eyes met Kirsten's. "What is happening? What are they doing?"

Kirsten recounted what had gone on before. "My father warned me that the Muscovites were cruel. He told me they tortured women until they begged for death. But until now, I did not know how truly he spoke."

Another shriek cut through the air, tearing at her sanity, shattering the sleep of the frightened prisoners who lay about her. One by one they rose to their knees, their hands clasped in prayer. A few of the village women, as yet unaware of the brutality of the Muscovites, prayed that the girl be released. But Kirsten, and most of the farm people who had so far survived the march, prayed that Irja's death would come soon.

All of the prisoners stared at the tent as they prayed, heedless of the laughter of the sentry. When the screaming stopped, leaving a stillness that was more terrible than the noise that had come before, a sigh of relief passed through the crowd.

The flap of the tent was thrown open and one of the soldiers stepped out, a white body draped on one arm. He tossed it to the ground like a rag and then, without another glance at the source of his recent pleasure, stepped into the darkness to relieve himself.

Kirsten closed her eyes, waiting for the soldier to return to the tent. But the sentry remained alert, daring someone to approach the white body. Far more terrifying than the thought of death by gunfire was the realization that any prisoner who moved to assist the battered Irja could easily become the next victim.

When morning came, Irja's body was half frozen, covered with a light dusting of snow. Kirsten, shielding Liisa's face from the sight, wondered helplessly who was the more fortunate: Irja, for whom the terror was over, or the rest of them, herself included, who still struggled to maintain lives that were fast becoming unbearable.

Days passed without any change in the horror that surrounded them. Each morning when Kirsten gazed into the faces of Liisa and her mother, she was thankful that they were still alive. But the starvation diet and the long marches were taking their toll. Liisa's bright face was solemn, her eyes dull. Her chubby arms and legs had become sticks that seemed unequal to the task of supporting her emaciated body. Her stomaach was swollen.

Food was scarce, even for the soldiers. Each evening they stopped a bit earlier and, on command of their officer, went out to hunt for edibles. Once they returned with a stag, and the starving prisoners sat, dull-eyed and patient, while the sweet aroma of roasting meat filled the air. When the bones were thrown out, the hungry captives rushed to pick them up, snarling and grabbing at the scraps like dogs. Kirsten, her thoughts on the child whom she had come to love, joined in the battle, and she emerged triumphantly, a section of ribs in her hands, with some meat still clinging to the bones. Both women watched hungrily as Liisa chewed at the food. But the child was too weak to eat much, and when she abandoned the effort, the two women finished what was left.

Kirsten kept the bones tucked in a pocket in her cape, aware that in the days to come the child might wish to chew on them. That night, all three slept more soundly than they had in many weeks.

On the road, long before the black cover of night was pulled from the sky, Kirsten tried to bolster Dorotea's courage. But Dorotea was wracked with convulsions brought on by the food in her empty stomach, and she moaned in pain with each step.

When she caught Kirsten's glance, she rolled her eyes. "When I think that we could have escaped! God is dead—or else he cares not a whit for our suffering!"

"Hush!" Kirsten met her friend's eyes. "You must not speak thus! It was not God who told you to sit idly by while your chance for freedom faded. You put your trust in a fragile woman, one not strong enough to bear the thought of what lay ahead. Had you listened to God and to your own hearts you would not have remained."

Dorotea cast a despairing glance toward Liisa and continued in silence. There was nothing left to be said.

Kirsten bit her tongue. Why, when Dorotea was suffering so much, did she insist upon reminding her of the folly that had brought on their woes? But the words had been said, and she could only pray that Dorotea would forgive her.

Feodor stamped past, his eyes touching her face with a sudden warmth. Kirsten shuddered. At night, she had feared that she might be next. Yet, despite his obvious interest, Feodor had not yet taken her. But her time would come, she was sure of that. And Dorotea's. And Liisa's. She shuddered at the thought. If she were still alive, she would kill the child before she would let her face such bestiality. If she had the strength. "Dear God," she prayed silently, "give me the courage to do what must be done."

That night they stopped in a clearing that had once been a prosperous farm. The soldiers set up their tents over the ashes of the farmhouse. The meager food was distributed and eaten.

But this night was to be different for Kirsten and her friends. Feodor stumbled over her as he made his rounds, and his eyes fell on Liisa, huddled close to her mother. Laughing wickedly, he bent and grabbed the girl by the arm, pulling her to her feet.

Immediately Dorotea was upon him. Her arms flailing, she hit at the thick fingers and pulled at the heavy beard. When she made no headway, she leaned forward and bit hard on his arm.

"Bitch!" The sharp cry seared the air, and he dropped Liisa to the ground. "You've hurt me! Damn you for a devil!" His fingers closed around Dorotea's neck. "I could kill you now! How dare you bite your master?"

Dorotea seemed unaware of her peril. With a snarl, she spit into the face of her tormentor.

Feodor roared again, and this time he lifted the woman and carried her by the neck to the tent. Liisa lay huddled at Kirsten's feet, temporarily forgotten.

Kirsten watched as he stopped before the tent. If God was good, Dorotea would strangle before she touched the ground. But the power of heaven seemed to have deserted the unfortunate woman. When Feodor put her on her feet, she swayed for a moment and then disappeared from view. She cast one glance at Kirsten and her daughter, who was standing now, too frightened to cry.

The hours that followed were more terrible to Kirsten than any she had endured in the past. She heard the screams and knew it was her friend who suffered. She heard the grunts of animalistic pleasure issue from the throats of the Muscovite soldiers, and she felt as if Dorotea's hurts were her own. She held Liisa to her breast, trying to shield the child from the sounds of her mother's torment, and she knew that she could do nothing to help her kind, loving, generous friend.

When at last the naked body was thrust into the cold, Kirsten sat in terror, knowing she should go to assist her companion, yet too frozen with fear to move. She stared at the white form, praying that Liisa would not look up.

Suddenly, the figure moved. It lifted its head and began to crawl into the shelter of the crowded prisoners. Their faces white with fear, those closest to her pulled away to let her pass. Kirsten could feel their terror, like some living thing, denying them the luxury of kindness.

Suddenly she moved toward Dorotea, her arms outstretched. She felt the shaking of the broken body, and she held her friend close, willing her strength to flow into Dorotea.

"Mama!" Liisa crawled into her mother's arms. Even in her pain, Dorotea could not reject her daughter. Settling into the folds of Kirsten's great cape, she held her arms open for her child. With a sob, Liisa settled into the circle of love."Mama! Oh, Mama!" The cry of anguish tore at Kirsten's heart.

Dorotea began to rock back and forth, her head pressed against the soft down of her daughter's hair. Her fingers pressed into the slender body, as if with her own failing strength she wanted to protect her child. She began to croon a lullaby, kissing the soft blonde head with lips still wet with blood and semen.

Kirsten took the woman deeper into her arms and the three rocked together, Dorotea singing a lullaby to her baby, Kirsten humming another song to the broken, battered mother.

Gradually, Liisa's sobs were stilled. The moon rose, casting a cold light on the silent mass of humanity. The other prisoners, freed of the fear that Dorotea's misfortune would affect them, had gone to sleep. Kirsten saw that Liisa, too, had lapsed into unconsciousness. But the rocking continued unabated.

A change in the body that she crushed in her arms made Kirsten pause in her song. For a time, Dorotea had seemed to grow warmer. Now she was cold again, and her skin felt tight against the bones of her cheeks. "Dorotea?" Kirsten whispered. "Dorotea?"

"Take care of her. Do not let them harm her. Please!" The words were barely audible.

"You will be all right. You will live to help her."

"No. God has not willed that I live. You must take care of her now." The face grew suddenly strong, filled with new determination. "If they try to take her, kill her. Do not let her know the horror I have been through."

"If I must, I will." Kirsten could hardly believe she was making the promise. "But I will pray—"

The face before her sagged abruptly. The light that had blazed in the blue eyes faded. And the weight she held in her arms grew suddenly heavy. Dorotea was dead.

Liisa woke as she was pulled from the unfeeling arms. "Mama?" She whispered the name, and when she saw her mother's face, her eyes grew wide.

Kirsten drew the child close to her breast. "Your mother is in heaven, Liisa. She will not be hurt again."

But when the girl returned to a restless sleep, Kirsten

144

sat awake, staring into the darkness. Maybe Dorotea was right, after all. Maybe God had deserted Finland.

From that day onward, Kirsten searched about her for a weapon, for she knew the time would come when she would have to use it on Liisa—and on herself.

Chapter 17

Viotto was the first to recognize Kirsten's subterfuge. Swinging his hands wildly at his sides, he stamped about the glen, searching the ground for some sign of her tracks. But the soil was hard and cold, and he could find no clue that would guide him in pursuit.

"Damn!" His anger could not be concealed. "To take such advantage of a child!"

Sirkka pulled Eila into her arms. "Of course Eila is not to blame. But did you expect otherwise? You cannot treat a proud, beautiful woman as you have treated Kirsten Gustafson and expect her to follow you like a faithful puppy! Young as she is, she cannot but be insulted by your behavior."

"How have I mistreated her or insulted her? When I spoke of her Muscovite lover, I told only the truth. She did not bother to deny anything."

"And why should she? Is she accountable to you for her actions? Oh, Viotto! You were more aware of the sensitivities of women when you were a child. What has changed you? Have you considered that she was a mere child who had been sheltered all her life, that she was alone and afraid? I do not know how she came to depend upon the Muscovite, but I am certain he has shown more cause to hold her trust than you, her own countryman."

Viotto sneered. Then, his voice heavy with anger, he

spit out the story as Kirsten had told it. And as he spoke, he heard it himself with new understanding. Sirkka was right. A child, a slip of a girl, suddenly bereft of her mother, not yet recovered from the loss of her father, accustomed to gentleness and love, faced with the reality of conquest. But the man who represents the enemy to her was not the beast she has been led to expect. Even after he forced himself upon her, he showed unexpected consideration. And in the end, Kirsten turned to him for protection as if to her own dead father.

Viotto met his sister's eyes. "You are probably right, as usual, little sister. Why is it that men need such assistance in understanding the simplest things about women? Do I treat you with no more sympathy?"

Sirkka took her brother's arm. "Sometimes, yes. But what you feel toward me is brotherly love, a closeness that stems from our childhood. I sense more in your relationship with Kirsten. My dear Viotto, wars destroy everything, even social barriers. What was far above you in your youth is now within your reach."

Viotto pulled his arm free and turned toward the river. Sirkka never knew when to stop! Ever the romantic, she had to weave a fable that satisfied her imagination. But she was wrong. What he felt toward Kirsten was guilt. He was ashamed of his actions. Sirkka was right that he no longer felt contempt for the lovely girl, that he forgave her for her dependence upon an enemy. But he did not feel love for her. That was going too far!

He did not speak again until they were safe inside the cellar. He sat with Eila on his lap, her soft hair tickling his nostrils. The child had shown obvious pleasure at not being blamed for Kirsten's escape, and her arm circled his neck affectionately.

He kissed the top of her head. "Sirkka, you know you cannot remain here. You have been fortunate to have escaped the Muscovites for so long."

Sirkka gestured toward a large bundle that lay in one corner of the cellar. "I have been ready to leave for many weeks. But I have waited, hoping to hear from you—or Veikko." Her eyes dimmed, but she forced the tears back. "Now that—he is dead—I can leave, for I know I have

148

nothing to hold me here." She rose and stood before him. "Brother, will you travel with me? Or have you a mind to search for your woman?"

Viotto scowled. "My woman is dead! Need I repeat it again?"

"My apologies, Viotto! I will ask my question in another way. Will you escort me and Eila to safety? In the woods, far from the farm, I will be lost. I have not traveled as you have, nor have I learned to fend for myself away from civilization. Eila and I will be in great danger if we travel alone."

Viotto looked down at his bandaged hands. They no longer ached, for the salve Sirkka had spread on them was potent. Yet he dared not use them until they were completely healed. "What good can I do you? I cannot gather food or hold a knife."

"But you can lead us. You can read the stars and keep us heading in the right direction. Viotto, think! If you wish to remain here so you can search for Kirsten, I will understand. But if you allow your niece, your best friend's only child, to wander through the forest without a guide because you are too set on vengeance to value her life, then you will disappoint me. God has taken vengeance upon his own shoulders. Do you honestly think that you have received his word and are acting on his command?"

Viotto lowered his eyes. "God has not seen what I have seen!"

"Oh, Viotto! What nonsense! God sees it all. He must be impatient with the foolishness of mankind. He gives us a fair land, with green fields and blue lakes. He gives us rain and sunshine. He populates the land with game, and stirs the seed we plant to life. He provides us with everything we need for happiness. And we choose to use the strength he gives us to kill our neighbors!"

Viotto rose, letting Eila slide to the floor. His face was red with anger. "We are not the ones who do the killing, nor are we the ones who rape helpless women. That is done by the Muscovites!"

He paused suddenly. The memory of the renegade raid on Kirsten's small company of women and their soldier husbands flashed into his mind.

149

Sirkka seemed to sense his indecision. "Is that so? Are the Swedes innocent? Are you innocent? Have you and they no blood on your hands? And do they not sometimes forget that they are defending their brothers and sisters?" She paused dramatically, forcing him to meet her gaze. "When you seek Kirsten's friend with vengeance in your heart, are you not as bad as he?"

"Never! He and his men are the ones who killed my Ruusu! He takes women against their will . . ." The words froze on his lips. Had he not taken Kirsten with equal disregard for her wishes? And had he, like Alexei, tried to right the wrong after it was done? He had rescued her mementos, that was true. And in the process he had burned his hands. In his heart, he had blamed her for his injury! He had shown her no affection since that fateful night.

Yet, despite his new understanding, he could not abandon the position he had cherished for so long. He paced the cellar without looking at his sister or the wide, questioning eyes of his niece.

At last he paused before them. "Maybe you are right, Sirkka. Maybe you are wrong. But I cannot deny certain facts. Kirsten is gone, and I realize I will not find her easily since she wishes to avoid me. The possibility is that she is already safe. If she is wise, she will go to the new Russian governor and ask for safe conduct to her lover." He did not really believe what he was saying, but the words still gave him comfort.

He chose to ignore Sirkka's frown. "As for her Muscovite protector, he is in all probability back in Russia, where I wish they would all go! I cannot, at least for the present, follow him there." He glanced at his bandaged hands. "I would gain nothing by finding him now."

He turned toward the bundle. "You will have to lift this thing onto my back and tie it securely. I will take you north, as you have requested. I owe Veikko that much." He smiled, suddenly warm and loving again. "And I must admit I would fear for your safety were you to travel alone."

"You will not regret letting Kirsten go without making a search?"

"Damn, little sister, how you can find the target! Yes, I will regret abandoning her. But there is little I can do. I was too long in recognizing my own feelings. My sister knows what is in my heart before I do!" His jaw clamped firmly, and he stared in silence at the sliver of light that stretched across the cellar floor. "Besides, she would not have me now. Anything I do will only inspire more hatred in her heart. She has made her choice, and I must learn to live with it."

He would not speak of Kirsten again, though she remained in his thoughts as the preparations for the journey were completed. What if she realized her danger and returned to the cellar for protection? Then he frowned and brushed the thought from his mind. Kirsten hated him, of that he had no doubt. But should it concern him? His love lay dead and buried with his child still in her belly.

Try as he would, however, he could not put the vision of Kirsten's sweet face from his thoughts. As he led the way into the shelter of the woods, he made a silent vow: when his sister and niece were safe, he would return. Despite his conviction that Kirsten meant nothing to him, he could not let her go. He would hunt for her until he learned that she was safe and happy. Only then could he put the memory of her soft surrender behind him.

"Viotto." Sirkka tugged his arm. "Viotto!"

He paused. The farm was still in sight, and he felt a surge of irritation at Sirkka's interference with their speedy departure. "Sirkka, you can't go back. If you have forgotten something, you must put it behind you."

"No, Viotto. I have forgotten nothing. It is Yrjo. Do you remember him?"

Viotto nodded. "I have not thought of him since I was a child. Why do you speak of him now?"

"Because his mother and sister might be at their farm. I have not dared to venture out to see them since the Muscovites arrived, but before, when our men had gone to war, we used to call on each other daily. Please. I cannot leave this place without knowing they are safe."

Viotto nodded. Yet why was it that when he had a feeling of urgency things conspired to delay him? If he stopped every hour on his journey north, he would never return to find Kirsten! Then he remembered that he had no wish to locate the girl. What was she to him? Nothing! All he wanted was to know that she was happy, that she had found the man she was seeking, or that she was dead and her search was ended. He shook his head angrily. He was a fool! What did it matter to him whether she was dead or alive? Either way, she had chosen another. And a Muscovite, at that!

Controlling his inclination to sigh impatiently, he turned toward the clearing that lay next to his brother-in-law's farm. "You're right, of course. We cannot ignore our neighbors." He slowed his walk. "But Sirkka, you must realize that the more people we have with us, the greater our danger. And my first aim is to bring you and Eila to safety."

"Yes, Viotto, I understand. But surely it will not delay us too much to see if our friends need assistance."

The farm appeared to be deserted. Sirkka hurried across the clearing to the cellar. It was empty. Viotto watched her with growing sympathy. He remembered now that the two girls had been as close as sisters, and that Yrjo's mother had been like a second mother to Sirkka.

It was then he relized that Eila had left his side and was running across the burned fields toward the river. With a curse, he raced after her. Damn! Why didn't the child learn caution?

Halfway across the field he knew what had attracted his niece's attention. In a grove of birch near the river was a spot of color. The sight set his heart beating. Could it be that Kirsten was foolish enough to have tried to hide in so obvious a place?

But her name died on his lips when Eila screamed. With a surge of speed, he reached her side and swept her into his arms, shielding her face from the sight. It was not Kirsten who lay dead before him, and for that blessing he felt an inner joy. But the sight of the two bodies sent a wave of fury through his soul. They had been attacked by the Muscovites and then left, dead or dying, their skirts pulled up over their hips, their faces distorted with pain, their legs covered with caked blood.

In spite of his realization of the danger involved, he remained long enough to bury the two white bodies. As he threw the last shovel of dirt over the graves, he gazed into the pinched little face of his niece. She stared ahead, her eyes still full of the horror of what she had seen. She jumped each time he let a shovel of dirt fall to the ground. When they resumed their journey, her face was solemn.

They moved swiftly now, giving wide berth to the small empty farmhouses that seemed to beckon them like ghostly ambushes. Viotto refused to listen to Sirkka's continued pleas to look in each house for some survivors. He hardened his heart to the possibility that behind some of the seemingly empty windows women lurked, gazing at the world outside with fear, praying for rescue—but expecting only death.

He told himself that he dared not risk Sirkka and Eila's safety again. Days passed before the child smiled again, and when she did, the brightness of her face filled his heart with delight. He dared not harm that joyful spirit with the sight of terror again.

But Sirkka refused to accept his concern. When they passed a farmhouse, she moved reluctantly, gazing long at the hollow windows as if hoping to see some sign of life. And at last she refused to continue until he would let her speak.

"Viotto, I know how terrible it was for Eila to see—what she saw. But we live in a time of terror. She will learn to survive, as have we all. And her ability to live will increase if she is aware of the dangers that surround her. We cannot protect her from life. Besides, she is considerably recovered. This morning she wanted to stop to gather berries." She paused. "I did not let her, but maybe I should have. We will need more food before we reach our destination."

Viotto nodded. "Yes. We can all take some time to find what food is available. The air is growing chill." He stared up at the sky. "It is difficult to decide whether to speed on or to stop to search for food. The first might make the second unnecessary."

"There is more. We will be derelict in our duty if we let our concern for our own safety, or for little Eila, harden

153

our hearts to the suffering of others. We do not have to take her with us when we hunt for survivors. You can stay with her and hunt for berries while I find out if there are other women who need to travel with us."

Viotto shook his head. "No, I will search and you will pick berries. But you must promise to be alert. If the soldiers come, they will give you little warning." He stared southward. "I cannot stand to lose another loved one."

Sirkka smiled as she watched Viotto depart toward the farmhouse. So Viotto did miss Kirsten! In the past, when life was filled with lightness and pleasure, she would have teased him with her new-found knowledge. Now she clutched it close to her heart. If Viotto loved Kirsten, then it had been wrong of her to ask him to accompany her to the north. He should be free to hunt for the woman he loved.

But she knew she could not persuade him to leave her now. He had committed himself to the journey, and he would see it through.

In spite of her new understanding, there was little she could do to hurry their passage. They found a woman and her three daughters huddled in their cellar, and Viotto, recognizing them as the family of one of his men, had to inform them that their man had fallen in battle. The four women took the news calmly, and he realized that they had already accepted their loss. Without speaking, they gathered their bundles and filed behind Sirkka.

Other women seemed drawn to the small caravan like moths to a flame. The travelers would stop for a night in a grove of trees and awake in the morning to find that there were more in their party than had been with them the night before. Often Viotto, sitting silently against a tree, keeping guard over his charges, would see the women arrive. And after the first time, he was careful not to acknowledge their presence until dawn.

All of these newcomers were frightened creatures, ready to flee into the woods if startled. They watched Viotto with guarded dependency, aware that he was essential to their safety, yet unwilling to trust any man completely.

He had risen when the first such lost woman appeared, and she had turned in terror and fled. He had no way of knowing whether she had returned again, after he learned to watch without moving, but he could not avoid a short prayer for her safety. She had been so like a startled doe, caught in the act of pilfering grain from the storehouse of a farmer.

Each night, he directed Sirkka and Eila to hide beneath fallen leaves or in a thatch of thick evergreens, and he waited until the other women did the same. Then, as was his custom, he settled himself against a tree, prepared to sleep in a sitting position, ready to leap to his feet at the first sound of danger.

On one such night, when the air was particularly crisp and the smell of snow was in the wind, he viewed the forest around him with a special uneasiness. With nature making such a disturbance, would he hear if soldiers approached?

One of the women stirred in her sleep, and he turned immediately in her direction. Like a mother hen protecting her chicks, he was aware of each of his charges and of those noises that meant harm to them. With a feeling of relief, he turned his gaze up to the sky.

Only a few stars sparkled overhead, peeking past the thick clouds like mischievous children in a game of hide-and-seek. Ten days had passed since Kirsten had run away. She could be dead. His thoughts recoiled from such a possibility.

He closed his eyes and immediately Kirsten appeared before him. Lovely, delicate, sensitive Kirsten! He had treated her so meanly. Was it any wonder she had learned to hate him?

With an angry curse, he shook his head and stared at the road. Why could he not put the girl from his thoughts? She had met his eyes with a burning inner fury when she spoke of her hatred. Surely her words came from her heart. For the thousandth time he cursed himself for his precipitate action that night in her house. He had fostered her anger—he deserved her contempt.

A new sound penetrated through the noises of the wind, and he was immediately alert, his eyes on the road. He had insisted that the caravan take shelter some distance from the gravel path each night, and now he was thankful for his wisdom.

As he watched, three soldiers appeared in the greyness of the night. They moved without caution, their guns rattling on their armor, their swords slapping their legs with each step.

He froze, pressing back into the shadow of the branches, thankful that the moon had not yet risen. But he had no reason to fear discovery. The three men were talking as they walked, and they seemed totally unaware of the countryside through which they were passing. They walked swiftly, as if pursued by Satan himself.

Viotto sat alert for the remainder of the night, waiting for more soldiers to appear. But the road remained empty. When the women awoke, he directed them to travel alongside the path, far enough into the woods to make concealment easy if the enemy were to appear suddenly.

His precautions were wise. A large encampment of Muscovite soldiers occupied the intersection of the next two roads they passed. The women moved like wraiths, slipping behind Viotto so quietly that the entire group succeeded in passing the danger without discovery.

But from that moment on, Viotto exercised even greater caution. The only safety they had lay in remaining hidden. For if they were discovered, the Muscovites would destroy them all. His one sword and gun would be no defense against an organized attack.

Chapter 18

"Liisa, please, you must eat. I have chewed the grain carefully, and it is soft enough for you to swallow." Kirsten held out the small lump of food. "And it tastes so very good! Sweet and delicious!"

She was speaking the truth. She had been surprisingly fortunate that night. As the marchers settled down to sleep in the snow-covered field, she had found herself staring at a stalk of wheat that had survived not only the destruction that had been visited upon the countryside when the Muscovite army swarmed over it, but the passage of other caravans as pathetic as her own. And on the pale stem was a full head of grain.

Jealously, she had stripped the single plant and separated the kernels from the chaff. She had chewed them slowly, relishing the sweet taste of the juices that washed down her parched throat. But, ever aware of little Liisa, she had resisted the urge to swallow it all. Liisa was too weak to chew the hard grain.

The child had grown sallow and listless in the days since her mother's death. Her eyes were set back in her head, dark caves that seemed to grow deeper by the hour. The hand of death was already on her shoulder. If Kirsten could not inspire some interest in life in the pallid face, there would be few days remaining for the little one.

157

"Please, Liisa. Just a little! It's so good!" Kirsten smacked her lips and smiled into the dull eyes.

Liisa's gaze remained glazed and empty. She did not respond to the food that was presented to her lips. And the sight of the wan face tore at Kirsten's breast. How could men be so cruel as to harm little children?

She took the small body into her arms and held it close. Liisa had fought with great courage until the day her mother died. Now she would not even eat when food was available.

Kirsten considered forcing the food into the child's mouth, but she knew the uselessness of such an act. Liisa would only spit it out onto the ground.

In despair, Kirsten returned the mush to her own mouth and began to chew it slowly. The delicious taste of wheat mixed with her saliva tricked down her throat. But even as she enjoyed the taste, she felt a disgust at her ability to preserve her own life when those around her were dying. She was showing cruelty. Her thoughts wandered back to all she had seen in the days of marching. No, she was showing lack of sympathy.

Cruelty was taking the clothes from the backs of dying men and women as they struggled to hold their places in the line. Cruelty was snatching food from the hands of children. Cruelty was pushing another forward when the soldiers came to pick a companion for the night.

But she felt a terrible pain in her heart when she gazed into the eyes of little Liisa. She longed to see the child well and strong again, with the same fervor that drove her to seek Alexei's face whenever a new contingent of Muscovite soldiers crossed the path of the caravan.

Kirsten knew that she was neither cruel nor lacking in understanding. She was not responsible for the selfishness that caused the young woman who marched ahead of her to pull her mother's clothing from her back as she died.

When Kirsten had protested, the girl had spat at her. "Mind your own business! She would want me to have it! What need have the dead for warmth?"

And Kirsten, covering little Liisa's eyes against the sight, had no answer to the question. It was only later that she realized that Liisa had shown no response either to the sight of the old woman falling or to the voice of the younger one as she shouted her anger and frustration. The realization added one more worry to the many Kirsten had regarding her young ward.

Little Liisa's body felt bony in Kirsten's arms. She made no attempt to pull away from the confinement. There had been a time when such patience would have been beyond her—in the days when Kirsten had first met her, when she ran free in the streets of Helsingfors.

Kirsten's thoughts wandered back to her own childhood. She, too, had been a happy child, wandering freely on her father's lands.

She chewed the lump of grain that was growing smaller in her mouth. She had always loved the taste and smell of bread. The fresh odor of newly roasted loaves never failed to bring her in from play, to stand restlessly at the kitchen door until the cook cut off a slice and handed it to her.

Kirsten bent and kissed the rumpled hair of the child. Poor Liisa might never live to have such memories of her childhood. And if she did live this would be better put behind her.

"Mama." The sound was so soft Kirsten barely heard it.

"Kirsten's here, Liisa. Just rest, my darling!"

Liisa opened her eyes wide and pulled out of Kirsten's embrace. "Mama!" There was no panic in the voice, only a joyful welcome. But to Kirsten, the very tone was frightening.

"She's all right, my darling. She'll never feel pain again. Don't worry about her."

The child did not seem to hear. "Mama?"

Kirsten had heard that sound back in the days when, tired from her play on the wharf, Liisa had come running home to nestle in her mother's arms, like a small bird returning to its nest. The sound filled Kirsten with terror.

"Liisa, don't leave me! You can live, if you only try. Here, there's a little grain left. Eat it now. Please!" Her cheeks were hot with tears, and she reached out to pull the child back to her bosom.

But Liisa's ears were tuned to another sound. She stumbled forward, her arms outstretched. The men and women who huddled around recoiled as she passed.

159

Kirsten rose and followed, ready to protect the helpless child from attack. She had reached Liisa's side when the small body stiffened and suddenly plummeted forward. With a cry, Kirsten caught the frail figure and wrapped it in her cloak. "Liisa, Kirsten's here. You're all right now."

But Liisa did not hear her. "Oh, Mama, I'm so tired!" The deep caverns of her eyes were shrouded, and her lips were still.

But Kirsten refused to recognize the face of death. She cradled the small body in her arms, crooning softly. As she sang, she wept. She was not aware when she passed into a troubled sleep.

It was almost dawn when a hand touched her shoulder, jerking her into immediate awareness. "Kirsten?"

She looked up in alarm. The woman who stood before her was gaunt, with a grey skin that spoke of frostbite. By her side was a child no bigger than Liisa. "Please, Kirsten. Let me have Liisa's clothing. My little one is freezing."

"No! Liisa needs all the clothes she has. How can you think of such a thing? Have you not seen how she suffers from the cold?"

The emaciated face twisted in sudden pity. "Kirsten, look at her. She needs warmth no longer. She is dead."

"No!" The sound tore through Kirsten's tender throat. But she could not avoid the pointing finger. The woman was right. The child in her arms was still, free at last from the torment that surrounded them all.

With the woman's help, she crawled to the center of the mob and hollowed out a hole in the wet ground. There the snow had melted under the warmth of the crush of bodies, exposing the earth. She removed Liisa's clothes before she laid her down and covered her with a pile of rocks. But she could not watch as the woman pulled the clothing on her living child. Covering her face with her hands, she prayed silently until the order was given to march.

"You! In there!" Kirsten stood watching dumbly as boys were torn from their mothers' arms and sent into one building with the men. Before her, half covered with snow, were two large barns.

160

The prisoners had crossed into Russia two days earlier, passing the sentries who seemed to ignore their condition while still making a close count of their numbers. Now, at last, it appeared that they had reached their destination.

Kirsten, waiting her turn to be directed into a building, gazed about her with dull curiosity. The land differed little from that over which they had passed in the last weeks of their journey: rolling hills leading to a lowland which in spring would be filled with water from melting snow. To the left tall mountains, to the right the bay. She looked left again. The mountains were far in the distance.

She had lost count of time during the long march, but she felt certain that winter had spent at least half of its fury on the land. If she managed to live until spring . . .

The thought sparked hopes that had lain dormant in her heart since Liisa's death. If she managed to live until spring, she might yet find Alexei. Alexei had been sent to St. Petersburg to serve the tsar. That was what Viotto had told her. And unless she was terribly wrong, the city was not too far from where she now stood.

She shifted back in the line, hoping to see beyond the wall of the barn. But the snow had begun to fall again, and she could barely see back to the heavy gate through which she had passed. Still the certainty that the city lay nearby gave her comfort. Whatever had been the reason for the long march, it was in some way connected to the city of St. Petersburg.

"You there! Get a move on!"

Kirsten stumbled forward, alert to the guards who stood over her, their eyes sharp and filled with warning. As had been her custom, partly from weakness and partly from fear, she crouched like a cripple and limped into the barn. The soldiers wanted young, attractive women for their pleasure.

She stepped away from the door as soon as she entered and stood gazing about her, waiting for her eyes to adjust to the dim light. Snow had filtered through cracks in the walls of the building, but the roof was solid, and the freedom from the wind gave her a feeling of sudden warmth.

The other women moved slowly into the barren interior, groping before them and stumbling on the uneven floor. There was a pervading odor of hay that filled Kirsten with nostalgia.

Her eyes darted about the large area until at last she located the source of the odor. In one corner, busily munching, was a herd of cows. They worked at their food with bovine concentration, undisturbed by the sudden appearance of humans in their quiet sanctuary.

A voice drew her attention back to the door.

"Here, all of you! Line up before me!"

She fell into line beside the others.

"When spring comes, you will prepare the ground for crops for the city of St. Petersburg. The tsar himself has provided food for you until that time. There are buckets and dippers hanging on the wall. You are responsible for the beasts. You will die if they do!" He turned and vanished through the doorway, slamming the door shut behind him.

Kirsten stood for a moment, too stunned to act. It was over! Now they had food and a warm shelter.

Her skin, accustomed to the cold, began to tingle with new life, and sharp pains shot down her arms and into her cold fingers. Her feet, too, were in pain, but she did not dare to rest. Not yet. Not until she had determined that the cows were real.

A few of the other women had reached them by the time she touched the flank of the first cow. But they seemed unable to grasp what should be done. Kirsten stared at them in surprise. And then she knew. City folk, they had grown accustomed to purchasing their milk from the farmers who lived on the outskirts of their town.

With sudden resolve, she removed a bucket from the wall and settled beside the first beast. Its udders were distended and the milk flowed easily under her touch, foaming into the pail and giving off a sweet fragrance.

Kirsten inhaled in anticipation. But before she could lift the pail to her lips, another woman grabbed it from her, tilted it up and, in her rush, spilled most of it over her gown. Other hands tore it from her and the remainder of the milk fell to the ground.

Kirsten leaped to her feet, filled with anger. "Stop! We have been beasts long enough! There is food here, but we will never get to eat it unless we stop fighting among our-selves. Someone help me. I will show you how to milk the cows, and there are ladles with which to drink. Let us not waste the food God has, at last, provided us!"

Subdued, the women backed away. One of the older women took a ladle from the wall. Another pulled down a bucket and stood watching Kirsten as she worked. Soon all the cows were being milked, and the rich white liquid was being distributed to the hungry wayfarers.

Some women, those who drank too much of the unex-pected nourishment, were sick that night. One, who had forced her way up to the ladle many times, died in convul-sions. But the rest woke in the morning with a small bit of their strength renewed. And with each passing day, they grew stronger.

The Muscovite soldier was true to his word. Food was provided, although the bread was moldy and often spoiled. There were no fresh vegetables. But on what they were fed, the prisoners began to recover some of their strength.

Those mothers whose boys had been torn away and put into the men's barracks worried constantly about their children, for there was no contact allowed between the two camps. Women with husbands or brothers or fathers shared in the worry. Yet there was some comfort. If the prisoners were to be required to farm when spring came, the men would be essential. And so, fearful and uneasy, the women comforted each other and looked toward the future.

Even in their treatment of those women chosen to share their beds, the soldiers seemed to show greater kindness. The nightly raids continued, but the victims lived to see the dawn. And when they returned, they were accepted back without rancor or reproach, at least by most of the others. There were only a few who seemed to resent the fact that the younger women who accepted the soldier's attentions received better food and even, on those nights when they visited the army barracks, a strong liquor to dull their minds against the force of the attack they had to endure.

Kirsten continued to exert every effort to avoid becoming one of those women. When the soldiers appeared, near the close of each day, she would hide in the shadows, and when she could not avoid their eyes, she twisted her face into a grimace and limped painfully, as if her body were terribly crippled.

Each night before she closed her eyes, she said a prayer for Liisa and Dorotea. And then, with the handle of one of the ladles, she scratched a line on the wall of the barn. Time was once more becoming important to her.

They had been confined in the barn for a month when a short, plump woman approached Kirsten. "Come. We have neglected God long enough. It is no wonder he deserted us. Kaisa, the pastor's wife, has decided that we should meet each morning to thank God for our deliverance. Will you join us?"

Kirsten stared into the chubby face which, only a month before, had been a skull. "Are we delivered? Is this our homeland?"

The woman looked abashed. "No. But we are alive. Does that not count for something?"

"Does it?" And Kirsten realized that she did not know the answer to her own question.

Nevertheless, when the women gathered together, she joined them, substituting prayers for her parents and for Liisa and Dorotea for their thanks. She tried to recall the different faces that had passed before her during the long ardurous journey, faces that had grown cold and still. And she prayed for each, one at a time, often without knowing the name to use.

As her prayers continued, she felt a new comfort fill her heart. She had been too long out of touch with her creator. In that Kaisa was right. Now, in the cold of Russia, she sought him again.

And with her search came new peace. When she rose from her knees, she possessed an inner strength that could withstand all future hardships. Whatever lay ahead, she could face it now with courage.

Chapter 19

Knut threw his shoulders back and stared in surprise at Halle. "Hide? Surely you jest. No soldier of the crown hides before the enemy."

"Sir, with all respect, things have changed. We who have fought . . ." Halle stopped, a flush suffusing his face. He marched for a time in silence beside his commanding officer, tugging nervously on his ear. He should have known better than to speak in such a manner to a superior. Even Viotto, friend that he was, required that minimum of discipline.

Yet the problem gnawed at him. This was different from any situation he had been in before, at least since he and Viotto and Tuomas had left the battlefield, the sole survivors of a doomed army. They had seen the success of the renegade bands, and they had learned from what they saw. When Viotto stayed in the south and sent his friends north with their families, he had given them only one order regarding the men they would find in hiding: "Form them into small bands and strike the enemy when he least expects it. Be a gnat that cannot be seen, but that drives the traveler mad nevertheless."

And it had been with that intent that Halle and Tuomas had arrived in the north country. They had set to work immediately, organizing the men into groups of threes and fours, usually by families. Where loyalties ran high, they could depend upon each other with greater confidence.

They had barely begun to have success in their forays when Knut recovered and took charge of training the men. And his calm authority left them helpless. At first they convinced the others to cooperate more to entertain the invalid than with any thought of seriousness. Even the marches were accepted more as a lark than serious soldiering.

Until now. Knut had announced in the middle of a march that they were on their way to Oulu, where they were to lay siege to that city and take it in the name of King Charles the Twelfth.

Halle knew the land they would cross far too well to take such information calmly. In the months since he and Tuomas had ceased to instigate forays against them, the Russians had become more prevalent in the countryside. He had even seen the Muscovites as far north as Tonio, where they sought to block attempts to cross into Sweden from the captive territory.

When Knut showed no inclination to alter his decision, Halle spoke up again, his face clearly showing his nervousness at such daring. "But, sir, shouldn't we wait until Viotto arrives?"

"And why should we do that? Can you say that the men are not well disciplined?"

Halle shook his head. The men had taken well to Knut's exercises, often practicing his drills during the late afternoon hours while the women gathered berries and prepared for the winter that lay ahead. He had never expected such cooperation. But neither had he expected Knut to take such advantage of it.

He marched on in silence, attempting to understand the reason for so sudden a decision on the part of his lieutenant. Then, suddenly, his eyes lit up. Of course! Knut was testing his willingness to obey orders. He would march the men for a few kilometers and then, when it became clear that they were disciplined enough to obey even when they were not certain of their destination, he would sound the retreat and they would return to safety.

Risky, true, but so like the taciturn young lieutenant.

He had required similar tests of the men's loyalty when they were practicing drills.

With a smile of smug satisfaction, Halle saluted and stepped to the side of the road. It would be wise were he to reach the advance force and inform them of what was happening. They would be confused and worried. If they knew, they would march a bit slower, and that would be good. He wanted none of his friends to march into real danger.

And when he was finished speaking with them, he would return to Tuomas, who led the rear. They must all be prepared for the sudden call to reverse direction and head for home. For the call would come. He was certain of that.

Knut turned as Halle stepped away. He was a good man, that Halle. A bit pig-headed, it was true, but dependable. His only fault lay in his continued reference to his former lieutenant, that Viotto. But even that was not a major crime, since in the end he always did as he was ordered. A good soldier, in all.

Tuomas, too. He considered the burly, tall man in his memory. Certainly he was an unlikely candidate for an officer, yet he was by far the best of the motley crew of men who populated the northern shelter. He had needed both men to help him create the army.

He turned and gazed into the faces of the soldiers who marched so stoically behind him. They were, in all, a good lot. A bit independent, possibly, with the tendency to evaluate orders before obeying them, as if they were given the authority to judge their betters.

Actually, they were the worst possible material for soldiers. Were they not the ones who had run rather than face conscription?

That very fact gave him a feeling of pride in what he had done. In spite of the difficulties, he had been successful at his self-appointed task. Now all that remained was to test the effectiveness of his teaching.

He had good reason for choosing Oulu as the focal point of his attack. Located as it was on the mouth of the Oulukoki, it resembled the town of Narva, where his king had broken the invaders' back at the beginning of the conflict. That fact gave him a considerable feeling of satisfaction. It was a right and proper place for him to begin the reconquest of Finland.

It happened also to be the only town of any size within marching distance of the north-country hideout. He and his men could attack it, wipe out the Muscovite defenses, and move south to greater victories.

He was well aware of the importance of rumor in the successful pursuit of military triumph. He would be sure to leave a few soldiers alive so they could take the news south. And the knowledge that he was moving toward them would strike terror in the hearts of the Russians all the way to the Gulf of Finland.

Underlying his thoughts was the steady tramp of feet on the gravel road. The world would hear that march! So would his friends back in Uppsala. They would hear of his victory, and they would know how truly great he was. And then they would rise up and follow him.

In his mind, he visualized a stream of boats traversing the Gulf of Bothnia, filled with young soldiers and led by his classmates. They would spill into Finland, forming a noose that would choke the invaders, forcing them back to their own land.

He smiled bitterly. There would be few Muscovites left to cross the border. He would give the order that they be slaughtered without mercy. Only such treatment would make sure that they would not try to return. And with his armies defeated and dead, Tsar Peter would be fair prey for King Charles. Maybe Charles would reward the man who provided him with such a victory with the right to rule over much of that conquered land.

And if the only reward he received was a duchy and a gift of land in Sweden or Finland itself, he would still be a man of great importance in the new world he had created. His portrait would hang in the great castle, and his name would be on the lips of students of military lore for generations to come. Best of all, he would be accepted as advisor to the king, not only in military matters, where his prowess had been proven, but in matters of state as well.

And he would have Kirsten beside him. Over the months, he had come to discount the shock she had shown when he told her he could not marry her. She loved him still, that was clear. She had consented to leave him only because she was hurt. But he would make it right with her. And when she understood, she would be properly thankful.

As for any questions regarding the circumstances of her rescue, he need not worry about it. He would say what he chose to say, and it would be accepted. Who would believe the word of a poor peasant woman against that of a nobleman—if, in fact, Lilja chose to dispute him?

In his fancy, he assumed that Kirsten had gone home where she could be found whenever he wished to seek her. She would hear of his prowess when the rumors filtered south, and she would be certain to wait, knowing with the sensitive awareness of a woman in love that he needed her.

Once more he gazed back at the straight lines of the marchers. In his optimistic fancy, the shallow lines seemed filled with men, dressed in smart uniforms and armed to the teeth. His army, in the service of the king!

The sound of gunfire brought him to an abrupt awareness. Suddenly alert, he waved his arm and ran forward, urging his men toward the battle. As he moved, he drew his sword, and it flashed in the sunshine when he raised it high over his head.

The gunfire continued steadily as he ran, and when he reached the advance force, he stopped in confusion. He had assumed that they had reached the city, but there was no city in view. No fortress, no buildings, not even a church. There was only a narrow road and a wide space between the scrub trees where the advance force, with Halle at the lead, was engaged in a battle for its very existence.

He threw himself into the fray with a whoop of encouragement. His sword sang as it cut through the air, and he felt the thud when it cut into the flesh of the enemy. Without bothering to wipe it clean, he pulled it up and dashed forward. "Victory! For Charles and for God!"

His cry served as a rally for the disorganized fighters. Halle, who had barely arrived at the front of the column when the Russians attacked, clutched his sword in a hand

169

bloodied from a wound in the wrist, and slashed about with renewed vigor. Those men still on their feet, though showing obvious confusion, fell in behind him.

As each line of men approached the field, they drew swords and joined in the battle, aware not so much of their military duty as that their friends were in trouble. But already they were too late.

The Muscovites had been taken by surprise. But they did not remain confused for long. At a command from the officer in charge they formed themselves into lines. As each line of Finnish soldiers reached the field they were mowed down by gunfire.

Tuomas, bringing up the rear, saw the disaster that had overcome his friends, and he entered the fight with a cry of rage. But he had no chance to use his shining blade. A bullet tore through his shoulder, but he ran onward until at last he fell, at the feet of the enemy.

Knut had fallen beneath the weight of a large soldier who had rushed behind him to rescue his friend. When first he opened his eyes, he assumed he was dead. But the moans of agony around him told him of his error.

He pulled himself erect and dragged himself out from under the body of the dead soldier. The field was empty, except for the dead and wounded. The few Finns who had survived the gunfire were straggling away, too weak to bury their dead, too sick with pain to look for long on the horror that was spread about them.

Knut tested each leg, He had not been injured there. His arms, too, were unhurt. When the realization came to him, he felt a momentary shame. He had been in the heat of battle, and he had escaped without injury!

He glanced quickly about him. But no one seemed to have noticed his presence. A lad at the edge of the field lay bent over the body of his father. An old man was lifting the slender body of a boy in his arms. Knut waited until both men had left the field. Then, once more, he searched for any observers of his shame.

No one alive remained. Gingerly, he lifted a musket from the ground. He loaded it carefully, and then, as he held it in his hands, he looked toward the camp. He could not use a musket; someone might hear the gunfire and wonder. Once more he resumed his search. When he found his sword, he grasped it in his fist. Bracing its handle on the ground, he pressed the point against his shoulder. He leaned in that manner for a moment, gaining courage, and then he fell forward.

He repressed a cry as the blade cut into his flesh, tearing at the bones of his shoulder. Blood gushed onto his uniform, spilling onto his hands, spotting the ground beneath him.

With one final thrust, he felt the blade cut through his back. And then, his jaw tight from the pain, he pulled the blade out and wiped it on the grass. With a last furtive glance, he slipped it into his scabbard. Without another look at the devastation, he stepped onto the road and, his hand to his shoulder to stem the flow of blood, returned to the camp.

No one greeted him when he entered the shelter of the woods where the camp was located. Lilja, who had nursed him to health through long summer months, turned her back as he approached, but not before he caught sight of the tears that covered her cheeks and spilled onto her ample bosom.

He felt a wave of anger. He had marched far to reach the camp, and he was exhausted. Besides, he was wounded! Already he had forgotten the source of his injury. He had been in battle and he had been hurt. It was the duty of the women to greet him as a hero.

A dog crossed his path, and he kicked at it sullenly. Was he to blame for the poor showing of his men? Certainly not! He had given his best in training them. He had spent hours teaching them to form proper military lines and to work together as a unit in the accepted, proper manner. Was it his fault that when they came under fire the men forgot all he had taught them and had resorted instead to some wild form of fighting that more resembled the attack of savages?

He saw that some of the men were gathered near the stream, waiting for their injuries to be bandaged, and he considered for a moment joining them. But then he changed his mind. He would not beg for their help. They would come to realize their duty to him, if he only remained patient.

Still, it was shameful that they should treat him so rudely. He crawled into the shelter that had been reserved for him from the time of his arrival and proceeded to wrap his shoulder in some of the rags that had been used on his earlier injury. Then, feeling thoroughly abused, he sat down to wait for the evening meal.

At first he thought there would be no food, for the women seemed intent upon mourning and weeping. But at last the sweet fragrance of venison filled the air, and he drew himself erect, waiting for Lilja to enter with his portion.

She did not arrive.

An hour passed, and his hunger grew more intense. At last, overcome by his hunger, he crawled from his shelter and joined the others beside the stream, his bowl in his hand. When no one served him, he approached the food himself and tore off a strip of meat. Then, glancing at the angry faces that surrounded him, he sought out a tree removed from the other diners and sat down.

There had been talk and quiet weeping before his arrival. All was quiet under his watchful eyes. The silence grew oppressive, and at last, unable to ignore their reproachful gaze, he lowered his dish.

"We have much to learn from this encounter. Clearly, the Muscovites have learned the art of ambush. If we are to survive, we must master the skill until we are more versed in it than they. But more than that, we must learn to stay together. We were destroyed because we let them make us forget our routines. And there were some who broke ranks and ran like cowards." As he spoke he looked accusingly at some of the younger men who had left the field before the fighting was over.

Lilja rose and carried her empty bowl to the stream where some young girls waited to wash it. As she passed Knut, she turned her face toward him and spit. "Cowards? Never were there braver men than those you killed today! They have made many journeys into the lands held by the Muscovites and they have returned each time with more of our countrymen. They have snatched prisoners from the hands of the fiercest guards. But, at such times, they fought as Tuomas and Halle had been told to teach them. They slipped in and out like ghosts!"

Knut had retreated when Lilja spit at him, but he advanced now, his face red with anger. "Are they Swedes, or savages? I have always believed that the people of Finland were equal to those of Sweden in every way. I learned that they were equally brave, equally strong, equally loyal to their king. Are you now saying that I was wrong? Are you telling me that the honorable men who taught me at the University in Uppsala were liars?"

"I am telling you that this war is not what you think it is. I am saying that we cannot march bravely, like trained soldiers. If we do, we cannot expect to survive. Viotto knew it, and he warned Halle and Tuomas. But you would not listen." She returned to her place among the women. The discussion was over.

Knut looked around. There was no understanding in the faces. Anger, yes, and sorrow. But recognition that he spoke the truth? Not at all! He had finished his bowl of food, and he went to the stream to give it to the girls. Then, without another word to the survivors of the day's disaster, he returned to his quarters.

The first sign to Viotto that everything was not all right at the camp came when, eager to reach his destination, he moved ahead of the women, inhaling deeply as he hurried forward. He had endured the long journey with surprising patience. Starting with only his sister and niece, he had soon found himself escorting four neighbor women, a half-crippled old lady who crept into his camp while he slept, and at least a dozen more women who, with their children, had appeared from nowhere to join in the exodus.

None of them had seemed willing to trust him entirely, though they recognized their need for his protection. And so they crept along, never too close, never speaking, as alert for danger as wild things.

The children were more trusting. Two girls joined Eila, and five boys formed a small band that trotted behind Viotto. The oldest of these was a lad of about twelve, and it was upon him that Viotto relied for much of his help.

Paavo was thin and tall for his age, but he was sturdy, and he seemed to gain the trust of the women as soon as he arrived. He was inordinately proud of his position as Viotto's right-hand man, and he performed his tasks seriously, but for all of that he still had a bright humor that served to keep the spirits of the small band high, even on the darkest days.

Now, at last, the journey was almost over. They had camped well into the thickets, separated so as to avoid notice, when Viotto heard the sound of troops marching toward them on the road. He glanced about quickly, but Paavo had already performed his duty with such perfection that Viotto could see no sign of anyone to warn.

He hid himself behind a bush close to the road. He had hoped that the Muscovites had not dared to venture so far north, and he felt uneasy to see them move about so openly. He had thought that Halle and Tuomas, in obedience to his instructions, would have kept them somewhat off balance.

He crouched lower as the first of the men reached his side. They looked sweaty, as if they had been exerting themselves more than usual, and their guns smelled of burned powder. But one man appeared to be injured, and three were dead, bodies thrown over a saddle like bales of grain.

He smiled smugly. Maybe Halle had been at work, after all. These soldiers might well have escaped from a sudden ambush.

He had instructed his two friends carefully before leaving them to return to Turku. First they were to deliver their women to the camp and see to it that the stranger was cared for. Then they were to take small bands of men and stage frequent attacks on the enemy. "Never approach the Muscovites openly," he had warned. "And never take many men with you at a time. Kill a few soldiers here and a few there. Destroy their munitions and their food stores. Nip at their heels when they march from one town to another. Steal their horses and set them free. Set their cattle loose to graze in the wild. Throw poison in their water."

Halle and Tuomas had nodded sagely, and Tuomas had

174

smiled broadly. "I can remove the shoes from their horses. An army can not travel far with lame horses."

"Good!" Viotto felt pleased with his friends' quickness. He watched their departure with confidence, certain that they would do as they had been told.

Now he began to wonder. These men did not march like soldiers who had suffered a sudden and unexplained defeat. They stepped proudly, their heads high, and they showed no fear that they might be attacked by another band of wandering fighters. Something had gone amiss with his plans. Halle and Tuomas had not obeyed him, and he swore quietly, determined to learn the reason why.

When darkness came, he gave the signal to move. Immediately Paavo bustled about, helping the women to their feet, herding the children together. Viotto smiled as he watched the child. Another good soldier to join his friends.

Sirkka, with Eila's hand clasped tightly in her own, came to his side. "Viotto, something is worrying you. Can you tell me what it is?"

He smiled in spite of his uneasiness. "I cannot understand why the Russians are so daring. Maybe Halle and Tuomas have moved the entire camp farther north, or maybe they are closer to the Swedish border."

Eila tugged at his coat. "Uncle Viotto, are we going to Sweden now? I don't want to go there! I'm so tired of walking!"

He made no attempt to release her hand. "We will do what we must. When I see Halle and Tuomas, I will know what has happened. Then I can decide what to do. Sirkka!"

"Yes?"

"Something is wrong ahead. The smell. Those soldiers. Wait here. And do not go on until I return."

She was a wonderful girl, strong, dependable. Almost like the brother he had prayed for when he was a child. Better, maybe, in some ways. She had not teased him about Kirsten once, though he had no doubt she knew he often had the girl on his mind. Once, as they journeyed, he had slipped and called her by the name that was so much in his thoughts, and she had only smiled secretly and remained silent.

He could not deny that Kirsten had been in his thoughts often during the long march. At first he had thought of her in anger, remembering that she had slipped away when he had wished to use her knowledge to point him toward his enemy. But as the days passed, his feelings changed. He remembered all she had said about her Russian protector and, unwillingly, he had begun to compare his own actions to those of the Muscovite.

Yet he could not forget that Alexei had been present when Ruusu was killed. So certain was he of that fact that he no longer thought of it only as a possibility. He was the culprit. He was the one whose death would even the scales.

He came upon the abandoned battleground without warning. The moon cast a pale glow on the white dead faces, and he stared at the sight with disbelief. He had no doubt that this was the battle from which the Muscovites had departed in victory. But the extent of their triumph filled him with despair.

Dead bodies lay all about him. Finnish bodies. He stepped into the clearing and walked among the corpses, looking at the ghostly faces of friends. There, face wrenched with pain, was Ville. And over there was Matti.

When he saw the body of Tuomas, he cursed and began to weep. And then, with a feeling of growing panic, he began to search the battlefield. He discovered Halle at last, face down in the mud, buried under the bodies of two hefty fighters. Most of the men had been killed by gunfire. They had never had a chance to use their muskets or their swords.

"Damn!" He bent to close some of the staring eyes. "Why?"

He could find no explanation. From the manner in which the bodies lay, it appeared that the men had marched in straight lines right into the face of the bullets. Exactly contrary to his instructions!

Another peculiarity caught his attention. Many of the men were garbed in makeshift uniforms, breastplates and helmets of leather, laced with hammered metal. Feeble protection! Useless against the guns of the Russians!

He stood for a moment in the middle of the field. His impulse was to bury every man before he continued on his journey. But he had his charges to consider. His shoulders sagging, he returned to where Sirkka waited.

"Follow me. We must take another route."

"Why? I thought you said they were directly ahead."

"I believe they still are. But you must not question me now. Get the women to follow you. I will tell you later what I have seen."

Like a good soldier, Sirkka helped Paavo mobilize the women into action. Viotto took a wide berth around the battleground. He was aware of grumbling at the added distance. But he refused to listen to their complaints. Only when he was certain that he had passed the scene of devastation did he return to the original path.

The men, the pitiful few who remained, woke at the sound of his voice and came staggering from their shelters. They rubbed their eyes to clear them of sleep and fell without thinking into neat lines. But they could not meet his eyes. As he stared into each face, he grew aware that he was looking at followers. These men might feel ashamed of what had occurred, but they were not responsible.

He gestured toward the women who straggled behind him. "Take care of these people. They have traveled a long way to reach safety."

He stood silently as women appeared to offer food to the newcomers. Little time was wasted in greetings.

Eila broke away from her mother and ran to Viotto's side. "Goodnight, Uncle. Thank you for saving our lives!"

He nodded absentmindedly. It seemed like a small thing he had done, now that it was over. A small thing compared to what had happened to his friends.

When the last woman was gone from the clearing, he turned again to the men. They had remained in ragged lines, as if they dared not go until they were dismissed.

His eyes again searched the sullen faces. "Well? Is someone going to tell me what happened?"

No one spoke. Again he let his eyes move down the line. "Damn you, speak! Halle and Tuomas were killed. Your sons and your brothers were killed. What happened? Tell me! What in hell happened?"

The youngest lad, one Viotto had held when he was christened, long ago before the fighting began, stepped forward. His young face was torn with doubt, and when he spoke, his words were considered. "Viotto, sir. We did not expect to meet them on the road."

Viotto exploded. "Did not expect to meet them! For God's sake, what did you expect? Tell me, have any of you gone on forays against the enemy?"

Immediately the men nodded, but something in their expressions caused him to pry further. "Recently?"

They lowered their heads.

"Then what did you expect? If the Muscovites came to feel that the roads were safe, if they encountered no trouble when they moved from city to city, did you expect them to stay locked in their fortresses?" He saw a frown flit over the silent faces. But he showed no mercy. "Yes, *their* cities! If you have abandoned the towns, they belong to the Russians! And so do the roads! So does your homeland!"

He saw now that the men were looking at him with a fixed stare. "Have you wondered where the soldiers might be going when you accidentally encountered them? No? Well, I will tell you what is most probably true. If what I have seen in my journey from Turku is typical, they were in search of prisoners to drive into Russia to do their farming. Is that the life you wish for your neighbors and your relatives?"

The shaggy heads shook uneasily, but no one, not even the youth who had spoken before, answered.

Viotto drew himself up, aware that he had to get an honest answer to his next question. Once more he turned to the youth. "Speak now, or you will rue the day you held your tongue! What reason had you for marching openly on the road? Have you all gone mad? Do you not know that you cannot stand against the hoards of the Muscovites? Answer me! Why have you all disobeyed my orders?"

178

There was no answer. But as he watched, the men drew themselves erect and formed into straighter lines, shoulder to shoulder, as if they were on review.

There was a rustling sound behind him, and Viotto turned to see what had caused the sudden change.

Knut Ivarson emerged from his shelter. Though he was dressed, as were the others, in scraps of a uniform, there was no mistaking the military bearing, the trained authority in his stance. He advanced toward Viotto without undue hurry, his eyes inspecting the men as he moved. And in spite of their confusion, the men shifted uneasily, looking sideways as he had taught them, making certain that their lines were straight.

Viotto, noting this, cursed under his breath. But he did not speak until the newcomer stood by his side.

"Dismissed!" Knut's voice rang out.

The response was instantaneous. Like small boys escaping from the wrath of a headmaster, the men vanished. Viotto watched them with growing despair. They had been ruined! All that was left now was for the Russians to learn where the camp was located. Then everyone would be slaughtered. Or taken to Russia as prisoners. Viotto had not lied when he spoke of seeing such marches. His country was being robbed of its people, and he knew that few, if any, would return when—and if—the war ended and Finland was free once more.

He turned to face Knut. "Who are you? What right had you to destroy my army?"

"Your army? I have every right! I am Knut Ivarson, lieutenant in His Majesty's army. And far from destroying 'your' army, I have turned them into a real fighting force. They were untrained dolts when I arrived. Now they march like soldiers!"

Viotto suppressed a desire to break the face that leered so smugly at him. "They *march* like soldiers, yes. And they stand at attention like soldiers. But they die like fools! You hold no rank on me, Lieutenant! I suspect you received your commission long after the fighting was over, so you have never had the chance to test your beautiful theories on the battlefield."

Knut snarled, but Viotto refused to be stopped. "You

think I showed ignorance when I had Halle and Tuomas teach these men to fight and run? You think that was a sign of cowardice? How wrong you are! They learned to fight like wolves, to attack before the Muscovites knew they were near. Imbecile! This is no time for organized battle. We are overpowered. We will be wiped out. Our women will be raped and our children will be taken off to forced labor in a foreign land. Is that what you want?"

Knut tried to respond, but Viotto held up his hand. "You have listened to your teachers, men who have been removed from the battlefield since the days of Charles the Eleventh. Have they had to watch as their wives were ravished by rude peasants? Have they seen their children split in half? They are fools, pompous fools! And you are twice the fool to have believed them without question. But what hurts me is that my friends were fools, too. They took your word when they knew better, and for that they are dead."

He turned on his heel then and stalked into the woods. He could stand the face of this complacent Swede no longer.

Chapter 20

"Faster! Do you expect to do nothing all your life?" The guard shoved Kirsten, almost throwing her to the ground. As she recovered her balance, another guard forced a hoe into her hands and pushed her toward the doorway.

The women had been awakened early. Before all of them were fed, the guards appeared and began to line them up, pushing the lame and halt mercilessly. Kirsten had pulled her robe over her head and bent low. She had escaped their lusts this far, and she had no wish to make them notice her when their attention was clearly on other projects.

The door, closed since the women had arrived except when a soldier entered with bread, stood wide open now, and the bright sunlight spilled into the darkness of the barn, blinding Kirsten as she approached it. But the soldiers gave her no time to recover her sight. She was jostled out into the sunshine, where she groped uneasily until she felt the others around her and then she stood quietly, blinking furiously and inhaling the sudden freshness of the spring air.

A warm breeze caught at her skirt and teased around her ankles. It whispered through the folds of her cape, lifting a strand of hair and brushing it against her cheek.

A shiver traveled down her spine. She had feared that winter would never end. But nature had moved inexorably on, unmindful of the suffering of mankind, and now she was celebrating the rebirth of the earth in her own private ceremony of joy.

Cautiously, Kirsten peered over the folds of her cape at the sky. The dark grey clouds of winter were gone. Overhead, sharing the deep blue with a soaring bird, were white puffs of clouds.

The line began once more to move. Lifting her hoe, Kirsten took her place and stepped forward. The ground was hard under her feet, still caught in the icy spell of winter. She looked up in alarm. If the soil was still frozen, what were they expected to do with their tools?

The line of women had passed the large barns and was moving down a gravel road between two fields. On either side, the men were already at work. Lines had been scratched on the surface of the earth, and they were being deepened in preparation for the planting of seed.

Soldiers guarded the workers, armed with guns and whips, and though they seemed adverse to using the former, they applied the latter liberally. If a man paused to rest, the whip rose to remind him that work was his lot. If he gazed too long at the sky, the whip touched his back, forcing him to look down at his labor.

Kirsten shuddered. Their treatment had been almost kind during the long winter days while they were waiting for spring. Now the kindness and the peace were over. She bent lower and pulled the cloak closer over her face. Soon she might have to remove it in the heat of the day. If the soldiers saw her, would they choose her for their pleasure?

A cry ahead focused her attention. The young woman who marched a short distance before her had spent the winter in great sorrow, weeping for her husband of only a week, who had been torn from her side when the march began. She had thought him dead. And now she saw him, chopping into the hard ground with the other men.

"Jussi!"

The young man raised his head. "Riita?"

Now the whips landed. "Move along!" The coarse voices bore no hint of sympathy for the young love. But Kirsten could see that Riita walked with a new lightness to her step, and when she cast a quick glance back at Jussi, she saw that he was digging into the hard soil with renewed vigor.

Throughout the morning, Kirsten wondered about the strange meeting. Had she imagined it, or had there been a light in the eyes of the soldiers as they watched the young couple call to each other? Kirsten shuddered. Was it possible that they now were planning other forms of entertainment, even more despicable than those they had enjoyed before?

Her mind recoiled at the thought, seeking the past for consolation. Once more she returned to her memories of Alexei. He had been kind to her. Despite all the cruelty she had seen since her capture, she could not allow herself to forget. Viotto was right about most of the Muscovites, but he was not right when he accused Alexei of murder.

The line in which she walked reached the crest of a hill and she cast a quick glance about her. Alexei! Would she ever find him now?

A rough hand shoved her from the road. "Start here! Now!"

She lifted her hoe and let it fall onto the ground.

"Use the corner! Fool! Have you never farmed before?"

She did as she was told. And when the guard passed on to speak to those who followed her, she looked again at what lay around her.

The field was wide, spreading for kilometers in all directions. Behind her the land stretched in a rolling evenness as far as she could see. But ahead, down the slope and nestled close to the bay, was the town of St. Petersburg. She knew it without being told. Travelers who had passed through the growing city had spoken in awe of its beauty. Other cities grew from necessity. St. Petersburg had been designed from the first to be the new capital of Russia, the tsar's "window to the west."

A shiver of admiration ran through her body. The morning sun caught at the spires and domes of the buildings, making them sparkle like jewels. She had heard that the city was built on a marsh, that it was too low, that it flooded every spring, but she could see now why the tsar persisted in his project.

"Back to work!" The whip caught her cape. "Do you think we bring you out here to gape at the scenery?"

Kirsten lowered her eyes. She did not look up again, but her heart was singing. She was within sight of St. Petersburg, and Alexei had been sent there!

By evening, Kirsten and the other women had barely made a scratch in the earth. The soldiers grumbled as they led the prisoners back to their barns, but they seemed content with what had been accomplished. Kirsten ached from head to toe. Her arms were so sore she wondered if she would be able to resume her labor when morning came.

For all of their labors, the food the women found waiting for them was most inadequate. The cows had been removed a few weeks before, when they calved, and their milk, at least for the present, was reserved for their young. And since all the women had been put to the task of farming, the only bread available was dry remnants from earlier bakings.

Kirsten took the small crumb that was offered her and crawled into a corner of the barn, too tired to protest. But some of the other women were unwilling to accept so meager a fare.

"Bread! Give us bread!" The cry grew louder as more women joined in until a mob of some fifty women crowded around the door, pushing and shoving and shouting at the top of their lungs. "Bread! Give us bread!"

Suddenly, the door flew open. A guard they had not seen before stepped inside.

A sudden stillness followed his appearance, and then the cry was resumed. "Bread! Give us bread!"

"Silence! Do you think we have nothing to do but fatten you up?" The soldier's shout went unheeded.

He looked about him and his jaw tightened. His sword rattled in his scabbard, and then it caught the glint of the setting sun. He lifted it over his head. "Silence!"

The women closest to him froze, staring at the blade with awe. But those in back saw nothing of his action. They continued the cry with more fury than before.

What happened next occurred so swiftly Kirsten could not be sure what took place. The women began to push forward, spurred by hunger and outrage. Those in the front began to scream. And the guard's sword fell with a whoosh that was heard throughout the chamber.

The shrieks that followed blended, for Kirsten, into one long wail. The calls for food were stilled at last. Those women nearest the guard began to push to get away, and soon the entire crowd was disbanding.

Kirsten remained huddled in her corner, staring at the horror that lay exposed. In the single band of light that shone through the open door, three figures remained. The soldier stood as he had when he entered, his legs braced, his shoulders squared, his head high. Before him were two women. One was kneeling, her head lowered. She was tearing her hair and moaning softly. On the ground before her lay the remains of what had been her sister.

Nausea overcame Kirsten and she turned away. Never, in her entire journey, had she seen anything so grisly.

When she regained control of herself, the door was closed and the corpse was gone. But there remained a pool of blood that was slowly soaking into the hard floor and the memory of the anger of the guard. The women crept about in terror, fearful that they might again bring his wrath down upon them. Kirsten lay awake for a long time, remembering now that she had not recognized the faces of the men who had directed the farming.

When morning came, she realized that none of the old guards remained. The familiar faces of men the prisoners had learned to understand and even, to some degree, manipulate, were gone. The new guards showed no sympathy for their charges.

At the end of the day's work, Riita and Jussi were pulled aside. Kirsten muttered a prayer for their safety as she was pushed into the barn. The worst was realized. Truly, the Muscovites were beasts.

But when the darkness was complete, the door opened and Riita was pushed into the barn. Immediately, all the women clustered around her. Kirsten voiced the question that was in everyone's heart. "Are you all right? Did they hurt you?"

Riita smiled at their worried faces. "We were forced to

work longer, Jussi and I, on a house." She seemed to bubble with unconcealed delight. "For ourselves!"

"A house?" Kirsten gaped in surprise. It was not like the soldiers to show such kindness.

"A very little one. Not much more than a pigsty, really. But we will be together, and we . . ." The girl blushed and lowered her head. "Please, don't make me question what is happening. I am so happy!"

Kirsten turned and walked back to her corner. Maybe Riita was right. In this new and terrible world, why not grasp at each small pleasure? But in her heart the question remained. Could Riita honestly consider raising a child in this terrible place?

Kirsten's premonitions were realized when, at last, Jussi and Riita completed their small hovel. That night, like bride and groom, they entered their own quarters, removed from the others at last. The few other couples who had been allowed to start their own construction looked with envy on the two and Kirsten heard the women mutter that soon, very soon, they would have the same pleasure.

That night, Kirsten ate her small portion in silence and crawled into her usual corner. Sleep came quickly, as it did every night, for she was exhausted from her labors.

She awoke with a start. Outside, the guards were shouting ribald calls. Shifting her position on the hard ground, she tried to return to sleep. They were drunk again.

But this time they would not quiet down. And in spite of her wish to block out their words, she could not but listen. What she heard filled her with sadness. They were chanting obscene comments at top volume. She knew that they were surrounding the small hovel in which Riita and Jussi lay together.

What she heard both comforted her and frightened her. Jussi and Riita had not been as irresponsible as she had feared. Though they longed to be together, they refused to copulate. And the guards were cursing them loudly.

Suddenly, the voices stopped, and one rang out over the stillness. "If you do not take her, we will give her to another man! Or, if she chooses, one of us will plant the seed that will start a new race of workers. Decide! The tsar has

186

decreed that there be a colony of workers here. And what the tsar orders must be done!"

In the silence that followed, Kirsten found herself covered with a fine sweat. The young couple had been given no choice. They would comply. And the child that would result? Kirsten shuddered. Born into slavery, would it ever see the light of freedom?

In the days that followed, more couples followed the path taken by Jussi and Riita. Some were man and wife when they left Finland. But others, children at the start of the journey, took what pleasure they could in their difficult environment. And the guards gave them many special preferences. Their food was better. Each received a cow to care for and to milk. And when Jussi found some bits of wood to enlarge his hovel, the guards made no protest.

Kaisa railed against the sinfulness of their unions. In a voice that sounded much like that of her dead husband, she spoke of the punishment that would come down on sinners who forgot the word of God and who reveled in the evils of Sodom and Gomorrah. But the young people did not heed her. As the summer advanced, more couples joined them, to form a colony of families who seemed content to make this strange new land their home. And the soldiers continued to treat them with special consideration.

With each day, it grew more difficult for Kirsten to remain unnoticed by the guards. She continued to wear her cape, even in the warmest weather, when the crops were high and the workers spent their days hoeing weeds. When a guard attempted to pull it from her, she shrank back, crying that she was not well, and that the sun would burn her unmercifully. The man laughed coarsely, remarked on what little loss there would be if a hag such as she were to die, and went his way. But from that day onward, she trembled with fear whenever he approached.

The time came when all that were left in the barns were the old people and the very young children. At the end of the day's labor, a guard stepped into the women's quarters and ordered the small ones to line up. The women watched nervously, but no one moved to protect the children. Kirsten, torn between concern for the little ones and

187

her own need for anonymity, hesitated for a second too long.

The children were marched out of the barn into the clearing where the young families were gathered. When all stood in full view, one of the guards stepped forward.

"These children must be taken in. You!" He pointed to the first child, a small girl who was sniveling fearfully. "Go with them!" He gestured toward Jussi and Riita. "You! There!" The next one had been given a home. And in this manner each child was placed.

The old women in the barn hovered at the door, for the first time unguarded, but they dared not move forward. And when the soldiers marched away, they returned to their pallets.

They were herded to the fields without food the following morning. Kirsten, hobbling behind one of the most feeble of them all, listened to the old one's complaints with a feeling of disbelief. Could the old hag not understand what was happening? The old ones produced little labor, though they spent the day in the fields. The soldiers had concluded that they were no longer worth their keep. They would be worked until they dropped from hunger and exhaustion. But they would not be fed again, no matter how loudly they cried for food.

For the first time since her captivity, Kirsten wondered at the wisdom of her decision to act the part of an old woman. Had she accepted her imprisonment, she would now be living as Riita was, in a small home of her own. She would have a man—and some love. She would have a child to care for, and others on the way.

Now she had nothing. Nothing but death by starvation.

But, in spite of her uncertainty, she did not speak to the guards as they passed her. Clutching her cape about her, she lifted her hoe and began to work. Death was better than a life of slavery! No amount of mistreatment could make her forget that she was born a free woman.

She raised her head and gazed for a moment at the beauty that lay below her. St. Petersburg glowed golden in the morning sunlight, its glistening domes and spires pointing heavenward like the roofs of a fairy city.

Was the life in that wonderful place as beautiful as it appeared it must be?

She saw the guard move toward her, and she resumed her work. But her thoughts were in the city below. Alexei was there. So close, yet so unattainable! Often, exhausted from her labors, she had considered breaking away from the line of workers and running down to where he was. But she had never dared to try. Her common sense told her she would be dead long before she left the farm. And he would never know she was so near.

The guard passed, and she looked again toward the glistening water. A movement at the gate of the city drew her attention. A carriage was leaving, heading directly toward the rise where the prison farm was located.

Her first reaction was one of disinterest. Carriages had arrived before, carrying officers who gave new orders or who rescinded the old ones.

A beam of light flashed from the fittings on the carriage, and she looked once more in its direction. This one was not like the others. Even from a distance, she could see that it was ornately decorated, and that the coachmen were dressed in bright livery. The horses were decorated with tall plumes that bobbed as they trotted. Dividing her attention between her labors and the oncoming carriage, she waited, aware that her heart was pounding as it had not done for many months.

There was a fork in the road at the foot of the hill, and she feared for a moment that the carriage would take the left turn and avoid passing the place where she worked. She did not bother to try to understand why it was important to her to see the carriage more closely.

A rattling of harness told her the coach was approaching. As it drew abreast, she straightened up, tossing her hood from her head. There was a single occupant in the carriage, a man. When he saw her, he seemed to grow. Suddenly, he was waving out the window, shouting to the driver.

In a billow of dust the carriage came to a halt. Kirsten, suddenly aware of the danger in which she had placed herself, pulled the cape back over her head and crouched

189

down again, praying silently that none of the guards had seen her. But she need not have worried. They were all circling the carriage, holding the horses, rushing to bring a step for the gentleman to use as he descended.

The prisoners had ceased their work. They stood, resting on their tools, gazing in awe at the magnificence of their sudden visitor. Kirsten watched in amazement.

The first thing to appear was a hand, plump and smooth, decorated with rings on every finger. Half covering the hands were fine lace cuffs. And then a leg appeared. Wrapped in satin of the palest blue, it glistened like the wings of a butterfly. The shoe was brightly polished, with a large silver buckle.

Then his head appeared. On his long wig he wore a large hat of the latest style, with an enormous plume that matched exactly the color of his breeches. His dark curls draped over his shoulders, half concealing his face. Kirsten stared at him transfixed. She had seen him before. But where?

He beckoned to one of the guards, who stepped smartly before him, bowing as he approached. The guard nodded, turned and fastened a curious glance at Kirsten, and nodded again. Then, with a quick salute, he stepped into the field.

When he approached Kirsten, she felt herself grow weak. She had tried so hard and so long to avoid notice. And now this!

The guard gave an order, and she moved forward. When she reached the magnificent stranger, she paused, her eyes lowered. But the guard was not finished with her yet. With one gesture, he removed the cape from her shoulders and pulled her head up, his fingers buried in her hair to keep her from slouching. She could hide no longer.

"Kirsten? Is that really you?"

She knew that voice. The man who stood before her was Alexei himself!

She could not find words to respond. Suddenly she was aware of her ragged gown and the worn, dirt-covered shoes that hung on her bare feet. She remembered that she had not had the chance to comb her hair or wash her face. And she felt ashamed.

He looked at her solemnly. "Is this what Finland has come to? Is this the land we have liberated?"

This time he did not give her a chance to speak. He turned, and for one terrible moment she feared he was leaving her.

But when he gestured, his coachman stepped to her side, a look of obvious distaste on his face. He took her arm, led her to the carriage and helped her enter. He was careful to place her with her back to the horses, so that she would not share a seat with his master.

The next thing Kirsten knew, Alexei was sitting opposite her and the carriage was beginning to move. Alexei rested his hands on the golden handle of his cane. "Tell me what happened to you. I thought you were dead, or escaped to Sweden. How did you come to be here, in a prison camp, and among the old, who have been condemned to die?"

Kirsten cleared her throat. At first her words came haltingly. But as she continued her story, she gained courage. She spoke of the search she had made for him in Finland. She told how she had finally reached Helsingfors and been captured with the others and marched to Russia. She spoke of Dorotea and Liisa, who had died during the long march. And as she spoke she began to weep.

Alexei listened in silence. In the middle of her narrative, the carriage came to a halt and he excused himself. When he returned, he looked solemn. "I have spoken to the commander. There may be some changes for the good, at least for a time. But it is difficult to control the soldiers. They feel the power they have over the prisoners, and they use it unwisely. But I can do nothing about the old ones. There is barely enough food for our soldiers. We have none to spare for unproductive prisoners."

She thought to reply with anger, but then she saw his face. He took no pleasure in these deaths. He had not changed, despite his magnificent appearance. His heart was still warm and kind.

He looked again into her face. "You are thin, but your beauty cannot so easily be hidden. Tell me now what you were doing with the old ones."

She explained how she had acted the part of a cripple after Dorotea's death in order to keep the guards' attention away from her. It had been easy, through the winter months, to continue the pretense, even to add to her appearance of age. She had allowed her hair to mat, and she bent over always, whenever the soldiers were near. "I did not want to serve for their pleasure."

Alexei smiled with delight. "Oh, Kirsten, how I have missed you! I looked for you, while I could, before I had to leave to attend the tsar. But I wondered about you. I saw your face on every woman I passed. I did not know, that fine spring morning, what a charmer I had rescued. You have me in your spell. My life has been dismal without you."

Suddenly his face darkened. "You were not stolen from my bed. You dressed in warm clothing and sturdy shoes."

For one moment, Kirsten considered trying to conceal the truth. But something in his eyes held her back. Haltingly, she spoke of Knut and his attempt to bring her to Sweden. She told how he had rejected her. "He would not marry me, because of you."

Alexei smiled. "Then you are no worse off here, with me."

She thought of Knut's stiff pride. "I am better with you. You show me love. Knut showed me only condescension."

She rode for a while in silence. When she spoke again, her eyes were pools of confusion. "What is better for the tsar now that Finland is his? Is it worth the suffering he has caused?"

He smiled a sad smile. "It is not only the tsar who wants war. Your King Charles seeks it with great earnestness. But there is nothing noble about war. For the few who are warriors and who love battle there is excitement and the joy of personal encounter, a test of strength between two strong men. But for the masses, war is a terrible thing. They die and they know not why. They suffer and there is no reason for their pain. And when the fighting is over they can see no change, except that they are poorer, and their loved ones are dead."

The carriage had turned, and it now traveled past the fields in which Kirsten had labored. She gazed out at the young couples, working side by side, at the old ones, weak from hunger and lack of water. And she knew she could not help them at all. There would be no difference in their lives because she had known them.

Yet, in spite of her knowledge, she felt guilty at her new-found luxury. She rode while they struggled with insects and burning heat from the sun. She would soon soak in a hot bath, would have maids comb her hair. And they would die. She could not find any reason for God to punish them and reward her.

At last, exhausted from the struggle to understand the impossible, she closed her eyes. It was fate. She would have to accept what happened without question. "Thank you, Alexei!" She smiled across the carriage. "Thank you for finding me."

Chapter 21

Knut stepped from his shelter and gazed about the clearing. The pall that had hung over the camp ever since the battle was still oppressive. He missed the cheerful chatter of the children and the quiet murmur of women busy at their daily tasks.

The work was done now, but the women moved as if in a dream, and the children were silent, even in their most active play. Most of the boys engaged in mock battle, but always in the style he had striven so hard to eradicate. They would slink about in the bushes and, when they came upon each other, slash with their wooden swords until one was "mortally wounded." The victor would then go on in search of other prey, and the "injured" boy would rise and intensify his drill in thrusts and roustabout fencing.

The men still saluted him when he passed, but there were far too few of them to matter, and even they had abandoned the drill teams he had worked so laboriously to establish. Viotto had taken control of the camp as if he, Knut Ivarson, had never existed, as if he were among the dead. The insult burned deep in Knut's soul.

His resentment against the arrogant Finn had increased during the days of waiting. Knut had grown accustomed to the barely concealed anger that smoldered behind the faces of the widows and orphans. He had learned to live and to hold up his head in the presence of the men who had survived the disaster. But he had not reconciled himself to the sudden loss of his power. He had been the leader. Now he was nothing. And Viotto was to blame.

There was another reason for his hatred of the Finnish lieutenant. When he lay injured in the woods with Kirsten beside him, it had been Viotto who had taken her away. When Knut was too weak to protest and Kirsten too confused, Viotto had led her back to Turku. And she had not returned with him.

Always in the back of his thoughts was the expectation that she would realize her foolishness in choosing to return to her home, and that she would arrive beside Viotto, contrite and filled with a desire to stay forever close to her chosen mate. Knut had no doubt that he filled her dreams. How could it be otherwise? She had responded to him with such passion.

He thought again of the lovely girl, swept into the ecstasy of love. True, he had been offended that she was not a virgin. But that was not surprising. His was an honorable name, not to be given lightly.

Yet, with the passage of time, he had become reconciled to her shame. He had told himself that she was not to blame. She had been helpless and frightened. And she had, after all, tried to do the honorable thing. Only a cruel fate had kept her from joining her mother in heaven.

His anger turned now to the man who had despoiled his bride. Kirsten had called him Alexei, hardly the proper address for a man who deserved her hatred. Yet, it was the *man* who was to blame, at least in this case, and so, magnanimously, he had at last reached a decision. He would marry her, after all.

And now a Finnish farmer turned lieutenant refused to give any explanation for her absence. He could not believe that she was dead, though he held little faith in Viotto's protection. He continued to believe that she lived because he wanted her to live; because, proud as he was, he wanted her forgiveness and her love.

He found Viotto sitting with the few remaining men, those who, for one reason or another, had not marched into the ambush. Seeing them reminded Knut of his injury. It had been treated at last by the women. But no one had shown any sympathy toward him. He felt uneasy, uncertain as to whether he had been seen inflicting it upon himself, and he wished, fervently, that he knew for certain. Now, he held his arm closer to his body, supporting it with his good hand.

Viotto did not rise when Knut appeared, and when the other men made as if to salute, he frowned in their direction. "Knut!" His voice was harsh. "What brings you out among the living? Are you in search of a few more victims to lead to their deaths? If so, look elsewhere. We have given enough good men to the devil."

Knut's anger rose. The impertinent bastard! Impulsively, his hand went from his injured shoulder to the hilt of his sword. Viotto's smile grew broader and more bitter.

Knut was panting with fury, but he made no move toward the grinning face that seemed determined to torment him. He had come to speak to Viotto, not to fight with him. He bit back a sharp retort. He would not be put aside again. "Viotto, I must speak to you—alone."

Viotto smiled sardonically. "Alone? Surely you do not intend to fight for dominance here! Remember, I have the use of both my arms."

Knut clenched his jaw and hugged his arm closer to his body. Damn the man! Just like a bantam cock, spoiling for a fight! "It is most important." He kept his voice deliberately low and calm. The men must know which of the two was in control.

Viotto rose. He nodded to his companions who had at last decided that they need not show respect to an officer like Knut. But they stood as Viotto departed.

With his hand on his sword, Viotto stepped into the shadows of a nearby grove. "You can speak here. The men cannot hear us, though I cannot imagine what you wish to say that should not be heard by all."

"You cannot understand what I might wish to say to you?" Knut's face was growing red again, and his breath came more quickly. "You charge into the camp and destroy all the work I have done—the months of labor to train these men to be soldiers. And you cannot think of what we should discuss?"

197

Viotto did not respond. He stared into Knut's face, and waited. When Knut did not resume his speech, Viotto's lips turned up in a sneer. "You want to talk about soldiering, is that it? You wish to question my authority here? If so, the matter is closed. You have demonstrated your military skills. Before we are all killed, it is time for someone else to take charge." He pulled his sword half out of its scabbard. "Unless you simply want a duel. Then, let us have at it. I would love to give you a real wound—into your black heart!"

Knut reached for his sword and leaped lightly into a fencing stance. Even with one arm bandaged, he had no doubt of his victory. He had been the best fencer in the academy, and he had kept up the skills throughout his university years.

The two men stood facing each other. Then, abruptly, Knut sheathed his sword. "No. I did not come here now to fight you, though I, too, will enjoy a confrontation in the future—when we no longer have an enemy to battle. We will never rid our land of the invaders unless we avoid bickering among ourselves." He deliberately allowed his body to relax, and seeing him, Viotto also sheathed his sword and stood once again beside him. "I have come to ask you what happened to Kirsten Gustafson, the girl you took with you. Remember? Where is she?"

Viotto felt a shock at the mention of Kirsten's name. He had completely forgotten that there was another who had a claim to her.

Then he remembered her words when she asked to accompany him back to Turku. She had shown no love for this imperious Swede. It was his decision not to marry her that had sent her back to the Russian. Poor, frightened child! No wonder she had gone running back to the only tenderness she had ever known. And now this snake had the audacity to inquire about her!

"Well? Surely you did not just let her get lost—or be taken captive again!"

"No. I had little to do with her departure. She ran away from my niece when they were playing. Eila has worried a great deal about her. The poor child feels responsible. Yet

198

from what was said before her departure, I assume that she has returned to her Russian protector."

"You mean you let a mere child—a delicate lady—wander alone on the roads of Finland? Are you mad? You should have gone after her immediately!"

"And left my sister and niece in similar straits? Or should I have dragged them with me, endangering their lives and safety for someone who chose to go off alone? No, Knut, Kirsten seemed unduly eager to spend the rest of her days with the Muscovites. I trust she was successful in her quest and is at this moment safe in the parlor of her colonel's love nest."

He could not keep the bitterness from his voice. The memory of her sweet body in his arms, of the softness of her lips, haunted him. She had left a void when she departed, a void no one else could ever fill.

Knut looked into the shadowed eyes. He did not see the pain. To him, it appeared that Viotto was so overcome with disgust and disdain for poor little Kirsten that he could hardly speak her name. He wondered, suddenly, what this man had done to make her run away. *If he forced himself upon her, I will kill him!* But he could see neither affirmation nor rejection in the closed features.

At last he spoke quietly, his voice firm. "Then I shall have to go and rescue her again."

"Don't be a fool! I, too, have thought of that, in spite of the trouble she caused me, and I have concluded that she should not be followed, after all. She has made her choice. Can you honestly believe that she wants you to steal her back, like some piece of baggage?"

"Is she to be left where she is, like an object of no value? She is my fiancée! When we return to Sweden, she will be my bride."

Viotto could not repress a derisive laugh. "Bride? That is not what Kirsten told me. She said you had rejected her, that you no longer chose to besmirch your good name by marrying a woman who had been a victim of the Muscovite invasion."

"Well, she was hysterical. Of course I was shocked! Who wouldn't be, especially when she showed no animosity toward her attacker. But I realize now, she was a child.

She can be taught to understand her shame, and to strive to overcome it. And my father need never know. I am an experienced man of the world. I can make allowances for the hardships of warfare."

Viotto felt again the urge to kill. He had known many Swedish officers during his years of training in Uppsala, and most of them had filled him with great respect. They were gentlemen, honorable and fair. But this young whipper-snapper was insolent and completely unfeeling.

He snarled his answer. "You can make allowances, can you? How very generous! No wonder Kirsten chose the Muscovite. He, at least, was honest with her. She believed that with him she would receive affection and some respect. And I pray to God she was right. There is nothing for her here."

"I am here! Her fiancé! Do you know that she is with him now?" Knut could not conceal the rage of jealousy that threatened to overpower him.

The question caught Viotto unawares. "No." The answer was barely audible.

"No?" Knut's voice rose to a shriek. "Would to God I were healthy now! I would leave this minute in search of her! And I would not rest until I found her and took her back with me to Uppsala!"

Viotto met the challenging eyes with unconcealed hate. This popinjay was causing altogether too much trouble. And now he was attempting to suggest that he, Viotto, did not care what happened to a woman who had been put in his charge. If it had not been for Knut's wild attack into enemy territory, the search for Kirsten would have already begun. He had planned to leave immediately upon delivering the women to safety.

He did not bother to hide his disgust. "Well, sir, you cannot go, can you, so you are safe to make such wild claims. Your arm has only begun to heal—and you do not know the country." He stared for a moment at the small circle of men just visible through the trees. "Look! See those men? They are the only adult males left to protect this colony. You have seen to it that the others are dead." Knut winced at the intimation of his guilt, but he did not interrupt.

200

Viotto turned again to face his opponent. "I had intended to search for Kirsten, not to bring her back, but to make certain she has what she desired. But you have made it impossible for me to leave. I cannot trust you not to try again. If you give me your word as a gentleman that you will not interfere with these men, if you will allow them to live as they choose, then I will leave now to search for Kirsten."

Knut stared grimly ahead, his lips sealed.

"The dead are buried now, and we must move on. This place is not safe. The Muscovites are not fools. They know that an army the size of the one they defeated had to come from somewhere. They are probably searching for us already."

Knut looked about the camp. "We traveled the roads. They cannot trace us here!" He cursed under his breath. He had not thought of trackers. Maybe there was a telltale line of footmarks leading to this hideout. "Well, then, if you insist upon moving them, do so. I can begin the search for Kirsten!" He stared into Viotto's face. He had admitted to Lilja, during the first weeks of healing, that he knew little of Finland other than the land immediately surrounding Turku. Now that slip was being thrown in his teeth by a man he hated more than any one on earth. "You have listened to an old woman. She has no love for me. I can do well enough already."

"Well enough for what?" Viotto did not bother to meet Knut's eyes. "Yes, Lilja has spoken to me. But do you honestly believe that she has no reason to hate you? Was it not you who led her husband and her son to their deaths?"

"Damn! They were soldiers, and they died like soldiers!"

"They were sheep, and they were led to the slaughter by a Judas goat!"

Knut reached for his sword. But this time it was Viotto who showed restraint. "Enough! I cannot bring my friends back to life by cursing you, no matter how loudly I might rail. What has been done is done. I am still waiting for your answer. Shall I go in search of Kirsten? Will you promise to leave the men alone? Will you swear that you will not try another assault against the enemy? My men are practiced woodsmen; you are not. If they wish to fight, they must be allowed to do it their way." Now he forced Knut to meet his flashing eyes. "Have I your word?"

Knut spoke sullenly. "You have it." His shoulders sagged. "God knows I have searched my heart for what might have been the cause of the disaster! It was the forward scouts, obviously. They had not received enough training, possibly. They sent no warning back to the lines. It was a terrible disaster. I needed those men! I had no wish to lead them to their deaths. We were marching toward a great battle and a greater victory! With them, I could have—" He paused, suddenly aware that he had almost spoken aloud of his deepest dreams.

"I am truly sorry for the women who have been left widows. I would like to help them. But they refuse to speak to me. Surely they cannot blame me for the fortunes of war."

Viotto studied Knut's face. The man was not begging for understanding. He had the strength of a good soldier. It was his pride that stood in the way of his learning from the past. When he spoke, his anger was dissipated. "I will speak to the women and to the men who remain. I will tell them that you recognize your error, but that, as an officer, you should not be expected to explain to them. They will understand. They are loyal soldiers. But you will have to prove the sincerity of your concern for them. I can only lay the groundwork."

Knut nodded. "I would prefer to leave here and return to Uppsala. But I cannot—will not—go without Kirsten. And there are Russian soldiers blocking the pass."

Viotto did not bother to listen. He was looking at the circle of men sitting silently together, comforting themselves with cups of strong ale.

Long before dawn the next day, the camp was broken and prepared to move. Knut took his place with the other men, carrying the heavier bundles, though it was clear that his arm gave him some pain. The women, Lilja included, seemed little impressed by his show of concern. They walked grim-faced, their eyes focused on the dark mounds of dirt where their men lay buried.

The weapons that had been salvaged from the battle-field were now in the hands of the young boys. Nervous at the delay, the youths moved restlessly about, and despite their grief at the disaster that had turned them into soldiers prematurely, they could not conceal their excitement at their new positions of responsibility. Viotto, watching them, made a mental note to speak to the older men about them. Such boyish glee at carrying a gun could be dangerous, both to the youths and to the women they were trying to guard.

Knut paid careful attention to the direction the caravan took, and he noted each change of direction with interest. But by the end of a day's march, they seemed to have gotten nowhere. The following morning, the zig-zagging began once more. Up a hill, down, not the opposite side, but at an angle. Across a stream, around a small lake, across a stream again.

When he tried to speak to Viotto, he was greeted with a curt "Good day," and a question regarding the comfort of the oldest woman, who was being carried on a litter.

"She is doing as well as can be expected, with this senseless wandering. I have watched the sky, and some of the farthest landmarks. We have made little headway."

"Nor shall we. If we go directly to another location, even the stupidest serf will be able to follow us. The snows should come soon. I am hoping to reach our new campsite just after they begin, so they can cover any tracks I have left unobscured."

Knut grunted and fell back in line. Viotto at least did not demand anything of others that he was not willing to do. He carried a heavier bundle than any of them.

The snow began the following morning. Viotto gave the signal to march before the children were totally awake, but no one protested his impatience. Now, at last, they moved swiftly. Knut cursed under his breath. Viotto had known all along where he wanted to go. Had he moved about so much in order to assure himself that Knut would have to keep his word?

When they reached the top of a small rise, Knut stared about him. As far as he could see, the land was empty of life. The sky was too overcast for him to determine for certain where Oulu might lie. He was, in truth, lost, and at the mercy of this wild man who seemed to choose not to fight.

They journeyed all day and far into the night. Knut grew fatigued, but when he glanced about him, he could see that the women and even the children seemed willing to continue all night if Viotto demanded it. He could not repress his amazement at the endurance of these peasants. In his years of training, he had often led marches across the mountains of Sweden, strenuous marches that separated the men from the boys, and he had never weakened. Yet he had a reason now for his easy tiring: his shoulder. It ached unmercifully now, and more than once he feared he might lose consciousness because of the pain. Only his determination not to be outdone by a farmer kept him going. He would not be the first to cry out for a rest.

"Halt! Who goes there?"

The caravan came to a stop as a young soldier, his musket ready, advanced toward them. Viotto, at the lead, suddenly let out a whoop of joy. "Errki!" He dropped his bundle to the ground and threw his arms around the boy. "I worried when you were not in the camp and I could not find you with Halle and Tuomas. What led you here?"

Errki was gazing at the older man with open admiration. He saluted smartly and then relaxed his guard. "When I approached the north, there was intense fighting near Oulu. So I led my people away, to the east. And then, when we found this lake, we decided to remain separate from any others." The youth looked up, suddenly aware of the line of strangers waiting silently behind Viotto. "Who are these people? Have you brought them up from the south? Oh, Viotto, how often I wished I dared to attack the Muscovites! Have you seen? They are taking our people away from the land. They are driving them into Russia to live as slaves."

"Yes, Errki, I have seen. You spoke of other camps?"

"Yes, there are many about. I have sent scouts out and made contact with many of them." He looked at the line of men who had gathered around Viotto. "Where are Halle and Tuomas?"

Viotto told of the ambush and of the death of his friends. As he spoke, he stared darkly at Knut and thought again that he had made a poor bargain. This pots and pans tradesman for two good fighting men! If Knut knew what was best, he would stay near Lilja, carrying her bundles, and leave the fighting to men who could change with the times!

Errki led the way into camp with cheerful calls. Soon the women were being helped to unload their bundles and were guided, with much clucking and expressions of sympathy, into the small shelters to rest. Viotto gazed about him. The men had wasted no time in more than cursory welcomes. They had asked only if the caravan of people wanted to remain with them, and when the answer was given, had set about building more shelters.

The snow was falling steadily. Viotto sought shelter with Errki and the other men of the village. He signalled his followers to rest, and all but Knut obeyed his order. Pushing back his fatigue, Knut took his place beside Viotto.

"This is Knut Ivarson, Errki."

"*Lieutenant* Knut Ivarson!" Knut's face was hard. Errki rose automatically and gave a salute. But when he saw Viotto's frown he paused, a look of confusion on his face.

"Errki, I am suddenly most exhausted. May I sleep in your shelter?" Viotto yawned elaborately.

Errki nodded. "If you wish. Will we talk later, then? I have much to report."

Viotto glanced at Knut. "Yes, Errki, we will talk later."

But when Errki led the way to his shelter, Viotto caught his arm. "Do not leave yet. I have some questions that are not for the lieutenant's ear. Sit down for a time. I can sleep later."

He settled himself on the floor that was covered with piles of well-seasoned pelts. "You say you knew of Halle and Tuomas's encampment. Why did you not contact them?"

"But we did! Though it was an odd thing. I met Halle in the woods, and he told me it was important that the people in his camp not know about mine. Said something about being too close to Oulu. If he thought he was too close to the Muscovites, why did he not move?"

Viotto was silent. So Halle had known there were other men nearby! He had kept the secret in order to limit the damage the Swedish lieutenant could do. Had there been more men in Knut's "army," there would have been a larger disaster—one that could have wiped out the settlements!

"How many fighting men have you?"

"Almost an entire company. We have been joined by others. Most of them are out now, hunting for food."

"The cattle you took with you, and the horses?"

"Gone. Many were lost on the journey. The chickens are all we kept, and they are housed one in each home. Mine is sitting on a nest of eggs that should hatch soon. The chicks will add to our food supply through the winter."

"You are a good leader, Errki."

"Not as good as Halle and Tuomas." Errki spoke with quiet reserve. But his eyes were wet when he spoke again. "Did they not warn the lieutenant? There are too many Muscovites near Oulu. They must be approached in the night, when most of the soldiers are sleeping, or on an evening when the officers hold a ball. They have begun to act as if they own our homeland, Viotto."

Viotto looked long at the youthful face. "How do your men fight now?"

"We do little fighting with the Russians. But when we hear of a band of soldiers leading people toward the border, we go to their aid. And usually we win the battle. We take the guards by surprise."

"Good. Do not try to start an organized assault against the Russians. Not yet. It must begin from Sweden. When the troops land in numbers again and start to push the Muscovites back, that is when you must be ready. For then your men can join the others and have a hope of victory."

Errki nodded. "It will happen, won't it? We will not live forever under the shadow of the tsar?"

Viotto stared toward the small doorway. The sun was up, but the day was still grey and the air was filled with

206

snowflakes. "I fear that we face that danger forever." When he looked again at Errki's face, he saw a new maturity in the eyes. "You ask if we will have peace. Do you not know the answer? Has Finland ever had peace? We live in a perilous time. Our people are being taken from the land and led away into slavery. But can we trust the Swedes to protect us? After this debacle, can we ever trust them again?"

The two men sat in silence. At last, Errki rose and crept from the shelter. There was work to be done. Viotto, seeing him go, smiled with a mixture of pride and admiration. Errki was a good man. With him in charge, there was time for sleep.

Chapter 22

When Viotto awoke the sun was setting, and in the darkness that covered the woods, the great northern lights shimmered like curtains of brilliant colors. He crawled from his shelter and stood for a time, drinking in the beauty of his land.

He became aware of a murmuring below him in a grove of trees, and it was in that direction he walked. The men of the settlement were returning from their hunt.

Knut sat alone, a bit removed from the others, watching the new arrivals. His eyes seemed to glow with the reflected light, and what Viotto saw in them filled him with a fear for the future.

He stepped to Knut's side. "Knut, I have been thinking about our conversation regarding Kirsten. And I have changed my mind. Our finding this camp has altered things. Now that our women are under the protection of a competent soldier—" He saw Knut's raised eyebrows and hurried on. "I think it would be wise for you to travel with me in the search for Kirsten."

Knut seemed to not have heard what Viotto said. He was watching the men come in from the hunt, and Viotto could see that he was counting them with growing excitement. When he did not respond, Viotto grasped his uninjured shoulder. "Knut! Did you hear me? We must go in search of Kirsten!"

Knut turned then, and the light in his eyes filled Viotto with terror. Here was a man with a purpose, a man who would let nothing, not even his word, interfere with his goals. "I too have been thinking, Viotto, my friend." Viotto wondered when he had earned such a title. "You are so much better skilled at skulking about in enemy territory. And you seem to know the man you seek. I would only delay you. My arm is still causing me trouble."

Viotto had no opportunity to respond. Knut had moved away, to where the men appeared to be reporting in to young Errki.

So that is what he is planning! Viotto watched as Knut circulated among the men, greeting them warmly, patting some on their backs as they delivered their game. Errki glanced toward Viotto, a look of consternation on his face. But Viotto turned away. Knut could not do too much harm in one night. Now was the time for thought.

He had seen the look of interest in Knut's eyes, and he had no doubt in his mind as to its interpretation. His instincts hammered at him to shout at Knut, to force him away from the men. But he restrained himself. Knut would not give heed to so obvious a warning.

How was it that Knut had led Halle and Tuomas, both seasoned warriors, into so useless an ambush? By subterfuge! He had claimed to be going for a march, and had directed them toward Oulu. Well, two could play at that game. He sauntered slowly over to where Knut stood.

"Maybe you are right, at that. I am impatient to leave. But there is one chore I must do before I depart. Errki has told me of other encampments like his own. I need to visit them and see what manpower we have with which we can work."

The brightness in Knut's eyes grew. "You are going now?"

"Soon. I travel best at night, and there is less danger that I will encounter any Muscovites."

"You think they are this far north?"

"Probably not. But I do not intend to take any chances on exposing the whereabouts of our camps to any that might be about."

Knut glanced at him slyly. "I think it will be dangerous

210

for you to travel alone. I will go with you. I am strong enough for such a short expedition. And I can rest after you leave for the south tomorrow."

Viotto frowned. "It isn't necessary, Knut. I do not fear the night."

Knut's voice deepened. "I insist. You are the only one who can find my Kirsten. I do not wish to have you harmed now."

Viotto nodded, his eyes veiled. *We will see how good a soldier you are and just how much Kirsten's welfare really means to you. We will see before this night is over.*

"Will we reach the next encampment soon?" Knut paused to wipe his brow. In spite of the snow and the chill wind, he was dripping with perspiration, and his shoulder ached.

"Where?" Viotto paused and met his eyes. Viotto seemed to travel more like a fox than a man. He padded over the soft snow so quietly and with such ease that Knut felt certain he could travel all night without tiring.

"The encampment! The next group of men!"

"Oh, we have seen them all. Have you kept count?"

Knut pushed the fatigue back and tried to remember all the faces he had seen that night. He was aware of a growing irritation. Could it be that Viotto knew all along that all the men of fighting age had joined Errki? And if Viotto knew, then why was he making this journey?

He shifted his musket to a more comfortable position and trudged on. He had counted almost a company of men that evening, far more than he had worked with before. Even if they were the only ones available, he could start a new army, and this time he would not put them to the test until they had trained longer. He had been too impatient before.

He glanced up at Viotto. Despite their differences of opinion regarding the best way to fight, he did not doubt the Finn's loyalty. Yet he resented the pressure that had forced him to give his word that he would not attempt the same thing again, were he to have the chance.

In Errki's company, he saw that chance. He was not comfortable in the position of follower. As long as he had

211

life, he would continue to lead men into battle to fight for their freedom. The king would expect it of him, and he wanted, above all, to be admired by his monarch. He would scheme, even lie, to reach his goal. His fatherland was worth even his honor.

This mixture of patriotism and self-interest was so fused in his thoughts that he was totally unable to separate one from the other. If he fought—and as a soldier, he expected to fight—he fought in a way most expected to bring him honor. Small strikes against an enemy (like gnats, as Viotto so aptly put it) did not fit in his picture.

Once more he looked up at Viotto's back. The snow was heavier and it clung to the fur of his jacket. *I am willing to lie to this man for my country. Could I kill him for the same cause?*

He had no illusions as to the extent to which Viotto stood in his way. Viotto valued the individual lives of his men more highly than he did their freedom. He rescued people from the Muscovites, and left the land in their control.

Knut's right hand fell onto his sword. It would be swift. In the back. Viotto would be dead, and he would tell the others that he had been killed by a Muscovite. Hadn't Viotto himself suggested the possibility that they might be nearby?

But his wish to be rid of his opponent could not overcome his natural aversion to killing a strong man with such a shameful blow. His hand fell to his side. Later they could fight an equal duel. Then Viotto's death would at least be an honorable one.

Viotto turned into a thicket. "We will rest here. It will soon be dawn."

"Rest? Are we not close to our encampment? We traveled but a short distance to . . ." His voice trailed off, and he was filled with a murderous rage. He had been duped! Unacquainted as he was with the woods, it had been easy for Viotto to lead him away from the camps, where they would not be disturbed by others. Had he the same thought in mind? Was he going to try to kill him while he slept?

He placed his hand on his sword. He would be alert.

212

He was not so easy to trap as all that! He held his place until, at last, Viotto was forced to look back. "Come along! We have far to travel tomorrow. We need to sleep now."

Knut stood his ground. "Coward! You need deceive me no longer! I know your nefarious scheme, and I call your hand. We will fight now, like soldiers! I will not close my eyes so I can receive a knife in my back."

Viotto settled on a rock. He gazed at Knut with a strange mixture of surprise and amusement. "If we fight, and you were to win, as you most probably would, since you are the better swordsman, then how would you find your way to safety? Have you dropped breadcrumbs to guide you home?"

Knut looked about him. The snow lay thick all around him. Already Viotto's footprints were partially obscured. "Where are we going? Where have you taken me, and why?"

"We are a distance south of the camp." Viotto spoke quickly. "But not due south. You would run a great risk were you to seek it alone. As for why, well, we have not come here to fight, at least not in my plans. We are simply on the way to find Kirsten. It became obvious that I could not trust you to remain among an entire company of men and not try again what failed so badly before. So you are coming with me. It's that simple. And when we find Kirsten—" In his mind, he finished the sentence. *She will decide which of the three of us she wants.*

Knut stared at him with mounting anger. "Have you no honor, sir? No loyalty to your king? Can you compare one woman's life with the fate of the nation? We must fight the enemy until we can fight no longer! And we must fight like soldiers. Then we will die with honor, if we must, for we will have given our all."

Viotto rose. "I can see I owe you an apology, Knut Ivarson. When I returned and found my friends dead, I thought you were irresponsible. Now I know that is not true. You are far more dangerous. You are a patriot. You put your country above your countrymen. You would kill every man and woman in Finland if it meant that you could plant the flag of Sweden in the empty land. But what would you have then? Nothing! Finland would be dead, and though the king might give you honors for courage, you would be a murderer."

Knut listened with shock, his eyes narrowing in disgust at the words. "You speak like a traitor. It is the land that matters, can you not see? You speak of Finland as if it were separate from Sweden, but that is not so. We are one. We have been for generations. Our prosperity has spread throughout your land and made it rich. Your farmers, like those in Sweden proper, are free men, not serfs. And now Finland is being destroyed by the plague of Muscovites. We must cut out that sickness, destroy it, even if it means that many men will fall in the fighting. It is our duty as soldiers!"

Viotto rose and faced Knut. His face was red with anger, but he kept his hand far from the hilt of his sword. "God save me from such self-righteousness! Can you not see that the serfs of Russia are no different from the farmers of Finland except in the extent of control forced upon them from above? They all have the same desire for peace and plenty. It is the leaders, with their dreams of imperialism, who lust for the property of others!"

"If that is so, why do the common soldiers fight with such viciousness? Why is it always the common foot soldiers who sack and rape and burn? No, they feel hate for the enemy, as any good man will!"

"They feel hate, that is true. And it can be directed against the enemy, because most men are stupid. But the peasant fights because he has nothing left of his life. He is filled with terror. He is deprived of hope. He is fed lies about the enemy and he is deprived of his women. He rapes because he needs women and because he believes that the enemy has already raped his wife. No, do not speak to me of the loyalty and patriotism of the common soldier. I know them too well. They can be—and are—led by the officers, and by the rulers of our countries. But left alone, they would not form armies. They would not seek territories far from their homes. They are followers! The responsibility for sanity lies higher up."

Knut sneered. "An officer is not to blame if his men are cowards and bolt when the fighting begins. He is not responsible when they sack a village after the victory has been won."

"You are wrong! An officer is responsible for everything his men do. But the greatest responsibility lies far higher. It is the king who is in the end responsible for his country. It is his God-given duty. If he uses their lives to advance his personal ambitions, he is a bad ruler, and history will show him up for what he is. He has the trust of the stupid, the dull, the helpless. He must lead them into goodness and peace. A ruler who behaves in any other manner is a bad ruler, no matter how many honors and awards he heaps on the shoulders of his underlings."

Now Knut had his sword half out of his scabbard. "You speak treason! You dare to criticize our king—you, a peasant turned soldier, dare to judge your betters! On guard, for now I shall surely kill you!"

But Viotto had resumed his seat on the stone, and he refused to rise. "Do it, then. Kill me. And then, if you are wise, you will run your blade through your own heart. For you will not survive in the wilderness without my guidance."

Knut stood for a moment, his sword poised. Then, with a curse, he slammed it back into its scabbard. He could wait. "You are right. I will not kill you now. But when we are back safely, beware, for I will have my due. No loyal soldier can hear his king maligned without rising to his defense."

Viotto shrugged. "The very thing of which I speak. You insult your king far more than I do, for by your acts you suggest that he is not capable of defending himself."

"He is not here to defend himself!"

"Then he is not here to be insulted, is he?"

Knut turned away, his chest heaving. When he saw Viotto crawl into the shelter of a pine tree, he did the same, wrapping himself close to the warmth of the trunk. But he lay awake long after his companion was snoring. He would not kill the man in his sleep. He wanted the pleasure of victory in a duel. And then the taste of revenge would be sweet.

* * *

215

When the two men drew close to the towns, after days of travel, Viotto produced new clothing from his roll. They covered themselves with capes of sheepskin and darkened their faces with tar. Knut, observing Viotto's appearance, saw that he now looked like an old man, gaunt and sickly. Viotto picked up a broken branch and bent over it. Then he straightened up and met Knut's gaze.

"We will carry sticks. And we will leave our swords here, for they will endanger our lives if we are found with them."

Knut's eyes widened. "Leave my sword? Never! If I am to act the old man, stiff from the cold, I will wrap my sword in fur and bury it in my clothing. But I will carry it. I assure you of that!" As he finished speaking, he unbuckled his sword and pushed the end of its sheath into the top of his boot. Then he wrapped his leg with fur. When he was finished the sword was hidden, but he walked with a heavy limp. Viotto watched him move. Then, slowly, he concealed his sword in a similar manner. When he finished, he handed Knut a strong branch to use as a cane. "If we are to walk like cripples, we will need these. And our journey will be slower." He paused and met Knut's eyes squarely. "But you are right. It is wise that we bring our swords."

They moved slower now, passing few people on the road. But even when they saw Muscovite soldiers ahead, they did not run to hide. They only limped the harder and bent lower over their canes.

Then suddenly Viotto grew alert. With a tap on Knut's shoulder, he led the way from the road and hid behind a protruding rock. Knut followed him in silence. He had learned early in their journey to respect Viotto's sharp ears.

When they crouched together, he leaned close. "What is it? What do you hear?"

"People coming. A number of them. Maybe a caravan on its way to Russia."

Just when Knut was beginning to conclude that this time Viotto had been wrong, the first men and women came into view. They pulled a cart behind them; the cart

216

held a coffin. Other people followed. They moved slowly, as if it were an effort to walk.

At first, Knut assumed that all the participants in this macabre funeral were old. But then he saw a child, and he knew it was more than age that made them struggle to move. As the line advanced, another cart came into view, and on it were two small coffins, obviously those of children. But it was not the last of the terrible cargo. More carts followed. One old man, pulling a cart, stumbled on the icy road, but no one hurried to his assistance. He recovered his footing and struggled on without a sound.

Viotto remained still until the procession had passed. Then he rose and warily resumed the road. "We will go far around this town. Kirsten is not here."

"How do you know? How can you be so certain? She could have been in that terrible march! I could see little of the faces of those who passed by."

Viotto did not slow his pace as he turned from the road and began to skirt the empty village. "I saw enough to know. They have the plague. They will all be dead soon. Some may not live to return from the cemetery."

The plague! It had decimated Finland once before, during the early years of the fighting. Was it returning now to wipe out those few who had survived its earlier assault? "But if Kirsten *is* there . . ."

"If she is there, she is lost. But I am sure she is not. Come, we must make a wide berth. We will not dare to approach her when we do find her if we carry the infection with us."

He did not bother to wait for Knut. Impatient with his self-imposed limp he hurried into the forest. This was too much for any man to bear! He and his countrymen had put their trust in King Charles, and they had been betrayed. The king had roused the Great Bear of Russia, and then had abandoned them to its wrath. When he spoke, his voice was thick with fury. "Had Charles returned to Sweden before you left Uppsala?"

Knut shook his head. "No. He was still in Turkey, or so I was informed. His plan is to enlist the Turks to attack the Russians from the south so that together we can drive them back forever."

Viotto winced at the word. Forever was such a meaningless period of time! "Are you privy to his intentions?"

Knut's voice filled with pride. "Though you seem to find it surprising, yes. Through my father, who has great standing in the court." He threw back his shoulders. "Do you think I would try to organize the rescue of Finland were I but an ordinary soldier? I come from a long line of leaders! My grandfather . . ." He realized that Viotto had moved ahead, out of range of his voice, and he grew silent. It mattered little whether this man appreciated his importance.

Viotto led the way through the forest until they came again to a road. Then he resumed the journey, his back to the doomed village. Knut shuffled up to his side. "On what basis will you decide where to look? Surely Kirsten could be in any city."

"No. She was searching for a soldier, a colonel. He was on his way back to St. Petersburg at the time. But you must understand that he, too, was seeking her. I heard it from the soldiers in Turku, when I went to find him. We can let him do some of our searching for us."

"How? Surely, he is home by now, and has found himself another woman."

"Maybe. But if he searched at all, people will remember. And we will begin to ask questions when we reach Turku. Then we turn east. If there is anything to be learned, we will ferret it out." He paused and rested on his staff. "You must be prepared for the possibility that she will not want to leave him. If she succeeded in her quest, she may now be living in luxury. And there are few women who, given the choice, would choose cold and poverty over a soft bed and tasty delicacies."

"Kirsten would! She is a patriot. Her father was a—"

"I am sure. But she is not her father. She is a woman, and she is alone except for the Muscovite. She will be a fool if she does not take his beneficence. Do not harbor any fond dreams of her loyalty. She is loyal to only one person—herself! She is selfish, frivolous, easily diverted by a new gown or a bauble, and her loyalty can be purchased." As he spoke, the memory of her in his arms threatened to overwhelm him. She had appeared imper-

218

vious to him. But, then, he had not offered her gold. "Throw her into a bed and dangle a jewel before her eyes and she will be loyal to any cause you choose to espouse."

He watched Knut as he spoke. Despite the conviction in his voice, he did not truly believe what he was saying. Kirsten had haunted his dreams for too long. She was not an ordinary woman. She had not shown herself to be frivolous and self-seeking. It was her deep-rooted need for security that had sent her running to the Muscovites.

Kirsten was not asking for rescue. She had made her choice without compulsion. When Knut was injured, she had left him by her own choice to seek Alexei. And she had slipped away from little Eila. She did not care for either of them.

He growled angrily. What perversity in his nature kept him so restless? He had had women before, many women, and all had shown their appreciation of him. But he had chosen Ruusu. His frown grew darker when he realized that he could not recall her gentle face. Kirsten's forced itself forward instead.

The anger he felt at his own disloyalty increased his fury. Ruusu had been a good wife, a cheerful, happy, joyous spirit. And he had almost forgotten that it had been Kirsten's friend who had been responsible for his wife's death. He held back his anger and let his guilt touch his spirit. How could he have forgotten his vow? Knut might have other reasons for seeking Kirsten, but his was revenge. He would travel to St. Petersburg if he had to, and he would find Kirsten's Alexei. If she was there with him, he would rescue her, if that was what she wished. But that would not be his goal.

When he found Alexei, he would kill the man!

For the first time in the months since he had held Kirsten in his arms, Viotto put her away from his awareness. He felt certain that she would be destroyed if he killed Alexei, but he did not allow himself to care. She deserved no better than any traitor. He would have his vengeance—and he would die happy.

Chapter 23

The major-domo's long staff bit into the hardwood floor at the head of the winding staircase. At the sound, the elite of St. Petersburg grew quiet and gazed upward. "His Royal Majesty, Peter, Tsar of all Russia!"

The orchestra struck up a fanfare composed specifically for the occasion, and when it reached its peak, two figures appeared high above the dance floor. Kirsten gazed toward them with unconcealed excitement.

Alexei, standing a short distance away, watched her graceful movements with open admiration. She was no longer the ragged waif he had found in the prison camp. Her flesh had filled out with good eating and plenty of rest. Her eyes sparkled in anticipation of the wonders life offered her.

He let his gaze wander over her slender form and the pile of fine golden hair that, set in the latest style, crowned her beauty. Truly, she was the most attractive woman present! He had chosen her dress himself, a royal blue satin that clung to her like a second skin and then burst out into drapes and pleats that swept the floor around her daintily slippered feet. The neckline was as low as the new styles allowed, and shining around her white throat was his latest gift to her—a necklace of rubies set in gold. In her ears were stones to match, and on her wrist was a large gold-encrusted bracelet set with rubies.

But all the jewels in the world did not bring him the pleasure he received from looking at Kirsten's face. She was alive with youth and an innocent joy of living. Her close brush with death had increased her lust for life, and he fostered that pleasure within her, honing it to a fine point and stirring it up with new gifts on those rare occasions when memories of the past threatened her happiness.

There was a tug on his arm, and his expression changed. His day had been difficult, spent fighting with his shrew of a wife. He had married Vera Feodorovna Leonidovna when he was quite young in order to establish himself in the court. There had never been any pretense of love between them, and until Kirsten's arrival, Vera had seemed quite content with the arrangement. Her position was enhanced by his authority in the court. She had been aware of his long line of mistresses. But none before had threatened her security. Gazing at Kirsten's alert interest in all that was happening around her, Alexei realized that none of his mistresses before had been as intelligent—or as innocent of intrigue and subterfuge.

Kirsten occupied most of his time when he was not with the tsar. He much preferred to spend his evening in her drawing room, sitting quietly with a book as she sat nearby. She was sewing on some small sampler that reminded him of the piece he had found on the stone bench at her home just before he rescued her from the airless death chamber that had killed her mother.

Vera was most disturbed by Kirsten's youth. "She's less than half your age! She isn't even as old as your own daughter!"

Alexei winced at his wife's words. He had known from the moment she conceived that the child she bore was not his. But he had concealed his anger, aware that he could never sire one of his own. An injury he had received in a duel had taken care of that. "True." He stared pensively ahead. "But she gives me more pleasure and love than Anastasia ever did." He could not quite hide the sarcasm in his voice. "She renews my youth. But, then, you would not know of such things, since you were never young."

But for all of his arguments with his wife, he was careful to keep her good will. He gave her gifts of great value, and when there was a ball, he appointed a young officer in his charge to attend Kirsten. This night, the young man who held Kirsten's arm was Dmitri Antonovich, a lieutenant in the army, and a most ambitious man who had his sights on a place at the tsar's conference table. Alexei had not given him the assignment with a free spirit. Dmitri was far too handsome. His dark hair and swarthy skin seemed to set off Kirsten's blonde beauty. Silently, Alexei vowed to find another escort for her in the morning.

The royal couple moved slowly, descending the staircase. Kirsten gasped in open awe, and some of the women closest to her cast deprecatory glances in her direction. To Alexei, her innocent admiration seemed only charming.

Tsar Peter was a man guaranteed to stand out in any crowd. Six-and-a-half feet tall, he towered over his tallest soldiers. He had strong, manly features, with a heavy brow and broad nostrils that flared as he walked, as if he were sniffing the air to get the feel of the gathering. Unlike his courtiers, he wore no wig, and his natural hair hung loosely about his ears in unpatterned waves. A small mustache that matched the width of his broad lips emphasized the strength of his jaw.

Holding his arm, and looking like a small child for all her finery, was his queen, Catherine. Despite her common background, she had all the poise of royalty. Her slender neck supported a head of frolicking curls, topped with a crown of diamonds. In the few years since her wedding to the tsar, she had heard all the unkind remarks that could possibly have been made, yet she remained calm and friendly, seeming to hold no grudges. But it was clear that she had the tsar's ear, and Alexei, along with many others, had used her influence to gain some worthy end.

Alexei knew her well. He had seen evidence of her kindness, of her sympathy for the common people, and of her devotion to Russia. All of these traits endeared her to her husband. But what solidified her position as his consort was her fecundity. She had already borne him one son, and there were rumors that another child was already on the way.

It was by observing Peter's devotion to his wife that Alexei came to understand how much respect the tsar had

223

for the family as a unit of his new society. He maintained a front of decorousness that guaranteed his queen no embarrassment, despite his many mistresses, and he expected his courtiers to do the same.

The tsar and tsarina descended the stairs and moved across the room to the dais on which the thrones were located. They stood for a moment before their seats, and then Peter nodded toward the major-domo, who gave the signal for the dance to begin.

Immediately, the orchestra began a galliard. With a stately bow, the tsar took the tsarina's hand and led her to the floor, which had been cleared of all other persons. They moved gracefully together in a wide circle around the dance floor, and only when they were again before the dais did the others join in.

This dance, by tradition, Alexei had to dance with his wife. He bowed to her and waited while she rested her hand on his fingers. And then they were moving lightly with the others. As soon as they began to dance, Vera began to speak. She complained first of her pains, most of which Alexei was sure were imaginary. Then, as they passed other dancers, she began to criticize their clothing and the manner in which they held their bodies while they moved.

Alexei paid no attention to her chatter. After ascertaining that Kirsten was dancing with Dmitri, he let his gaze wander to the face of his monarch. Peter had returned to his throne, and he sat now in conversation with Catherine. His head rested on one hand, as if he were too fatigued to hold it up by himself, and his eyes, when they swept the ballroom, seemed devoid of light.

There was no question that the tsar was tired. He had returned only the day before from the Turkish front, and his thoughts seemed still to be with that conflict. But he had shown no desire to delay the ball. It was already a tradition in the sparkling city. He had held the first ball only months after moving the capital of Russia to this port from Moscow, and now, four years later, he showed pride in what had been accomplished.

There was certainly reason for celebration. The tsar had quelled the Turks even after King Charles of Sweden formed an alliance with the southern kingdom, and even though Peter's forces had seemed at first to suffer a defeat. The treaty that first was signed gave Azov back to the Turks, but no one considered the loss important. But before Peter could leave the area, Charles stirred up the Turks to attack again. This time, though the same treaty was accepted, there was no doubt in anyone's mind that the Muscovites had won. The Turks, though they did not send Charles packing back to Sweden immediately, actually considered imprisoning him until they could send him home under escort.

Charles had escaped and, with Peter's assent, traveled across Europe back to Denmark, where he took ship for Sweden. Alexei had been disappointed when the tsar did not take advantage of Charles's retreat to have the man murdered, for he felt certain that as long as Charles lived, war with Sweden would be inevitable.

But Peter had been adamant regarding the safe-passage for his opponent. "Charles is a good soldier and a brave man. If he dies at the hand of a Russian, it will be in battle, like an honorable warrior."

But Alexei had shaken his head when he heard that Charles was at last in Uppsala. The entire direction of the conflict could change suddenly.

Dmitri and Kirsten brushed past his arm, and Alexei turned his attention to his charming mistress. For the thousandth time he muttered a prayer of thanks that he had found her in time. His months of searching had been filled with disappointment and private anguish. Rather than diminishing his desire to locate the delicate Swedish girl, he found that each unsuccessful attempt only served to increase his need to see her again. She represented Finland to him, that was true. But more and more she came to represent his own youth and his own idealism. He had to find her and preserve those qualities in her if he was to maintain his hold on life.

Starting in Turku, he had been able to trail her through the woods to the shore of the Gulf of Bothnia. When his men discovered the shallow graves of the slain, he had felt a momentary panic. But her body was not among those dead, and his hopes were stirred again. With a company of men behind him, he began to scour the country for information regarding her passage. A week passed before he turned again toward Turku.

The acrid smell of charred wood assailed his nostrils as he approached the hill on which her home was built, and a feeling of *déjà vu* threatened to overcome him. Fear tore at him. Was she trying again what she had failed at before?

When he saw the destruction, he stopped in horror. And when his men reached his side, he ordered them to search for any victims of the conflagration.

His lieutenant called him to the lawn. "Look, footprints. It appears there were two people who fled the building. See?"

Alexei studied the prints. There was no question of his man's accuracy, nor of his claim that one of them belonged to a man. Had they been the ones to set fire to this old landmark?

The thought was unacceptable. Kirsten loved her birthplace far too much to destroy it. She had been a victim of the fire, though she had apparently lived to depart in safety. But where had she gone? Alexei returned to Turku a saddened man.

The following morning, his chief officer produced a very frightened woman who admitted that she had set the fire when she saw Kirsten enter the house. The violence and fury that the woman spouted filled Alexei with anger. "Bitch!" The woman's voice cracked with emotion. "Traitor! She deserved to die! My only disappointment is that you were not the man with her. I had thought you were both destroyed."

Despite his dislike of killing, Alexei gave the word for the woman to be destroyed, or she would try again, and maybe the next time more than a building would be burned.

More information arrived shortly. Footprints had been found on the hill: fresh prints, a man's and a woman's. On this fragile evidence, Alexei concluded that Kirsten had survived the fire and was fleeing Turku, possibly with her Swedish lover.

It had been more difficult to follow her path thereafter.

He had been forced to search each town he passed, but she had been nowhere. It was as if she had vanished from the earth. He spent an entire day in the town of Helsingfors, but he had left it at last, convinced that she was not there.

It was not until months later, when he had returned in despair to St. Petersburg, that Alexei learned that his informant at Helsingfors had not been entirely truthful. After he had left, more Finns had been permitted to infiltrate the city, many of them coming from secret hiding places that had not been found when the Russian soldiers had scoured the woods.

Alexei had fretted at his duties that kept him in the city. Peter was absent, and he had been assigned the task of supervising the completion of the docks so that shipping to European ports could begin with the coming spring. The work had been difficult. Slaves from Finland had been put to labor beside serfs from Moscow and its environs, and there had been considerable dissension between the two groups. But he had persevered, and the task was at last completed.

His efforts had been generously regarded. Peter had confirmed his position as advisor, and had shared with him his dreams for the future. "We have already done many good things for our country. The trade we have established through these ports will serve to secure our power in the west. France, England, and Sweden will not soon forget that we are a force with which they must contend. And the trade is making our land rich. We are at war now, my friend, but we will have peace soon, and it will be a prosperous one. Wait and see!"

Alexei had remained silent. His memories of the destruction of Finland were too fresh in his mind. He could not be sure that the price of this new prosperity was not too high.

The music stopped, and Alexei stood for a moment, reorienting himself to his surroundings. Immediately, Vera's high-pitched whine assailed his ears and he winced. He bowed gracefully. "My thanks, my dear, for the dance. I trust your book is filled?"

Vera was already searching the floor for her next partner. The man appeared suddenly at her side, bowed, took her hand, and spoke to Alexei. "With your leave, sir!"

"Fine, fine! Take her. And may you enjoy the evening!"

When they were gone, Alexei sought out Kirsten. She was standing beside Dmitri, her cheeks rosy with delight, and a smile lighting her face. When she saw him, she called his name and stepped toward him.

He felt a rush of pride at her eagerness. He had begun the search of the prison camps as soon as he realized she might still be alive, but it had nevertheless been a surprise when he saw her standing among the old people. Yet he could not but admire her skill in avoiding the soldiers' lust.

He had driven her directly to the home of a doxy he had used occasionally in the past and paid her to bathe and dress the ragged prisoner. Then he had gone on his way, intending to return that night to pick up his prize. But it was not easy to find the house he wanted for her, and so he had not returned until the following evening. What he saw when Kirsten came to greet him set his heart racing and filled him with pleasure.

Kirsten had slept much of the time. Bathed and with her hair washed and piled in soft curls on the top of her head, she appeared fresh and lovely, like a child stepping into spring. Only her eyes were haunted and deep. Looking at them, he vowed silently that he would not rest until they again sparkled with the joy of living.

This night was more than a formal celebration for him. He had carried Kirsten to her new home, introduced her to her maid, Katerina, and instructed the cook to feed her well. He had visited her daily, watching as the color returned to her cheeks and the sparkle to her eyes. Now, at last, she was as he remembered her. Never had she seemed more alive. The past torments were, as far as he could tell, forgotten. She glowed with good health. Her skin, pale compared to that of most Russian women, looked like alabaster.

With a sign to Dmitri, he turned to Kirsten. "We have this dance, I believe."

Kirsten's eyes met his. "Yes. Oh, isn't everything wonderful?"

He beamed as he took her hand and placed it on his arm. The dance was a gavotte, and he felt her lightness beside him. "Are you happy, my dear?"

"Oh, yes! You are so good to me!" Kirsten lowered her eyes, and Alexei knew immediately that she was thinking of the prisoners she had left behind on the hill.

He cursed under his breath. He had hoped she would put that terror behind her. Those godforsaken skeletons meant nothing to him, but he gave them his attention for her sake. "I have good news for you, news that will make you even happier. I have arranged for you to visit the camp and see the children. I know you miss your countrymen and worry about their treatment. I hope you realize there is a limit to what can be done for them. In some ways, they live better than our own serfs. They are not subject to conscription in our army." He paused. "Maybe after tomorrow you can put them out of your mind and think more of me. I hope I mean enough to you."

"Oh, yes, Alexei! You mean everything! You are good and kind, and you are so noble. I beg your forgiveness if I seem to be ungrateful. I truly am not! I know there are limits even to what you can do. We are, after all, still in a war."

He smiled indulgently. "Well, then, let us forget prisons and labor, at least for the present. Tomorrow, if you still wish to, you may ride up to see how they are. But now you must rejoice with me in our reunion. Oh, Kirsten, I had so feared I would never see you again!"

Kirsten let herself relax into the music. She had learned to dance as a child, and it had always given her great pleasure. But even more than the dancing and the music, she enjoyed the beauty that surrounded her. The balls given by the mayor of Turku paled in comparison to the magnificence that was all around her now.

As they danced, she commented on the beautiful gowns of the other women and on the sparkling jewels they wore. To Alexei's delight, she seemed completely unaware that of all the women present, she was the most striking.

Toward the end of the evening, Catherine retired with the "respectable" women to a quiet drawing room for tea and biscuits, a pastime far more agreeable to her simple

229

tastes. Alexei and the other men, with their doxies, remained in the ballroom, where the dances now became more lively, and the conversation a bit more ribald.

It was then he led Kirsten to the throne and introduced her to the tsar. Kirsten curtsied low before the towering monarch. "Your majesty, I am honored!"

Peter bent slightly at the waist, and took her hand in his. "Look up, my dear. We wish to see the wench our chief advisor dotes on so devotedly." He took her chin in his hand and tilted her face upward. "Alexei, you rascal! You have outdone us all again. Where did you find such a precious jewel?"

"In Finland, sire. A diamond in a sea of mud."

A faint look of surprise flitted across the broad features. "Finland? And did she not fight you all the way to her bed? It is my understanding that those fair-haired females are all spit and gristle!"

"She was an orphan, sire, and she has a real fondness for me."

Peter laughed slyly, his eyes sweeping Kirsten from head to foot with such intensity that she felt suddenly unclothed. "Yes, we would think that she would have to—and that you would be equally fond of her. But can you fill the needs of so lusty a wench? Or have you already enlisted the assistance of—" he cast a glance toward Dmitri— "others?"

Alexei flushed, but his voice remained on the same light, bantering tone it had held before. "Kirsten knows that I will brook no rivals. She would not risk her happiness for a momentary pleasure, even with so handsome a companion."

Peter met Kirsten's eyes. "Is that true? Do you find our friend here all that you want in a man?"

Kirsten blushed. She had not yet become accustomed to the forthrightness of the lusty tsar. "Sir, Alexei is my master. I have no wish for other companions."

Peter laughed at her seriousness and turned back to his friend. "Well, Alexei, for your peace of mind, we hope she remains so loyal. But we find her most attractive. If you decide to seek other companionship for her, send her first to our room."

Kirsten curtsied and backed away, too embarrassed to meet the tsar's continued gaze. Her heart was beating wildly, and Alexei felt that the flush on her cheeks was far more lovely than any rouge would ever produce. But Kirsten could not forget her lover's warning. When it was time for her to leave, and Dmitri resumed his place at her side, she did not allow herself to look up at him. When he delivered her to her door, she refused to allow him to come even into the entryway. Yet when he turned and trudged down the steps to his carriage, she watched him with a feeling of terror.

Dmitri was not in himself a danger to her. He was handsome, that was true, but his threat—and the threat every young man she met carried with him—lay in the memories their youth and vitality evoked. Whenever she saw a youthful soldier, especially a lieutenant, pass her house, she was reminded of Viotto Hannunen. Their intense eyes brought to mind the deep blue eyes that had bored into her very soul and seen her inner weaknesses.

Despite her vow to put Viotto from her thoughts, she had not forgotten him. And the memory of his embrace hovered close, threatening to destroy the pleasure and security that, for the first time since her father's death, lay within her grasp.

Chapter 24

Kirsten rose late the following day and rang for her maid. Katerina appeared immediately at her side, a tray of food in her hands. She adjusted the covers and puffed up the pillows so Kirsten could sit up and enjoy her breakfast. Her soft, pale face was wreathed in smiles. "Did you sleep well last night, my lady?"

Kirsten smiled. It still embarrassed her to be addressed in such a manner. "Yes, very well, thank you. When will the colonel arrive?"

"He is downstairs now, my lady, waiting your awakening. He insisted that I allow you to sleep until you were fully rested."

Kirsten nodded. Alexei often followed that procedure, spending his time in the study reading, until she rose and sent for him.

She took a sip of the thick beverage and bit a small piece from the cake, which was still warm from the oven. "Delicious! Tell the cook I am most fond of his chocolate. And never have I tasted a sweeter bread."

Katerina curtsied. "He will appreciate the compliment, my lady. Will you have more now? Or will you wait and eat later, with his lordship?"

Kirsten put down the empty cup and pushed the dish away. "I will eat more later, thank you. Tell the cook to keep the ovens hot."

Katerina raised her eyebrows, but she said nothing. She lifted the dish from the bed and headed for the door.

"Is Dmitri arrived yet? When he does come, tell him I wish to go shopping this afternoon."

"My lady, Dmitri is no longer here. He has been replaced by Sascha Vasilievich Gregorovich. Shall I call him now?"

"While Alexei is waiting? Of course not! Just tell him to be ready. Do you know why Dmitri was dismissed?"

Katerina smiled broadly, but she shook her head. "No, my lady. Shall I call the colonel now?"

"Yes, please. And do not return until we ring for you. We will order a full breakfast then."

Alexei paused as the door closed behind him. Kirsten sat on a chair near the window, her soft silken gown flowing about her like a cloud of pale blue. She had piled her hair loosely on her head, and some of the curls cascaded down over one shoulder, giving her a look of delightful dishabille. The thought that soon it would tumble down over his bare shoulders and bury him in its softness caused an excitement to grow in his groin.

"Good morning, Kirsten, my love. I trust you rested well."

"Oh, very well, dear Alexei. It was such a marvelous ball!" As she spoke, Kirsten rose and began to dance across the room, her arms extended, her body swaying to the memory of some light melody. Alexei groaned with delight. She was more than he could bear—so lovely, so desirable!

She floated into his embrace like a butterfly, and he held her lightly, afraid to crush her delicate wings.

"Kiss me, my dear, and then let us to bed. I long to hold your fair body close to me again. All night I lusted for you. Were you aware of my need? Did you feel the longing, too?"

Kirsten nodded, dropping a light kiss on his cheek. Then, before he could hold her closer, she slipped from his grasp and floated again across the room, this time coming to rest on the bed. "Come, Alexei, I have forgotten how to remove all this finery you have provided me. Help, or I will be forever wrapped in this blue cocoon."

234

Alexei moved swiftly across the room. Much as he loved Kirsten, he loved even more her sensitive awareness of his need for play. Since the first, she had known when to tease and when to welcome him with open pleasure. And now, fresh from his nagging wife, he valued Kirsten's playfulness even more.

Kneeling before her, he took her fingers into his hands and brought them to his lips. He held them there as he kissed each one, loving it with his tongue. Then he rose, pulling her up with him and holding her close. Her breasts, swelling above the firm neckline of her peignoir, pressed against his chest, and he touched them with his fingers. He kissed her lips, her ears, her eyelids. Then, with a youthful laugh, he began to fumble with her ties.

She slipped again from his grasp and ran to the window. The bright spring sunshine had already warmed the air, and a slight breeze pushed the curtains against her as she approached. He followed, caught another tie, and pulled it open. Her peignoir fell from her shoulders, exposing the thinnest of camisoles, through which he could see the dark aerola of her nipples and the shadow of the mound of Venus. With a cry of joy, he pulled her to him again, crushing her against his body. Then he lifted her and carried her to the bed.

Kirsten squealed when she felt her feet leave the floor, and she kicked in mock fear as he carried her across the room. Her arms flailed against his body, tearing his coat open, mussing his hair, and pulling, as if by accident, at the small buttons that held her camisole in place. It fell away as he dropped her onto the bed.

She lay naked before him, and he paused to gaze at her beauty. In the first days after he took her in her father's study, he had been charmed by her youth and innocence. The youth was still there in her smooth body and open warmth. But the innocence had been replaced by a quiet maturity that was, for him, irresistible.

There had been a gentle roundness to her belly that was gone now, a victim of the starvation and terror of the march. But that was the only indication of her past suffering. Her limbs were perfect, shapely and white. Her waist was narrow, and her breasts, full and round with the bloom of youth, were like two roses on an ivory vine.

There was a translucence to her skin that never failed to excite him. He gazed at her, aware that he felt as if he were Pygmalion, the ancient Greek sculptor, and Kirsten were his creation come to life. Her alabaster skin was warm to his touch. He bent down and stroked her breast with his hand.

The contact stirred his passion anew. Throwing his coat onto a nearby chair, he began to unbutton his breeches. He could feel his desire swelling, and his fingers stumbled at their task.

Kirsten lay watching him, waiting for the last button to open, for him to slide his breeches down and climb above her on the bed. For one moment, the magic that surrounded her faded, and she saw him for what he was—an old man, seeking youth in a young girl's arms.

For one moment the thought came that all this was make-believe, that she could not play the game again, and then she brushed the idea aside. She had heard Alexei's warning. He wanted her enthusiasm, her life, her excitement. If she lost it, he would find another, more stimulating woman to take her place. Forcing the joy back in her eyes, she held out her arms to receive him.

When he lay panting beside her, she aped his exhaustion, throwing her arms akimbo over her head, as if weak from love. He smiled with pleasure at her show of being spent.

He leaned on one elbow and brought his lips close to hers. "Is it good, my dear? Do I give you pleasure?"

"Oh, yes." Her voice was husky, and her eyes were wet.

He rested his hand on the moistness between her legs. "I have a confession to make. I cannot give you a child, though God knows I wish it were possible. An old wound . . ." He let his voice trail off. Better if she believed there had been a time when he had been virile. He himself knew he had never been capable of siring a child. His daughter, whom he had always accepted as his own, was certainly another's spawn. Vera had been attractive when first they married, and he had been away so much.

He kissed Kirsten's moist lips. It no longer mattered to

him that his daughter was not his own. What mattered now was that Kirsten knew she could not deceive him. He would know if she let another share her bed.

He pulled her once more into his arms and then, with a sigh, rose and began to dress. Kirsten washed herself in a basin and then, her peignoir properly tied, rang for Katerina. The girl stood at the door. "You are ready for breakfast, now, my lady?"

"Yes. We will eat on the balcony. It is such a lovely morning!" Kirsten smiled secretly at Alexei as she spoke.

Alexei felt a glow of pride at her calm assumption of authority. There had been a time in his life when he would not have told his mistress of his weakness, using it instead to trap her in an affair with another. But he had passed the need for such games.

"Kirsten?"

"Yes, Alexei?"

"Are you happy?"

"Oh, yes, Alexei. I have told you that." Her voice was sweet, but he could sense her impatience at his constant need for assurance.

"What are you going to do today?"

She repressed a sigh. Every day, he asked her for an accounting. "I am having tea with Sonia and Tamara, at Olga's house. And then I have it in mind to go shopping. You told me something last night which requires some preparation on my part."

He raised his eyebrows.

"You spoke of my visiting the children on the hill. Is it true? Have you at last been able to work out the details?"

A small frown creased his forehead. "I wish you did not want to visit that mournful place, or to revive the memories of your past misfortunes. Yes, my dear, I have made the arrangements. But I must exact one promise from you. If you are depressed after the visit, you must not return. I have no use for a morbid woman."

Kirsten smiled brightly, aware of the hidden threat in his words. Alexei was not a simple man. He loved her sprightliness, and, in a way, he actually loved her. But he had reached his own compromise with the terrors and miseries of war. In his beautiful home in St. Petersburg, he ignored the suffering of others, and he expected her to do the same. There might have been a time when he tried to lighten the burdens of the miserable victims of others' greed, but that time was past. He knew now that he could do nothing lasting that would alleviate their pain. So he wiped his mind clear of the memories. It was that or go mad with frustration and anger.

"Don't worry, Alexei. I will not allow anything to depress me. How could I? How could anyone be sad in such lovely surroundings as these?" As she finished speaking, Katerina appeared with a large tray of food. She busied herself at the table on the balcony, and when she left Kirsten and Alexei took their places. A breeze from the harbor brought the scent of salt air, and below them in the garden, a bird settled on a bush and began to sing.

Kirsten poured some chocolate into his cup. "Is it true that the tsarina is holding a garden show in the new conservatory? And am I really invited?"

"Yes, to both of your questions." Alexei smiled indulgently. She was being the innocent child again, and he loved it. "Do you think of me when I am away?"

The question was unexpected, but Kirsten did not allow herself to show her surprise. "Oh, yes, Alexei! I always do. My life is built around you. You know that." She paused, her expression suddenly serious. "But there are times when I think of other things as well."

"Oh?"

"Yes. I think of my friends. And I think of my country. Alexei, will I ever be allowed to return to my homeland? Sometimes, in spite of my happiness here, I am filled with a longing to see the green countryside and the blue lakes of Finland."

"We might visit there again. It is peaceful, now that the conquest is over." He stared down toward the street, where a carriage was clopping past. "Is that all you think about?"

He knew her answer before she spoke. They had covered this ground before. He would press her about her travels through town. Did she see any other men? Were they as exciting to her as he was? Were they younger,

238

more handsome? And she would reply in the words he wanted most to hear. No, they were—well, she didn't really remember how other men looked. She paid no attention to them. And then, reassured, he would kiss her and change the subject.

He pushed his plate away, suddenly no longer hungry. He hated his jealousy, yet he could not control the feeling that swelled inside him whenever he thought of Kirsten. He had pressed her with questions until she had admitted that it had been her fiancé who engineered her initial escape. He had even forced her to acknowledge that she had not resisted the young Swede's embrace. But he had been unable to elicit more information from her, no matter how hard he tried.

She had left the Swede, Knut Ivarson, and returned to Turku. Only when he informed her of the two sets of footprints did she acknowledge that she had had a companion as she watched her house burn.

Then who had he been? Knut Ivarson?

She had at last admitted that it had been a Finnish soldier, and that he had given her cause to hate him. But he had learned no more. Now he was determined to press the questions further.

"When you left your house, after the fire, did you travel long with that Finnish fellow?"

"No." She did not appear at all surprised at the direction the conversation was taking. "I escaped from him as soon as I could and went in search of you. I returned first to Turku, and then I traveled east."

"Kirsten." His expression was solemn. "You have teased me long enough. Indulge my weakness. I must know more of this man. Was he tall? Strong or weak? Did he mistreat you? If I know, I will be relieved of my torment."

Kirsten met his gaze. She had no illusions that what he promised would be true. She knew him well enough to know that more knowledge would only feed his jealousy. And she saw in that weakness the eventual end of her security.

"Please, Alexei, I do not wish to remember those days. I wanted to find you so very much, and I was frustrated in my search. In those dark days, I feared I would never see you again!"

The frown vanished from his face. "Thank you, my dear. I know you are right. I must learn to be content with the knowledge that you wanted me, that you searched for me. Come, give me a kiss. I must be off." He was smiling again, and he held out his arms.

Kirsten rose and went to his side. She kissed him passionately. But when he closed the door behind him, she turned to gaze at the two portraits of her parents which stood on her dresser.

The frames were scarred and the paintings were faded, but to her they were invaluable. She settled herself on a stool before them and gazed long into her mother's eyes. The memories flooded back. Viotto had rescued them, at the risk of his own life. He had carried them in hands raw from the flames, and put them in her arms.

Tears began to flow down her cheeks. "Oh, Mama! Why didn't I understand when you told me about love? Why didn't I know when I found it? I could be with him now, wherever he is!"

She leaned closer. "I know now what you meant, but I threw it away. I left him to search for Alexei, and so I must settle for what I have."

She sat up again, and brushed the tears away. "I have a good life, Mama. A good life!" The tears were flowing again. "Alexei treats me very well. And maybe, someday, I will learn to forget."

She rose and threw herself down on the bed, giving free rein to her unhappiness. "Will I ever forget him? Is it possible to forget the only man you have ever loved?"

She did not move when Katerina entered to clear the room, and by the time she had recovered her composure, she barely had time to dress for her luncheon appointment.

Chapter 25

Kirsten surveyed her image in the large mirror that Alexei had imported from Italy for her. She was garbed in a soft velvet gown of dusty brown, the least elaborate of the many gowns that had been made for her in the months since her arrival in St. Petersburg.

Her hair, normally piled into riotous curls atop her head, was combed back in a simple bun and covered with a bonnet of the same brown velvet. There were no ornaments on the crown, only a simple dark ribbon, with streamers that hung down her back.

She studied herself in silence and then, impatiently, applied more powder to her cheeks. But her attempt to conceal their rosy proof of her robust health was unsuccessful. No amount of powder could hide the fullness of her smooth skin or the sparkle in her clear blue eyes.

This was not the first time she had been concerned with this problem. Every time she visited the prison camp, she was made acutely aware of her own good fortune.

"The carriage has arrived, my lady." Katerina stood at the door, a dark cape over her arm. "Sascha is waiting to escort you."

"Thank you, Katerina. Have you heard from the colonel yet?"

"No, ma'am. The colonel has not returned to St. Petersburg. Did he tell you he would be back today?"

"No." Kirsten felt the same vague uneasiness that troubled her whenever Alexei was away from the city. "It is just that I would have preferred his companionship today. I . . ." She let her voice trail into silence. There was no advantage in troubling her maid. Still, she always felt so unprotected when he was not available to her.

With a final pat of the bun that covered the back of her neck, Kirsten swept from the room and down the stairs. Katerina fluttered behind, the cape still folded over her arm. When they reached the door, Kirsten paused and waited while her maid draped the robe over her shoulders. Then, with a smile of thanks, she stepped into the cold winter morning.

Sascha leaped from the carriage when she appeared. There was no question in Kirsten's mind as to why he had been chosen to replace Dmitri. He was a scrawny youth, who looked like a vulture. His eyes were small and sharp, and they darted about as if he were continually in search of living prey. He was strong, too.

He bowed politely as she approached. There was nothing wrong with his manners. He had shown her the most proper decorum since he first was appointed as her escort. Yet she did not feel comfortable in his presence. He was too alert to her every move, too quick to step between her and any other person she might encounter. And she knew that he disapproved of her regular visits to the prison camp.

Nevertheless, he had given her no cause to request his release from his duties. And so she continued to accept his presence. She was aware that she would only arouse Alexei's jealousy were she to ask for any unexplained change.

She knew that Alexei had no more sympathy for her concern with the prisoners. Under her barrage of questions, he had made attempts to improve their lot. But would he have done as much had she shown no concern? She doubted it. What she was sure of was that he resented the time she spent on her countrymen. He often did not visit her on the evening after her drive up the hill, and she was convinced that he sometimes left town so as not to be reminded of her preoccupation with the suffering of others.

This morning, however, she let none of these worries bother her. This was a special day: December the thirteenth, the festival of the lights, the Lucia Festival. She pictured the lovely face of young Siiri, whom she had decided would wear the crown of candles at the ceremony. It would be the first time since their imprisonment that the prisoners were allowed a break in their labors.

She checked the contents of the boxes that filled the carriage. Everything was there, the crown she had had made specially for the occasion, the clear white tapers. With a signal to Sascha, she settled back.

The heavy gate of the prison compound swung open as her carriage approached. In the months since her first visit, the soldiers had come to anticipate her arrival, and though they showed no particular pleasure at her presence, they showed no antagonism. Today they even appeared pleased. She had already spoken to their commander regarding the unique quality of this celebration, and with his permission arrangements had been made for all of the Finns, adults as well as children, to leave their work and join in the ceremony.

She nodded to the guard who stood at the barn door. But only when Sascha gave a signal was the lock opened. Then she stood aside while some of the male prisoners unloaded her carriage and carried her bundles into the dark interior. There was an air of expectancy that sent a thrill of excitement through Kirsten. Then, amid a murmur of quiet voices, she stepped into the building that had been her prison for the first months of her stay in Russia.

The murmuring grew louder. She was clearly not the only one to feel the excitement, the specialness of this occasion. The prisoners, most of whom usually showed little pleasure at her arrival, were smiling openly. Young couples with infants in their arms stood behind the older children, who were gathered closest to the doorway.

They barely whispered their greeting, but she felt the warmth of their happiness. She had not been wrong in wishing to share this holiday with her countrymen.

There were many familiar faces that greeted her. The young folk who had been permitted to establish families had benefited from her solicitude. She had stood beside

Alexei and heard his command that they be given greater privacy, that the soldiers no longer be permitted to harass them after their work was done.

Everyone seemed healthier than before. Another order from Alexei had increased their rations and decreased their hours of labor. But her help had come too late for the old ones. Their faces were gone. Kirsten wondered if those who remained regretted their loss.

"Good morning!" Kirsten smiled down at the ring of young children. "Are you ready for the ceremony?"

"Yes, my lady!" She felt a momentary discomfort. She had tried to get the children to address her in a more familiar manner, but they seemed unable to change, or unwilling to accept her as one of themselves. Irja, a particularly charming child with deep solemn eyes, squirmed nervously. Kirsten touched her golden curls. "Some day you will bear the Lucia candles!"

Irja smiled shyly. "Yes, my lady."

Kirsten glanced around, her eyes now accustomed to the dusky light. "Siiri!" Her voice rang out, and silence followed. "Come up here, Siiri. You are to be the Lucia maiden."

Siiri did not move. Even in the darkness, Kirsten was aware that the girl's thin face was flushed. "Siiri, don't be shy!"

Still, Siiri did not approach her benefactress. Kirsten glanced at Sascha, who made a barely perceptible gesture. A guard stepped into the crowd. As he approached, Siiri drew back, and then, as if to avoid his touch, began to move toward Kirsten.

She stood at last in the center of the circle of children. But there was no pride in her posture. She cowered, her head bent toward the ground.

Smiling grandly, Kirsten turned to Sascha. Immediately, he produced the crown and put the candles in place. Kirsten took it from him and held it while he lit the tapers.

A glow suffused the circle, and in the golden light, Siiri's face appeared sallow. She met Kirsten's glance with eyes filled with tears. "Please, my lady, not me! I will disgrace the holy feast!"

Kirsten had already lifted the crown up to place it on

244

Siiri's head, but she paused. She gazed into the troubled face with surprise. Then, slowly, the realization came. Sirri, lovely, delicate little Siiri, had already served the guards' lust. She was no longer the virgin required by custom for this holy celebration.

A hush fell over the crowd. Kirsten stared into the agonized face and knew that much of her work had been in vain. And in that moment, she had a flash of understanding. It was not that Alexei had deceived her. He had tried, he had done his best. But no one could watch the soldiers all the time. They were accustomed to thinking of the prisoners as their property, to use as they wished. A few changes in the rules did not alter their behavior. For all of her efforts, she had done little to help her friends. Their lives were still as hopeless as hers was filled with joy.

Siiri turned toward Irja. "Please, my lady, let Irja take my place. She is still—still pure."

Kirsten looked at the child's face. So Irja was as yet untouched. But how long would that last? When would her bright eyes be dulled by shame? When would her trust be destroyed by cruelty and lust?

With a nervous trembling, Siiri took Irja's hand and led her to the front of the crowd. Irja smiled uneasily, her eyes on the heavy crown of candles. But she did not shrink back when Kirsten lowered it onto her tiny head.

A sigh traveled through the mob when it became clear that the crown would fit, and suddenly a feeble voice began a song. One by one others joined in, until it swelled into an anthem of rememberance. Smiles lit the thin faces; heads were raised. And Kirsten knew that she had been right, after all. In this one moment, the terrors of war were forgotten. Once more, her countrymen knew their heritage, and the memory had given them renewed courage.

A woman who Kirsten assumed was Irja's mother called out a direction, and the child began to walk around, moving among the other children like a queen. Her head was high, and a small smile lit her lips.

A warmth filled Kirsten's breast. Even the young ones knew the stories. Finland had not died in the hearts of these exiled ones. She was alive! She would always be alive, no matter what hardships they faced. And as the realization came, Kirsten knew why she had returned so often to the hill. She needed these courageous people far more than they needed her. She was the one who was tempted to put her country aside.

The singing continued. Youthful voices merged with those of mature men and women as little Irja completed her circle and returned to where Kirsten stood waiting. The crown was removed, and the child seemed to grow in stature. When she returned to her place among her friends, she was still glowing with pride and excitement.

Kirsten gazed about her. These were her friends, it was true. They had been her companions through the agony of the march. But they did not resent her fortune. They accepted her—but they did not need her visits.

She let her eyes sweep the circle of prisoners. Up until this moment, she had needed them. But, in the songs that swelled from their deepest memories, they had let her know that her heritage was too ingrained for her to forget it.

Irja's mother pushed forward and stood beside Kirsten. "Thank you, Kirsten Gustafson. We will remember this day for the rest of our lives."

There were tears in Kirsten's eyes. "I am the one to be thankful. You have given me so much."

The woman reached out and touched Kirsten's hand. "Then we are even." She smiled down at her daughter, and then met Kirsten's eyes. "Goodbye, then. God be with you!"

Kirsten lowered her head. With the songs of the prisoners ringing in her ears, she stepped from the barn.

Sascha was waiting for her, his fingers tapping restlessly on the door of the carriage. He straightened up when she approached. "You are ready to go now, my lady?"

"Yes, Sascha. I am ready to return to the city."

She let herself be assisted into her carriage. Sascha leaped in beside her, and called out to the coachman. The horses, their coats steaming, began to trot down the hill. Kirsten looked back. The Russian soldiers seemed as affected by the singing as she had been. They stood quietly, their usual eagerness to intrude upon the lives of their charges gone—at least for the moment. She turned and looked toward the city.

It was only then that she became aware of a strange pressure against her thigh. Sascha was sitting too close. She shifted to her left, widening the gap between them.

Sascha moved closer once more, and again the pressure came. She shifted once more, but this time she could move only a short distance.

Almost immediately, the pressure was renewed. She looked up at him with a frown. "Sascha, you are being offensive! Please remember your place, and behave like a gentleman!"

Never before had she realized how ugly his face really was. He leered at her, and his pinpoint eyes seemed to glow like hot coals. "No one can see us, Kirsten Gustafson! Why do you deny the hunger that is within you?"

With a sudden lunge, she rose from her seat and dropped onto the opposite bench, facing her tormentor. "I will speak to Alexei. You are being impertinent, sir!"

His knees caught hers and held her immobile. "You need not pretend with me, Kirsten. I have heard the rumors that circulate through the city. And I recognized the honor that was bestowed upon me when I received this appointment. But you have been coy long enough. I expect my reward. I grow tired of waiting."

A frown creased her brow. "Reward? Honor? What are you talking about?"

His voice grew sharp. "Do not pretend that you do not know! I have heard the stories of each of your 'escorts.' I know how you have used them, and how, when you grew tired of them, you cast them off. Dmitri told me of his visits to your chamber. And I am growing impatient. I have been in your service longer than any of the others, yet I have received none of the pleasures. When do we begin?"

"Sir!" Kirsten brought all of her anger into her response. "How dare you? Whatever you have heard from your fellows is a lie! I have never had anyone in my chamber but Alexei!"

"Ah, but I understand now. That is why I have approached you." Sascha leaned froward and took her hands in his. "The colonel is away now. And that is what you have been waiting for. I know he will be out of the city for at least two days more." The carriage entered the city, and he sat back, letting her hands fall in her lap. "I will come tonight. We do not have to wait any longer."

The horses clopped through the brick-paved street. Kirsten stared through the window at the snow-covered facades. This was unreal! How could Sascha have reached so wild a conclusion?

Time was running short. Soon she would be at her home, and Sascha would leap from the carriage. "Do not dare such a thing!" She tried to keep her voice steady, but it shook with anger. "If you try to do such a thing, I will kill you!"

He smiled, moving his shoulders to display the strength of his muscles. "Ah, you wish to be conquered! Good! I find a woman with spirit more exciting." His eyes burned into hers. "I felt that Dmitri was holding something back. Now I know what it is. I will bring a whip with me."

Kirsten began to protest. But the carriage came to a halt, and the face of the lackey appeared at the window, cutting short any further conversation. Nevertheless, as Sascha helped her to the ground, she hissed her reply. "I will kill you!"

But she could see that her words fell on deaf ears.

"My lady, are you ill?" Katerina hovered beside the large armchair in which Kirsten sat. "You have eaten nothing since your return, and you have not heard my words at all."

Kirsten forced a smile. "I'm sorry, Katerina. I didn't realize you were speaking."

"I asked you about the visit. Was the celebration all you had anticipated?"

It seemed to Kirsten that the singing in the prison camp had occurred many ages ago. "Celebration?" Had it really been just this morning?

"The Lucia Festival! Was Siiri proud to wear the crown?"

Kirsten stared for a moment at her maid. She had described the entire ceremony many times before this day, and Katerina was well acquainted with what was to have happened. Slowly, Kirsten began to recount the events of the morning.

As she spoke, the fear that had invaded her happiness seemed to fade. She spoke at last of the feeling she had had as the singing continued. A new security had filled her soul. Without knowing it, she had been afraid she would forget her homeland. The songs of the prisoners had told her that she had no need to be afraid of such an eventuality. Finland, Sweden, both were so ingrained in her heart that she could never put them behind her. However much she enjoyed her life with Alexei, she would remain a true subject of Charles the Twelfth until her death.

And then, suddenly, her pleasure vanished. She remembered Sascha and his unexpected threat, and her face grew solemn.

Kateriana noted the change with alarm. "My lady, what is the matter? Why are you so sad? You tell me of pleasure and good thoughts, and then you begin to weep. Did something go wrong, after all? Or are you thinking of Siiri? How sad that she could not take her place as the Lucia maiden!"

Kirsten continued to weep, but she shook her head in reply to her maid's query. And so Katerina persisted. "What is it, then? Please, my lady, tell me. Who knows, maybe I can be of help to you."

Still Kirsten sobbed without replying. At last, Katerina's eyes widened. "My lady! Is it Sascha?"

Kirsten looked up.

"What did he mean just before he left you? I heard him say 'tonight!' in a voice filled with overtones of conspiracy. What has he said to destroy your happiness?"

The floodgates opened, and Kirsten leaned forward, resting her head on Katerina's shoulder. "Oh, Katerina! I don't know what do do! He said terrible things about Dmitri and me. And he spoke as if I had accepted every other escort into my bedroom. Where could he have received such an impression? You know I never let Dmitri onto the second level of the house, nor any of the others. Oh, Katerina, what am I going to say to Alexei? If such rumors are circulating about me, he will be filled with jealousy!"

Katerina stroked the smooth silken head. "Don't cry, my lady. Tonight is not here yet. We will prepare a reception for Sascha that he will not forget."

"But Alexei, what will he think? How can I face him, knowing the terrible rumors that are being spread about the city?"

Katerina smiled reassuringly. "One trouble at a time, my lady. First, we must make certain that Sascha has a reception worthy of his daring."

She spent the rest of the day in planning. Kirsten, still too afraid of what Alexei might think, was at first reluctant to comply with her maid's directions. But in the end she did as she was told.

Katerina was openly amused at Kirsten's naïveté. "My lady, is there no intrigue in your homeland? Do not people conspire to advance themselves at the expense of others? Here at the court of the tsar, it has been perfected through years of practice. A man or woman who ignores the importance of intrigue does not last long. One must learn duplicity in order to survive."

Kirsten knew then how helpless she was. Her father had required honesty at all times. She knew nothing of deceit. "I will do as you tell me, Katerina. Only help me to keep Alexei from learning of this terrible thing!"

Katerina smiled. "Whatever happens, my lady, do not worry. I have prepared for any eventuality."

That night, Kirsten slept, not in her bed, but on the chaise near the window. Katernia, her hair covered with a nightcap, assumed her mistress's place in the canopied bed. The curtains were opened slightly, and a streak of silver cut across the carpet, lighting the heavy door. Katerina spoke, "When he comes, you must be very quiet. And when I tell you, you must begin to scream." She settled back on the soft pillows. "Remember, we must not speak again until it is over."

Kirsten lay stiffly, her hands close against her sides, and stared at the door. He would come through it soon, of that she was certain. She wondered if she would be able to contain her fright.

Outside, the snow had started to fall. A carriage clopped by, its wheels squeaking on the frozen street. Somewhere, far in the distance, a watchman sang out his call. For the first time in months, she wished that Viotto were at her side. Viotto! The curve of the chaise against her body reminded her of the pressure of his hips against her. She felt again the growing desire. And she knew that never again would she enjoy the release he had given her that night so long ago. Fearful of her own emotions, she pulled her thoughts back to the present trouble.

The only sound in the room was the slow, steady breathing of Katerina. Kirsten felt a momentary alarm. What if the girl fell asleep? Then, surely, her plans would go awry.

She raised herself on one elbow and strained to see the form on the bed. At that moment, she heard a board squeak outside her door. She was too late. Sascha had arrived!

Trembling, she lay back on the chaise and stared at the moonlit doorway. Nothing happened. Had she been mistaken? But before she could sit up to see better, the door moved.

It opened slowly, as if whoever moved it was listening for danger. Then Sascha slipped into the room. He stood in the moonlight, his eyes fastened on the still form that lay in the bed.

Kirsten suppressed a gasp of alarm. She wanted to cry out to wake Katerina, but her throat was dry. She watched as the silent figure approached her bed.

He would learn soon enough that it was not Kirsten who lay asleep before him. And what would he do then? Maybe kill the girl, and turn to hunt for his intended victim. Kirsten shuddered.

He was leaning toward the bed when Katerina suddenly sprang into motion. She turned in the bed, and Kirsten thought she saw something bright flash before her.

"Now, my lady, scream loudly!" The command came like a shout. "Scream, and come quickly to the bed."

Kirsten rose and hurried to Katerina's side. When she saw what had happened, she needed no urging to cry out. The stiletto that she used for her embroidery had been

251

thrust through Sascha's heart. His blood was spilling out onto her covers. Katerina wiped her hand clean and slipped out from beneath his body. "Quick! Lie down in my place."

Kirsten stood as if frozen to the floor. "Hurry! You have no time to lose!" Katerina half-pushed her into the bed. She took Kirsten's hand and placed it over the handle of the stiletto. Kirsten's screams grew more frantic. She could feel the blood oozing over her fingers.

With a sudden convulsion, she pushed the body away. It slid to the floor.

Suddenly, there was a pounding on the door below. Katerina scurried from the room. Kirsten, overcome with horror and fear, felt her head begin to spin. She fell back on the bed, too weak from shock to think of the gore in which she lay.

"My lady! Are you all right?" Katerina was leaning over the bed, her face furrowed with concern.

Kirsten opened her eyes. Very little had changed. Her hand was sticky from the blood, and she was aware that her stomach was unsettled. But there was another man beside the bed now, and a second one stood facing her at the foot. She opened her eyes wide in alarm. "Katerina? What is this? Who are these men?"

"Night watchmen, my lady! Do not be alarmed. They are friends of mine." A glance passed between the three, and Kirsten wondered for a moment just what Katerina meant by those words. "They heard your screams, and they have come to help you. I have told them what occurred."

Kirsten opened her mouth to speak, but Katerina continued without a pause. "I told them how you felt ill this afternoon, after your long visit at the prison camp, and that you requested that I sleep in your room so that I could nurse you if you grew uncomfortable. I explained that you worked for a while on your embroidery, and that you requested that I leave it beside your bed so that you could light a lamp and work more on it if you wakened during the night."

She was well into her story now, and Kirsten listened in amazement. "When Sascha entered, I was asleep. But I

252

heard your scream and tried to run to your rescue. But I was not needed to defend your honor. You were strong enough for the task. Oh, my lady, the colonel will be proud of your bravery!"

Kirsten closed her gaping mouth. This was a development she had not anticipated.

"By your leave, madam, we will remove the body. I will fill out the necessary reports." The man at the foot of the bed signaled to the other, who immediately lifted Sacha in his arms. "Do you wish to have the stiletto back? In a case such as this, there is no need for evidence. Clearly, you killed the gentleman in defense of your honor. No one will question what has occurred."

Kirsten nodded silently. But it was Katerina who spoke. "I think my lady would like to show the weapon to the colonel. He might want to see how strong she is in protecting his interests." She moved toward the door and opened it to let the men out. "Thank you for arriving so swiftly. If my lady had not been so brave, we might have needed your help." She held out her hand and took the blade from the watchman. Blood was encrusted on its handle, but she showed no distress. "And please, Evgeni, we will need a copy of your report. It will be important to the colonel."

"I will drop it by later today, Katerina." The officer bent and planted a kiss on Katerina's lips. He smiled into her face. "The same time?"

Katerina nodded, and the men left the room.

Kirsten slid out from between the covers. She stood quietly while Katerina rinsed her hands and wiped the streak of blood that had marred her face. But even when her skin was clean, Kirsten felt the taint. She wondered if she would ever feel clean again.

When she was settled once more on the chaise, Kirsten looked up at her maid. "How did you know they would come?"

"Don't fret, my lady. Evgeni knows that you are an honorable woman. His report will tell everything that I said and all that he saw. The colonel will have no reason to doubt your faithfulness." She tucked the blankets up over Kirsten's shoulders. "Sleep now. I have it on the best authority that the colonel will be home in the morning. You will want to be fresh to greet him."

She rose as if to leave, but Kirsten grasped her hand. "Don't go now. Please. I cannot endure being alone in this room now."

Katerina nodded. Without replying, she took a cape from the wardrobe and draped it over her shoulders. Then, her head resting on the chaise beside Kirsten, she fell asleep.

Kirsten lay staring up at the dimly lit ceiling. The vision of Sascha's empty dead face and the stream of blood that had covered her hand haunted her thoughts. She wondered at the ease with which Katerina had fallen asleep, and admitted to herself that for her it could never be that easy. Maybe she would never sleep again. Maybe the odor of death would never leave the room.

She woke suddenly, aware of voices below her window. Katerina sat up, rubbed the sleep from her eyes, and hurried to look out. When she turned, her face was bright with pleasure. "The colonel has returned. And, good fortune! He has just received the report Evgeni promised to deliver. I must hurry down and let him in."

Kirsten sat up as Katerina left the room. If Alexei did not believe all that was told him, she would soon know. But she did not have to wait for him to reach her side. He called her as soon as he entered the house, and she could hear his footsteps on the stairs. "Kirsten! Are you all right?"

Kirsten rose and stood facing the doorway. He burst in, his eyes flashing. Never had she seen him look so young. He saw her at once, and ran to her side. "Oh, Kirsten! How terrible! Thank God you were able to save yourself!"

She hardly knew how to answer him. But there was no need for a reply. He took her in his arms and kissed her lips. His hands roamed over her body, as if to assure him that she was unharmed. But when he carried her to the bed, he stopped abruptly. The pool of blood had hardened on the coverlet.

With a curse, he tore the bedding away. The sheet was unmarred, and he lifted her again and placed her on it.

254

She shrank away as she felt the bed beneath her, but he paid no attention to her weakness. He pulled off his clothing with an impatience she had not seen in months, and then he lay beside her.

"Oh, my love! How terrible it must have been! Forgive me for choosing so dangerous a companion for you!"

In answer, she kissed his lips. Suddenly the terror of the night was gone. A new, stronger passion than she had ever before felt in Alexei's arms consumed her body. Now, at last, she spoke. "Oh, Alexei, I was so frightened! I missed you so very much!"

And for the first time in their relationship, it was she who caressed him, and it was her desire that demanded his entry. But he had only so much to give. Long before she had reached satisfaction, he lay spent in her arms.

She lay still beneath him, waiting for him to awaken. And she knew then that her life would always be incomplete. Her dreams of Viotto would remain her only comfort. For Alexei was an old man, and he was too jealous to admit that he could not satisfy the desires of a woman in the bloom of her youth. There would be other Saschas in the future. And maybe, some day, there would be one who came on her invitation.

And when that happened, then her real danger would begin.

Chapter 26

"My lady, it's time to get up!" Katerina stood at the door, the usual morning tray in her hands.

"Yes, Katerina, I'm awake." Kirsten sat up in her bed. It had been thoroughly cleaned since that terrible night, and she could not smell the odor of death that had repelled her so terribly. "Has the colonel arrived yet?"

"Not yet, ma'am. But there is a gentleman at the door with a message for you."

Kirsten hesitated. Was Alexei sending her a note to inform her of another trip? He was gone so often these days on business for the tsar. "Send him in, please."

Katerina put the tray over Kirsten's extended legs. "I shall tell him you will see him as soon as you have finished your breakfast, my lady."

Kirsten felt a momentary impatience. There were times, since Sascha's death, when Katerina acted more like a nursemaid than a servant. "No, I will see him first. If he carries a message from Alexei, I might as well know what he has to say."

Katerina curtsied, her face a study of mixed uneasiness and amusement at her mistress's directness.

The young man who appeared at the door was both tall and handsome. His dark blue uniform was so new it still smelled of the tailor, and the salute he gave smacked of a recent graduation from a nearby military academy. "Mistress Kirsten?"

"Yes, I am she. What is the message you have for me?"

He advanced across the room, his eyes sweeping around as if he wished to see everything in one glance. And suddenly, she knew that he had heard of Sascha's death, and he wanted to see the chamber in which it had taken place. She wondered if the same rumors that had driven Sascha to such daring still circulated in the guardrooms and streets of the city.

The youth presented a small packet. "I was told to deliver this to you, madam."

Kirsten took the packet and tore it open. Inside was a small sheet of parchment on which a message was inscribed. Without bothering to read the words, she glanced at the messenger. "Were you told to wait for an answer?"

"No, madam." She was acutely aware that he was staring at her face, and at the bedclothes that protected her from his view. Did he expect that the bloodstain would still remain?

"Then you are dismissed. Thank you." The last words were spoken from habit.

He saluted again, and left the room. She stared at the door, aware of a strange uneasiness. She would have to ask Alexei to provide locks for her doors. She could not endure another night of terror.

Suddenly, she was aware of the packet that remained unread on her lap. Removing the parchment, she unfolded it. In a neat, careful hand, five words had been written: *Whore, prepare for the end!*

She stared at the even letters. Who would write such a cruel thing? And why? The paper burned in her hand, and she tossed it to the floor. It lay reprovingly at her feet, almost exactly where Sascha's body had fallen.

She leaped from the bed and snatched it up. She could not let Katerina see such insulting words. She could not let anyone see them! And Alexei was coming soon. With a feeling of panic, she tore at the parchment, shredding it to pieces. She dropped the shreds into her empty chocolate cup. Then she crawled back into the bed.

Katerina appeared at the door. "Was the message important?"

"No. Just a note from Sonia, asking me to tea. Has the colonel arrived?

"Yes, ma'am. He came just after the messenger left, but I do not believe that he saw the lad. Shall I let him come up?"

"Of course!" Kirsten could not hide her irritation. "When have we ever kept the colonel waiting?"

By the time he entered her room, she had recovered her good spirits. She leaped from the bed, her warm flannel nightgown flowing behind her. He chuckled at the sight. "Ah, Kirsten! My little maiden, rushing to meet her lord! I swear, you will retain your innocence even when you are as old as I am." He caught her and crushed her in his arms. "Kiss your Alexei! For I must leave again this afternoon."

He did not notice that her smile was shadowed with an inner fear. When he kissed her, he thought the trembling of her lips was due to passion.

It was not until he had left, taking with him her assurances that she had no intentions of leaving the house, that she remembered she had told Katerina that she had been invited to dine at Sonia's. Torn between the risk of deceiving Alexei and planting a doubt in Katerina's mind, she decided to go out. After all, Alexei had told her he would be away. And she did not want Katerina to question her about the content of the note.

Sonia was surprised to see her, but in spite of the short notice was the perfect hostess. When she kissed Kirsten in greeting, she whispered softly, "You are welcome to lunch with me. But then, if you do not mind, I will have to ask you to go. I have a visitor this afternoon."

Kirsten nodded. "Of course. Forgive me for intruding. But I have not seen you in days, and I wondered if you were well."

The guest appeared moments later, for he too had come for lunch. When Kirsten saw him, she felt a shiver of fear. Sonia was deceiving her patron. The young man who kissed her hand with such familiarity showed clearly that he anticipated greater intimacy. No wonder Alexei's jealousy was so easily aroused. In all probability, he had never had a mistress who did not take on additional bed partners.

She forgot the episode in the days that followed. Now that she no longer visited the prisoners, she had become involved in more domestic duties. She spent hours practicing the harpsichord, and a dancing master attended her every afternoon to improve her deportment on the floor.

She had just finished a session with the dance instructor when another messenger appeared at the door. Katerina stepped into the small bare room Kirsten used for her lessons. "Madam, a gentleman is waiting in the foyer."

"A gentleman? I have no appointment other than with Monsieur Jordeaux. Did he tell you what he wanted?"

"No, my lady. Shall I tell him to leave?"

Kirsten glanced at Jordeaux. He smiled politely and bowed with a graceful gesture of his hand. "Madam, do not let me detain you from other pleasures. The time for your instruction is past now. I will return tomorrow." The door remained open as he stepped into the hall, and Kirsten saw him cast an appraising glance at the newcomer.

The sight of his glance sent a damp chill down her back. Monsieur Jordeaux was a notorious gossip, and now he would have some news about her! Quickly, she rushed into the entryway. "Sir!" She extended her hand toward the newcomer. "You may deliver your message and leave." As she spoke, she looked toward Jordeaux, but he was smiling as if he shared some special secret with her. He bowed once more and stepped out into the snow.

Kirsten cursed the fate that had brought a messenger to her door before Jordeaux was gone. But there was nothing she could do now to allay his suspicions.

She started when the youthful messenger pushed a packet into her hand. "Is that all, ma'am?"

"No." She tore at the seal impatiently. "Wait, please. There may be an answer."

The note was brief—and provocative. *In the conservatory.*

She stared at it for a moment. "Who gave this to you?"

"I don't know, ma'am. The officer of the day called me

260

up to deliver it. He did not say who left it with him." He frowned. "Is there something the matter?"

"No. Of course not! Thank you. There is no reply."

The lad saluted smartly, clicked his heels, and disappeared. Kirsten stood staring at the large door as it closed behind him. She had made no arrangements to meet anyone, yet the cryptic message piqued her curiosity. Who—or what—was waiting in the conservatory?

There was a nagging worry in the back of her mind, warning her to ignore the message, to remain indoors, as she had planned. Yet she knew she could not resist the mystery.

Katerina cleared her throat. "Ma'am, are you well? Is something the matter?"

"No. I mean, I am fine. Nothing is the matter." She stared down at the packet in her hand. "Get my cape. I am going out."

"Oh, my lady, is that wise? You know how the master is about your changing your mind after you have talked with him."

"Please, Katerina. It will be all right. I will not be long."

A wave of hot, steamy air slapped Kirsten in the face as she stepped into the glass-domed shelter of the conservatory. This, above all the other structures in St. Petersburg, was the pride of the tsar, for in a climate suited only to the hardiest plant life, it provided the proper environment for exotic flowers and ferns from the far south.

Kirsten opened her collar and draped her cape over her arm. Already she could feel the perspiration forming on her brow. And already she was aware of the foolishness of her action. What had possessed her? She had told Alexei she was staying home, and here she was in this exotic place!

Katerina took her cape from her arm. "Is there some special flower you wish to see?"

"I . . . I don't know, Katerina. I just want to walk a bit." Why was she acting so secretive? Why not tell Katerina what this was all about?

Because she did not know what it was all about. Suddenly Kirsten felt like bursting into tears. Why, oh why had she done such a stupid thing?

The young man appeared so suddenly that she cried out in alarm. Katerina, ready to defend her mistress, scurried forward. But the youth seemed to have no ill intentions. He bowed politely and stepped close to Kirsten, so close she wondered for a moment if he intended to smother her.

He took her arm and led her to a nearby bench. "Please, my lady, I appear to have startled you. Rest assured, I have no intentions of harming you."

Her heart was pounding, and she was aware that her hand trembled. "What do you want of me? Why did you frighten me so?" She caught Katerina's eyes and signalled her to remain close. "Why are you tormenting me so?"

He seemed honestly surprised. "Tormenting you? How can that be? I have never seen you until this moment."

"Then what business have you with me?"

He drew a packet from his pocket. "I have been instructed to deliver a message to you."

Kirsten felt a chilling premonition. Her eyes wide, she extended her hand. As her fingers closed around the packet, she closed her eyes, too faint for a moment to consider leaving. Was it the heat, the humidity, after the chill of the street, that upset her so? Katerina rushed to her side, her arms extended, as if to keep her from falling.

The young man rose as the maid approached. Bending low, he brought her fingers to his lips. "Adieu, madam." He was gone before she could demand an explanation for his presence or for the strange method of delivery.

Katerina took his place, her eyes fastened on Kirsten's pale face. "Oh, madam, I knew we should not have come out! How can you explain this meeting to the colonel? What will he think?"

"Why . . ." Kirsten felt confused. Why would anyone go to such elaborate lengths to give her distress? "I don't know, Katerina. I don't know."

She was aware of the packet that she still clutched in one hand, and she stared at it dumbly. She had made no attempt to tear it open, but she felt sure of its contents. There was one word that would surely be written inside.

And that word she had no desire to read ever again. Slipping the packet, still unopened, into her pocket, she rose to her feet. "Come, Katerina. If we hurry back, maybe Alexei will not learn of our escapade."

Katerina watched her closely as they walked back to the carriage. When they were once more in the great hallway, she took the cape from Kirsten's shoulders. "Shall I burn that, madam?"

"Burn what?" Kirsten tore her mind from the fog that had encompassed it since the sudden encounter in the misty hall of the glass-domed building. She had struggled all the way home with the question that had presented itself when the young messenger arrived at her side. What was happening? Who was causing her this trouble? And why?

She grew aware that she still clutched the packet in her hand so tightly that her knuckles were white and her fingers ached. She pulled it from her pocket, tore it open, and stared at the paper it contained. As she had expected and feared, there was one word emblazoned in the center. *Whore.*

She reeled slightly, clutching at Katerina's arm for support. "Who is doing this? Why am I being tormented so?"

Katerina tore the missive from her hand. "Please, my lady, try to forget this insult. Someone is jealous of your beauty, and of the great man who is your patron."

Kirsten shook herself. Some feeling of order was returning. If she did not allow herself to become upset, whoever was perpetrating this terrible hoax would get no satisfaction. "Yes, of course. Throw it away. Or, better yet, burn it. I should not let such unimportant nonsense disturb me."

A week passed before she was again caused any upset. A young marine officer appeared at her door. He entered when Katerina invited him inside, and stood gazing about the entryway with obvious curiosity. Kirsten was in the library, studying a book that was written in Swedish.

When Katerina announced the visitor, she felt herself pale. It was beginning again, just when she thought it was over.

She was aware of the young man's eyes burning through

her clothing as she approached. *Insolent!* She almost spoke the word aloud. *You should be whipped!* But she smiled as she approached him. "You have a message for me, my maid informs me. I will take it."

He held out another red packet. She felt affronted by his behavior. He lounged before her, as if to show that he held her in little esteem. And his eyes pried under her dress.

She drew herself erect. "Sir, you have delivered your message. Why do you remain?"

He smiled. "Your pardon, miss. I was given to understand . . ." He flushed, suddenly aware that things were not as he had been led to believe. "I had been told . . ." His face turned crimson, and he backed toward the door. "Your pardon, madam! I—It must have been some of my comrades playing a trick on me. I can see I was mistaken. I pray that you will forgive me for my rudeness!" He stumbled back until his hand touched the doorknob, and, with obvious relief, he let himself out.

When he was gone, Katerina stepped to Kirsten's side. "My lady, I am worried. There is more than a youthful prank here. Someone is trying to destroy you."

Kirsten had felt such relief at the young man's embarrassment that she could not contain her pleasure. She smiled broadly "Come, now, Katerina. Destroy me? Whatever for? What have I done to anyone in St. Petersburg? Why, I hardly know many people here. And this, certainly cannot be related to the others. It surely was an accident, or a joke, as the young gentleman suggested."

As she spoke, she gazed at the packet she held in her hand. It was different from the others. When she tore it open, she felt a flood of relief. She had been right. But this time the word bore no shameful associations. She read it, and then repeated it aloud. *Lovers.*

Lovers? She met Katerina's worried gaze. Maybe, after all, her maid was right. Maybe someone was trying to ruin her. If it was true, then she knew only one thing about the perpetrator of this prank, or threat, whichever it might be. Whoever was at its core knew that colonel Alexei Mikhailovich Leonidovich was a very jealous man.

*   *   *

"Kirsten!'" Alexei's voice rang through the great hall. Kirsten rose from her bed. The faint morning light had hardly begun to tint the curtains that covered her windows, and Katerina had not yet brought in her morning chocolate.

"Kirsten!" He had mounted the stairs, and she could hear the violence in his step and the anger in his voice. She waited in silence until he stepped into her room. "Kirsten!" He was shouting now, even though she could have heard him whisper. "Why do you not answer me?"

"Why do you call me with such fury? Have I done something to offend you?" She spoke quietly, forcing her voice to remain steady in spite of the fear that brought a flush to her cheeks.

He seemed hardly to have heard her. "I see it all now!" He spoke bitterly, and his face was twisted with an inner agony. "What a fool I have been! To think that I believed that you killed Sascha in defense of your honor! What a fool! What better way could there be for a woman to rid herself of an unwanted lover!"

Kirsten braced herself against the bedpost. "Alexei, what are you talking about? Sascha has been dead for months! Why are you worrying about him now?"

"Because I am only now beginning to understand why he was murdered! What a doddering fool I have been, to trust my happiness to a heartless woman such as you!"

She felt as if he had slapped her in the face. "Heartless? Why do you call me that? Surely you do not think I could murder a man in cold blood!"

"If it served your purpose! You have never been completely honest with me concerning your past, and now I understand why. You developed many appetites during your months in the prison camp, and you have been unable to put them aside. How many guards did you service when you pretended to visit your countrymen on the hill? And how many have met you in other secret places?" He seemed suddenly aware of her confusion. "Tell me, madam, have you remained at home every day this week?"

She thought back quickly. "Yes, of course. Where should I want to go? It is too cold to go shopping, and I have all my needs cared for through your generosity."

"Every day? Are you certain?" Behind him, Katerina was blinking wildly, her hand over her mouth. Suddenly, Kirsten knew that she had made a grievous error.

"No, not every day. I forgot for a moment. I went to—"

"To the conservatory!" His voice rang triumphantly. "You thought I did not know! You thought that because no one was set to guard you, you could do as you pleased. You told me you were staying in all day, and no sooner did I leave than you dressed and hurried off. Do not deny it! I have witnesses!"

She remembered Monsieur Jordeaux. How could she have failed to see his carriage? "I do not deny it! I simply forgot. I went there because . . ." She paused. The enormity of the plot lay before her, as clearly as if she had heard the conspirator describe it. Someone, she knew not who, had arranged it all.

Alexei continued to speak, as if he had not heard her attempt to defend herself. "You have many guests, as well. I have witnesses who saw two, no, *three* different young men enter your house, the last one only yesterday. Do not try to deny it! I know it to be true!"

"But I must deny what you assume those visits to mean! The young men were messengers. They carried packets addressed to me. You must believe me! They were not lovers, nor did they stay for any length of time. They entered my house, delivered their packets, and left."

"And are you accustomed to receiving messengers gowned only in a peignoir? Do you receive every stranger who approaches your door in your boudoir?"

"No! Certainly not!"

"Do you honestly expect me to believe that they were mere messengers? One was a ship's officer, fresh from a voyage, and the other two were young officers. When did men of such caliber become carriers of letters?" He stared at her triumphantly. "And from whom did these letters come? Who do you know who needs to correspond with you in so secret a manner?"

She felt a growing terror. Never had she seen Alexei so angry. His face was red, and his temples throbbed wildly. He staggered as he approached, and grasped at a chair for support.

But his temporary weakness did not reduce his vitriol. His fist raised, he continued to shout. "I should kill you now! I should have you destroyed for filling my life with such bitterness!" He seemed to break before her, and suddenly he was bent over, tears streaming down his face. "What have I done to you that you should treat me so meanly?"

"Please." She felt the first glimmer of hope. Maybe now he would listen. "They are lies—all lies. I have never deceived you."

"You try to deceive me now. Wench, at least show the courage to admit your evil ways. Face me squarely and tell me all that has transpired. I demand that you speak now!" He had recovered his strength, and he stood above her, his hand raised to strike.

She dodged instinctively as his fist fell. She felt the breeze as it sped past her ear, and then he was pounding the bed with such fury she feared he might have a stroke. He fell to his knees, tears running down his cheeks, and his fists flew up and down, pounding the bed with unrelenting force.

When he made no move toward her, Kirsten glanced toward the door. Katerina had not moved since his arrival. She stood silently, ready, Kirsten knew, to rush to her aid. Silently, she signaled her loyal servant to leave. It was all right now. He would be calm when his crying fit was over.

The door closed softly. Kirsten looked again at Alexei. He continued to pound the bed and to sob loudly. She sat rigid beside him, just out of reach of his fists, and waited. Surely he would regain his composure soon! He was a strong man. He would recover, and then he would be willing to listen to reason.

But Alexei showed no sign of overcoming his delirium. He continued to hammer the mattress with wild fury.

As quietly as she could, Kirsten let herself slide to the floor. But she had hardly begun to move, when he grabbed at her legs, and held her so tightly that he bruised her tender skin. With a sudden lunge, he shifted his grasp to her shoulders, and she felt a pain shoot through her back. "Do not try to escape my vengeance!"

His voice was unrecognizable in his anger. "You must die for your perfidy!"

He rose and pushed her back onto the bed. They remained thus far a time, Kirsten cowering below, and Alexei towering above her. As she watched, anger, hurt, and lust fought for control of his body, and then, with a sudden roar, he fell upon her.

The peignoir was torn from her shoulders as he thrashed above her. He pulled at his breeches, and then, with an unexpected shout, he thrust himself into her. She cried out in surprise and hurt. Never, except that first time so long ago, had he entered her with such ferociousness.

But he was not satisfied with this humiliation. He rose and forced her to lie face down on the bed. And then he was upon her again. This time he tore into her with such violence that she screamed in pain. She felt a warm liquid flow over her thighs, and she screamed again.

He paid no heed to her cries. Grunting and panting, he thrust himself repeatedly into her until, at last, he stiffened and grew suddenly still. He rose to his feet then, and she touched her backside. Her fingers came away red with her own blood.

She listened without moving while he stormed across the room. Then, timidly, she rolled over and watched, fearful that he would return again to the assault. But he seemed to have forgotten her presence. He stood before the large mirror and smoothed his clothing.

He faced her again, and his expression was devoid of any affection. "Prepare yourself, woman! I am sure the guards on the hill will find many ways to entertain themselves, once you are returned to them."

He brushed past Katerina as he stormed through the door. Kirsten rolled over once more, and by the time Katerina reached her side, she was sobbing helplessly. Her entire body ached. But she felt certain that when Alexei's sentence was carried out, she would know even more agony.

Chapter 27

Viotto stopped abruptly, his arm raised in silent warning. In the months since they had left the encampment up north, they had endured many perils. There had been more than one village wasted by plague, and as winter passed into spring and spring into summer, the intensity of the sickness increased.

Where possible, Viotto had insisted upon burying the corpses, though both men had been most cautious when dealing with the stinking remains of the lonely dead. But there were times when they could only pass by quietly, aware that the presence of Muscovite soldiers denied them the opportunity to complete the task.

Now fall once more painted the land in red and gold. Drawn closer together by their shared dangers, the two men scoured the countryside. But they had little to feed their optimism. From all appearances, Kirsten had vanished from the face of the earth.

Now, his eyes on the small cottage that stood in the center of what appeared to be an empty barnyard, Viotto sniffed the air. There was a smell to the plague that could not be washed away even by the coldest weather. But this clearing smelled clean, and the fresh odor of refuse put him on the alert. There was someone—or something—living nearby.

Viotto gave another signal, and immediately began to

move forward. Knut rested against a nearby tree. The two men had reached an understanding long ago to risk only one life at a time. This time, it was Viotto's duty to see if the structure that lay ahead contained some hidden danger.

The earth crunched beneath his feet, packing tight under his weight, but Viotto paid little attention to the trail he was leaving. There would be time to eradicate it if this place was safe. In the months of searching, he had become acutely sensitive to the existence of life. An empty farm had a different smell and a different feel. What he felt here was the presence of some faint life. What he did not know was whether it was human.

His first attention was directed toward the cottage. There was no smoke floating up through the chimney. The windows were dark and empty. The one door he could see was tightly secured on the outside. He moved swiftly around the back. That door, too, was bolted.

Now he concentrated on the barnyard. Was it a wild beast he sensed? When he saw the movement, he was instantly alert, his gun ready in his hands. He moved toward it slowly, prepared to defend himself against an attack, and he put his gun aside and pulled out his knife.

He lunged suddenly. A squeal tore through the silence. He had made a clean kill. He wiped his blade and pushed it back into his belt. Then he lifted his prey into his arms. He had slaughtered an undernourished pig.

The sound of the creature's death cry rang through the woods, echoing faintly, and then everything was still once more. But neither Viotto nor Knut assumed safety. They remained where they stood, immobile, waiting.

Nothing moved. They were alone.

At last, Knut moved toward the house. As Viotto carried his kill from the barnyard, he unbolted the door and held it open. Viotto entered alone.

He stood for a moment just inside, waiting to grow accustomed to the dim light. Gradually, the shapes appeared. To his right, filling one wall, was the fireplace, with a stack of wood piled beside it. He could barely discern the iron arms and the big kettle that some earlier occupant had used for cooking.

In the center of the room was a small wooden table and some rough benches. On the far side of the room, at the greatest distance from the fire, were the beds.

The table was thick with dust, but the earthenware dishes and roughly shaped tools were stacked neatly in the center. The firebed was cleared of ashes, as if waiting for a new fire to be laid. The beds were covered with furs. This house had not been abandoned suddenly by death or by a raid. The occupants had left it with intent to return.

He shifted his burden to one arm and brushed the table clean with the other. Then, leaving the carcass on one edge of the board, he searched the corners of the room. It was empty. He lifted a log from the pile and moved toward the fireplace. A scurrying sent a warning through his tense body, and he froze in his tracks. Rats! With a sigh of relief, he finished the task of laying the fire.

Knut stepped inside when the fire was burning. Drawing his knife, he began to slice the pig into strips. The meat he speared on the metal braces that hung over the fire. The bones, still thick with flesh, he threw into a pot.

Viotto took another pot and stepped outside. When he returned, it was filled with clean water. Most of the water he poured over the bones. Then, together, the men lifted the large kettle and hung it on a hook over the flames.

Again, Viotto went outside. This time he climbed up to a small rise and studied the distant scene. There appeared to be no one nearby. At last, as satisfied as he could be that their smoke would not draw an attack, he returned to the warmth of the cottage.

Knut had added another log to the fire. "Too bad there are no vegetables. Soup would taste very good right now!"

Viotto shrugged. "I think there was a cellar in the back. It's worth a look. God, that meat smells good already!" He closed the door behind him and circled the building.

What he found only served to assure him that there had been no hurried exodus, and that the Russians had for some unknown reason left this house untouched. The cellar was filled with dry vegetables. Then he saw the small symbol over the door to the cellar.

He returned to the cottage with a basket of vegetables on his arm. "Good fortune! And I know the reason for all

271

this bounty. This farm has the symbol of a witch on its mantels. The Muscovites are too superstitious to enter."

Knut's eyes widened. "Maybe we, too, should be suspicious. I have heard that witches have marvelous powers."

Viotto settled on the bench and began to clean the vegetables. "I choose to risk an unseen witch's curse before I spend another night in the snow. I've known a few such women. They are usually fierce patriots. They will not object to offering us hospitality." He carried the vegetables to the fire and dropped them into the kettle. "But we must leave this place as we found it."

Knut nodded. Already the odor of cooking pork teased his appetite. God, he was hungry!

Viotto leaned on the table. "Too bad there is no ale. We could have quite a feast."

"Just like a Finn!" Knut smiled. "Never satisfied. No matter what bounty the good Lord provides, he asks for more."

Viotto chuckled. "Strange! I thought that was a proper description of a Swede!" Their eyes met, and they laughed. But they did not allow their good humor to interfere with their caution. Once more, Viotto bundled himself into his furs. "I will stand watch. Signal when the food is cooked." He tugged his cap over his ears. "I feel trapped with both of us inside."

Knut nodded. Now that he knew the reason for the unexpected bounty, he felt less perturbed. He found a feather duster and swept the table. Then he set out two plates. When he located a barrel at one end of the room, he smiled. Taking a cup from the table, he returned to the barrel and pulled out the plug. The odor of fermenting filled his nostrils. This witch thought of everything! He filled a second cup and returned to the fire.

The first weeks of the journey had been difficult for Knut. Angry at being trapped into taking the journey, he had resented Viotto's calm assumption of the lead. Every waking moment he spent in planning his return to the settlement. Had it not been for his awareness that he was not skilled enough in wilderness travel to survive alone, he would have killed his companion.

But very gradually, his feelings had altered. Viotto

talked of his wife and of the man he sought. "Kirsten knows that man, I am convinced of it. I suspect he is the same man who is her benefactor. That was why I took her with me when you went up north. But she ran away from me before I could find him."

Knut found the story of Ruusu's rape and murder infuriating. He had felt outraged that Kirsten's honor had been ruined, that he had been denied the right to introduce her to the pleasures of marriage. But when he tried to visualize her lying dead on the steps of her home, he understood Viotto's anger.

Another experience brought them closer together. Each time they saw the effects of the battles on the farmers, their hatred grew. Finland was destroyed. People lay dead and dying of the plague. Families were stripped of their menfolk, and women, assaulted by the enemy, were left to fend for themselves.

More than once, Knut wished he had a body of men behind him. When he crouched with Viotto as a company of Muscovites marched past, he had to exert all of his control to keep from rushing out with a cry of fury.

Not that he and Viotto never expressed their rage. When they came upon a company of Russian soldiers they were cautious. But when they encountered two or three men traveling alone, they made sure that none of the wanderers lived.

They spoke often of their years of training at Uppsala. Knut had assumed that Viotto was an officer. But he was more complex than that. He had studied at the university. His ancestry, though Finnish, was noble. Knut came to accept Viotto as his equal.

Their greatest bond lay in their mutual goal. Both longed to find Alexei and to see him dead. Their greatest disagreement lay in their assumption as to who would strike the death blow.

Searching for Kirsten presented them with many problems. She was one girl alone, herself seeking a Muscovite officer. But fortune had been with them. Starting from Sirkka's abandoned house, they had headed first toward Turku.

There they had learned only that Colonel Leonidovich

had returned to Russia, where he was settled in the new city of St. Petersburg. Of Kirsten they had heard nothing. They had traveled then to the west. Now, at last, they were on their way toward Helsingfors. If Kirsten was not already dead, she might have traveled that way in search of Alexei.

Knut stirred the soup, inhaling its savor. Was Kirsten hungry? He had heard rumors about a great exodus from Helsingfors. If Kirsten had been captured with the others, she might now be in a prison camp deep in Russia—if she had survived the terrible march. Knut pushed the fear from his mind. She had to be alive!

He leaned back against the stones of the fireplace and let the memory of her beauty wash over him. How could he ever have been foolish enough to deny her? She was his affianced! Pure and innocent in spite of her hardships, she had trusted him to save her. And what had he done? He had rejected her love. He had taken her like any whore, and he had threatened her with a life of lasting shame.

No wonder she had run from him and believed that her only security lay with her Muscovite lover. But she would understand when he explained how he felt. She would not remain with Alexei once she knew her rightful husband had come to his senses. He would show proper contriteness, of course, and he would vow endless devotion. Then he would take her back to Sweden.

And what if they could not cross the water and the land bridge was still guarded by the Muscovites? Then he would fight! And this time he would win. He would lead the men to a glorious victory. Under his leadership, they would start the liberation of Finland.

He felt a glow of anticipation. Yes, that was what he would do. It would be cowardly for him to rush back to his father. He and Kirsten would return with Viotto and change the course of history. His name would be remembered as long as men called Finland home.

They would be rewarded by King Charles for their bravery. Maybe, as a sign of his appreciation, the king would make Knut the new governor of the land. And then, at last, Kirsten would have the reward she deserved for her long suffering. As the wife of the leading citizen of Finland, she would be honored wherever she went.

He thought again of her soft blonde hair as it cascaded down over her shoulders. He saw her delicate face, aglow with the light of love, lying beneath him. He felt an ache in his groin.

"God! How I miss her! How I want her!" They would have to find her soon, or he would be forced to seek other means of relieving his needs. He rose and stirred at the pot. Maybe there would be some women in Helsingfors. He needed one soon, or his lust would eat him up.

He remembered with a wave of regret how he had been stirred to anger at Kirsten's sensual response to his caresses. She had shown no virginal fear of his approach, and he had known then that he was denied the joy of introducing her to passion. The realization had filled him with resentment. But now her open acceptance of his embrace seemed wonderful. Thinking of it, his longing grew. What a marvelous woman she had become, so sensuous, so seductive, so passionate! "When I find her, I will never let her go. Never!" He jabbed fiercely at the sizzling pork. "And I will kill the bastard who destroyed her innocence!"

Viotto settled against a tree, well within the shelter of the woods. Smoke curled from the chimney, and the air was filled with the fragrance of burning wood and roasting pork. He pressed his hands against his empty stomach. Soon the meat would be done. But now he had to keep watch. If any others caught the odor of the fire, he might have to fight.

The food had been discovered at a most propitious moment. He and Knut had not eaten in days, for they had come through an area overrun with the plague, and they had not dared to approach the few survivors to ask for assistance.

He blew on his fingers, watching his breath billow out before him. God, it was cold! Inside the cottage was warmth, food, and a bed. He had not slept in a bed in far too many months.

He and Knut had spent many nights huddled together for warmth, their fur robes draped over them to keep their body heat from escaping. And the closeness had rubbed away the antagonism he had initially felt toward the proud Swede.

Knut spoke of his dreams as they walked side by side, and as he talked, Viotto came to understand his ambitions. Knut was not as irresponsible as he had first appeared to be. He had not tried deliberately to ruin the colony. The son of a prominent Swedish official, he had grown up under the shadow of an illustrious father. He had a burning need to show his own worth. And his army training pointed the way toward achieving his ends.

Victory above all! Valor in the field! He had to gain a place for himself through his own skill and bravery. He was driven by a need to show his valor, and this forced him to seek new ways to overcome the enemy. He would try again. And if he failed, he would not be discouraged. He would never cease his efforts until he triumphed or lay dead.

Viotto sighed. How could he hate a man for such glorious ambitions? And if his friends had fallen in that first battle, it was not as innocents, led to the slaughter. They were seasoned soldiers. The enemy might have come upon them unexpectedly, but they had chosen to remain and fight. He shamed their memory when he thought of them as victims. They had fought an unequal battle and they had lost. But they might have won.

He knew now that he and Knut were not far apart in their aims. Both dreamed of the day when the Muscovites would be pushed from Finland. Their disagreement lay in how they would reach their goal. And who was to say which way was the best? Men who fought as he directed, striking quickly and vanishing into the woods, lived to fight again, that was true. But they were never in a position to achieve great victories. A gnat might annoy a horse, but it would hardly kill it.

He located a tree stump and sat down on it, slapping his arms around his chest to increase the circulation. A light snow had begun to fall. He tried to visualize Kirsten trudging through the white countryside, but he could not picture her in such an inhospitable surrounding. She was

276

brightness and light. The night had been warm when he took her in his arms, and she had been beautiful in the pale moonlight.

He felt a familiar ache when he thought of her delicate white skin and her wide blue eyes. How could he have taken her with such rude force? What had possessed him, that he invaded her as if she were a whore?

He knew the answer. He had thought of her as nothing more. He had failed to recognize her helpless innocence and her fright. And only when she stood gazing at the burning house, watching all that she knew and loved go up in flames, did he admit his commitment to her happiness. He had shamed her, as had every other man she met. He had taken her body and ignored her needs. When he rushed in to save the portraits of her parents, it had been with the hope that he might show his penance for his sin. He did not wish to be like the other men, wanting her and giving no security.

He knew as he thought it that there was one who had offered her more. Alexei, the man who had been responsible for the death of Ruusu, was also the only man who had comforted Kirsten. She looked to him for protection. "Pray God she found what she sought!"

He started at the sound of his own voice. He had tried to face the possibility that Kirsten had been killed, and he had been unable to accept such a fate. He needed no portrait to bring her delicate features to mind: her fair skin, smooth as alabaster and translucent as the moonlight; her trusting eyes, deep and frightened, yet filled with a faith that could not be shaken. She had been terrified of him. And then, under his hands, her fear had turned to wild, abandoned passion.

He groaned at the memory. Early in his journey he had admitted that he no longer sought Kirsten so that he might kill her protector. He remembered her with a greater poignancy than he did the face of his bride, Ruusu. He needed her, as he had never needed the trusting farm girl who had died, his unborn child still in her belly.

He remembered Kirsten's touch, the feel of her skin against his own. That one night had sealed his affection.

He wanted her for his own. But he had been too pig-headed to heed the message of his heart until it was too late.

On this point only he could not converse with Knut Ivarson. The Swede spoke of Kirsten as if she were already his wife. He had no doubt that she would run to his arms if—when—they found her. But Viotto knew that he could not accept such an arrangement.

Yet he hesitated to argue about Kirsten's fate until they knew for certain that she was still alive. He took comfort from his memory of her response to his caresses and from the look he had seen on her face when she bade the injured Knut farewell. There had been no love in her eyes then, only resentment and a deep disappointment.

Knut appeared at the door of the cottage and waved his arms. Immediately, Viotto rose and left his hiding place. No unwanted visitors had disturbed his reverie.

Yet he remained alert throughout the meal. They laughed a bit from the ale, and in the end they drank too much, but even then they did not ignore the dangers that surrounded them. When they rose from the table, Knut lifted his musket to his shoulder. "You sleep first, Viotto. I will stand watch."

Viotto nodded. When Knut left the cottage, he threw himself onto the bed. He was asleep before Knut reached his post.

Chapter 28

The sun was barely touching the treetops when Viotto, his watch ended, stepped into the cottage and roused his companion. The night had been uneventful, and he had even dozed as he sat overlooking the clearing. Knut had banked the fire before he lay down to sleep, and the odor of burning wood and roast pork had slowly dissipated.

With the rising sun, his spirits rose. Breakfast had been filling. They carried a small jar of ale in their packs, and what was left of the pork had been divided between them and stuffed in their knapsacks. With a full belly and a good night's sleep, Viotto felt more optimistic than he had in many days.

They came upon the next cottage unexpectedly, long before noon. Knut approached the cottage cautiously, but he was startled nevertheless when the door swung open and a woman appeared. She approached him with open arms. "Arne! Oh, Arne! You've come home!"

He paused, and then he saw her eyes. They were fixed on his face with a strange wildness. She was mad, totally mad! He cast a quick glance toward Viotto's hiding place and then, with a shrug, let the woman lead him into the house. If he did not appear within a reasonable length of time, Viotto could come and rescue him.

The woman almost pushed him into a chair and proceeded to set an empty bowl before him. Then, with a smile of happiness on her twisted face, she began to spoon out some imaginary gruel from an empty container. "Sit, Arne! Sit and eat. I have kept breakfast for you."

Knut took his spoon and pretended to eat. "Ma'am, I am searching for a girl named Kirsten. Has anyone by that name passed your cottage?"

"Kirsten? Your sister's name is Kerttu. I know no Kirsten."

"You're sure? Has no young woman passed by here recently?"

"Kerttu visited me a few months ago. But she ran away. I tried to protect her from the Muscovites, but she ran away." The old woman was weeping. "She ran away, and I don't know when she will be back. I tried to help her, I tried!" Suddenly, her expression changed. Her eyes grew dreamy, and she stared before her as if he were no longer in the room. "Kerttu is so lovely! The Muscovites would take her for sure. She had to be saved. I had to . . ." Her right arm was moving up and down, and Knut realized that she was thrusting a nonexistent knife into a long-dead breast. He stared at the woman with growing horror. She had killed her own daughter to save her from the Muscovites and she had gone mad from the memory.

He rose and pushed his way to the door. "Ma, I must go out and feed the animals. Keep my gruel warm. I will be back."

As soon as he was outside, he began to run. When he reached Viotto's side, he was panting. "Quickly! We must leave this place. The woman is mad. But I have learned something. Kirsten was here, I am sure of it!" Half dragging Viotto back to the road, he told what he had surmised from what he heard.

Viotto listened in silence. The girl the mad woman spoke of could have been anyone. Yet, he, like Knut, felt light-hearted. It had to be Kirsten! And so he hurried on, unmindful of the cold, refusing to allow the doubts that crowded in to destroy his optimism.

They entered Helsingfors the following day. Viotto was telling a story about his adventures with Halle and Tuomas, but he grew silent as they approached the quiet streets.

The town was abandoned. Houses stood open and empty. Furniture lay in piles near the unlocked doors. Yet there were some signs of life. Dogs, half-wild and starving, slinked through the shadows.

The two men had heard the story of this unhappy town many times as they approached its abandoned houses. The people had been duped, first by one of their own, who had quieted their worries with stories of God's salvation, and then by the Muscovites themselves, who allowed many farmers to enter the town and who then threw a cordon around it. Trapped between the enemy and the sea, the people had capitulated without a fight, though some had drowned in a final abortive attempt to flee.

Viotto was certain that Kirsten had reached this village. "I have no proof, I know that. But I have a feeling about her. She was a determined woman. And she might have hoped that Alexei would be in charge of the capture."

"You think she knew the Russians were planning to make all the villagers prisoners?"

Viotto shrugged. "You and I would have expected it. Maybe she did not. I don't know. But we have so little to give us any direction. She could be anywhere. She could be dead! But we cannot search everywhere, and we may never know if she is dead. The best we can do is to start somewhere. And I plan to begin here, in this city of disaster. These people were taken to Russia, and Kirsten wanted to go there. It is enough for me."

Knut frowned. There was no logic to Viotto's argument. But there was no better route to take. At least they had something to do.

They turned a corner, and a stench assailed their noses. Viotto cursed, his eyes fixed on the harbor. The source of the smell was the docks. The shallow bay was covered with ice and piles of drifted snow, but nature could not conceal the horror that man had wrought. Dogs and fish had done much to decimate the remains of the dead, but some bodies still floated, half-eaten, in the shallow water.

Knut put a kerchief over his nose. "We should search there."

"I will not accept the possibility that she is dead! It would be too horrible!"

"Yet—" Knut seemed surprised at Viotto's emotion. "If she is down there, we must find her. For then we can return to the battle."

Viotto had forgotten Knut's preoccupation with fighting. He had seen so much death, so much horror. Villages wiped out by plague, men killed or maimed, women, even young girls, victims of rape and assault—and now this. It was enough! No land was worth the death of its people!

Knut had begun the descent, his kerchief pressed over his nose and mouth. Following suit, Viotto trotted behind. Knut was right. They had to examine this disaster more closely.

They abandoned the task when they realized the extent of decay that had taken place. Knut's face was drained of color. "God forbid that she was among them. We will never know."

Viotto hurried up the street. He did not look again at the horror that filled the bay, but he took his time searching the empty houses. In one he found a rotten body of an old woman, who had evidently died as the Muscovites approached. They found the corpse of an infant in the street, its flesh torn from its body by dogs. And everywhere they found bits of clothing.

Suddenly, Knut pulled a scarf from a snow bank. "Viotto, look! I am certain this belonged to Kirsten. Do you recognize it?"

Viotto studied it in silence. Kirsten had worn a scarf when she ran from her home, and she had taken it with her when she escaped from his niece. But was this the one? He looked up into Knut's eager eyes. "Yes, I think it is. I am sure it is! Let us hurry. I am sure she is still ahead of us."

Knut smiled for the first time since entering the city. "Thank God! She left the town alive." He did not continue. They both knew that she still might not have survived. They had seen prisoners marching toward Russia, and they had picked their way among the corpses that littered the road after they were gone.

It was Viotto who took the scarf and stuffed it into his

knapsack. "Come. We're wasting time here. This city fills me with horror. It is a crypt. I can endure no more of it—it smells as foul as the breath of the devill"

They traveled the rest of the day without meeting a soul. When they slept, it was in a shallow cave Viotto found under a burned barn. Knut had difficulty falling asleep, for the visions of destruction he had seen as he walked through the city remained to haunt him. When sleep did at last come, he dreamed that Kirsten was struggling in a frozen pond, her hands reaching out to him for help. But he was too far away to be of assistance.

Viotto fought his own battle of despair. He could not believe that Kirsten could survive the march to Russia. She was too delicate, too fragile to endure such misery, and far too beautiful. The soldiers would not allow so lovely a creature to remain untouched.

He raged inwardly at the thought of her fair body being misused by the rough guards, and his urge to kill them all doubled. Convinced that their search was hopeless, he knew he should turn back. The settlement up north needed them.

But he could not follow the road of logic. He realized now that he could give up the dreams he had shared with Ruusu because he had seen her lying dead. He knew that that life was over. But in spite of the evidence that pointed to Kirsten's death, he had no solid proof. His hope would not leave him until he knew for certain.

He wondered if he would ever forget her deep blue eyes, her beautiful, soft body, and the unconquerable spirit that drove her to strive for good even in the midst of destruction. She was like no woman he had met before. When he fell into a fitful sleep, he held her once more. And he knew that she had become a part of him that he could never put aside, even if he saw her body dead before him. When he wakened, he had once again faced and acknowledged the truth of his search. He cared not at all about Alexei. He wanted only one thing: to find Kirsten.

At midday, they saw an old woman crouched near the side of the road. She seemed unaware of their arrival, so intent was she. Viotto approached slowly. In her hand was a handmade net. She was holding it over a rabbit hole.

283

"Go away! You will frighten my game!" The voice crackled with age.

Viotto paused. "Old lady, your game has gone out another hole. You will never catch a rabbit in that way."

She looked up at him, and he saw the despair and hunger in her face. "I must catch food! My daughter is dying."

Immediately, Viotto was alert. "Dying? Of the plague?"

"No! God forbid!" The old woman made an awkward sign of the cross. "She escaped from the soldiers that were taking her into Russia. I have no food with which to fill her belly."

Viotto reached into his leather pouch and pulled out one of his pork bones. "Here, old one. You need not seek rabbits this day. You can chew the meat from the bone, and you can make soup for your daughter. Eat. I must know about that march."

The hag's eyes lit up when she saw the food. But when she held the bone in her hands, she turned and ran into the woods. With a muffled curse, Viotto followed. Knut ran close behind.

The old woman did not stop until she reached a wooden lean-to deep in the woods. Viotto and Knut gathered the dryest wood they could find for her fire, and helped her fill an old kettle with snow. Only when the soup was cooking did she consent to listen to their questions.

"It was a terrible sight! The weak died as they walked, and they were stripped of their clothing by those who lived. My daughter . . ." She stared into the dark interior of the shelter. "My daughter was attacked by the soldiers and left for dead. I found her lying naked, half frozen from the cold. She is still not well. God only knows if she will ever be fully right again!"

The two men nodded in sympathy. Viotto continued. "Old lady, we are looking for a woman we think was in that march. Would your daughter be able to help us?"

The old woman shook her head. "I do not think so. She does nothing but stare before her, as if the angel of death had already come to free her from her misery. But you may ask. I owe you that, in thanks for the food."

Viotto nodded, and before Knut could move ahead of him, stooped and entered the lean-to. The younger woman lay on a pallet of furs on a litter made of dry branches. She did not move as he approached her bed, but he thought he saw a trembling shake her as he drew near. He paused. "Do not be afraid. I have not come to hurt you. We have brought food, and your mother is preparing it now."

The trembling seemed to stop, but the eyes were on him now, filled with undisguised fear.

"I need information from you. I am seeking a woman named Kirsten Gustafson. I think she might have been in Helsingfors." He saw the trembling start again, and he stopped.

When the figure on the bed grew still again, he continued. "Please, I must know. Was there a woman by that name who entered Helsingfors before the soldiers came?"

For what seemed an age, the gaunt face remained still. Then, slowly, the lips began to move. "Kirsten? She warned us of the danger, but we would not listen. We are dead. We are all dead!" She burst into sobs.

The old woman appeared at Viotto's side. "Look what you have done! You have made her cry. Thank God! You have made her cry!" She knelt beside the pallet and lifted the frail creature into her arms. Keening loudly, she rocked back and forth, tears of joy and sorrow running down her cheeks. "You have brought my daughter back to me. Thank God!"

Viotto backed slowly from the hut. He pulled another bone from his knapsack and dropped it into the kettle. Then, with a signal to Knut, he returned to the road.

When they were again on their way, he told Knut what he had heard. "She was alive when she left Helsingfors." He could not conceal the relief in his voice. "At least we have that. She was alive and she warned the people of their danger. Maybe we will never learn why they ignored her." He felt fear and apprehension returning. "We must search the sides of the road carefully now. She might . . ." He could not complete his thought. His heart would not allow him to admit that she might yet be dead.

Knut flushed when Viotto began to speak. But his first joy at learning that they were, in truth, on Kirsten's trail was lost in his sudden awareness that Viotto had more than his avowed reason for searching so faithfully. Viotto loved her, too! He felt anger boil within him. That meant only one thing—Viotto had taken her. Viotto, the man who professed such nobility!

His hand touched his dagger, and he pulled it from his belt. "You will go no further! Stop now, and face your judgment!"

Viotto turned, immediately alert. "Knut? What are you doing? What are you talking about? We cannot kill each other! If we fight between ourselves, we will surely not live to rescue Kirsten."

"That is what you want, isn't it? You want Kirsten for yourself! What a stupid fool I have been, that I did not see!" He held the dagger out before him. "Fight me now! I will kill you, but first I will hear it from your own lips. Admit it! You took her! You the defender of innocence, the protector of women! You who have shamed me because of my need for a female! You have been lying!"

Viotto braced himself and then, suddenly, kicked out at Knut's wrist. The dagger flew into the air and landed in the snow. Immediately, Viotto was upon Knut, grabbing his hands and pulling his arms behind his back. When he had Knut in his control, he began to speak.

"Yes, I cannot deny it. But I had not intended to tell you."

"No, of course not!" Knut snarled in frustration. "You could not have lived long enough to see her again had I known of your perfidy! And to think that I have allowed myself to accept you as an equal, as a friend!"

"Damnation! Can you not hear?" Viotto moved suddenly, throwing Knut against a snowbank. "We may have reason to fight, that I do not know for certain. But we cannot fight now unless we are willing to leave Kirsten with the Muscovites. One man alone will never rescue her. We must work together." He watched Knut sharply, and only when he saw that the man no longer planned to attack him did he rise from his wrestling stance. "What

286

right have we to decide for Kirsten? When we find her, she can choose between us."

"You are truly depraved. Can you not understand? You have treated the woman I am to marry like a whore. What kind of a creature are you? Have you Finns no sense of honor? Do you give your woman to any man who wants her? Well, I have a more noble sense of pride! I expect that my woman will be mine and mine alone!"

"And what of the Muscovites? When we do find Kirsten, do you believe that the only man she will have known will be her Alexei? Did you not understand the old woman? Her daughter was taken by the guards as they rested from the march. Can you believe that Kirsten, lovely, beautiful Kirsten, has not faced a similar fate? She may be dead along the road ahead. And if she lived—" He clenched his fists to repress his agony. "If she lived through their torture she will need understanding and love. She will have no honor left."

"How dare you speak so of my bride!" Knut seemed to crumple as he spoke. Then he was sobbing, his face buried in his hands.

Viotto stared at him in silence. He, too, could shed tears when he contemplated Kirsten's probable fate. But he was too filled with anger to cry. He had to know. And if she was dead, he would devote the rest of his life to vengeance.

When Knut grew still, he said, "Knut Ivarson, we are men, not animals. Yes, I love Kirsten! I want her for myself as you want her. But if she is alive when we find her, she must be allowed to make her own decision. If she chooses the Russian, we must let her go. She was a child when last we saw her, but now she will be a woman, capable of making her own choice."

Knut bent down and picked up his dagger. But he did not again point it at Viotto. He tucked it into his belt and began to walk up the road. When Viotto fell in beside him, he began to speak. "I will not forget that you violated my woman. Nor will I forgive what you have done. You are right. We must work together until we find her. But you are wrong to think she will be the one to choose. Her father pledged her to me when we were children. She is a Swede! She is mine!"

Viotto did not reply. When he did speak, he said, "I wonder, Knut Ivarson, lieutenant in the king's army, whether Finland has been wrong all these years. We felt that we were a part of Sweden. You did not give us full equality, but we were too involved in our loyalty to the crown to care about our liberty. We comforted ourselves for our loss of honor by reminding ourselves that Sweden was strong. Under the blue and yellow banner, we were safe from the aggression of the Muscovites. But Finland is being torn apart, and the king we trusted has done nothing to save us."

"Spoken like a true Finn! Why should the king save you when you are not willing to save yourselves? You fought me when I wanted to form another army to attack the Muscovites. You tricked me into this search just to keep me from training the men we found into a company capable of fighting for their own freedom. Do you expect to go about your business and let others defend you? In spite of your crime against Kirsten, I would let you live if I had your word that you would put aside our enmity and help me train the few men who are left. All that matters now is that we fight!"

"You want to give up the search, when we are so close?"

"No! Need I remind you again that she is *my* affianced? But we will have to stop the hunt eventually. We will find her—or we will find her body." His voice broke, but he forced himself to continue. "And when that happens, we will either fight—or we will return to the north country. We have been fortunate so far. We have avoided the Muscovites. Though my heart cried out to kill them, I knew you were right in hiding. As long as we search for Kirsten, our safety comes ahead of our wish to fight. Tell me, will you help me fight the enemy? Or will you face me in defense of Kirsten's honor?"

"When Kirsten is found, I will help you train the men. And we will let Kirsten choose between us."

"She will not make a choice. And when the Russians

288

have been driven from the land, we will settle our personal score."

Viotto nodded. Maybe it was good that his feelings were no longer hidden. Now Knut would be careful of what he said. For the thousandth time, Viotto remembered the expression on Kirsten's face as she saw Knut carried away. *She does not love him!* That thought comforted him.

Chapter 29

Too furious to endure the confinement of his carriage, Alexei dismissed it and walked from Kirsten's residence to his home. The cold air stung his face and cooled down the anger that boiled within him. He knew now that he had left because he had come close to strangling her with his bare hands. "I could have killed her!" He slipped on a spot of ice and stretched out his arms to recover his balance. "I *should* have killed her!"

But if he had killed her she would have suffered very little for her deception. No, death was too swift a punishment. "She belongs on the hill. Ah, to see her face when she has to explain to her countrymen why she no longer has my favor! And the guards! I will tell them they may deal with her as they wish. No more protection, no more special kindness. Maybe they will fill that hungry void within her that drives her to bring strangers into her bed. Deceitful bitch! May she rot in hell!"

He stormed into his house and stamped up the stairs. Vera, his wife, approached him as he entered, but when she saw his face, she bade him a swift good-day and hurried away. He was too preoccupied to notice a strange, satisfied smile on her usually bland face.

He left the house soon thereafter, too restless to read, and hurried to the palace, where work awaited his attention. There he remained for the rest of the day. He worked with a furiousness that was unlike his usual calm order. Plans for a floating bridge, a new concept in engineering, were on his desk when he arrived, and he was able to lose himself in their complications. On an ordinary day that would have given him pleasure. Now he cast them aside impatiently.

Kirsten's face floated before him. She had actually had the gall to act surprised, and she had tried to protest. Was she fool enough to believe that she could still deceive him?

Yet he had behaved more like an animal than a man. He cursed under his breath. Damn! How could he have been so crude? She had cried out in pain when he forced himself upon her—and he had found her struggle exciting. He was no better than the men whose rudeness he had so often cursed.

There was a sharp rap on the door. He looked up. "Yes?"

The door opened, and a lackey looked in. "Master, there is a woman here to see you. She says her name is Katerina."

He rose automatically, his heart pounding. "Katerina?"

"Shall I send her away?"

"No . . ." He sat down again. "No. Send her in. I will see her alone."

"Master, she carries a bundle in her arms. Shall I take it from her?"

"Dammit, fool! Send her in! Do you think I cannot deal with a woman without your help?"

"Yes, master. No, master."

The door closed. When it opened again, Katerina stepped timidly into the room. She clutched a small red package to her breast. She curtsied deeply without advancing.

"Come here, woman! Do you expect me to shout?"

"No, your lordship." She stepped forward.

He observed her with a feeling of growing annoyance. So this was Kirsten's response to his accusations. She sent a woman to beg for mercy. "Speak up! What is it you want? If you have come to intervene for your mistress, you waste my time. The question is settled. Tomorrow she will be carried up the hill."

Katerina crouched lower, as if to ward off a blow. He could see that she was trembling with fear, but she did not succumb to her terror. Some inner compulsion drove her. She would speak, even if he had her killed for her trouble.

She paused when she reached his desk, and she shoved the package across its smooth surface. "Master, you must look at these. My lady had no chance to explain. The young men who came to the house all carried things like this, messages. She—" Katerina began to straighten up, as if her courage grew as she spoke. "She was so horrified by these messages that she gave them to me to burn. But I kept them. Now I am glad I did, for you can see for yourself that the men who brought them did not come for love."

The bundle lay before him. Alexei stared at it in silence. All of his instincts cried out to grab it, to tear it open, to find proof that he had misjudged his mistress. But he had suffered enough already.

"Please, your lordship, please look at them. She is innocent, I swear it! I have been with her night and day. I swear on my immortal soul that she has done nothing to earn your anger."

He reached out and touched the parcel. The red cloth fell away, and the three packets spilled out. His eyes widened in surprise, and he drew himself upright. He knew the pattern on the plush covers, and the seal. There was only one place where they could have originated. His own study!

The packets had been a special gift from the tsar himself at the time of Alexei's appointment. And in the flush of excitement, Alexei had imprinted each one with his seal. His fingers shook as he tore the first one open and withdrew the letter it contained. He kept these packets in a locked drawer in his desk. Only one person might possibly be in a position to steal them—his wife!

The letter opened, and he read the one word written in a careful hand. *Lovers.*

With a curse, he ripped open the other two. The second had a new message, one terrible word: *Whore.* But the third had more. *Whore, prepare for the end!* He stared at the three parchments in horrified silence. He could hear

293

Katerina's breathing, and he knew that she was waiting for him to speak.

His premonition had been true. Vera had not always been the dour, angry woman she was today. Long ago, when he was first wed to her, he had taught her to read and write, though such skills were considered unnecessary for a woman. It had made him proud to have a talented wife, and he had hoped that she might be of eventual value to him because of her unusual abilities.

He abandoned that hope quickly. But she had not forgotten what she had learned, though she used it seldom. Her hand was recognizable. Vera had spelled out those ugly words. She had sent them to Kirsten! She had been the source of the rumors that had driven him mad.

"You swear these are the packets Kirsten received from her visitors?"

"Yes, master! She did not choose to take the warnings seriously. She could not believe that anyone wished to do her harm. Had I not saved them—"

"Yes, yes, you told me. Were there others?"

"Yes, master. But she destroyed them. She would have destroyed these, too. She was shocked by what they said."

"Damn her for a witch!"

Katerina recoiled. "She is not a witch, master! She is a good woman, a woman who has never violated her promise to you!"

Alexei waved his hand impatiently. "I do not speak of Kirsten. Be quiet, while I think." He stared again at the three notes. He had taught Kirsten to read French, the official language of the Russian court. And it had been French that Vera had learned. Unknowingly, he had assisted his wife in her diabolical plan.

Suddenly he was on his feet. "How is she?"

"Very ill, master." He could see her mind working now. She hoped to punish him for his mistreatment of her mistress.

"I will see for myself. Come, I will take you back." He shouted for his lackey. "Order my carriage to the front! Hurry!" Then, with Katerina trailing behind him, he almost ran from the room.

They mounted the great stone steps together, but it was

Alexei who pushed open the door and stepped first into the hallway. He caught a glimpse of his image in the large mirror he had given Kirsten for her birthday, and he grimaced. There was no gift in the world that he could give her to assuage his guilt for this terrible deed!

He tossed his cape on the railing as he ran up the circular staircase that led to her room. "Kirsten!" He barely whispered her name.

Kirsten lay as Katerina had left her, half on her side, her face toward the door. When Alexei appeared, she cowered under the covers, and a small animal-like cry of fear escaped her lips.

He slowed his step as he approached the bed. "Kirsten, my love, you must listen to me. I was wrong! I know it now, and I beg your forgiveness! I swear I did not know what I was doing."

Kirsten did not reply.

"Please." He knew his heart was beating wildly and his face was flushed with emotion. Did she fear that he had returned to do her further injury? "I will explain. I have been subjected to weeks of lies and innuendoes. At first I refused to believe what I heard. I had faith in your fidelity. But it continued, and each time there seemed to be greater proof that you were deceiving me. When at last I could no longer deny the stories that were circulating about you, I went mad. As God is my witness, I did not know what I was doing!"

She did not leave the protection of her covers. "You hurt me! Why did you hurt me?"

He grasped at the bedpost for support. She had said those words long ago, that first time. He had hurt her then, but he had made it up to her. "Kirsten, you must listen. I have had many mistresses before you. You must know that. I am a man of power. My wife has known about them all—or at least most."

He could see that Kirsten was beginning to release her tension. Slowly, he sat on the bed beside her. "She accepted them all without any outward sign of jealousy, for she knew they meant little to me." He inhaled deeply. "I did not know she was wise enough to recognize that you are different."

"Your wife?" Kirsten pushed the covers down from her shoulders. "But you believed what you heard! You did not let me answer you! I was condemned without a chance to defend myself!"

He rested his hand on her arm. Her body was shaking with a fear he had created. He lowered his eyes. "It is my shame, my dearest. My shame and my sorrow. I am an old man, and I love you. But you are so beautiful, so witty and wise! You could have the tsar himself for your lover, if you said the word. How can I believe that you remain faithful to me? Each one of the men who came to you was handsome and virile. What have I to offer when compared to them?"

She crawled from the covers and took him in her arms. "Oh, Alexei! How can you fail to understand me? You give me love and tenderness. You have protected me. You saved me from death, not once, but twice! You are a good man, a kind man. There is no one who deserves my love more than you do. I owe you my entire existence!"

He removed her arms from his shoulders and walked to the windows. There he stood staring into the street. When he faced her again, his expression was filled with sadness. "Oh, Kirsten, can you understand? I do not want thankfulness and admiration from you. I am not satisfied to be a substitute father. I want your passion! I desire nothing greater than to stir you to rapture! And it appears that is the one thing I cannot do. Love, passionate love, is the one thing you cannot give to me." He continued quickly, unwilling to allow her to respond. "You must recognize that I can live with what we have, but only because I cannot live without you."

He began to walk toward the bed. "But it tears at my heart, sometimes, and erodes my pleasure. Knowing that I can never be the lover you deserve makes me easy prey for—all of this!"

He drew her into his arms. She did not resist, though she winced at the pain. "My sweet Kirsten, I pray that you will forgive me for my anger, and for what I have done to you. But you must give me your word that if ever you are confronted with some unexplainable thing such as this, do not hide it from me. Tell me immediately. I may forget, and I may become temporarily angered. But I will remember this day always, and I will listen to what you have to say." He kissed her eyes, her cheeks, her lips. "I fear that Vera will not stop when she knows this attempt has failed. She fears you as she has feared no one before."

He laid her back in the bed and sat once more beside her. "You have caused me to see things I ignored before I knew you. You have stirred my concern for my fellow men, and my desire for peace. With your inspiration, I have convinced the tsar to improve life in all of Russia. And I have dealt harshly with prison guards who mistreat their charges."

She began to speak, but he rested a finger on her lips. "Let me finish, my dear. I know what a worthless labor it is to try to improve the lot of prisoners. I know that the guards forget all I have said as soon as I leave them. But I have at least tried. Maybe, because of you, I have been the first man in power to try to do something for the helpless and the oppressed."

She smiled at his strange combination of humility and pride, but she did not contradict what he said.

"My love for you has changed the face of Russia." He was growing poetic, and she began to relax, assured that things were again as they should be. "Your gentleness overcomes anger. Your love is stronger than hate. That is why Vera resents you so. She will try again to destroy you. But now we are prepared."

He rose and pulled the covers about her shoulders. "I must reward Katerina. By her daring, she has served us both."

He turned then and left the room. When Katerina entered with a bowl of soup, she propped herself up and reached out to hold it. The pain in her body was no longer so terrible. •

"What am I to do, Alexei?" Kirsten dropped beside him on the settee and buried her head in his shoulder. The tears she had suppressed during the ride home from Sonia's party flowed freely now. "What am I to do? Everywhere I go I am greeted with the same taunts. I thought Sonia was my friend, but she is no better than the others.

She asked me—" She raised her head and met his gaze. "She asked me what hidden thing it was that I knew about your past that gave me such power over you. She—everyone—is aware of your anger at me, and—oh, Alexei! What shall I do?"

Alexei stroked her soft hair. It did not please him to see her cry. Yet he had spent many more hours in the past months comforting her than he had spent in pleasure in her bed. He lifted her face to his and kissed her cheeks. "I understand, my love. I have encountered the same kind of stupidity, but with greater subtlety. Even the tsar has asked me what I am hiding, though his question was posed in jest. He finds my predicament amusing. I find it greatly disturbing."

Kirsten wiped the corners of her eyes with her kerchief and forced a smile to her lips. "He is right. We should—I should find this a cause for laughter, not for tears."

Alexei's expression brightened. Maybe Kirsten was at last coming to her senses.

She brushed her cheeks, and he saw with delight that the tears did not return. "Forgive me, Alexei. I know you have said you want a mistress who could give you happiness. I have indulged myself too long. What need have I for other companionship when I have you?"

He nodded and met her upturned lips. It was a generous remark, but not true. He knew she would struggle to retain her spirits. But in spite of her efforts, she would gradually grow morose. She would not cry, but she would not be happy, either.

"I have spoken to Vera. She knows now that I am wise to her scheming. Maybe now it will stop." He watched Kirsten's face closely as he spoke. But she showed no sudden optimism. She had learned to suspect those who did not like her, even when they appeared to be powerless.

Her eyes narrowed. "I have been thinking, Alexei. Surely there is some secret she wants to keep hidden. Maybe I could—Maybe we could use it against her, to keep her silent."

He was on his feet, pacing angrily before her. "No!" His voice resounded through the room. "Never! Kirsten, you must not allow yourself to become like Vera!" He paused before the open window and stared down into the street. Summer had draped the city in a flowered cloak. He thought of Kirsten as she had been in the days just after he found her. She had skipped lightly over the grass, singing songs. Why had she changed? Was it the scheming that surrounded her?

He could not deny the reality of it in her life. When she had gone up the hill regularly, she had had a protection against the intrigue that occupied most of the time of her companions. But now she had no such diversion. Her dancing lessons only increased her self-consciousness, although, where before she had moved with the natural grace of youth, she now walked with controlled elegance.

He turned and drew her into his arms. "Kirsten, my love, be patient. Stay away from your thoughtless friends. I will find a kitten to occupy your solitude."

Her eyes lit up, and for a moment the sight raised his spirits. But when she thanked him politely, he knew he had little time left to him. If he did not do something, he would soon have a mistress who differed in no way from all the other women in St. Petersburg. Kirsten was a strong-minded girl, but even she could not resist their influence forever.

His first duty upon leaving her house was to send his lackey to search for a kitten. His next was to seek a special audience with the tsar.

He came away smiling. Now all that was needed was to begin work on his plan.

Kirsten sat sewing on a sampler. She had felt a brightening of her mood when Alexei spoke of a kitten, but that had passed. Resting the sampler in her lap, she gazed up at the portraits of her parents. In spite of her resolve not to cry, tears crept from her eyes. "Oh, Mama! Will life always be so tedious? Will the days never speed up, so I can again be with you and Papa? Alexei is good to me, but he does not understand why I am sad. It isn't the rumors."

She resumed her embroidery. She had designed the sampler herself, drawing from memory the house in which she had been born. With each stitch, her longing grew stronger.

There had been a time when the luxury in which she lived provided pleasure enough. But that time was past. Luxury alone was hollow. She glanced again at the portrait. "If you can come back, please take care of him for me. Keep him safe, and don't let him forget me!"

She brushed the tears from her cheeks. It would not do to let Katerina see her weeping. She would tell Alexei, and he would worry.

There was a knock on her chamber door, and Katerina entered. "Look, Kirsten! Look what his lordship has sent you!"

The kitten was white, with pink ears that pointed upward and bright green eyes. Katerina held it out awkwardly, and it meowed piteously.

"Oh, what a darling!" Kirsten took the tiny ball of fur in her arms and held it close to her breast. It meowed again, and she cuddled it in her hands. "It's hungry! Quick, Katerina, bring me some meat. Oh, what a sweet little face! Look at its eyes! I think it likes me."

Katerina hurried from the room and returned with two dishes, one filled with water, the other with a mixture of food left over from last night's table. "You must take it into the garden and show it—"

"Yes, Katerina. I know. What shall we call it?" She lifted the kitten up and gazed into its face. Immediately, it began to complain. "I will call it Angel. Where did he find it?"

"It was not easy. There are many who still believe that a cat is a slave of the devil. Kirsten, you must watch it when it is outside. It is quite the fashion for young boys to catch and kill cats."

"How terrible! Back home, we always loved them. They kept our barns free of rats."

Nevertheless, she heeded Katerina's warning. Little Angel grew up indoors, and spent most of her time cuddled on Kirsten's lap. And the mischievous little creature did what Alexei had hoped she would. Kirsten's spells of weeping grew less common. She continued her work on her sampler, but now she smiled at the antics of her pet as the kitten chased her ball of yarn across the rug.

At night the kitten wandered. Kirsten worried at first,

but when little Angel greeted her every morning, she forgot her fears.

Alexei seemed unusually preoccupied in the days that followed. He was busy, Kirsten knew, with the task of putting the tsar's latest plans into effect. But there seemed to be more. At last she decided to confront him.

He arrived, as was his custom, just as she finished her morning toilette, and he lifted the kitten from her bed and sat petting it as he spoke. "Kirsten, my love, it pleases me to see that you are happy once more. What power a small creature like this has, when it can banish the sadness that has oppressed you for so long."

Kirsten sat beside him. "I cannot thank you enough for sending her to me." She stroked the tiny head. "I was afraid, at first, that she would remind me of my other kitten." Her voice brightened. "She does, in a way. But it does not make me sad. Thank you."

He put the kitten on the floor and fumbled with the tie that held her peignoir in place. Kirsten brushed his hands aside and loosed the knot. There would be time to talk later.

He lay beside her at last, panting from the exertion that his passion had inspired. "Have you been bothered by Sonia?"

"No, Alexei. I have not attended her parties. I've been busy with my sampler and with Angel. Have there been new rumors?"

"A few. Katerina tells me there were two young men who tried to see you last week. She stopped them at the door, and delivered their letters directly to me. Vera has begun again, my love. There is no way I can stop her unless I resort to her own wiles. I have been thinking. Would you like to see Finland again?"

Kirsten sat up and stared wide-eyed into his face. "Finland! Oh, Alexei! Is it possible?"

"Of course it is possible. I have been planning for weeks. Prepare yourself. You can take Katerina with you, or you may find a new maid when you are settled."

"When I am settled? You are sending me away?"

"I am going with you. I have received permission from the tsar to inspect the nonmilitary government that has been established in Finland. And I wish you to accompany me. You would not be safe here without my protection. And I have no intentions of giving you to Peter. He has enough women of his own."

She was out of bed now, bouncing with delight. She picked up the kitten, and began to pull gowns from her wardrobe. At last she turned to Alexei, who had not moved from the bed. "Oh, what shall I take with me? Where will we be? Am I to travel with you on your inspection? When are we leaving? The snows start in October, sometimes. We should hurry!"

He chuckled in delight. How good it was to have Kirsten her old self again! "We will leave within the week. Unfortunately, you will have to travel with me, for the house I have under construction for you will not be finished. My sweet one, there is a settlement of Finns who are loyal to Russia close to the border. It is there you will live, after our journey is completed."

Kirsten stared at him in surprise. "Then you *are* sending me away! Why? I am not sad any more!"

"No, my love, I could never send you away. I am only moving you away from Vera and from the intrigue of the court. You do not belong here. You are too lovely, too unspoiled. I want you to remain that way. I will visit you every week, for it is only a short ride. Please, my dear, it will be better for us both."

He saw that she was still troubled. "Don't worry about it now. We will be together for the entire year, at least. I intend to make a very thorough inspection."

Now that she knew she would be leaving the city, Kirsten found herself liking it more. She resumed her shopping, and when she encountered her former friends, she greeted them warmly, unheeding of their whispers. She carried Angel with her wherever she went. Katerina held the kitten while Kirsten tried on new clothes. And both mistress and maid ignored the looks that were pointed in their direction when the cat's presence was noted.

Trunks were purchased and carried up to her chambers. Kirsten spent much of her time deciding what she would take with her and what would be sent to her new home to await her arrival.

When the task was at last finished, she looked about for Angel. The white ball of fur was nowhere to be seen.

"Katerina, have you seen the kitten?"

"No, not for a time. She's probably in the garden, digging at the flowers. Shall I get her?"

"No. I'll find her myself. She comes more quickly when I call her."

The garden was empty. Kirsten began to search the flowerbeds. Sometimes the cat crouched among the blossoms.

When she saw Angel, she did not realize what had happened. The kitten lay on her side, as if she had fallen asleep. Kirsten bent to pick her up.

"Katerina! Oh, my God! Katerina! My little Angel is dead!"

She was holding the small body in her hands when Katerina reached her side. Angel's throat had been cut, and she had been thrown into the garden to die.

Alexei arrived the following morning. He had a closed carriage for himself and Kirsten, and a wagon for her luggage. With Katerina's help, he led the stunned girl to the waiting conveyance.

Kirsten said nothing as she watched her trunks being carried out. She had said her farewell to her little pet before sunrise. Alexei climbed into the carriage and took his seat beside her. "Away, now!" He waved at the coachman. Slowly, the horses began to move.

Kirsten glanced back then at the house that had been her home in exile. She had believed, for a time, that she would never leave it. Now she wanted nothing more than to forget it, to wipe its image from her memory. St. Petersburg, the heavenly city by the sea, was a place of horror and hate.

"Goodbye, Angel!" she thought. "I will never forget what you meant to me."

And then she turned her face forward, toward the land she had once called home.

eyes

Chapter 30

"Wake up, Kirsten, my love! We have crossed the border into Finland. You are home once more!"

Kirsten opened her eyes and met Alexei's eager glance. She smiled gently, and gazed through the window of the carriage. The view was little changed from what she had seen before she closed her eyes: flat land, covered with verdant grasses, a few clumps of birch trees. The road dipped slightly occasionally, and once they even reached a high ridge that overlooked a deep blue lake. She had traveled through this land before, as a prisoner on her way to Russia. But then everything had been covered with snow.

"Are we stopping at my new home?"

"No, my dear. Not now. We passed the road already but I decided not to wake you. There is little to see. I fear the builder is far slower than I had expected." He saw the disappointment in her face. "I'm sorry. I would much prefer to surprise you when it is finished. Are you unhappy with me?"

"No, of course not. I can wait. Are there more trees around it than along the road? I loved the woods surrounding me, as they did when I lived near Turku."

"Then we will plant more trees. But if there are not enough, I hope it will not make you too sad. I felt it was more important for me to have you near me than for you to have your home in the middle of a forest."

She flushed. "I'm sorry, Alexei. You are more important to me than trees." She settled back and gazed into the gathering shadows. "Will we stop at an inn?"

"Yes, there's one a few kilometers from here. We will eat soon."

When he fastened his attention on the road, she breathed a sigh of relief. She felt a sudden need to be alone. The memories she had repressed during her months in St. Petersburg were beginning to return.

Back in the Russian capital, she had been able to dismiss her dreams of Viotto and, in time, to repress them altogether. Or almost. When she did think of him, it was as he had been that night before the fire, when they shared her mother's bed.

And later, too, the following morning. He had rushed into the fire to save her mementos. He had been forceful then, but he had also been kind.

Now other things about him were coming back: his burning anger, his relentless search for vengeance. "Alexei, maybe after all it would be best if I did not stay in Finland. Surely there is some town near St. Petersburg where I could live and where you could visit me. There are men here who seek your death."

He leaned back abruptly and laughed. Now that they were away from his wife, he was again the lighthearted lover she had known before. But she could not share his laughter. This time there were important problems. She had to convince him to take her seriously.

When he regained control, he met her gaze. "Oh, my dearest, you worry unnecessarily. I have lived a long time, and I have made enemies. I know how to protect myself!"

She took his hand. "Please, Alexei, do not mock me. I am serious." She had avoided the subject of his safety as long as they remained in St. Petersburg. But now it was necessary that she speak.

"Please listen to me. There is a man in Finland who is searching for you. He has vowed to kill you. If word gets out that I am living in Finland and you are visiting me, he will come. He will learn where you are, and he will kill you."

Alexei heard far more than her words. He saw the

306

quiver in her lips when she spoke of the unknown assailant. He could tell that there was much she was leaving unsaid.

"Kirsten." He took her hands and forced her to meet his eyes. "You have been hiding something from me. I have asked you to speak about it before, and you have always remained silent. Is it possible that you are ready to tell me now?"

She tried to lower her eyes, but he forced her to meet his gaze. "No, Alexei, there is nothing. It is just that I worry about you."

"Worry about me? Why, if you do not know that there is some specific danger? Kirsten, you must tell me. I know you have more to say about what transpired before I found you than you have divulged so far. Please, speak."

"I . . ." She hesitated. The words seemed to stick on her tongue. "When I reached the coast, after—that night— Knut was injured defending me against an attack by some renegades. I told you that they left him for dead, and that we were rescued by some Finnish soldiers going up north."

She paused. It was too painful! She could not speak of those days. Viotto had treated her so cruelly. He had despised her, and she had been so frightened. But she had to continue. "Their leader brought me back to Turku. He—" She forced herself to go on. Alexei's safety depended on his knowing. "His wife had been raped and killed by Muscovite soldiers."

"But that was commonplace at that time. Had he been victorious, he would have taken Russian women. And many would have died." He frowned at the memories that rushed in. "It is a terrible thing, I agree. But it is part and parcel of battle."

She did not want to continue. But now that she had begun, the words spilled out, as if removed from her control. "She was hurt very badly before she died, and his unborn child died with her. He found a piece of a scarf on a fence near the body, and he was certain it belonged to the colonel who had permitted the outrage to occur." She paused. What had this to do with Alexei? Was it possible that she had begun to believe Viotto's mad accusations?

307

"He was searching for the colonel who tore his sash?" Alexei spoke very quietly. "Did he describe where the woman was? And the farm, was it near Turku?"

Kirsten was screaming inside. No! He could not be the man, not her Alexei! "Yes. Just east of the city."

"And the sash, it was blue? And it hung on a fence near the gate to the barnyard?"

"Yes." She wanted him to stop. But he did not heed her unspoken plea.

"She was left to die at the door to her house?"

"Yes." Kirsten wondered that he could not hear her heart pounding. "Please, Alexei. I know it could not have been you! There were other colonels in the forces that approached Turku."

"But no other with a torn sash. No, Kirsten, I was the man. But you are right that I did not approve of what my men did. I had allowed them to march ahead of me, for I was aware of their eagerness to reach Turku. Kirsten, you must understand, not all officers are in charge of their men at all times. I was not the best of officers. I never had much heart for war."

He saw the hurt in her face. "I tried to stop them, but I arrived too late. They left her on my command—but—" He knew he could never explain. "Thank God such acts have ceased! Most of the soldiers have returned to Russia, and Finland is at peace again."

Kirsten barely whispered her reply. "It still continues in the prison camps. I never told you, but when I went up the hill to celebrate the Lucia Festival, the only virgin I could find was a child of five. All the older girls had been—taken—by the guards."

"Ah, but that is in the prison camps! I have already explained to you that it is impossible to regulate the behavior of the guards continuously. But here in Finland, things are back to normal. All reports indicate that farming is again encouraged, that families are working undisturbed on tilling the soil." He gazed out the window, and Kirsten marveled that he could not see what he passed.

The farm houses still stood empty. The fields were still unplowed. No crops waved in the summer breeze. Alexei might have been told that Finland was back to normal, but she could see that little had changed.

He frowned suddenly. "Is that all you have hidden all these years? That a man you met wishes me dead?" His eyes pierced into her heart, tearing away any chance she had to pretend that she was finished. "What is it about this man that caused you to remain silent? Do you fear that, knowing of his search for vengeance, I might have him killed?"

She shook her head. That had never been her fear. Alexei was too kind, and Viotto had proven that he could care for himself.

When Alexei did not press her for an answer, she let her thoughts drift to Viotto. Immediately, the vision of his strong, firm features flashed before her. She blanched. What if she met him now? Would he still try to kill Alexei? If he did, she would have to stop him!

Maybe he would not even remember her. She felt a wave of relief. He probably had forgotten her altogether. Even when he held her in his arms, he had spoken the name of his dead wife. She had known it then, and she could not deny it now. Hatred had scarred him forever. He had no room in his heart for love. All he could think of was revenge.

She should have met him long ago, before the war began. The thought brought a smile to her lips. His sister had told of watching the Gustafson carriage roll past their farmhouse. He had seen her then, and she had been far above him.

And now? Now his anger barred the door to love.

She became aware that Alexei's eyes were burning into hers. When he spoke, his voice was quiet, as if he were deep in thought. "So that is how it is! I thought, all these years, that you did not love me because I was old. I struggled to maintain my youth, to remain as eager for life as I had been when I was a lad. But it never made a difference. You were always so gentle, so accepting. I felt all along that you were not giving yourself to me fully."

She felt a sudden alarm. But when she met his eyes, she saw no anger, only a great sadness. He continued, as if he were speaking to himself, "Now, at last, I know. It was not me, or what I did or did not do. It was not that you thought of me as old. You did not think of me at all! Your heart was already taken. You learned true passion in another's arms."

She began to protest, but he held up his hand to quiet her. "Please, Kirsten, do not tell me another lie. You have been as loyal to me as you possibly could, under the circumstances. But I think I have always known there was something you kept hidden. I know now that though I had your maidenhead, there was another who awakened you to rapture and ecstasy."

He stared at the dark trees. The inn lay ahead, and soon he would hold her in his arms. Did he want her still?

He knew the answer. He wanted her however he could get her!

"So he is the man who wishes to kill me. I wonder if he has any idea how passionately I long to run my sword through his heart!"

Chapter 31

Viotto leaned heavily on his staff and gazed out from under the cowl of his robe. There had been times during their journey when he and Knut put aside their disguises and walked upright. But when they approached Muscovite strongholds, they hid their swords in wrappings around their legs, tucked their daggers into their belts, and assumed again the roles of old men, exhausted from kilometers of walking.

Knut drew alongside his companion. "How far is it to the Russian border?"

"I believe not much more than thirty kilometers. The inn ahead is one of the last before we reach Russia."

"I would trade my weapons for a chance to sleep in a real bed this one night." Knut rubbed his shoulder. "I find it far more tiring to walk bent like this than to fight a dozen battles."

"We have no money. But I share your wish for some comfort, and for shelter. Have you noted the greater freedom these peasants near the border seem to have? There seems little enmity between them and the Russians."

"It is common knowledge at home that the eastern Finns share more with the Russians than with their countrymen. They even cling to the icons and domed churches of their neighbors."

"Maybe we can put this to our advantage. If there is

less antagonism to natives here, maybe the innkeeper will allow us to sleep in the stables."

Knut moved down the road. "Come, then. It is growing dark. I have no wish to spend another night in a cave."

The ancient building that stood alongside the road showed the ravages of war. Many of the wooden slats of the fence had been torn down by passing Russian soldiers for use as firewood. The inn, its roof patched with roughly hewn shingles, had been allowed to stand only because of the service it provided to traveling dignitaries.

The sign, Wayfarer's Rest, hung from a post that had been tilted by the heavy snows, and the lettering was so faint as to be almost unreadable. It protruded over the road with such precariousness that Viotto wondered how coachmen, turning in for shelter, had avoided losing their heads.

The inn, like the fence, was a dull brownish grey, weathered through heavy snows and pounding rains and bleached by the relentless summer sun. It occupied one side of the courtyard. On the opposite side of the manure-strewn clearing was the barn.

The two men paused as they entered the courtyard, and Viotto gestured toward the littered ground. "I believe we are in luck. This innkeeper must be short of help." He looked sharply at Knut. "You must let me do the talking. Your accent might be noticed."

Knut nodded sullenly. "You think you have none? You are as much out of place here as I."

"Please." Viotto lowered his voice. "We must not argue again. I share your wish that we could separate. But we have agreed that we have a greater chance of rescuing Kirsten—when we find her—if we remain together. I cannot hold you because you have learned to deal with the wilderness. So now it must be our love for Kirsten that keeps us together—as it remains the cause of our dissension."

"You need not fear that I will leave you. If you find her, I will be beside you. She will hear no lies from you regarding me!"

"Good. But we have attracted the attention of the stableboy. Come on now, before we arouse any suspicions."

Viotto pulled his cowl forward and limped toward the door of the inn.

The stableboy, who had begun to approach them, backed away, calling loudly to the innkeeper. That gentleman appeared at the door of the common room, a small riding crop in his hand. "Go away! I have no room!"

Viotto limped forward and gazed up at the well-fed, neatly dressed proprietor. "Please, master, take pity on two old men who have traveled far." He spoke slowly, like a man feeble with age, and his voice wavered. "Surely you have room in your barn for men who can pay for their comfort with labor."

"What can old grandfathers like you do that will be of service to me?"

"Oh, master, we may be bent from age, but that only makes easier the task of cleaning the courtyard of dung. We know animals well, for we have spent our lives on farms. Can you say that we will serve you any worse than that callow youth?" He waved his staff toward the stableboy.

The innkeeper's eyes narrowed. "What reason have you to leave your homes? I can tell you are not from this region."

Knut cast an angry glance toward Viotto, but he remained silent. Viotto bobbed politely. "Our daughters were taken by the Muscovites and marched this way. We seek them."

"Your search is foolish! You would be better to return to your farms and raise food once more. I speak from authority. The Russians grow angry at the stubbornness of the farmers. If you continue to refuse to raise crops, they will bring in their own people and take your land from you!"

Viotto peered out from under his hood. The innkeeper was a stout man with a rotund face and a protruding belly. If there had ever been a time when he went hungry, that time was long past. Now he catered to the Russians, and his reward was a full larder. "You may be right, master. But we are old men, and we might not live to return to our homes. Is this youth your only stableboy?"

"I had more, but two of them vanished but a week ago. Anti here tells me they have run away toward the northland, where all cowards who cannot face the difficulties of life have gathered. Those of us who show strength, remain to keep what we can from the—" He paused, as if suddenly aware that he was telling these two men far more than they needed to know. "I will let you stay, but you must start now to show me I have made a good decision. Anti will give you rakes. When I come out again, I want the ground clean."

"Thank you, master! God will reward you for your generosity!" Viotto bowed again. But Knut remained still. When the innkeeper was gone, he spit angrily.

"My, you act the poor beggar well! I see no reason to thank a man for giving us work. It is food and a bed I desire."

"We will have both. Did you not hear that this great man has need of workers in his stables? He will feed us well, and if we choose, we can remain here."

"I heard only that he will give us rakes. And I saw only that he eats well himself."

"Then look at the stableboy." The lad was approaching, two rakes in his hands. "He is almost as plump as his master!"

Viotto grew silent as the lad approached, and when the rake was put into his hands, he began to work swiftly. Knut moved more slowly at first, but gradually he increased his speed. When the manure was raked behind the barn, they followed Anti into the dimly lit interior.

The months of travel had had its effect on both Viotto and Knut. Their shoes were worn and covered with dirt. Fatigue gave credence to their assumption of age, and the strain of walking with one leg bound to a sword increased their appearance of age. Their hands and arms were grey from the road. They settled clumsily on piles of hay and waited.

When Anti did not leave the barn, Viotto spoke. "Young man, when will we eat?"

The boy looked from Viotto to Knut, as if trying to penetrate the shadows cast by their deep cowls. "We eat after the guests are through. And tonight there is no one in the common room. If no Russians stop, we will get the scraps from the master's table."

"And when will that be given us?"

"Soon, if no guests arrive. If a carriage comes in, we will wait until we have curried the horses. And then our food will be better."

"Yes, and we will be even hungrier than we are now!" Knut shifted angrily.

"Be patient. What prospects for a full belly did we have before we saw the inn?" Viotto lay back, making sure he remained in the shadows. There was a peacefulness about the barn. The odor of fresh manure was not unpleasant. The quiet nickering of the horses reminded him of his days as a farmer—and of Ruusu. And then his thoughts centered on Kirsten. Was his search for her as hopeless as his earlier drive for revenge? Russia was an immense country. How could he hope to find one woman in its endless wastes?

His only hope lay in the importance of her companion—if, in truth, she had found Alexei. But that chance was so slight!

He sat up abruptly. Nothing was gained by such morbid thinking. If he did not continue to believe that Kirsten was alive and safe, there was no reason to continue.

Suddenly, Anti leaped to his feet. "A carriage! I hear a carriage!" He ran to the barn door and threw it open. Only then did Viotto hear the sound. The faint rattle of harness and the clop of hoofs on the hard road grew louder and louder. Anti was right. A carriage was approaching—from Russia!

Viotto and Knut moved more slowly toward the barn door. As they stepped into the yard, the carriage turned in through the gate. It was a well-appointed vehicle, clearly belonging to someone of importance. Sturdy as it was, and built for hard travel, it was etched with gold trim, and over the windows were heavy curtains. The coachman was dressed in a smart livery, as were all the other attendants. Behind the carriage came a wagon, loaded with trunks and large crates. Two soldiers brought up the rear.

The innkeeper appeared at the door of the common room, his arms flailing wildly about. "Aino! Kaisa! Hurry now! Guests are coming! On your toes! Hurry, or you will feel the whip!"

Viotto put a restraining hand on Knut's arm. "Anti can unharness the horses without our help. We will do well to stay away from too close contact with unknown strangers."

Yet, in spite of his awareness of the danger inherent in the presence of so many Russians, he felt a new excitement. Now, at last, they were approaching their goal. If ever they found Kirsten, it would be with the conquerors.

Kirsten leaned forward and gazed up at the darkening sky. The setting sun had tinted the clouds with reds and golds, but now the purples were pushing the bright colors aside. Ahead, the inn seemed like a ghostly structure, leaning hard against the road for support.

Had she passed so large a building on her march to Russia? She could not remember. There had been towns alongside the road and a few isolated buildings. But the prisoners had not been allowed to take shelter in them.

She settled back and let the curtain fall into place. A restlessness she could not explain possessed her.

"We will be stopping here for the night." Alexei took her hand in his. "I do not wish to tire you overly much."

"Thank you. I did not expect the journey to be so fatiguing." She leaned her head back against the cushions. "Besides, I am eager to put my feet on Finnish soil."

"Little Kirsten! Are you happy, then?"

She leaned forward impulsively and kissed his cheek. "Oh, yes, Alexei! Thank you for taking me with you! I had not realized that I missed my homeland so much!"

As she spoke, the coachman cried out, and the horses turned into the courtyard. Amid much noise and chattering, the carriage drew to a stop.

Immediately, there was a bouncing as the coachman leaped to the ground and tugged at the door. It opened with a smoothness that proved the quality of workmanship that had gone into the construction of the vehicle. The liveried servant stood with his arm outstretched, waiting for Kirsten to step down.

She put one foot on the edge of the doorframe and bent to exit. And then her foot was on the step, and she stood

316

for a moment, surveying the scene. Even in the faint light, she could see the little signs that told her she was home at last: the peak in the roof of the barn, the yellow hair of the stableboy. The innkeeper shouted an order, and she felt a glow of delight. He spoke Finnish! But when he turned toward her, his words were Russian. "Welcome, my lady! Welcome to Finland!" He turned toward Alexei, who had dismounted on the other side. "Welcome, my lord! I am honored to welcome you to my humble inn."

Alexei leaped to the ground and hurried around to stand beside Kirsten. They waited until the carriage moved forward and turned toward the barn. Then, arms entwined, they mounted the steps. They paused once more as they reached the door, and Kirsten turned for one more look at the quiet scene. In the torchlight, her face seemed to glow. She threw her hood back and lifted her face toward the sky. "Oh, Alexei! How beautiful it all is!"

He chuckled and placed her hand on his arm again. "You will recognize more as we move westward. Come, now, I have a great wish for a draught of ale and a side of pork! Our friend the innkeeper knows how to make a weary traveler welcome."

The door closed behind them, and the courtyard was once more wrapped in shadows.

Viotto had watched the arrival with minimal interest until he saw the woman emerge. Yet even as she exited from the carriage, he had been aware of little more than mild curiosity. She was a wealthy woman, that was obvious, and well formed. Like most women on a long journey, she wore simple clothing, devoid of ruffles or lace that might soil. But she was clearly not an ordinary woman nor, for all of her wealth, a matron. Her narrow waist was held snugly in the firm fit of her bodice, and her full skirt draped in even pleats. She was young and he felt certain she was beautiful. The appreciation in the innkeeper's voice was unmistakable.

When she paused on the stairs and threw her hood back, he felt a shock through his body. In the torchlight, her features were clear. "Knut, look!"

Knut, too, had watched the arrival with interest. He

had shared Viotto's appreciation of the figure that emerged. When she dropped her hood and spoke, he gasped. "Kirsten! My God, it's Kirsten!"

Viotto caught him as he stepped forward. "Fool! Do you want to get us both killed? We are old men, remember? We cannot race across the barnyard, screaming the name of a Russian lady. Do you think you can help her by letting her know you are here?" In spite of his concern, he kept his voice low.

Knut faced him, pulling his arm free. "Now you show your true colors! Can you see her there and not feel the urge to fight? Does it not anger you to see the Russian treat her with such familiarity?"

"What I feel now does not matter, nor do your wild responses. Look, observe them well!"

Alexei, like Kirsten, wore subdued colors, yet there was no question as to the quality of his dress. His coat was a dark wool, neatly tailored in the latest fashion, and his wig was topped with a wide-brimmed hat decorated with a large white plume. He was older than Viotto had imagined him to be, but the lines on his face seemed to give greater evidence of kindness than cruelty. And when he took Kirsten's arm, it was with such gentleness that Viotto understood at last why Kirsten had run to him for help. This Alexei was a gentleman. And his fondness for Kirsten was sincere.

Yet Viotto shared Knut's longing for action. They had found her! He wanted to call her name and run to her side. He resented the gentleness of her escort, for he saw in Alexei's kindness a greater danger than cruelty would have offered.

"Come!" Anti was approaching, leading the horses, and the door to the inn was closed. "Hurry, we have work to do."

Knut pulled his arm free. "Did you see him? An old man! You lied to me! She would not choose an old man when she could have stayed with me!"

"He offered her love and protection. What did you give her?"

"My name! I was willing to marry her!"

"If that is true, she was not aware of your generosity.

318

We have gone over all of this many times already. You are wasting time. What does it matter why she chose to return to the Muscovite? She is safe! I had feared for her life!"

He shuffled ahead and picked up a brush. When Anti led the horses into the stable, he was ready to begin his chores.

He worked with a ferociousness born of his inner impatience. Kirsten's face, glowing in the light of the lantern, burned in his consciousness. Had he been hungry before her arrival? His need for food was forgotten. Had he been exhausted from the long kilometers he had walked that day? He was charged with energy now. His hands moved swiftly over the steaming backs of the horses, and Anti, surprised by his energetic behavior, stepped back and let him work.

Knut moved with equal speed. The smell of heated horse-flesh assailed his nostrils as he worked, and the smell was good. Never before had he traveled so far without a mount. As he worked, he devised one plan after another for absconding with Kirsten, and with horses on which they could ride. He had seen enough of the conquerors to know that they were already growing careless. He could make a quick move, and if he rode hard, he would not be caught. As for reaching Sweden, that did not worry him. There were rumors that some vessels plied the shoreline in search of those who were successful in escaping the Russian oppression. He would seek one of them, and sail to freedom with his bride.

He glanced over the rump of his charge and met Viotto's sharp gaze. Somehow, he would have to get Kirsten alone and convince her to leave with him. And, somehow, he would have to keep her from knowing that Viotto was with him.

Anti settled down on a bag of grain. "You are fast for old men. I will see if there is any food yet."

Night had wrapped its dark blanket on the earth, and the yellow light of the torch by which Viotto and Knut had been working cast a square of brightness into the dark courtyard. Viotto put his brush down. "I will be back, Knut. I think I saw an outhouse nearby."

Knut nodded and sat down on a bag of grain. He would

have to wait until Viotto and the stableboy returned. But then, when he could be certain he would not be disturbed, he would slip into the yard and peer into the common room. He would not rest until he had a chance to see Kirsten once more.

Kirsten settled herself on the wooden bench. Her arms and legs ached from the hours of inactivity, and her head was throbbing.

Alexei helped her remove her cloak. "Are you very tired, my dear? I regret we had to ride so far, but there are very few inns with good enough service."

She forced a smile. "I'm fine, Alexei. Just fine. I am sure I will feel better when I have had something to eat."

"Then rest, my dear. I will order food and wine for you. The women are already preparing our chamber." He looked deep into her face. "Was I wrong to take you with me? Is the journey too exhausting? I thought you might be eager to see Turku."

A bitter sadness filled her heart. "Why Turku? There is nothing there to draw me back."

"Forgive me, my dear. I forgot that your home was destroyed. Maybe you would be happier were we to pass it by."

"No. I do not wish to cause you to neglect your duties. I believe that Helsingfors will give me greater pain, for I know the horror that devastated that town."

Just then the galley boy arrived with two dishes and placed them on the table. Alexei picked up his knife. "Eat now, my love. I will do what I can to spare you when we reach Helsingfors." He signaled to the boy, who poured wine into Kirsten's glass.

They ate in silence. Kirsten was actually more tired than she let Alexei know, and yet she could tell from his attentiveness that he expected to enjoy her before he fell asleep.

The food served to revive her. When she finished the last of the wine, she rose and slipped away from the bench. "I believe I saw the building on the other side of the barn. By your leave, I will step out there before I retire."

He lifted the candle and put it in her hand. "Carry this. You will need it to see your way."

She took the candle and hurried to the door. Behind her, Alexei shouted for another mug of ale.

The courtyard was black, except for a square of light that poured through the half-open door of the barn. Using it as a beacon, she picked her way across the clearing, tilting the candle slightly to light the ground at her feet.

When she emerged from the shed, she tilted the candle again and focused her eyes on the ground. When she heard footsteps behind her, she increased her pace, but they moved more quickly than she.

A man materialized from the darkness, an old man, limping heavily as he approached. He straightened up as he entered the circle of her candlelight, and threw the cowl back from his face.

She gasped. The face before her was covered with dust, and the blond hair was thick with dirt. But the features were unmistakable. They had been burned into her consciousness far too deeply for her to forget them. "Viotto!" It was a whisper, no more.

He brushed the dust from his face. "Kirsten. Oh, my dearest!" His arms encircled her waist, and she was pushing against him, her lips pressed against his. The touch was like a flame. He had come! He loved her!

And then the fear returned. She pulled free of his arms. "Viotto! You must not do it! Please, for my sake, you must not kill Alexei!"

He seemed dumbfounded by the suddenness of her words. "Kill? Oh—" He understood immediately. When she left him, he was still determined on revenge. She did not know that his love for her had freed him.

She did not let him finish. "Do you not see that you will be killed if you seek to avenge yourself on Alexei? You cannot bring Ruusu back to life. And he was not to blame for her death. He is a good man!"

"But he is the one, isn't he?"

She backed up defiantly. "Yes. He told me what happened. He had allowed his men to go ahead, and when he heard the woman—Ruusu—cry out, he ran forward. But he was too late. She had already been injured too severely. She

321

must have fought without any outcry, for she had no idea there was someone close by who could save her."

He met her gaze. "You believe him?"

"Oh, yes. I know him very well. He is a good man, but he is not always strong. And he hates violence. He is not like the others. His sleep is disturbed by his memories. He would have gladly spared Ruusu, had he been able."

Viotto smiled gently. "Do not fear, my dearest. I have abandoned my need for vengeance long ago. You have brought life back into my heart. When I realized that your face outshone Ruusu's in my memory, then I knew that the need for vengeance was past. I have traveled for months searching for you. And now . . ."

She stepped toward him, her lips parted. He loved her! And his heart was free of hate!

The door of the inn swung open and a wide shaft of light cut through the darkness, touching the hem of her robe. "Kirsten?" Alexei's voice was heavy with concern. "Are you all right?"

Viotto stepped into the shadow. "Kirsten, you must come with me. Tell me you will!"

"Oh, Viotto, if you knew how I dreamed of seeing you again! But how can I run from Alexei? He has been good to me." She turned then and faced the inn. "I am here, Alexei! I was just looking up at the sky."

He laughed softly. "Ah, my sweet! It will be there in the morning."

"But not so filled with stars! Please, do not worry, I will be in shortly."

He stood for a moment, and then he turned and vanished into the brightness of the common room. Kirsten turned toward the shadows where Viotto was hidden. "Please, you must go now. If I can—if I find it possible—I will meet you later. But you must promise me you will not kill him."

"You have my word." His voice sounded hoarse with emotion. "I will promise you even more. If you choose to remain with him, I will not pursue you. You have the right to live as you please."

She felt the yearning that so often possessed her in her dreams. He was so close! Her every wish was to fall into his arms once more and never leave his side again. But she could not make so hasty a decision. Alexei had told her of his need for her. He had laid his heart bare before her. Could she reject him now? Duty demanded that she stay with him. Viotto could survive without her, he was strong. But Alexei? She knew him too well. He would grow old quickly were she to leave, and he would die alone.

"I will wait. There is a cave a kilometer west of the inn. If you choose to come with me, seek it out. It is to the north of the road, in a pile of rocks near the point of the lake. I will hide there."

She held herself still. "A kilometer west? I cannot run that far!"

The door to the inn was thrown open once more. Again Alexei stood in the square of light. "Kirsten! I have been speaking to the innkeeper. Come, we must get ourselves to bed. There is a herd of deer nearby, and I have decided to remain so I can hunt. Please, my love, you will have tomorrow night to look at the stars."

She turned when she heard his voice. "Yes, Alexei. I will be right there." She lowered her voice. "Do you not see? He needs me!"

Viotto was nowhere to be seen. But his whisper reached her ears. "I will wait for you. When you return from the hunt, come out again to the shed. We will make plans tomorrow."

She brought her hand to her face. Why, when she should be happy, did she feel so old and tired? Without answering, she turned and headed for the stairs. She wanted Viotto; she could no longer deny it. But Alexei deserved her loyalty. Her heart was beating wildly, and in her innermost thoughts, she said her farewell. *I love you, Viotto! I will always love you! But I cannot leave Alexei. Maybe some day you will understand.*

Chapter 32

"Come to bed, my dearest." Alexei rested his hands on Kirsten's shoulders. "I have decided you may accompany me on the hunt. It will be a diversion for you." He stroked her cheek. "I worry that you appear so peaked. Is something troubling you?"

When she could not avoid his eyes, she forced a smile. "I am just tired—and I suppose I am more excited at reaching Finland than I expected to be." She pulled herself from his arms and stepped to the window. "It is so beautiful! Filled with the wonderful sounds of night!"

"We have heard those sounds in Russia, my dear. The last inn we stayed at was, if anything, more rustic than this one."

"I know. But this—" She held out her arms toward the darkness. "This is my home!" Impulsively, she twirled about and threw herself into Alexei's embrace. "Oh, thank you for being so kind to me!"

He chuckled. "What occasions this outpouring of appreciation?" Her lips were on his, and he paused to receive her kiss. "No, you need not explain! I have determined that I will never ask you to account for your affection for me. Let me show you the depths of my love for you!"

She stood quietly as he closed and latched the shutters. Out there, somewhere, Viotto was sleeping. The thought of his nearness drained her. She felt weak with longing for more of his kisses.

Yet she had dreaded the day when she would meet him. How foolish she had been! She had feared he would strike out at Alexei and destroy her life. But in that one thing he had changed. He had admitted to her that he no longer had a need for vengeance. She let herself taste the joy his words stirred in her heart. He had rid himself of his hatred toward one man.

She thought of the hardships she had endured, and of the many who had died. There was much room for anger— but at the war, not at one person. And now Viotto understood. When she thought that she would never see him again, she felt terribly empty and alone.

Alexei began to undo the buttons of her gown. "Come, my love, I am eager to hold you in my arms." He opened the front of her bodice and kissed her exposed breasts. But she felt no response. He bared her shoulders, and touched them lightly with his lips. It was as if he had not touched her. She stood frozen, waiting for his caresses to end.

"You are so lovely!" He pulled her close. "I do not care if you hold another in the secret depth of your heart, as long as I am the one who feels your kiss. I told you it saddened me to know you had loved another. But I was not completely honest. It makes me far happier to know that you love me now." She felt his breath on her cheek, but its warmth did not stir her desire. "You have given me the greatest proof of your loyalty. You have told me of the danger this stranger is to me. What more can I ask than that you warn me of his presence so that I may destroy him?"

She felt a shock at his words. Did he know that Viotto was nearby? Was he testing her now, waiting for her to tell of her meeting?

She had no time to consider such a terrible possibility. He lifted her into his arms and carried her across the room. Her gown fell to the floor, and he kicked it aside. "Now!" He put her down beside the bed. "Remove your chemise. I wish to see your loveliness again."

As she finished her disrobing, he tore his clothes from

326

his body. He stood for a moment, admiring her alabaster skin, and then he guided her to the bed.

He spent little time with kisses; his need for her was too great. She felt him move above her, felt him press between her thighs. And she knew in the innermost part of her heart that he would never arouse her desire again. She would accept him always, for he was kind and attentive to her wishes. But that would be all.

Alexei seemed unaware of her passivity. He moved above her, and she felt his passion grow. He moaned her name at last, and fell heavily upon her, panting from the exertion. She could feel the pounding of his heart against his chest, and she wondered, sadly, if he was aware that hers did not echo his rhythm.

With a sigh of pleasure, he rolled beside her. Immediately, the cool night breeze touched the moistness of her body, washing away the heat his passion had induced. "Thank you, my dear. You are, as always, my perfect love."

She reached out then and touched his lips with her fingers. This was all she had. She could not leave Alexei to grow old alone.

He kissed her fingers. "Sleep, my love. I will return shortly." She felt him rise from the bed, and immediately her heart began to pound. Was he going now to confront Viotto?

"Please, Alexei, don't leave me!"

His laugh was light-hearted, almost youthful. "You honor me, my dearest! I will return as swiftly as I can. But I, too, must tend to my needs before retiring." He pulled on a robe as he moved toward the door. "Sleep, my love. You have made me very happy—as always." And then he was gone.

She lay immobile, trying to follow his descent. When she heard the outer door slam closed, she began to pray. "Dear God, do not let him see Viotto! He must never know!"

Suddenly she rose and hurried to the trunk that stood at the foot of the bed. Her parent's portraits lay between the folds of her favorite gown, and she pulled them out. She needed to touch the one thing that reminded her most of Viotto—the frames that had felt so hot to her touch when he rescued them from her burning home.

She pressed them against her breast, and the passion Alexei had been unable to arouse stirred within her. She stood for a time, tears streaming down her cheeks, and then she returned the mementos to their resting place and lay back on the bed.

Alexei strode swiftly across the courtyard. He paused once and glanced back at the inn. The room he shared with Kirsten was dark. She was so tired. Poor child.

That was the matter, of course. He expected too much of her at times. He should not have insisted upon taking her. But she still had the power to rouse his desire, even when she was herself too exhausted to respond.

Yet when he turned and continued on his way, he knew that the uneasiness had not been explained. She had stayed out so long. What was it, then, that had charmed her?

She had said she was looking at the sky. He studied it quietly. It was not changed from the way it looked above her garden in St. Petersburg. No, it had not been the sky that kept her attention.

As he passed the barn, another sound drew his attention. The stableboys, their chores completed, were talking together. He could hear their voices faintly over the nickering of the beasts. Impulsively, he stepped to the barn door and pushed it ajar. Yet something held him back. He stood quietly, listening to the mumbling voices. They had not noticed him yet.

Three men were visible. One, the youngest, lay sprawled on the hay, his arms akimbo. He was breathing steadily, and every so often he snored softly.

The other two sat some distance removed. Unlike the sleeper, they were mature men, with firmly etched features and beards that bushed out around their cheeks. They leaned back in the hay, their robes thrown back from their blond heads.

He stared for some time before he realized what it was about the scene that perturbed him. He had seen old men in Finland, wandering about like lost souls, searching for the peace they would never find again. But these two were of an age to be soldiers.

He felt his body tense. But he had little time for surmising. One of the two began to speak again. "You say he is staying here for a time?"

"Yes." The second man's voice was deeper. "I heard him say it himself. He is planning to hunt deer tomorrow. We will have time to make our plans—if she decides to leave him."

"If she decides!" The first man rose on one elbow, his face red with sudden anger. "You persist in this foolishness! She is not the one to make such a decision. She is my affianced and I will have her. Where are the herds? I will follow them in the morning and rescue her."

The second man spoke again, and Alexei inhaled sharply at his words. "I forbid it! We have agreed to let her make up her own mind. You cannot change now! Do you think it does not give me pain to think she might choose the Russian? Yet I have seen her, and I know she is a woman. She cannot be treated any longer as if she were still a child."

"It is easy for you to speak thus!" The first man touched the sword that lay beside him in the hay. "What do you know of her feelings? I have known her since she was a child. I played with her in the quiet of her garden. She is a loyal Swede, and an obedient daughter. She will be my wife, for that was her father's wish. Neither you nor the Muscovite will stand in my way."

Alexei let the door fall closed. He was shaking with emotion. He should kill them now—both of them! Yet he did not cry out for the soldiers, nor did he scurry back to the inn to get his musket. Instead, he rested his ear against the door.

The deep voice was the first he heard. "Quiet! Did you hear a noise?"

"I hear many noises! Viotto, you are losing your manhood! I thought, when you first proposed it, that you used the idea of giving Kirsten her choice only to keep peace between us as we traveled. But now I see that you were serious. It gives me pleasure to hear your sniveling, for it proves to me that you do not love her, though you continue to say you do. You could not even consider leaving her with another if you did!"

"Quiet, or you will wake the boy. There will come a time, Knut, when we will meet and settle our differences. But this is not the time. Our duty now is to Kirsten, and that means we must let her be."

Alexei leaned against the barn door, waiting for the pounding of his heart to slow. She had seen the man named Viotto. That was what had kept her so long in the night. He understood now why she had been so quiet upon her return. But if she had chosen the Finn, would she have accepted the love he, Alexei, had offered her?

"She accepted me! But she was not mine." He began slowly to cross the courtyard. He needed time to recover his control.

Which was the one Kirsten loved? He paused as he reached the steps. The one with the deep voice, the one who seemed willing to let her remain where she was? Was he, then, the one who had threatened revenge?

Alexei scratched his brow. It made no sense! She had described that man as filled with anger.

Well, it mattered little. Both were a danger to his safety and to his happiness. Both must die.

But they could not be killed where they lay. Kirsten must think they fought each other and died at each other's swords. Yes, that was it! He would work it out tomorrow. There was plenty of time. They had said they would wait.

When he entered the room, Kirsten lay uncovered on the bed. Her smooth white skin seemed to glow in the pale light of the stars. So lovely!

Was he only imagining that she had been less responsive to him this night? Had she accepted his love and given nothing? He shook his head. He would not concern himself with such fine variations. She did not love him fully, that he already knew. He would be content that she had made her choice. She had said nothing, and she had let him love her. For the present, that was all he asked. Later, when the two men were dead, she would learn to forget them.

Yet his mind did not rest. Was it the angry one she

longed for? The one who threatened to follow tomorrow and confront her? If so, he had no need to worry. If the Swede made an attempt to approach, the soldiers would kill him.

But what if it was the other? Though he had made no threats, Alexei had felt the strength of that man. He would pose a greater danger. "Did he hold you in his arms, my love?" His whisper did not carry across the room. "Is that why you showed so little interest in my caresses?"

There was no answer. Kirsten was asleep. Alexei sighed and crawled into the bed. In this one thing he agreed with the angry one. Kirsten's decision did not matter. Her life would be decided by others.

If the Swede attacked, he would be killed by the soldiers. No, he would not take the soldiers along. If the Swede approached, he would enjoy killing him. And Kirsten would understand.

But he would let his own men take care of the other one. If both men were dead, she would have no reason to leave him.

If neither of the men followed him in the morning, he would arrange to have his soldiers capture them and kill them some distance from the inn. They would both just disappear. Kirsten would be upset for a time, of course, but he, Alexei, would comfort her. He raised himself on his elbow and kissed her cheek. "You are mine, little Kirsten. I cannot live without you. Nor will I. You can be sure of that!"

Chapter 33

Alexei raised his hand and at the same moment pulled up on the reins of his horse. This was the location the innkeeper had described. Now it was time to leave the road.

He tried to move gracefully as he swung his leg over the saddle and slid to the ground. There had been a time, ages ago, when he could leap down like a cat. But those days were long past. Now all he could ask was that he not stumble as he dismounted, and that Kirsten not observe his clumsiness.

She was not watching him now. The same reserve that had possessed her the night before subdued her usual effervescence. She had said hardly a word all the way from the inn. And she stared absentmindedly into the woods as she waited for him to help her dismount.

Patience, that was what he needed most of all. He must not allow his jealousy to override his common sense. Not now, when he was so close to triumph. He was prepared to endure her sadness when she learned what had happened. He was ready, even, to comfort her. For he was convinced that her sorrow would not last long. One way or another, the two men who threatened his happiness would be killed. And then, when it was all over, she would resume her life with him. No one would destroy what he had so carefully constructed.

There were, of course, a few unknowns. Was the Swede hiding somewhere in the woods beside the lake, as he had said he would? Had the man Viotto persuaded him to wait? *I hope he did not abandon his plan. One man at a time. It is easier that way.*

He threw the reins of his horse to the nearest of the two soldiers who had accompanied him from the inn and stepped beside Kirsten's mount, his arms extended. As she slid into his arms, his thoughts returned to what lay ahead.

He would learn soon enough what the Swede had decided. Alexei counted on an impulsive attack. He depended upon it. Kirsten could not blame him for killing in defense of her safety.

"Shall I wait with the soldiers?" Kirsten met his glance, her eyes clear and innocent. He frowned. Was it possible that she had learned at last to deceive? Now, when she was far from the center of all intrigue?

He brushed the thought aside impatiently. Not his Kirsten! She had made her choice and she was still beside him. All she attempted to hide now was her sadness. He watched the play of light on her finely etched features.

"No, my dear. You will enjoy the stalking as much, if not more, than I. And if you tire, you can sit near the lake and watch the geese. I have heard them honking all the way from the inn." He reached up and took a basket from the soldier's outstretched hand. "You may carry our lunch. The innkeeper assured me there were many tasty treats for us to enjoy."

Kirsten's face brightened. "Oh, I will love that! Please, let me go there directly. I have not seen wild geese for many years. And they are such beautiful creatures."

"No more lovely than you, my dear." He took her hand. "Sergei!" One of the soldiers saluted. "You both are to remain here. Too many hunters only frighten the game. When I have made my kill, I will signal you to come and fetch it back to the inn."

"Yes, sir!" The salute was proper. "Will you be safe, sir?"

Alexei snorted and rested his hand on his musket. "I am well armed. I have plenty of ammunition. There is no beast that can stand up against a firearm!" He glanced at

334

Kirsten. "On second thought, come to the lake at noon. I should have made my kill by then, and it will save me the trouble of devising a signal."

"Yes, sir!" Sergei saluted once more. As Alexei and Kirsten entered the woods, he and his companion dismounted.

Kirsten listened to Alexei's conversation with the soldiers as if it came from a dream. Why, at so early a stage of his inspection of the Russian fortifications in Finland, did Alexei suddenly become so obsessed with hunting? She tried to remember back to the same season in St. Petersburg. Had he gone to hunt then? She did not know. There were many days and weeks when he was gone, and the tsar was fond of hunting.

And why, if he were in truth hunting deer, did he insist that the soldiers remain behind? Deer were among the most foolish of beasts. Approach them from downwind and move slowly, and one could almost walk up beside them. Two more people on a hunting expedition would not scare them away. The uneasiness she had felt ever since her meeting with Viotto increased. But she could find no immediate cause for her concern. Alexei seemed, if anything, more pleased with himself—and with the world in general—than he had been for many days.

He caught her glance and smiled warmly. "Are you happy, my dear? Is it good to be home again?"

"Yes, Alexei." She felt increasingly confused. He had asked her that question so often. "But what will we do with the deer, once you have killed it?"

"We will have its head prepared and shipped back to my home, where it will grace a wall in my private study. And when I see it, when Vera is her most troublesome, I will look up at the deer and think of you. I will know that you are waiting for me, and I will be comforted. I will think of this day with you. Oh, Kirsten, my dearest! The future lies open before us, and it is good."

She did not immediately respond. He had stepped onto a narrow path that led from the road, and he held back a branch to let her pass. A bramble caught at her cape, and she stopped to pull it free. "Are you sure the deer were sighted here? What if they have moved on?"

"No worry! The innkeeper told me they water close by every morning. There, through the trees. See, you can catch the sparkle as the sun hits the lake. The deer will be nearby, I am sure."

Kirsten paused. Ahead, the shine of the lake was bright. Behind her the woods were still dark, filled with deep shadows. Suddenly she felt afraid. Alexei was walking slowly forward, as if he expected to encounter some enemy, and yet he made no attempt to be quiet. Any deer within shooting distance would hear him and run away. What then—who—was he hunting?

She gasped in alarm. Ahead on the path stood a man. He was covered from head to foot in a dark brown robe that concealed his features. The dark shadows that surrounded him, backlit by the light from the lake, gave him the appearance of Death himself! Only his hand, protruding from the robe, proved his humanity. And in it, pointed directly at Alexei's heart, was a sword. Alexei leaped back, his own sword drawn.

With a sudden motion, the newcomer pulled the robe from his head and tossed it to the ground. It lay in a crumpled heap beside him. Kirsten clutched her breast. "Knut! What are you doing? How—?"

He did not lower his guard. "I have come to rescue you. Step around him and get behind me, quickly! He will not stop you as long as I have my sword at his neck!"

She backed farther into the woods. "Knut! No!" But she did not move in his direction.

"Hurry, Kirsten! I cannot hold him at bay forever!"

Gradually, her voice returned, and her reason. She drew farther away from him, behind Alexei. "What right have you to come and demand that I follow you? You rejected me! And who are you to order me around? Leave us be!"

Alexei's sword tapped Knut's blade. "You heard her, sir! She has told you to leave her alone! Are you a rude peasant, that you do not heed the word of a lady?"

Knut appeared surprised at Kirsten's response, but when Alexei spoke, his face grew red. "Who are you to speak of rudeness? You despoiled an innocent woman—my affianced! You took what was rightfully mine! You forced her to travel with you to Russia! Do you now think you can make amends by showing her little kindnesses? You are a cur, sir! A despicable lecher! An old man who preys on young women! You deserve to die!"

Alexei seemed to actually enjoy the confrontation. "Ah, then you are Knut Ivarson!" He grinned when Knut showed surprise. "Yes, I know your name, for Kirsten has told me all about you. It is you who have shamed a good woman! You do not deserve a lady as pure and beautiful as Kirsten Gustafson!"

Now at last Kirsten moved. "No! Knut, you do not understand! Alexei is good to me. He saved my life, not once, but twice! If it were not for him, I would be dead in a Russian prison!"

Knut twirled the tip of his sword, but he did not take his eyes from Alexei. "I offer you my thanks, Colonel, for preserving my love for me. But you still must die! I cannot rest while the man who ruined my virgin bride still lives! Yet, for all of your evil, she is mine. She will come with me now because she knows what is right. Step aside, sir, and let the lady pass."

Alexei seemed to plant himself across the path. "I will not allow you to take that which does not belong to you. She is mine, for I have created her. Yes, I have made her what she is! She was a child when I found her. Look at her now! Can you say she is the same? No! She is a beautiful, loyal woman who knows where her security lies. You may have been pledged to the child—but the woman is mine!"

Kirsten drew back once more, but neither Knut nor Alexei noted her movement. They stood face to face, swords poised, each waiting for the other to make the first attack.

Knut raised his voice. "Move now, Kirsten! You will be safe behind me."

She remained in the shadow, her eyes wide. They were the same, these two men. Both considered her no more than a sweet possession. They did not ask her to make a choice. They were ready to fight, and they expected her to accept whatever decision fate decreed.

"Kirsten! Do you not hear me? Now! Behind me!" Knut was growing impatient. "You do not appreciate all I have done for you!"

Alexei snorted. "Have you killed your companion? Then you have saved me the trouble. Ah, what a brave man you are, to kill your friend while he sleeps!"

Alexei's words tore at Kirsten's mind. Viotto dead? She tried to penetrate Knut's angry features, searching for denial or confirmation.

Knut flicked his sword and stepped closer to his enemy. "Why would I kill Viotto? No, Kirsten, do not let him deceive you with his lies. If Viotto is dead, it is because he ordered it. I left him snoring in a haystack."

The relief flowed over her like a balm. Viotto was still alive!

Alexei's voice cut into her thoughts. "Come, sir! You waste my time! You say you have presented yourself to rescue your lady. Then make your move. I grow impatient with your inactivity!"

Knut leaped back, his arm ready. "On guard!"

Now, at last, their swords met in earnest. The clash of metal upon metal drowned out the call of the geese, and silenced the sounds of the forest. Kirsten stepped behind a tree, her eyes wide with fright. "Stop it! Stop! I will make my own decision!"

But neither of the fighters heeded her cries. They moved lightly, swords meeting, thrusting, parrying. She ceased her protests. They would do as they willed. They were not concerned with her desires.

Knut was, she knew, a skilled swordsman, for he had studied under the best teachers in Uppsala. What surprised her was Alexei's ability. The men were far more evenly matched than she had expected. Alexei made up in technique for any weakness caused by age. And it was clear that Knut was out of practice. His foot slipped on a root and he fell to his knees. But his sword parried the thrust, and he was up again before Alexei could take advantage of his accident.

Now it was Knut who took the offensive. He pushed inexorably forward, crowding Alexei against a clump of trees. Kirsten cried out, but neither man heard her. And then Alexei shouted suddenly and forced his younger opponent back.

As he drew away, Knut caught his heel on a rock and

338

fell backward. His sword went up and out, catching Alexei, who was still rushing forward. It entered his body below the chest.

Alexei cried out in rage and fell forward onto the ground. His sword flew from his hand and landed at Kirsten's feet. In that instant, he drew his musket and fired.

The sound of the shot reverberated through the woods, and Kirsten's scream was lost in the echos. She ran first toward Knut. His head had been torn open by the bullet, and he lay dead, killed instantly.

Alexei groaned, and she hurried to his side. He called her name as she approached. "Kirsten, oh, my dearest! I did not want it to end like this!"

She dropped to the ground beside him, holding his head in her lap. "Alexei, you must not die! It is only a little wound. You will be better soon. I will call the soldiers!"

He looked up into her face, and she could see the gleam of light fade from his eyes. "I love you, Kirsten. Do not forget that I have loved you dearly."

"You will love me again! I will get help."

"No. Do not leave me. I have so little time. Listen now. The other one, Viotto. You must find him. Do not return to the soldiers! They cannot be trusted once I am dead." His voice grew fainter. "Promise me! Do not return to the inn."

"I promise. But you will live! You must live!"

"I cannot. Goodbye, my love!" His head sagged forward, and he was still.

She held his head on her lap, and slowly she began to rock. Was she on the road again, marching toward Russia? It was still continuing, the killing and the dying. "Alexei! Oh, Alexei!'

She looked up again at the body of Knut, but she averted her gaze quickly. He had loved her, too. Her senses were too shocked to recover quickly. First she felt nothing. Then, slowly, the pain came. They were dead, and without reason. What right had either of them to make her decisions? If they had asked her, the fight would have been avoided.

If they had asked her.

But neither one was willing to let her make up her own mind. They had spoken of her as if she were chattel.

She rose slowly, letting Alexei's head rest on the ground. The soldiers would come soon. She glanced up at the sky. In a few hours, maybe four, the sun would be at its zenith. It was time for her to go.

She staggered as she took her first steps, and clutched at a tree for balance. It was then she remembered the basket. Hurrying into the woods, she picked it up from where it had fallen. Viotto had said he would be waiting for her in the cave. They would need the food.

The sun almost blinded her as she stepped from the shelter of the trees. Where was it Viotto had said the cave was located? In the rocks at the west end of the lake.

Somewhere ahead the cave was waiting. It offered her the only shelter she could trust. And maybe Viotto would be there when she arrived.

Chapter 34

Viotto woke with a start. He had planned to rouse himself early and help Knut conceal his weapon. From the start, the two men had disagreed on how to deal with their swords during the night. Viotto always kept his wrapped against his leg so that, were he disturbed, he could maintain his role as an elderly man.

But Knut insisted upon removing his and laying it beside him. "If someone attacks me as I sleep, I want to have a chance to defend myself. You're a fool, Viotto! You will be murdered in your sleep some night."

"And you will be found out! I do not know yet which is the worse fate." Viotto had resigned himself to Knut's stubbornness.

Below the haystack on which they rested, Viotto could hear Anti moving about, spreading grain for the chickens and raking hay into the manger for the cattle. If the boy had seen Knut, it was already too late for action. Their disguise was exposed.

But Knut was not sleeping where he had thrown himself on the straw the night before. Viotto rose to his feet, rubbing the sleep from his eyes. Never, in all their journey, had he slept so late!

Anti looked up. "Good morning! I was surprised to see that you did not go with the others."

"Go? Where?"

"The Russian and his lady and the soldiers. Your friend helped me ready the horses, and then, when the guests rode off, he went for a walk in the woods. I have been expecting him to return any moment. Do you know where he went?"

Viotto slid down from his resting place. He remembered now. Knut had said something about confronting the Russian. But had he not agreed to wait? Was he fool enough to risk Kirsten's life through his eagerness?

Kirsten! He had told her he would be waiting at the cave. Yet he had little hope that she would seek him there. Even in the dark, he had sensed her commitment to the Muscovite. What was it she had said? *Alexei needs me.*

He limped into the barnyard, dragging his bound leg behind him, and drew a bucket of water from the well. Some of it he drank. Then, with a quick glance around to make certain he was not observed, he pulled the cowl away from his face and poured the rest of the water over his head. He sputtered as it flowed over his nose and mouth and then, refreshed, he buried himself once more under the folds of cloth.

He needed her, too. Many a night he had lain awake remembering the softness of her embrace. Surely his need was equal to that of an old man.

He knew the foolishness of his claim even as he made it. He did not need Kirsten to give him courage or strength, as the Muscovite did. He wanted her desperately. But he could live without her. He had learned that lesson well when Ruusu died. His strength was in himself. But his life would be richer were she beside him. Richer and filled with joy.

Anti appeared at the barn door. "Old man! Can you help me move some bags of grain?"

Viotto glanced at the road. He should be going. He had promised to be at the cave, and though it was doubtful that she would arrive, he did not wish to renege on his word. Yet the lad was sorely overworked. He hobbled into the stable. "I will help you. But when I am through, I must go in search of my friend. If he left when you say he did, he has been gone far too long a time."

"Thank you, Grandfather!" The lad lifted a sack and

carried it toward the back of the barn. "We must pile these here. They are in the way when I curry the horses." He watched as Viotto swung a sack onto his shoulder. "You are hardy for so old a man. And your friend, too. He seems well able to care for himself. He will be back by the time you are finished. Wait and see."

But Knut did not appear. The morning passed swiftly. When the chores were completed, Anti went into the cook house and emerged with two bowls of gruel. Viotto settled himself on the edge of a manger and ate.

He loved the smells of the barnyard, for they reminded him of the past, before the fighting began, when he had lived on his own small plot of ground with Ruusu beside him. They were pleasant memories now, for Kirsten had rid him of his hatred. But they were only memories, nevertheless.

It did not surprise him that Knut did not return. He had said he was going to confront the Muscovite and fight for Kirsten. Fool! Did he not know that Alexei was too wise to allow himself to be caught unawares? And the soldiers, would they stand aside and watch their master be attacked? Knut undoubtedly lay dead. And soon Alexei and Kirsten would return to the inn.

Would Kirsten mourn the death of her Swedish fiancé? Viotto shook his head. He was not certain. Surely she had shown no love for him that day so long ago when he had been injured fighting the renegades. Nor had she expressed a wish to remain with him to nurse his injury. She had been eager to hurry back to her Muscovite.

Damn! What hold did the old man have on her?

It was not love that kept her where she was. Viotto had felt the passion in her kiss. And yet, with her eyes speaking of her desire, she had walked away, back to the arms of the Russian. Why? She was grateful to him, that was obvious. He had saved her life once. Under what circumstances had they met for the second time?

He needs me! Did she pity the old man? Yes, it was pity that held her to him. *But he cannot want her pity! I would not want a woman to stay with me out of pity!*

The sun was well up in the sky when Viotto crossed the courtyard and stepped onto the road. Anti had offered to

343

accompany him, and it had been clear he would have enjoyed the walk.

"No, thank you." Viotto searched for some reason to leave the boy behind. "The innkeeper would not be pleased were we all to disappear. What if he wanted a horse? Or what if the Russian returned? You would deserve the beating he would give you when he got his hands on you."

"Yes, Grandfather. But I could search for your friend far faster than you can. Let me go out. You stay and watch the animals."

But Viotto did not give the boy a chance to depart. He took his leave quickly, and scurried across the courtyard as fast as his bound leg would allow.

Had Knut actually accosted the Russian? Viotto muttered an angry curse. Fool! Was it possible he was that stupid? Yet, if he had not, where was he?

Viotto glanced back. The barn was out of sight, and no one else was near. Quickly he slipped into the woods. If the Russian did return, he had no wish to encounter him.

When he was no longer in sight of the road he paused and released his sword from where it lay bound to his leg. Leaning against a tree, he flexed his knee and rotated his ankle. Then he hurried on his way.

He had traveled no more than a kilometer when he drew up short. In a small clearing some distance ahead, two figures were moving. He stepped into a shadow. Had they seen him?

No. The two soldiers who had accompanied the Russian and Kirsten when they arrived at the inn now stood together. They seemed stunned, as if something unexpected had occurred. Viotto moved slowly closer.

When next he paused, what he saw made him freeze. Two bodies lay on the path. Knut's was closest, but he recognized it only by its clothing. The corpse lay face down, and the head was a red smear on the ground.

The second corpse lay in a more relaxed position. Alexei had fallen on his back, and he lay staring up into the bright sky. Kirsten was not to be seen.

One soldier knelt and closed the eyelids. Then he lifted the body into his arms and walked slowly toward the road.

The other stood gazing at Knut's corpse. Viotto repressed a bitter smile. There was no doubt what the Russian was thinking. If Knut had not died already, he would not have lived any longer. Then, abruptly, the man turned and followed his companion.

The woods grew still. Yet Viotto waited. Was Kirsten already at the road, waiting for the soldiers to join her? He almost ran down the path, but even in his hurry he was as silent as a wild animal. He paused when the road came into view. Four horses stood tethered to a nearby tree. One held the body of Alexei. The soldiers released the reins and mounted two others. But the fourth trotted behind with no rider. Kirsten had not remained with the body of her lover.

Then she was at the cave! Quickly, Viotto turned and ran back along the path. Alexei and Knut were both dead. But Kirsten was alive—and she was waiting for him!

Kirsten crouched in the dark cave, trying to sort out her jumbled thoughts. Alexei was dead. She had held him in her arms and listened to his warning.

She tried to stir some regret in her heart at the thought of Knut's sudden death, but she felt too stunned for any emotion. All this time she had feared Viotto! All this time, she had been certain that the day would come when Viotto and Alexei would face each other in combat! But Knut had held the sword that ended Alexei's life.

She heard a rustling in the leaves outside the cave and she began to tremble. A wild animal?

No, the wind. And Viotto was not waiting for her, as he had promised.

She thought back on the meeting in the courtyard. She had made her decision then, though she had not voiced it. Had he guessed what was in her heart? Was Viotto even now on his way back north, convinced that she had chosen Alexei?

But he had promised he would wait for her. He had given his word. Surely, even if he had no hope that she would arrive, he should have waited.

What would become of her if he did not arrive? She slipped her hand into the deep pocket of her skirt and felt the frames of the small portraits. She would follow him. She would turn her face toward the north, and she would travel as far as fate allowed.

Maybe she would reach safety. And if she failed, it would not matter. Now that she was free from Alexei, she wanted to be with Viotto. Without him, her life was meaningless.

She crept toward the entrance and stared out into the bright sunlight. Should she go now? He had said he would be waiting.

Or had he told her to wait? Now, when it mattered so terribly, she could not remember.

Well, then, she would have to wait, at least for the remainder of the day. Once more she crawled back into the darkness. There was food in the basket. She would not be hungry.

But what if the soldiers found her?

She shuddered. Would they hunt for her? If they found her, then all the terrors her father had predicted would happen! The Muscovites would rape her not once, but many times. And then she would die violently, her torture providing the last amusement for their hardened lust.

She began to weep at last. And as the tears flowed, she thought once more of Knut. He had loved her too, in his own way. Was he to blame because he considered her more of a possession than a partner? He had loved her enough to risk his life for her.

She wept until there were no more tears left. Then she wiped her eyes and lifted the lid of the basket. She would eat now. Later, when the sun set, she would decide where she would go.

It was then she heard the sound. Once more she crawled forward. If it was the soldiers, she wanted to be prepared. The innkeeper had provided a knife for cutting the meat. She was determined that she would not remain alive to be tortured.

But the rocks lay bare and hot in the midday sun, and the only sound she heard was the call of the wild geese as they settled down on the surface of the water. The wind rustled through the jumble of rocks, picking up loose

346

leaves and tossing them wildly about. That was what had disturbed her. No one was coming, not even Viotto!

Overcome with despair, she crawled back once more to the basket. She ate, and each mouthful tasted sweet to her tongue. Sweet and sad. There was no doubt in her mind any longer. Viotto was not going to come.

Suddenly she drew herself erect. Was that a voice she heard?

She crawled forward. This time there was no doubt. It was the sound of steel against a rock. The soldiers were coming after all!

Quickly she returned to the basket and lifted the blade to her breast. She held it there, poised, but she could not drive it home. Turning, she stared at the bright entrance. They would appear, and then she would have no difficulty pushing the blade into her breast. She drew in a breath and waited. Soon it would all be over.

A figure appeared at the opening, and she gasped. It was tall. But it was not garbed in a soldier's uniform.

"Kirsten?"

She exhaled with relief. Viotto!

"Kirsten? Are you here?"

She dropped the knife with a clatter and crawled toward him. "Viotto! Oh, Viotto!"

He caught her as she approached him and pulled her out into the golden sunlight. She felt his arms circle her waist as he pulled her to him. She breathed his name once more. It was over, her longing, her loneliness, the terror of fear!

She felt his hand on her chin, and then his lips were pressed against hers. Did she hear him speak, or did the words come from his heart directly to her own? "Kirsten, thank God! I love you so!"

She did not try to respond. Her lips spoke a far more meaningful message. She was home at last. And she would never be lonely or afraid again.